ALSO BY ALISON ESPACH

Notes on Your Sudden Disappearance

The Adults

THE
WEDDING
PEOPLE

THE
WEDDING
PEOPLE

a novel

ALISON ESPACH

Henry Holt and Company
New York

Henry Holt and Company
Publishers since 1866
120 Broadway
New York, New York 10271

Henry Holt® and ⒽＨ® are registered trademarks of
Macmillan Publishing Group, LLC.

Copyright © 2024 by Alison Espach
All rights reserved.
Distributed in Canada by Raincoast Book Distribution Limited

ISBN 9781250899576

Designed by Kelly S. Too

Printed in the United States of America

To all the strangers who made
a dreary moment magical

It was awful, he cried, awful, awful!
Still, the sun was hot. Still, one got over things.
Still, life had a way of adding day to day.

VIRGINIA WOOLF, *MRS. DALLOWAY*

THE
WEDDING
PEOPLE

TUESDAY

≈

The Opening Reception

The hotel looks exactly as Phoebe hoped. It sits on the edge of the cliff like an old and stately dog, patiently waiting for her arrival. She can't see the ocean behind it, but she knows it's there, the same way she could pull into her driveway and feel her husband in his office typing his manuscript.

Love was an invisible wire, connecting them always.

Phoebe steps out of the cab. A man in burgundy approaches with such seriousness, the moment feels as if it has been choreographed long ago. It makes her certain that what she is doing is right.

"Good evening," the man says. "Welcome to the Cornwall Inn. May I take your luggage?"

"I don't have any luggage," Phoebe says.

When she left St. Louis, it felt important to leave everything behind— the husband, the house, the luggage. It was time to move on, which she knew because that was what they had all agreed to last year at the end of the divorce hearing. Phoebe was so stunned by the finality of their conversation, by the way her husband said, "Okay, take care now," like he was the mailman wishing her well. She could not bring herself to do a single thing after except climb in bed and drink gin and tonics and listen to the sound of the refrigerator making ice. Not that there was anywhere to go. This was mid-lockdown, when she only left the house for gin and toilet paper and taught her virtual classes in the same black blouse every day because what else were people supposed to wear? By the time lockdown was over, she couldn't remember.

But now Phoebe stands before a nineteenth-century Newport hotel in an emerald silk dress, the only item in her closet she can honestly say she still loves, probably because it was the one thing she had never worn. She and her husband never did anything fancy enough for it. They were professors. They were easygoing. Relaxed. So comfortable by the fire with the little cat on their laps. They liked regular things, whatever was on tap, whatever was on TV, whatever was in the fridge, whatever shirt looked the most normal, because wasn't that the point of clothing? To prove that you were normal? To prove that every day, no matter what, you were a person who could put on a shirt?

But that morning, before she got on the plane, Phoebe woke and knew she was no longer normal. Yet she made toast. Took a shower. Dried her hair. Gathered her lecture notes for her second day of the fall semester. Opened her closet and looked at all the clothes she once bought simply because they looked like shirts a professor should wear to work. Rows of solid-colored blouses, the female versions of things her husband wore. She pulled out a gray one, held it up in front of the mirror, but could not bring herself to put it on. Could not go to work and stand at the office printer and hold her face in a steady expression of interest while her colleague talked at length about the surprising importance of cheese in medieval theology.

Instead, she slipped on the emerald dress. The gold heels from her wedding. The thick pearls her husband had lain across her eyes like a blindfold on their wedding night. She got on a plane, drank an impressively good gin and tonic, and it was so nice and cool down her throat she hardly felt her blisters exiting the plane.

"Right this way, ma'am," the man in burgundy says.

Phoebe gives the man twenty dollars, and he seems surprised to be tipped for doing nothing, but to Phoebe it is not nothing. It's been a long time since a man has stood up immediately upon seeing her get out of a car. Years since her husband emerged from his office to greet her when she got home. It is nice to be stood for, to feel like her arrival is an important event. To hear her heels click as she walks up the old brick entranceway. She always wanted to make this sound, to feel grand and dignified when walking into a lecture hall, but her university was made of carpet.

She goes up the stairs, passes the big black lanterns and the granite lions guarding the doors. She walks through the curtains into the lobby, and this feels right, too. Like stepping back in time to an older world that probably was not better, but at least was heavily draped in velvet.

Then she sees the check-in line.

It's so long—the kind of line she expected to see at the airport, and not at a Victorian mansion overlooking the ocean. Yet there the line is, stretching all the way through the lobby and past the historic oak staircase. The people in it look wrong, too—wearing windbreakers and jeans and sneakers. The normal shirts Phoebe used to wear. They look comically ordinary next to the velvet drapes and the gilt-framed portraits of bearded men lining the walls. They look like solid, modern people, tethered to the earth by their titanium-strength suitcases. Some are talking on their phones. Some are reading off their phones, like they're prepared to be in this line forever and maybe they are. Maybe they don't have families anymore, either. It's tempting for Phoebe to think like this now—to believe that everybody is as alone as she is.

But they're not alone. They stand in pairs of two or three, some with linked arms, some with single hands resting on a back. They're happy, which Phoebe knows because every so often one of them announces how happy they are.

"Jim!" an old man says, opening up his arms like a bear. "I'm so happy to see you!"

"Hey, Grandpa Jim," a younger man says back, because it seems practically everyone in line is named Jim. The Jims exchange violent hugs and hellos. "Where's Uncle Jim? Already on the course?"

Even the young woman working the front desk seems happy—so dedicated to looking each guest deeply in the eye, asking them why they're here, even though they all say the same thing, and so she replies with the same thing: "Oh, you're here for the wedding! How wonderful." She sounds genuinely excited about the wedding and maybe she is. Maybe she's still so young that she believes everybody else's wedding is somehow about her. That's how Phoebe always felt when she was young, worrying about what dress to wear for a month, even though she sat in the outer orbit of every wedding she attended.

Phoebe gets in line. She stands behind two young women carrying matching green dresses on their arms. One still wears her cheetah-print airplane neck pillow. The other has a bun so high the messy red tendrils dangle over her forehead as she flips through a *People* magazine. They are engaged in whispery debate over whose flight here was worse and how old is this hotel really and why are people so obsessed with Kylie

Jenner now? Are we supposed to care that she's hotter than Kim Kardashian?

"Is she?" Neck Pillow asks. "I've actually always thought they were both ugly in some way."

"I think that's true about all people, though," High Bun says. "All people have one thing that makes them ugly. Even people who are like, professionally hot. It's like the golden rule or something."

"I think you mean cardinal rule."

"Maybe." High Bun says that even though she understands she's baseline attractive, something that has taken her five years of therapy to admit, she knows that her gums show too much when she smiles.

"I've never noticed that," Neck Pillow says.

"That's because I don't smile all the way."

"This entire time I've known you, you haven't been fully smiling?"

"Not since high school."

The line moves forward, and Phoebe looks up at the coffered ceiling, which is so high, she starts to wonder how they clean it.

Another "Oh! You're here for the wedding!" and Phoebe begins to realize just how many wedding people there are in the lobby. It's unsettling, like in that movie *The Birds* her husband loved so much. Once she spots a few, she sees them everywhere. Wedding people lounging on the mauve velvet bench. Wedding people leaning on the built-in bookcase. Wedding people pulling luggage so futuristic it looks like it could survive a trip to the moon. The men in burgundy pile it all into high, sturdy towers of suitcases, right next to a large white sign that says WELCOME TO THE WEDDING OF LILA AND GARY.

"Your rule is definitely not true about Lila, though," Neck Pillow says. "I mean, I seriously can't think of one way she's ugly."

"That's true," High Bun says.

"Remember when she was chosen to be the bride in our fashion show senior year?"

"Oh yeah. Sometimes I forget about that."

"How can you forget about that? I think about how weird it was once a week."

"You mean because our guidance counselor insisted on walking down the aisle with her?"

"I mean more like, some people are just born to be brides."

"I actually think our guidance counselor is coming to the wedding."

"That's weird. But good. Then I'll actually know someone at this wedding," Neck Pillow says.

"I know. I pretty much don't know anyone anymore," High Bun says.

"I know, ever since the pandemic, I'm like, okay, I guess I just have no friends now."

"Right? The only person I know now is basically my mom."

They laugh and then trade war stories of their terrible flights here and Phoebe does her best to ignore them, to keep her eyes focused on the magnificence of the lobby. But it's hard. Wedding people are much louder than regular people.

She closes her eyes. Her feet begin to ache, and she wonders for the first time since she left home if she should have brought a pair of sensible shoes. She has so many lined up in her closet, being navy, doing nothing.

"So what do you know about the groom?" Neck Pillow whispers.

High Bun only knows what Lila briefly told her over the phone and what she learned from stalking him on the internet.

"Gary is actually kind of boring to stalk," High Bun says, then whispers something about him being a Gen X doctor with a receding hairline so minor, it seems like there's a good chance he'll die with most of his hair. "How did you *not* stalk him after Lila asked you to be a bridesmaid?"

"I've been off the internet," Neck Pillow says. "My therapist demanded it."

"For two years?"

"They've been engaged that long?"

"He proposed just before the pandemic."

They inch forward in line again.

"God—Look at this wallpaper!"

Neck Pillow hopes that her room faces the ocean. "Staring at the ocean makes you five percent happier. I read a study."

Finally, they are quiet. In their silence, Phoebe is grateful. She can think again. She closes her eyes and pretends she's looking at her husband across the kitchen, admiring his laugh. Phoebe always loved his laugh, the way it sounded from afar. Like a foghorn in the distance, reminding her of where to go. But then one of the Jims yells, "Here comes the bride!"

"Jim!" the bride says.

The bride steps out of the elevator and into the lobby wearing a glittering sash that says BRIDE so there is no confusion. Not that there could be any confusion. She is clearly the bride; she walks like the bride and smiles like the bride and twirls bride-ishly when she approaches High Bun and Neck Pillow in line, because the bride gets to do things like this for two or three days. She is a momentary celebrity, the reason everybody has paid thousands of dollars to come here.

"I'm so happy to see you!" the bride cries. She opens her arms for a hug, gift bags hanging from her wrists like bracelets made of woven seagrass.

Neck Pillow and High Bun were right. Phoebe can't identify one thing that is ugly about the bride, which might be the one thing that's ugly about her. She looks exactly how she is supposed to look—somehow both willowy and petite in her white summer dress, with no trace of any undergarment beneath. Her blond hair is arranged in such a romantic and complicated tangle of braids, Phoebe wonders how many tutorials she watched on Instagram.

"You look beautiful," High Bun says.

"Thank you, thank you," the bride says. "How were your flights?"

"Uneventful," Neck Pillow lies.

They do not mention the surprise flock of seagulls or the emergency landing because the bride is here. It is their job for the entire wedding to lie to the bride, to have loved their journeys here, to be thrilled by the prospect of a Newport wedding after two years of doing practically nothing.

"When do we meet Gary?" High Bun asks.

"He'll be at the reception later, obviously."

"I mean, obviously," Neck Pillow says, and they laugh.

The bride hands out the seagrass bags (with "emergency supplies") and the women gasp as they pull out full-sized bottles of liquor. All different kinds, the bride explains. Things she picked up when she and Gary were traveling in Europe last month.

Scotch. Rioja. Vodka.

"Oh, how fancy," High Bun says.

The bride smiles, proud of herself. Proud to be the kind of woman who thinks of other, less fortunate women while traveling Europe with her doctor fiancé. Proud that she returned a woman who knows what to drink and not to drink.

"Here you go," the bride says to Phoebe with such intimacy it makes Phoebe feel like she is a long-lost cousin from childhood. Like maybe once upon a time, they played checkers together in their grandfather's dodgy basement or something. She hands Phoebe one of the bags, then gives her a really strong hug, as if she has been practicing bridal hugs the way Phoebe's husband used to practice professorial handshakes before interviews. "Just a little something to say thank you for coming all this way. We know it wasn't easy to get here!"

It was actually very easy for Phoebe to get here. She didn't stop the mail or line up a kid in the neighborhood to water the garden or get Bob to cover her classes like she always did before vacations. She didn't even clean up the crumbs from her toast on the counter. She just put on the dress and walked out of the house and left in a way she's never left anything before.

"Oh, I . . ." Phoebe begins to say.

"I know, I know what you're thinking," the bride says. "Who the hell drinks chocolate wine?"

The bride is good. A very good bride. It's startling to be spoken to like this after two years of intense isolation, of saying, "What is literature?" to a sea of black boxes on her computer, and none of the boxes knew, or none of the boxes cared, or none of the boxes were even listening. "What is literature?" Phoebe asked, again and again, until not even she knew the answer.

And now to be given a hug and a bag of chocolate wine for no reason. To be looked in the eye by a beautiful stranger after so many years of her husband not looking her in the eye. It makes Phoebe want to cry. It makes her wish she were here for the wedding.

"But it's better than you think," the bride says. "Germans love it, apparently."

The bride smiles and Phoebe sees a bit of food stuck between her two front teeth. There it is: the one thing that makes the bride ugly today.

"Next?" the front desk woman calls.

It takes a moment for Phoebe to realize it's her turn. She sees High Bun and Neck Pillow already walking into the elevator. She takes the bag, thanks the bride, and walks toward the front desk.

"You must be here for the wedding, too?" the woman asks. Her name is Pauline.

"No," Phoebe admits. "I'm not."

"Oh," Pauline says. She sounds disappointed. Confused, actually. Her eyes flicker to the bride in the distance. "I thought everybody here was here for the wedding."

"I am definitely not here for the wedding. But I made a reservation this morning."

"Oh, I believe you," Pauline says, typing as she speaks. "I just think that someone here has made a very big mistake. It might have even been me! You'll have to excuse us, we're a little understaffed since Covid."

Phoebe nods. "Labor shortage."

"Exactly," Pauline says. "Okay, what's your name?"

"Phoebe Stone."

This is true. This is her name, the name she has come to think of as hers. Yet it feels like she's lying when she says it now, because it's her husband's family's name. Whenever she hears herself say it, it somehow pushes her outside of her body. It makes her see herself from up above like a bird, the way the wedding people must see her, and she's sure from up there, they can spot the one thing that is ugly about her, too: her hair. Something should be done about that hair. She completely forgot to comb it this morning.

"Here you are," Pauline says. She is so focused now on giving quality service she does not even look up when one of the wedding people walks through the doors and slips on the floor behind Phoebe.

"Uncle Jim! Oh my God! Are you okay?" the bride shouts.

Uncle Jim is not okay. He is on the floor, yelling something about his ankle, and also the floor, which is a terrible floor, he says, not to mention, total bullshit. The men in burgundy gather around him and start apologizing to him about the floor, which yes, yes, they agree is the worst floor, even though Phoebe can see it's some kind of Italian marble.

"There it is," Pauline says. Pauline is a hero. "You're in the Roaring Twenties."

"Is each room a decade?" Phoebe asks. She pictures each room having its own hairstyle. Its own war. Its own set of stock market triumphs and failures. Its own definition of feminism.

"You know, I don't actually know what all the themes are!" Pauline says. "I'm new. They seem kind of random to me. But that's a *great* question."

She opens the drawer, searches for the right key.

"It's our penthouse suite," she says. "The only one with a proper view of the ocean."

It feels practiced, as if Pauline whispers something to each guest to make them feel special. *It's our only room with a desk from the Vanderbilts' family home. It's our only room with an infinite supply of toilet paper.*

"Wonderful," Phoebe says.

"So what brings you to the Cornwall Inn?"

Even though she knew this question was coming, Phoebe is startled by it. When she imagined herself here, she didn't imagine herself having to speak to anybody. She is, simply, out of practice.

"This is my happy place," Phoebe blurts out. It's not the entire truth, but it's not a lie.

"Oh, so you've stayed with us before?" Pauline asks.

"No," Phoebe says.

Two years ago, Phoebe saw the hotel advertised in some magazine, the kind she only ever read while waiting in the fertility clinic. She looked at the pictures of the Victorian canopy bed, overlooking the ocean, and she thought, Who actually plans their vacations by looking through a travel magazine? She felt angry at these people, not that she knew anybody who did things like that. Yet days later, when her therapist asked her to close her eyes and describe her happy place, she pictured herself on that canopy bed because she could only imagine herself happy in a place she had never been, a bed she had never slept in.

"Well, this is a happy place, indeed," Pauline says.

Phoebe picks up the key. It's already been too much conversation. Too much pretending to be normal, and she is not paying eight hundred dollars just to stay here and pretend to be normal. She could have easily done that at home. She feels herself grow weary, but Pauline has so many more questions. Would she like to add a spa package? Would she like to book a visit with their in-house tarot reader? Would she like a normal pillow or a coconut pillow?

"What's a coconut pillow?" Phoebe asks.

"A pillow," Pauline says, "with coconut in it."

"Are pillows better that way?" she asks. "With coconut inside them?"

That's what her husband would have asked. A bad habit of hers, a product of being married for a decade—always imagining what her husband might say. Even when he's not around. Especially when he's not around. Phoebe didn't think she'd end up being a woman like this. But if the last few years have taught her anything, it's that you really can't ever know who you are going to become.

"Pillows are much better that way," Pauline says. "Trust me. We'll have one sent right up."

Phoebe walks into the elevator and feels relief when the doors start to close. Finally, to be getting away from the wedding people. To be doing something for a change. To have a key to a place that is not her house.

"Hold the elevator!" a woman calls out.

Phoebe knows it's the bride before she sees her. She yells like she deserves this elevator. But nobody deserves anything. Not even the bride. Phoebe presses the button to close the doors, but the bride slides a hand between them. They don't bounce open like they're supposed to, maybe because the Cornwall was built in 1864. An old hotel has no mercy, not even for the bride.

"Fuck!" the bride shouts.

"Oh, God!" Phoebe says. She pries the doors back open, then stares at the bride's hand in disbelief. "You're bleeding."

The bride holds up the gash across the back of her knuckles like a child and takes the tissue Phoebe offers without saying thank you. Phoebe presses the button, and the doors close again. The women don't say anything as the bride politely bleeds into the tissue and they begin to ascend. Phoebe hears the bride try to steady her breath, watches the tissue darken.

"I'm really sorry," Phoebe says. "I didn't realize that would happen."

"Oh, I'm sure it'll be fine," the bride struggles to say. She clears her throat. "So, are you in Gary's family?"

"No," Phoebe says.

"Are you in my family?"

"You don't know who's in your own family?" Phoebe asks. The question makes Phoebe want to laugh, and it's a strange feeling. The first time she has wanted to laugh in months. Years maybe. Because how does the bride not know her own family? Phoebe knew everybody in her family. She had no choice. It was so small. Just Phoebe and her father, tiny enough to fit inside his old fishing cabin.

"I have a very large family," the bride says, like it's a big problem.

"Well, I'm not in your family," Phoebe clarifies.

"But you have to be in one of our families."

"No," Phoebe says. "I'm not in any family."

It had been a crushing realization, one that started slowly after the divorce, and got stronger with each passing holiday, until she woke up this morning to such a quiet house, she finally understood what it meant to have no family. She understood it would always be like this—just her, in bed, alone. No longer even the sound of her cat, Harry, meowing at the door.

"But everybody is here for the wedding. I made sure of it." The bride eyes the gift bag in Phoebe's hands, confused. "This has to be some kind of mistake."

The bride says it as if Phoebe is the big nightmare she has always been dreading. Phoebe is something going wrong at a time when nothing is supposed to go wrong. Because every little thing during a wedding has the power to feel like an omen—like the high winds through the park that flipped over the paper plates and sent a chill down Phoebe's spine on her own wedding day. We should have gotten real plates, she thought, something with weight and substance.

"There's no mistake," Phoebe says.

This is Phoebe's happy place. The place Phoebe has chosen out of all the possible places. How dare the bride make Phoebe feel like she's not supposed to be here.

"But if you're not here for the wedding, then what are you here for?" the bride asks in a much lower pitch, as if her real voice has finally emerged. Because now in this private space with a person not attending the wedding, the bride doesn't have to be the bride. She can speak however she wants. And so can Phoebe. Phoebe is not High Bun or Neck Pillow. She is nobody, and the only good thing about being nobody is that she can now say whatever the fuck she wants. Even to the bride.

"I'm here to kill myself," Phoebe says.

She says it without drama or emotion, as if it's just a fact. Because that's what it is. She waits for the truth of it to stun the bride into an awkward silence, but the bride only looks confused.

"Um, what did you just say?" the bride asks.

"I said, I'm here to kill myself," Phoebe repeats, more firmly this time. It feels good to say it out loud. If she can't say it aloud, then she probably won't be able to do it. And she has to do it. She has decided. She has come all this way. She feels relief as the doors begin to open, but the bride presses the button to close them.

"No," the bride says.

"No?" Phoebe asks.

"No. You definitely cannot kill yourself. This is my *wedding* week."

"Your wedding is a *week*?"

"Well, like, six days, if you want to be technical about it."

"That's a . . . long wedding."

Phoebe's wedding was a single night. She had tried not to make a big deal out of it. And why? It seems silly now, to have not celebrated something good when she had the chance. But Phoebe and her husband were a year out of graduate school, trained to live on a stipend with a cheap bottle of wine and a nice tree in the distance. And a wedding was such a spectacle, Phoebe thought. Every time she ordered flowers or sampled another piece of cake or told her friends how happy she was, she got this horrible feeling that she was bragging.

"A week is actually pretty standard now," the bride says with a tone that makes Phoebe feel old. "And people are coming a long way to be here."

But Phoebe doesn't care.

"This is the most important week of my life," the bride pleads.

"Same," Phoebe says.

Phoebe presses for the doors to open, but the bride closes them again, and it makes Phoebe angry, the way she gets only when she's stuck in traffic on the way to work. All those taillights ahead made her want to scream, and yet she never did, not even in the privacy of her own car. She was not a screamer. Not the kind of woman who ever made demands of the world, did not expect the streets to clear just because she was in a rush. She was not like the bride, who stands so entitled in her glittering sash like she's the only bride to have ever existed. It makes Phoebe want to rip off the sash, whip out her own wedding photo, show her that she had been a bride once, and brides can become anything. Even Phoebe.

But then the bloody tissue falls to the ground. As the bride picks it up, she lets out a half sob, then looks at Phoebe as though her entire life has already been ruined.

"Please don't do this," the bride begs, and it gives Phoebe that feeling again, as if she knows her, like the bride is asking from one cousin to another.

"I'll be very quiet," Phoebe promises. "I mean, I might put on some light jazz in the background, but you won't hear it."

"Are you joking? Is this a sick prank or something? Did Jim put you up to this?"

From her purse, Phoebe pulls out her ancient Discman and a CD titled *Sax for Lovers*. One of the only things she brought from home. From the first night of their honeymoon in the Ozarks. A small motel on the side of a canyon with a heart-shaped hot tub that made the whole room humid. Her husband found the CD in the stereo. Sax for Lovers, he read aloud, and they laughed and laughed. Well, put it on, lover, she said, and they danced until they undressed each other.

"Oh my God," the bride says. "You're serious. You're going to do it here? In your room? When?"

"Tonight," Phoebe says. "At sunset."

She is going to smoke a cigarette on the balcony. She is going to order room service. Have a nice meal while looking out at the water. Eat an elaborate dessert. Listen to the CD. Take a bottle of her cat's painkillers and fall asleep in the large king-sized canopy bed as the sun goes down. It is going to be quick, beautiful, and entirely bloodless, because Phoebe refuses to make the staff clean like her friend Mia cleaned after her husband Tom slit his wrists. That's just selfish, Phoebe's husband said when they heard, and Phoebe agreed, because Tom survived. Because it felt important for a husband and wife to agree on something like that. But also because Phoebe is a tidy person, afflicted by the belief that each book has its rightful place on the shelf and blood should always be inside our bodies, even after death, especially after death, and how awful for Mia, to have to kneel down and scrub her husband's blood out of the grout.

"There will be no mess," Phoebe promises.

"No," the bride says firmly. "Absolutely not. This can't happen. This can't be real."

But her wound is a red circle that keeps expanding. The bride looks at it and says, "How could you *do* this to me?"

Is Phoebe really doing anything to her, though? If it's not Phoebe, something else will ruin it. That's how weddings go. That's how life goes. It's always one thing after another. Time the bride learns.

"Believe it or not, this actually has nothing to do with you," Phoebe says.

"Of course it does!" the bride says. "This is my wedding! I've been planning this my entire life!"

"I've been planning this my entire life."

It's not until Phoebe says it that she realizes it's true. Not that she's always wanted to end her life. But it's been an idea, a self-destruct button Phoebe never forgot was there, even during her happiest moments. And where did this sadness come from? Did her father pass it on like a blood disease?

"Please," the bride says. "Please don't do this here."

But she has to. This is the only place that feels right: a five-star hotel a thousand miles from home, full of rich strangers who won't be upset about her death and a staff so well trained that they will simply nod over her corpse and then quietly move her through the service elevator in the morning.

But here is the bride, already upset.

"Please," the bride says again, like a child, and it occurs to Phoebe that that is what she is. Twenty-six. Twenty-eight, maybe? A child the way she and her husband were children when they got married. The bride doesn't understand yet, what it means to be married. To share everything. To have one bank account. To pee with the door wide open while telling your husband a story about penguins at the zoo. And then one day, to wake up entirely alone. To look back at your whole life like it was just a dream and think, *What the fuck was that?*

"What about your husband?" the bride tries, noticing Phoebe's wedding ring. "Your children?"

Phoebe is done explaining herself. She hands her one last tissue.

"Consider it a wedding gift," Phoebe says. "I hope you two will be very happy."

The doors open. The top floor. Phoebe is finally here. But of course, it doesn't really matter where she is. She can be on the top floor, by the ocean, or in the small bedroom of her house. There is no such thing as a happy place. Because when you are happy, everywhere is a happy place.

And when you are sad, everywhere is a sad place. When they went on those terrible vacations in the Ozarks, they were so happy, they laughed at nearly everything. And the towels were so shitty and short, but it was fine, because they revealed her husband's athletic legs up to the thigh. You're scandalizing me, she said.

"Lila!" High Bun shouts from the end of the hall.

There is no escaping for either of them. The bride flattens out her dress, prepares herself to be the bride again, but then spots a red dot on her hem.

"Is that blood?" she asks Phoebe.

The dress is ruined. They both know it. They are two women who have bled on their underwear for the majority of their lives, and they know there is no unruining it. But the bride takes a deep breath as High Bun and Neck Pillow approach, holds out her arms wide to greet them all over again. Phoebe wonders how many times tonight the bride will have to do this.

"We're on the same floor!" High Bun says, while Neck Pillow eyes the gash on Lila's hand but says nothing. They are good bridesmaids, refusing to point out the things that make the bride ugly.

"What room are you in?" Lila asks.

"The Gloucester," High Bun says. "Is that how you pronounce it?"

"I think you're supposed to say Gloster," Neck Pillow says.

Phoebe begins walking down the hall, leaving the bride fully caught in the web of her wedding, the one she spun for herself as a small girl, dreaming of this moment.

And will High Bun and Neck Pillow remember her tomorrow morning after her body is removed? Will they think, Is the dead woman that one we saw you with in the elevator? Or will they only remember seeing the bride?

The hall gets darker as she goes, lit up by only one perfectly placed copper sconce. Phoebe walks by an alcove with an ice machine that reminds her of other hotels, lesser hotels, the kind she would stay at in her old life when she used to go to conferences and give talks on the marriage plots of the nineteenth century. There is a vending machine, too, but it's hidden behind a tall gold-leaf wall, like some kind of agreement among rich people. This is a nice hotel. If you want to do something you shouldn't, please do it in private.

Inside the room, Phoebe locks the door. She is satisfied by the sharp, metallic sound. She is alone again. She leans her back against the door, and before she admires the ocean view or the golden tassels on the lamps, she looks down to realize she is still holding the gift bag. She takes out the German chocolate wine. A small bottle of something called Everybody Water. A candle hand-poured by the maid of honor, whoever she is. A pack of cookies that look as much like Oreos as they legally can. I will never have another Oreo, Phoebe thinks. And it's these small things she can't accept. The never drinking wine again. The never again feeling her husband's finger down her spine. The body always wanting to be a body.

She opens the German chocolate wine and takes a sip. The bride is right. It's better than you'd think.

"At the Cornwall, we can go sailing on an America's Cup winner," Phoebe said to her husband, Matt.

"We can rent a vintage car and drive it around like dumb bastards," Matt said.

This was January two years ago. They were in bed, searching the internet, trying to plan their most indulgent vacation ever—a thing Phoebe and Matt decided they needed after their final visit to the fertility clinic. The embryos had been bad, it had all been a waste, and Phoebe had miscarried—though the doctor would never say it like that. He said, "It was a nonviable pregnancy," and "I'd suggest not doing a sixth cycle at this point," and the whole drive home, Phoebe couldn't stop feeling like her body had nothing to do with her. Her body was just some piece of land, like the overharvested soybean fields along the highway. Phoebe drank whiskey for the first time in months, and Matt stared at the moon through the window until he said, "Let's go somewhere fun for spring break."

That's when Phoebe remembered the Victorian hotel from the magazine. She found the Cornwall Inn online.

"Look, we can sit in the hot tub while staring at the ocean," Phoebe said.

"We can slurp oysters and somehow laugh at the same exact time," he added, and it felt good to make this list of new things they suddenly wanted together.

Eventually, Matt fell asleep, but Phoebe's body was still too uncomfortable to sleep. She was still bleeding. She stayed up looking at the hotel, analyzing the rooms and the excursions—there were so many possible excursions. They could paddleboard with seals. Go on a "water journey" at a nearby spa. Visit Edith Wharton's house on the Cliff Walk. Do yoga by the ocean, not that she had ever done yoga. But she liked the thought of becoming a woman who casually did yoga by the sea.

She made a detailed spreadsheet of excursions, because she was a researcher by profession. Kept a long list of every book she ever read and her favorite lines from them. Wrote a dissertation tracking each time Jane Eyre went on a walk in Brontë's novel. Became proficient in German one year, then Middle English the next. And after sex with her husband, she always wanted to think more deeply about it, like: What was the first use of the word *cunt* in the English language? And Matt would laugh and say, "Shakespeare, probably?" and Phoebe would continue: "I bet it was Chaucer." And then they both looked it up to learn that two hundred years before Chaucer, there was a street in Oxfordshire called Gropecunt Lane.

She loved the way Matt indulged her. They were very similar—he was a researcher, too, though he would never call himself that. He was a philosopher. He read books on Friday nights and overanalyzed commercials with her, and engaged her in long debates about what they should call their private parts during sex, even if all they could agree on was that they would never call them private parts.

But when Phoebe showed him the spreadsheet the next morning, Matt said, "You made a spreadsheet of fun?" the same way he once said, "You made a spreadsheet of sex?" And yes. Phoebe was thirty-eight. They couldn't afford to be casual anymore about trying to have a baby. But when the time came for sex, he looked at her across the bed like, Okay, are we on schedule? and she looked at him like he was nothing at all, just the vase on the end table.

"You honestly expect me to believe that people go on vacations without making a spreadsheet of fun first?" Phoebe asked.

It was a joke, but he didn't take it as one, so it didn't feel like one. He just looked at her like he was deciding something about her. A short glance, but her husband did not need much to come to a conclusion. Her husband was a careful and astute reader of text. He once wrote a thirty-four-page article about a single word in Plato.

"I'm sure it's great," he said, and then kissed her goodbye.

Matt was not the most handsome man in the world, but he had been to her. And he seemed to get better-looking with age. The light gray taking over his brown hair, the smile that devastated her every time. Her husband could still go out into the world and have children without her—it was a thought she had every time he left the house for work. She wondered if he thought it, too.

"See you at dinner," she said, and they went to teach at the same university in separate cars. She taught literature, while he taught philosophy. She ate a CLIF bar at her desk. She left for a meeting and passed Bob's giant office, the consolation prize for having to be department chair. He was listening to a string quartet loud enough for her to hear. "'Ello," he said, even though he was not British. She went upstairs, walked by her husband's door, which was open, but not really, because he was with a student. A brunette. A girl. He always kept the door open if a girl was in his office, even when all he was doing was listening to her describe her relationship to the Bible.

"I never realized you could read it like it was just a book," the girl said. "I never understood that actual human beings wrote the Bible. I thought God wrote it. Is that stupid?"

"That is not stupid," Phoebe's husband assured her.

Then Phoebe went to the Adjunct Lounge Committee meeting, made up entirely of men with monosyllabic nicknames that somehow passed as professional names. Jack. Jeff. Stan. Russ. Vince. Mike. Phoebe was the only woman and the only adjunct, brought in to answer questions about what a woman and an adjunct might want from this future office space.

"Phoebe?" Mike asked. "What do you think?"

It was a nonviable pregnancy.

"Do you think the chairs should have tablets or no tablets? Russ thinks the tablets look too industrial," he said. "We want you to feel at home. But the tablets do eliminate the need for coffee tables."

Successful men all over the world are always celebrated for their ability to eliminate something so they can make more room for something else. Like the three polyps Dr. Barr removed from her uterus to make room for her future children.

"I think the real coffee tables would be nice," Phoebe said. And then they all went home—the men to their wives and Phoebe to her husband. But he was not there yet.

Getting a drink with some work people, he texted.

She poured herself some leftover wine and wondered who the work people were. She couldn't ask, because she knew that would get classified as overbearing, and she tried so hard never to be overbearing, especially at this delicate stage of their marriage. She tried so hard not to give a shit about the ways she was losing her husband, but why? Of course, she gave a shit. He was her husband.

Was he drinking with Bob? Bob kept a bottle of something in his desk the way professors do in movies about professors. But she knew that her husband didn't really like drinking with Bob. "The man drinks to annihilate himself," he said one night, coming home from a faculty party that went on for too long, mostly because of Bob.

It's possible that he drinks with Rick or Adam or Paula from his department. Maybe Mia? Though ever since Mia and Tom had a baby nine months ago, Mia hadn't really reentered the world yet. And Matt would have invited her if he went with Mia, because Mia was Phoebe's best friend at work, if people at work were allowed to have best friends. Phoebe was never sure. But they had grown close in their adjacent offices, and even closer after Mia's husband attempted suicide two years ago. Phoebe had made it a point to invite Mia and Tom over for dinner nearly every weekend, because Mia made it a point to talk to Phoebe when many of the other tenured professors did not. At these dinners, Tom would talk about all the things he was doing to feel better—meditating three times a day, subscribing to hiking magazines, and quitting refined sugar because that was his trigger, something he explained to them one night when they offered him cake. Tom needed to be honest and open about his depression now, because being ashamed of his depression only made him more depressed. They all nodded in agreement, they totally got it, and yet Phoebe and Matt couldn't help but exchange glances after Mia and Tom left the house.

"I don't know what Tom could be so depressed about. Aren't they trying to have a baby? And Mia is beautiful," Phoebe had said to Matt, because that's how confident she was in her husband's love for her. She could admit when other women were more beautiful, had learned at a young age that she was not the most attractive woman in the room. It had been fine then.

But that night, she drank the wine and added to her spreadsheet of fun and it did not feel fine. It did not feel fun, either, which was what her husband specifically asked for. "We need to have some fun," he had said. And he was right. They were never laughing anymore. They were hardly sleeping together. It was tricky, with her body always feeling so wrong. But she wanted to do something for him. Something she had never done. Something fun.

"When you get home, I want to make you cum," she typed out on her phone to her husband. But just looking at the word *cum* made her nervous. So she deleted it, wrote *come* instead of *cum*, and then turned it back to *cum*, because she didn't know if it was better to be correct or fun, and why did it feel like she always had to choose between the two?

WHEN MATT CAME home from drinks, he came with champagne. Very rarely did he buy champagne. When he did, he felt compelled to make a joke about it.

"I hunted and gathered us some champagne," he said.

"Are we celebrating something?" Phoebe asked. "Or are we just drinking champagne?"

She watched him get two flutes. She waited for him to say something about her text, but he didn't. Did she send it to the wrong person? She picked up her phone, but no, there was the text, dangling so awkwardly at the end of the thread.

"We're celebrating," he said. "I have news."

They never came home from work with real news. Work was always the same. It was either good or bad or busy or just fine. The students were either lazy or enthusiastic or inspiring or depressing. They were misspelling the names of historical figures or they were drawing graduate-level comparisons between Virginia Woolf and Cubism. They were missing the midterm because their grandmother died again (so suddenly and in the night!) or they were ready to go, pens upright.

"What's the news?" she asked.

The champagne bottle stood on the counter like a green god. She hated this bad feeling in her stomach. This assumption that her husband's good news couldn't possibly be hers.

"I found out that I won the Arts and Letters Scholar of the Year award," he said. Her husband twisted off the cork, and it made a loud gunshot noise across the room.

"Oh, wow," Phoebe said.

How did people celebrate? Phoebe remembered throwing confetti in the air on New Year's Eve. She remembered *yip-yip-yipp*ing at the top of the canyon in Arkansas. But overall, they were pretty out of practice.

"I kind of can't believe it," he said.

Phoebe could believe it—she knew he'd win the award at some point. The College of Arts and Letters was one of the smallest programs at their university, and they used to joke that the award would happen to most of the professors if they stayed there long enough—though it would never happen to Phoebe, because adjuncts did not get awards. They did not get health benefits, either, even though she did the exact same job as her husband, a now tenured professor of philosophy with a health insurance plan that covered their cat's visit to the dentist. And that was okay then, because they were married and had enough love and money between them to buy a house and do the things that people who recently bought houses do, like start a garden and renovate the kitchen with a quartzite slab and make six embryos at a lab.

But it did not feel okay when her husband won awards. It did not feel okay when they were at a faculty event, and someone suggested she apply for the new tenure-track job in English. What an opportunity, what a fortuitous time for Jack Hayes to die. But she knew they wouldn't seriously consider her for the position. She'd only had one publication since graduation, and that was not enough. It was Matt who had to say the things Phoebe couldn't, like, "Phoebe is still working on her book," and then they asked what the book was about, but Phoebe found that she couldn't describe it. She said something about the domestic spaces in *Jane Eyre*. Something about the walking culture of the Victorian era. About feminism? But Phoebe didn't really know anymore. The whole thing bored her now. Every time she opened her dissertation on the computer, it felt like sitting down for coffee with an old boyfriend she couldn't imagine ever loving again.

"Congratulations," Phoebe said to her husband. "That's really great." Phoebe smiled and kissed Matt on the cheek. Squeezed his arm like she might fuck him silly later, and maybe she would. Maybe he'd notice the text and pull her upstairs and tonight would be the night when everything changed, when she would lean over the bed as he took her from behind. Or maybe they'd do it face-forward, look into each other's eyes, like they did when they first fell in love.

"I'll have to give a speech at the awards dinner in February," her husband said.

"Is a speech bad?"

If Phoebe had to give a speech in February, that would be very bad. Phoebe had started to hate standing in front of her students each day, all of them waiting in silence for her to prove herself. Because hadn't she proved herself yesterday? And the day before? Why did she have to wake up every day just to prove herself if it didn't seem to matter how often she proved herself? By the end of the hour, she was exhausted, and didn't feel better until she was at home, drinking a glass of wine.

"A speech is great," Matt said. "We need things to look forward to."

He was right. They had nothing to look forward to, which was the entire point of planning the vacation.

"Here." He handed her a champagne flute. It was flimsy and delicate. It made her nervous, just holding it. "I know it doesn't really mean anything for promotion, but it's got to help at least a little."

Her husband's goal used to be marrying her and starting a family. Now he was concentrating very hard on promotion.

"Of course," she said. "Everything helps."

"Cheers."

She drank.

"This is good champagne," he said.

She couldn't help but note that in the history of her husband's life, he had never yet purchased bad champagne.

"It is," she said. She really loved the first sip of champagne. The first sip always brought her back to life. To the park where they made their first toast as a married couple. To the warm and snowy balconies on New Year's Eve. But the second and third sip were always so dry, they killed her again. "It really is."

Her husband—what a great scholar. And the students loved him.

They were always gathered outside his office, eyes glowing with worship, saying, "He's a genius, and yet not even an asshole about it." And it was true. He knew a lot. He spoke three languages and could hold a long conversation about everything from the drinking culture of ancient Greece to the local politics of St. Louis to the problem of blood-doping in the Olympics to the species of bird at their feeder. His intelligence was one of the reasons that she fell in love with him. But it was annoying to see young women worship it, because nobody worshipped hers. People were either surprised by it or disapproving of it. Not even Bob was a fan anymore.

"You know what your problem is, Phoebe?" Bob had asked a few days prior. Bob was technically her colleague now, no longer her dissertation advisor, no longer required to worry about her publication record. Yet he did. And Phoebe understood. Phoebe was worried, too. It had been ten years since she graduated, and she was still here at the same university, walking the same academic halls, teaching as an adjunct, never having moved on like the others in her program, never able to turn her dissertation into an actual book. She didn't know what her problem was, and she hated how eager she was for Bob to tell her: How much of her life had she spent in this moment, waiting for someone else to decide something conclusive about her? That was her problem, she knew. But Bob said, "You think too much," and it genuinely surprised her. Wasn't that a good thing? Wasn't that the entire point of being an academic?

IT WAS NOT until later in bed when Matt saw the text.

"Oh, shit," he said. "I didn't see this. I'm sorry."

He apologized but didn't reach over to touch her. She was so embarrassed by that point, she changed the subject.

"We should book the Cornwall," Phoebe said.

"Huh?" Matt asked.

"The hotel. For spring break. The Cornwall."

"Was that the expensive one?"

"Very expensive."

"Like remortgaging the house expensive?"

"Like, eight hundred a night."

"That's . . . too much, Phoebe."

But wasn't that the point? To be too much? To be reckless? To be extravagant? To do whatever the fuck they wanted because if they couldn't have children, they could at least have fun spending the savings account that Phoebe had started ten years ago for their children?

Phoebe needed that. But she could feel that he no longer did. He had changed his mind today. He had won his award. He had his fun thing to look forward to, and he didn't even have to buy it. He simply earned it, and how wonderful that must feel for him now—to have earned back his dignified place in the world.

"Why don't we just go to the Ozarks?" Matt said. "We always like it there."

Phoebe looked up at the dark ceiling. She felt a panicked feeling, like when she was a kid, lost in the supermarket looking around and realizing everybody in town sort of looked like her father. They all wore the same jeans.

"No," Phoebe said.

They always went to the Ozarks. They honeymooned in the Ozarks and they took spring breaks in the Ozarks, and the hikes were long and beautiful things that made Phoebe feel proud enough to enjoy their evening happy hour. Phoebe had always felt her fun must be earned, her vacations must also be work, require a lot of gear.

But Phoebe was tired of work. Her whole life felt like work now. Even the parts that used to be the most fun, like reading over the summer or orgasming during sex or having conversations with her husband at dinner. They felt like things she had to be really good at now, in order to prove that everything was normal. That even without a baby, they would be happy. And even without a book, the ten years she had spent trying to write one had been worth it. Because it was getting harder to believe that. Most nights, she looked back at all of her research, all of her spreadsheets, all of her journals and her papers and her injections and thought, *What the fuck?*

"The Ozarks are for families," Phoebe said to Matt.

They were full of kids flying kites. Parents that wore matching hats and walked through the woods eating American flag ice pops.

"We're a family," Matt said.

"But we don't *have* a family."

"We have Harry."

Harry was their cat, always curled up between them just before bed. They bought him ten years ago when they really wanted a dog but then decided it was not the right time for a dog. Yet they went to the shelter "just to browse" only to learn that there was no browsing at a shelter. There was a little orange kitten with its nose pressed up to the cage, going, *Meowmeowmeowmeow.*

Harry, Matt read off the adoption file, and it sounded wrong to them, overly human, but they spent a decade loving Harry more than they thought normal. They gave Harry treats for doing nothing at all and then wondered whether it was wrong to give Harry a treat for doing nothing at all. For just being a cat? "Why do I expect you to be more than a cat when all I want is for you to just be a cat?" Phoebe asked Harry, like he was a psychiatrist sitting between them, and often that's what Harry looked like—so dignified, with one little paw crossed over the other like he was patiently waiting his turn to say something wise.

"Harry is not our family," Phoebe reminded him. "He's our psychiatrist."

"Oh right. It's such a blurry line."

They used to crack themselves up by asking Harry deep, dark, existential questions. *Am I self-sabotaging at work because I had no mother, Harry?* And Matt would say, *Absolutely*, in Harry's voice—she had no idea how to describe it other than it was the voice they both knew to be Harry's.

"Harry thinks we should go to the Ozarks," Matt said, and she softened for a moment. She always felt deeply connected to Matt when they were talking to each other like this, through Harry. It made her feel like maybe the three of them really could be a family. "Harry wants to hike the canyon again."

"Fine, but you can tell Harry that if we wind up staying in that really shitty motel one more time, I will kill myself," Phoebe said.

They both laughed a little because Harry opened his eyes and looked at Phoebe like he had understood, but also because they knew that Phoebe was not the type to kill herself. Phoebe had taken a multivitamin every day since she was a child. Phoebe brushed her hair before bed. Phoebe was very normal, and her husband liked that. Being normal was his big dream—something her husband confessed on their very first date.

"Ever since I was a kid, I just knew I wanted to grow up and be normal," he had joked. "But seriously. It's true." And Phoebe understood. Her childhood had been exceptionally lonely—with a dead mother and a depressed father and no siblings to talk to at night, which is why she started reading books. Fairy tales at first, because they were about girls just like her, girls whose mothers were killed off in one quick sentence. "Your mother was a wonderful woman who died giving birth to you," was how her father put it one morning and she felt awful. She felt like she had ruined something just by existing, and she had. Her mother! That beautiful woman who was always hiking in all their photographs. And her father—he was in the picture, too. He was smiling and hiking through the Ozarks with his pregnant wife, and Phoebe had ached for that normal man she never got to know. The normal girl she never got to be.

"But why does being normal feel like a crime here?" Phoebe had asked Matt.

In graduate school, it had been embarrassing to be normal. Everyone Phoebe had met was on a mission to be spectacularly, deliciously weird, and she was impressed and confused by how her colleagues looked so good in socks and high heels. Phoebe could not wear things like that, could not push fashion boundaries, and she didn't know why exactly, except for the reason that she never wanted anyone to know she was strange.

So, she wore jean shorts and Tevas as soon as the temperatures rose above fifty. She never dyed her hair and had no idea what to say when a poet brought her to a noise concert on a date except, This is a little noisy. The poet kissed her at the end of the night, laughed in her mouth a little as he said, You're so, like, normal, and it felt like a compliment at the time, but days of his silence later, she saw her collection of cardigans from Banana Republic lined up neatly in the same direction and knew it wasn't.

"Well, good, because I'm very normal," she had said to Matt. It was a relief not to feel like she had to buy a whole new wardrobe just to go to a pub with him.

"It's settled then," he said. "Where's the preacher?"

And that's how everything had felt for years—so wonderfully normal. They got married in a public park, invited only their closest friends and family, because they were suspicious of money, of grand gesture. The bigger the gesture, the emptier the feeling. The more wedding you need, the less happy you must be.

Phoebe truly believed this then. But now the utter simplicity of their lives felt crushing. When Matt reached over to touch her, Phoebe could see and feel the whole experience even before it started.

"I wish I saw your text earlier," Matt said. "I really wish I did."

When he leaned over to kiss her, she flinched at his tenderness. She hated his softness. She had been fantasizing, lately, about him doing terrible things to her. Things so awful she couldn't ever tell him, because she knew it meant something was changing inside of her, some darkness was hardening into sludge. So, she just said, "I love you."

THEY BOOKED A hotel in the Ozarks for March. And every day after, Matt was up early in a tie and then off to work. But Phoebe moved a little slower. Some mornings, she felt wildly emotional, and some mornings impenetrably numb. She didn't know how to explain the contradiction to her new therapist when he asked. She kept saying, I feel . . . disconnected. No, I feel sad. No, I feel . . . and she would trail off and hope the therapist would fill in the blank, but he never did.

"I feel fucking crazy," she said to Harry the night before her husband's awards ceremony. Harry was the only one who knew how often she said fuck while grading papers. "I mean, seriously, what the fuck?"

When she proposed the Fairy Tale course, she thought it would be fun. But she was increasingly disturbed by each student paper that compared Rapunzel's mother's infertility to "a kind of poison." She had forgotten about all the barren women in these stories or maybe she just never noticed them before. She had been too distracted by all the dead mothers.

"And why are all the mothers in fairy tales always dead?" Phoebe asked Matt, who was grading on the couch next to her.

"Because they were premodern. The mothers were often . . . dead."

But it had to be about more than that. It seemed like the story wouldn't even work if the mother wasn't dead—the dead mother was an important plot point, a necessary precondition for the girl's story. Because Cinderella never would have been at the center of the novel if her mother had lived. (Neither would Jane Eyre, she thought). The mother had to die so that the girl started in a place of desperation, because that's what the story was always about. That's why she had liked them. Watch the good girl grow up, watch the girl try very hard to get everything she wants, then watch how happy she becomes.

The end.

And that had been Phoebe's story, too—she had been so good. So quiet. So studious. Valedictorian of her high school, then college, and then went off to graduate school to make a life for herself, which she did. She fell in love, got a PhD, got married. Bought a house with her husband. And then, after five grueling cycles of IVF, when all seemed lost, she finally got pregnant using their last embryo. For ten weeks, she rubbed lotion on her belly, and she could feel it, how she was hurtling toward the happy ending that would make everything, even her mother's death, seem like a necessary part of the story.

But then it was over, in under a sentence. One day she had been pregnant, and then the next day, she was not. She had felt the blood between her legs, and every time she remembered the blood, she thought, No, no, no, this can't be how it ends. Because this ending made a mockery of her mother's death. This ending was just tragic. More like a Russian novel, where all the characters go on a great wild adventure just to be killed off in the end.

"The Russians got it right," Phoebe said the morning of the awards ceremony, and she loved that she could say things like this to Matt. "Maybe I just need to accept that my life is a Russian novel."

"You forget I haven't read the Russian novels," Matt said, pouring coffee in his to-go mug.

"I just mean, a story can be beautiful not because of the way it ends. But because of the way it's written."

"That's true," Matt said. "But you're not at the end."

Matt clearly wasn't ready to be a character in a Russian novel. He wasn't ready for his life to be a tragedy, albeit a beautiful one. He was off to work, where he was going to write his speech and pitch a new book to his editor about the philosophy of doing things, while Phoebe stayed at home to write. "Why are all the mothers dead?" she typed, but then felt too depressed to continue. So she got up and made an elaborate breakfast. She touched herself in bed and thought of her husband holding her against a wall by her neck, calling her terrible things. Then, she went for a walk and admired novelty door knockers. She stopped at Joe's wine shop on the way home. They bought wine exclusively from Joe, a bald man with big thick muscles who asked a lot of questions about the English language every time she purchased something.

"Hey, Professor. Is *conversate* a word?" Joe asked. "Never heard of it. But girlie over here says it's a word."

He pointed to the young girlie, who was always sitting on the stool next to the register, all eyeliner and purple nails. There was always a young girlie—sometimes they worked in the store, and sometimes they just came to visit Joe and sit on a stool for hours because that's what girlies seemed to like.

"Everything's a word," the girlie said. "If you say it enough. Isn't that right, Dr. Stone?"

This girlie was a student at the university, dark brown hair, dark eyes. Studying psychology. She had never had Phoebe as a professor, but said she had "heard about" her.

"That's true," Phoebe said. "Say it for ten years, and it ends up in the dictionary."

"Ten years," Joe said. "That's all it takes?"

Joe wanted Phoebe to like him because Joe wanted all women to like him. Liking him seemed to be the first step to fucking him. And sometimes, she liked Joe. When Joe was railing against the authoritarian undertones of popular politicians or watching a Disney movie on his computer and laughing at all the slapstick. But then she saw the girlie on his stool and the cup in front of the register that said PUSSY FUND.

Right then, it was half-full.

"That's right," Phoebe said.

Her husband never commented on the Pussy Fund after they left, as if it were not right to call out another man on his Pussy Fund, or like, if they actually called him out on it, they'd have to find another place to buy wine, and this one was really the most convenient with the best selection. So, she paid for the bottles, and she said, "See ya, Joe," and she tried not to wonder if her husband ever dropped his spare change in the Pussy Fund when she was not there.

EVERY FEBRUARY, THE awards ceremony, and every year they went, and every time, Phoebe wore the same dress. A black Calvin Klein that she bought years ago for her job orientation. A dress that nobody ever complimented but nobody ever insulted. A dress designed not to be noticed.

She was surprised that it still fit, still made her look the way she always looked, and this depressed her. Tonight, she wanted to feel different. She wanted to walk into the awards ceremony and be noticed. Because if she wasn't going to have children, she should at least have magnificent dresses. So she drove to the mall and didn't stop shopping until the emerald dress caught her eye. The silk felt amazing, like cool water dripping down her body—why had she always been afraid to wear silk? To wear color? She looked good in emerald. It highlighted the red tones of her brown hair. The green specks of her eyes. Her olive skin.

She bought it without thinking, without wondering what her husband might think, what Bob might think, what Mia might think. That's how much she loved it.

But before the dinner, when she put it on again, she felt ridiculous standing on her beige carpet next to her flannel sheets. The silk dress was too much. Five hundred dollars. And the dinner was going to be in the gymnasium. What was she thinking? It was floor-length, a dress meant for a wedding, not for an awards ceremony at a cash-strapped university in Missouri.

She put the black dress on again. She didn't want to embarrass her husband. She knew she had been embarrassing her husband lately. She knew she had been a little sloppy, sometimes too drunk when he came home.

"Did you write today?" he asked her when he returned to pick her up. He suggested they take one car.

"Yes," she lied.

She looked at herself in the mirror. There she was again, she thought, and yet, she felt like she was somewhere far away, still in the fertility clinic, watching Matt shake hands with the doctor. Or maybe she was at the River Ouse, watching Virginia Woolf fill her pockets with stones. She wondered how many stones Woolf used. How cold was the water?

"You look beautiful," he said, and when he said it, she felt it.

She combed her hair and off they went to dinner.

THE DINNER WAS an elaborate affair for a gymnasium. The university paid five grand a year to bring in a guest speaker, some celebrity scholar who could talk both about the crisis in the Middle East and the value of a liberal arts education or the labor conditions in China and the value of a liberal arts education or the recession and the value of a liberal arts education.

"You really look so beautiful," her husband said again before they entered the gym. He seemed to be telling both of them. He put his arm around her and just like that, they were husband and wife again.

They drank white wine and ate chicken marsala with steamed vegetables. They sat at a table of people just like her husband. People with real jobs. Bob. Susan. Brian. Mia.

Then, a series of speeches and applauses for the various achievements of other people and then, chocolate lava cake. They ate the cake and talked about how the cake was not very lavalike. They talked about their students, their jobs as a whole, and the consensus at the table was that they were very rewarding but also very hard.

"Hard?" Bob's wife asked. She was a surgeon at a local hospital. "All Bob ever does in his office is drink German beers and listen to Bach."

"And not to mention your summers off!" said Tom. With his doctor's schedule, Tom and Mia could only take a one-week vacation each year, and then they talked about that vacation for the rest of the year. "So, no complaining, you professors!"

They laughed. Tom was right. Their jobs were wonderful, her husband confessed with his hands up.

The lights dimmed and the student choir began singing from the stage with candles. But even in the dark, Phoebe could feel the truth: the gym underneath her feet. The foul line that cut across the dance floor. The way they looked at her like she was just Matt's wife. Especially the ones who didn't really know her, like Susan from the philosophy department who forgot her name every year. She always had the same question for Phoebe: "And what do you do?"

"I teach," Phoebe said.

"Phoebe actually teaches here," her husband said.

"Oh wonderful, what do you teach?" Susan asked.

"Pretty much whatever Bob asks me to teach," Phoebe said. "Mostly the survey lit courses that all freshmen are required to take. Everything from the beginning of literature to the internet."

"But what's your field?" Susan asked.

"Victorian literature," Phoebe said.

"Phoebe actually teaches a seminar on the fairy tale right now," Matt added. "And she's finishing a book on *Jane Eyre*."

For ten years, Phoebe has been finishing her book on *Jane Eyre*.

Then more awards. When her husband's name was called, he smiled. He put down his napkin. He walked onstage. He took his award, and everybody at the table clapped and smiled at him. Mia leaned into Phoebe's shoulder.

"You must be proud," Mia said.

She was. Look at my husband, she thought, as he took his place behind the podium. He gave a short speech about the value of a liberal arts education, but Phoebe barely heard a word. Look at him, she thought, as he returned to the table smiling. My husband. He sat back down, and everybody congratulated him, while he tried very hard not to appear too pleased.

"They've got to give it to everybody at some point," he said, which felt like a small betrayal, because this had been their joke. "I bet you even Bob will get it one day."

Bob laughed.

"The students just love him," Mia said, and it was something about the way she said it, as if she knew the students better than Phoebe. As if Mia and Matt occupied a house together without her.

But she didn't say anything. She felt ill and said, "Excuse me." She went to the bathroom. She looked at herself in the mirror.

Your husband thinks you are beautiful, she thought, until she felt better.

But before she returned to the table, she saw her husband talking to Mia. Mia threw her head back to laugh, and her husband laughed, too, opened his mouth wide, wider than Phoebe had seen in months. Even when they watched TV and Phoebe curled into him, he kept his mouth pressed shut.

But in this moment with Mia, she could see the old Matt, the one she first met years ago in the computer room, who was light and funny and happy. And Mia looked happy, too. Something she had not really seemed since Tom got depressed years ago.

Phoebe sat back down at the table, and all of a sudden Mia's beauty seemed different. It was not just a basic fact. It was a situation.

PHOEBE DIDN'T BRING Mia up until they were home, back inside the house.

"It doesn't seem fair that Mia can have three books and also be so goddamned beautiful," Phoebe said. She hoped it sounded like a joke.

"Oh," Matt said. "Yeah. She is a good laugh."

"I didn't say that. I said she was beautiful."

"What are you doing?" he asked. "I thought we had a nice time tonight."

"We did," she said.

He kissed her. "*You* looked beautiful tonight."

He wanted to have sex; she could tell. But she didn't want to. Or maybe she didn't want him to be sweet in that moment. In her fantasies, he was never sweet to her anymore. In her fantasies, it was no longer even her that he was fucking, though the therapist had insisted the fantasy was still good news.

"It's good that it at least involves your husband," he had said.

As she went to undress, her husband said, "No, keep the dress on." He took off his shirt, his pants, and when he walked toward her, she imagined him walking into Joe's wine shop, seeing the girlie sitting on the stool like usual. She's doing homework for her class. No, she doesn't know where Joe is.

"Anything new today?" her husband asks, and the girlie says, "Let me show you what we've got." She is bringing her husband to the back to show him the latest shipment of wine. She bends over to pick up a few bottles and her husband walks toward her, puts his hands on her waist, and centers her the way he does when he really wants to fuck, when he wants her to just be tits and ass and ponytail. He pulls on her hair, and that's when her thighs clench tight around him—and it is only then, when Phoebe pretended that she didn't know her husband at all, that she could come.

After they had sex, they couldn't look each other in the eye. She took off her black dress and her husband poured himself a glass of whiskey and he didn't bother with ice cubes and he went outside to look at the stars because that's what people have done since the beginning of time. And still, Phoebe did not think it was the end. She couldn't really conceive of the end. She thought that in a few weeks, they'd go to the Ozarks for spring break, and then maybe, just maybe, she would try IVF one more time, because who knows? Maybe it would work the sixth time. Maybe the doctors were wrong.

But a few weeks later, in March, the world shut down and they did nothing at all. They sat in the house. They taught through their computers. They looked out windows a lot. She cried too much, and he drank too much, and sometimes, she worried he might leave her. Sometimes, she wanted to leave. But when she imagined herself leaving, her husband always begged her to stay. He got on his knees, pressed his face against her thighs, and clutched her like a child. Please, Phoebe, he said in the fantasy. Please. I need you. Then he explained all the ways he needed her, and how the kids needed her, too. And so, she stayed. Every time she imagined leaving her husband, she always ended up staying. It was a fantasy, in which there were children and the children always needed her. She had to imagine leaving only so she could imagine staying. She had to imagine herself at the door and her husband shouting, "No, Phoebe, no!" like she was a dog. And she really didn't know why, in her fantasy, she wanted to be treated like this.

"So, how was your day?" Matt asked.

It was August, the night before their fall semester began. Their last dinner together, but Phoebe didn't know it yet. Maybe Matt didn't know it yet, either. Maybe during that dinner, he was still deciding. Maybe if she had said something more interesting in response, something other than, "Good," he might have stayed.

"Good!" he said. "Good. Did you write today?"

"A little."

That morning, Phoebe tried so hard to write. Their summer break was ending, and she had nothing to show for it, so she set up her coffee and her computer and closed the blinds and put out two fingers of whiskey and one cigarette on her desk, her future reward for finishing a page, and then she finished, and she slowly sipped on the whiskey, and she lit the cigarette but didn't smoke it. She just liked the smell, the feeling of holding it between her fingers, and it started to feel like she was in her office not to write but to drink and pretend to smoke.

Matt left his office, a door slam, and she put out the cigarette. She finally understood what her advisor meant when he said, "Don't combine your good habits with your bad habits." When Bob had said it years ago, she only had good habits. She ran 3.1 miles every other day, she drank ginger shots at the local café, she always did her laundry on Sundays, she planned her courses in June before the summer got away from her, and these good things had always been enough. They had been at the center of her life. Her house. Her students. Her research. Her husband, her physical tether to this world from the day she met him. But now they could not even look each other in the eye when they asked each other questions.

"Were you smoking in your office earlier?" Matt asked.

"No," she said, and it was not technically a lie. But Matt didn't understand. Matt said he could smell the smoke, said it was bad for her body, which ironically made her want to smoke. For years all she had been thinking about was what she should put in her body to make it a super womb, and she was tired of it. Fuck my body, she thought, but did not say it.

"How was your day?" she asked, and felt like one of the awful characters in a T. S. Eliot poem.

What shall I do now? What shall I do? I shall rush out as I am, and walk the street with my hair down, so. What shall we do to-morrow? What shall we ever do?

Yet when Matt left her later that night, it truly did surprise her. Nothing had ever shocked her more. He did what he always did before sleep. Took off his belt and rolled it into a ball. Took a shower and then put on the kind of junk shirt he only wore around the house. But then he put on jeans, slipped on his belt, and packed a bag. "I am in love with Mia," he kept saying, and she didn't really believe it. This was not how her fantasy went.

But this wasn't her fantasy. It was his, and she didn't know how it worked. She just watched him, waited for him to drop his bag, but he didn't.

The golden tassel lamps of the Roaring Twenties make Phoebe want to drink before she should be drinking, and it's ridiculous that she still thinks things like that, still tries to impose rules on herself like, I should not be drinking, when she is hours from taking her own life.

She pours herself a full glass of the German chocolate wine. She refuses to spend her last hours on this planet worrying. She has spent too much time worrying about what to drink, where to vacation, what to wear, what to say, was it hotter to write *cum* or *come*, and what was the point? What did it matter how she spelled it? Her husband left anyway.

Phoebe takes a sip of wine. She opens the drapes. They are heavy and teal, fit for a queen or a movie star. They could block out all the world's light if she wanted them to, but Phoebe wants to see the ocean. Phoebe has never been to the ocean before, a fact that appalled most people but charmed her husband. He once liked that Phoebe did not run around feeling the pressure to conquer each worldly experience.

Yet Phoebe thought it was wrong to leave the world before seeing the ocean, the way she thought it was wrong for Matt to ask for a divorce thirty miles away on Zoom. He should have returned from Mia's house one last time to remind himself of the beauty of their world. The trim he had hand-painted himself. But it was five months into the pandemic when he asked for the divorce, and he said he couldn't return. Matt, Mia, and her baby were already a "pod." He sat in front of a shelf lined with Mia's trinkets from Paris like they were his and said, "I'm so sorry." And "Are you okay?" And "Please tell me you're okay."

Phoebe sets the cat's painkillers on the nightstand. She looks out at the ocean spread before her. From up here, the water looks calm. Like a flat and reliable rug, as if it knows nothing about what is to come. Phoebe expected more from the ocean, maybe because she read too many Herman Melville books in which the ocean knows everything about the future—foreshadows death with every wild and loud crash of a wave.

But so be it. She picks up the phone.

"Hello," she says. "May I place an order for room service, please?"

Phoebe wants to have a big, decadent meal before she dies. She wants to have lobster and crab. She wants to eat oysters and drink wine and crack a crème brûlée top one last time.

"Unfortunately, we've suspended room service for the opening reception tonight," Pauline says.

"The opening reception?" Phoebe asks. "That's what she's calling it?"

"Yes. I'm so sorry for the inconvenience," Pauline says. She sounds truly devastated. "Please understand we are a little understaffed from Covid."

"Right, okay," Phoebe says, but she feels panicked by the news. "There's really nothing at all?"

"Well, there's food down at the reception," Pauline says.

Phoebe hangs up. She can't go downstairs. She definitely can't go to the reception. She did not come all this way just to watch happy people eat expensive food. And she refuses to have her last meal be imitation Oreos from the wedding bag or Doritos from the vending machine. There's something just too sad about that.

So, fine, she will not eat. What's the point anyway? Why take perfectly good oysters down with her?

But then she doesn't know what to do with herself. She had planned on eating for an hour or two. She had planned on the meal feeling like the final event of her life. She sits on the bed and stares at the water and it's an odd feeling—this having nothing at all to do except feel the ocean breeze on her face. For the past ten years, there has been too much to do and not enough time. There was the dissertation that needed to become a book, the research that needed to become PowerPoints, the sex that needed to become a baby, and the students that needed her to run their lives. That's how her student Adam put it yesterday morning when he came into her office and announced that Phoebe was now in charge of his life.

"But I'm not your advisor," Phoebe told him.

"You're not?"

"No," Phoebe said.

The conversation would have ended there, had her husband and Mia not walked into her office, which was also the photocopier room and the coffee station. The university never built the adjunct faculty lounge—the committee went bust after pandemic budget cuts. Then Bob had given away her old office to the new hire after Phoebe chose to continue teaching virtually during the second year of the pandemic. And now that she was back, Bob was at a loss. There was nowhere else to put her except next to the Keurig and the pound cake that Jane the admin brought in.

Mia and Matt looked shocked to see Phoebe there but then quickly said, "Hello," as if she were any other colleague in the department, and Phoebe could not think. Could not breathe. Could not say hello. She just stared at her student Adam, focused intensely on his nose as she said, "But maybe I can still help you?"

"Well, I'm thinking of dropping out of college," Adam said. She heard her husband pour the two coffees, and Mia put in the cream. "I want to make pants."

"You want to make pants?" Phoebe asked, and she did not know what a person asked next, so she said, "What kind of pants?"

Her husband stirred in the sugar, and maybe her husband was looking at her, maybe he recognized the black Calvin Klein dress she wore just so he might remember the last time he fucked her in it. But she could not bring herself to look.

"Any kind, all the pants," Adam said.

Her husband and Mia put the lids on their cups.

"But can't you make pants and also be in school at the same time?" Phoebe asked, and then her husband and Mia were gone, and Adam said, "Maybe," and Phoebe felt like she might throw up or faint.

After, she packed up her books and went to class where she tried to teach a John Donne poem, but her Brit Lit students weren't fans.

"Why is the speaker being, like, ravished by God?" a student asked.

Everyone laughed. They were waiting for Phoebe to say something, for context, a frame in which to put all the confusing and strange things.

"It is, essentially, a love letter to the Lord," Phoebe said.

"Why would anyone write a love letter to the Lord?" another student asked.

"Oh my God, it's not a *love* letter," the girl said. "He's basically asking for God to rape him."

"That's what I got from the poem, too," another kid said. "But I'm glad you said it."

This made a few kids snicker, which made another student raise her hand and proclaim that there was "nothing funny about rape, not in the 1600s, not now, and not even when it happened to a dead white man."

"It's not *supposed* to be funny," Phoebe clarified.

"Well, of course it's not funny, the man is being *raped*, Dr. Stone. By God!"

"So is it like, a gay poem? Is God gay?"

"God is like, famously not gay."

"Why are you all laughing? It's seriously not funny!"

"I'm not trying to be funny! You *know* I'm gay!"

Phoebe stumbled backward into the desk.

"It's about knowing you want to be better," Phoebe says. "But not knowing how to fix yourself. That's why he's begging the Lord to force him to be better, to fix him."

"That's like, messed up," a student said, and Phoebe agreed.

"It is," she said, and Phoebe can't remember much after that except one of the boys standing at her desk, saying, "You okay, Dr. Stone?"

"I'm fine," Phoebe said.

The students seemed completely unchanged as they left, except the girl who was still ranting about the poem to a friend, "I just don't think anybody should *teach* that poem."

Phoebe went back to her office that wasn't really an office. She was not fine—but maybe she could be fine. She just needed a cup of coffee. And to make copies of a Whitman poem before her Intro to Lit class. She didn't have time to do it yesterday—she had been too busy, too overwhelmed, getting her nails done, touching up her roots, getting herself ready for her big return to campus. Was the black dress too much for the first day or not enough? she wondered, because she hadn't seen her husband since the divorce hearing, and a tiny part of her still felt like if she wore the black dress, it would turn them back into husband and wife again.

But there was only Mia—this time at the photocopier. There Mia would always be, Phoebe realized.

"Paper jam," Mia said, and Phoebe nodded because a paper jam was nobody's fault. It just happened sometimes, which is exactly what her husband had said about the affair. It just happened.

But why? Phoebe couldn't bring herself to ask her husband this. Because she knew why. She looked at Mia in her big wooden earrings and her cropped black jeans and an oversize pink blazer that somehow made her seem skinnier. It made Phoebe feel foolish to think that her husband would be wooed back by a simple A-line black dress. Was this why it was so hard to be mad at Mia? Because Phoebe knew on some level that Mia was just better? Always standing there in her big earrings, making Phoebe wonder why Phoebe always had to be herself.

"I'm sorry," Mia said.

Mia got down on her knees. In Phoebe's fantasies, this was how Mia always apologized to her: literally groveled at her feet. Phoebe couldn't believe it was actually happening and felt herself get excited.

But then Mia added, "I'm sorry, this will only take a minute," and it made Phoebe so angry. Because a paper jam always took longer than a minute. Phoebe knew this. Mia knew this. Mia started opening up all the drawers the machine told her to open, but even then, Mia couldn't figure it out, didn't know where drawer five was, and this is when Phoebe normally would have helped her look for drawer five, but she refused.

"*This* is what you're sorry about?" Phoebe asked.

Mia's eyes flickered over to the admin's desk, as if to suggest Phoebe not do this here, so close to Jane's pound cake, and Phoebe could suddenly understand why affairs ended with someone dead. Her rage felt ruinous, too big for the hum of this small, quiet office.

"You slept with my husband," Phoebe said, not so loud to be yelling but loud enough for Jane to hear.

"Look, I'm sorry I hurt you," Mia whispered. "I'm sorry it happened the way it did. But I'm not sorry it happened. I can't be. I love him."

"No, *I* love him," Phoebe said. "He's *my* husband."

It made her feel silly, fighting over her husband with a female colleague who had her arm wedged in drawer five, like she was about to help birth a document. This was not how it was supposed to go. In her fantasy, Phoebe doesn't ever mention her husband. Instead, Phoebe delivers an impassioned and loud monologue about what an awful woman Mia is, the biggest traitor of all the traitors, an embarrassment to women, and then Phoebe walks out of the office, out of the building, feeling victorious, never to return again.

"He's not your husband," Mia said. "Not anymore."

Phoebe felt crazy. She felt like she was a kid, crying over a bath her father wouldn't let her take because he had to go to work. "Fine, Phoebe, have a tantrum, see what good that will do," her father had said. And that's when she learned it did nothing except make her father leave a room.

"I thought you were my friend," Phoebe said calmly. She was trying to compose herself. She couldn't bear it if Mia walked out, if she left her alone with this horrible feeling.

"I was your friend," Mia said. "And I will always regret damaging our friendship."

"*Damaging?* You *ruined* it. You ruined everything. My life. My job. My marriage."

"I really do like you, Phoebe. And I hope we can somehow be friends at the end of this. But I did not ruin your marriage. That is not on me. The only reason Matt fell in love with me was because your marriage was already over."

As if to conclude her argument, Mia pulled out the piece of paper. Mia solved the jam, but it was too late. Class had started five minutes ago. Phoebe was already divorced. Phoebe had signed the final papers. There was nothing her anger could do here.

The door opened. Stan, the Americanist, took one look at her black dress and said, "Wowwee, Phoebe, nice dress!"

She didn't know what else to do but say, "Thanks."

Then Mia snuck out of the office with her papers, and Phoebe stood there for a moment, feeling utterly bereft and flattened, like land right after a bomb hits. She walked to class empty-handed, said hello to her students, and yes, she understood why they never said hello back—a lesson Phoebe learned in yoga class last month when the instructor said hello, and everyone waited for someone else to do it. Everyone always hoped it was someone else who would be bold. They were like Phoebe.

But Phoebe was sick of them. Sick of herself. Sick of everything.

She walked out of the class without a word, got in her car, and drove home. By the time she walked into her kitchen, her hands were shaking. Something was wrong. She called her therapist, thinking he might help, but he sounded wrong, too.

"Listen, before we have another session, there's something you need to know," he said, and why did he sound just like her husband before he left?

"I have thought long and hard about this, Phoebe, but unfortunately, I am going to have to drop your new health insurer," her therapist said. "They're just too unethical to do business with, and I refuse to work that way."

Then he reminded her that what he was doing was setting a boundary, like this might be a learning moment for her.

"You'll have to pay out of pocket for this session, and all future sessions, if you want to go forward," he added.

She hung up on him. She couldn't afford to go forward. She got small alimony payments from Matt, but they were only enough to cover the new insurance payments she made ever since losing coverage after the divorce. A thousand dollars a month, just for catastrophic. Trying to stay alive was starting to bankrupt her, and even though Phoebe had been as good a saver as she was a researcher, the children's savings fund was starting to run out. She was going to have to apply to teaching jobs all over again, which she already knew was hopeless, because she had tried it last August.

So she was going to have to sell the house. It was the only solution. But she couldn't bear to sell the house. The house was the only thing she had left. And Harry.

"Assuming you take United," she joked, and at least she could still joke. At least she still had Harry. Where was Harry anyway? She rattled his bottle of painkillers, which always made Harry come running because the pills were flavored like tuna. But Harry didn't come running, and she knew. Before she found him in the basement, curled up into himself, she knew.

She was too distraught to bury him. Instead, she just left Harry there, drove to Joe's, got mind-blisteringly drunk, and woke up the next morning with such a headache, such a weight on her chest, she knew her life was over.

But still, it was Tuesday. The second day of the semester. She had another Intro to Lit at ten-thirty. She made toast. She looked over her old lecture notes on *Leaves of Grass*. She saw the scribbles of her past self in the margins next to the lines, "The smallest sprout shows there is really no death . . . Has anyone supposed it lucky to be born? I hasten to inform him or her, it is just as lucky to die, and I know it." She had always secretly thought those lines were bullshit until that morning when she held up the gray blouse in front of the mirror. No, she wouldn't put on that blouse. She wouldn't go to work. Why bother? She could already see the whole day—the whole long and lonely life—before it happened.

Whitman was right. How lucky it would be to die, she thought—to just be the dirt. To just be a plant. To be made beautiful again by becoming part of the earth.

It is a lovely way to think about death. It's circular. And she always loved circular endings in literature, even if they were completely unrealistic. Probably why she was the only one in her Victorian literature class who actually liked the ending of *Jane Eyre*. She liked the endings of all marriage plots. The books were orderly and deliberate. They succeeded on their own terms. The endings always reflected the beginnings. The authors had powerful control of the narratives. The deaths were put into a kind of cosmic order that made everybody feel better about being alive, because they happened offstage, in the South of Italy or at the sea-side, where characters were given the grace and dignity to die on beds more beautiful than their own.

She put down the blouse. She looked at Harry's painkillers, and she booked a room at the Cornwall.

She sits on the canopy bed and tries to relax, but being relaxed about her death is proving to be difficult, even on this king-sized pillow-top. She still feels like she should be doing something significant. She still feels too much like herself in her head, worrying about all the small things that are already ruining her beautiful ending, like the blood on the bride's dress. The sound of the toilet flushing next door. The smell of the air conditioner, not to mention the wedding people gathering on the patio below.

The bride's opening reception has begun.

She puts on the headphones of her old Discman to drown out the people talking below. But the CD is so scratched, the music skips. Instead of making her feel calm, it makes her anxious. So she takes them off, goes out to the balcony, and lights a cigarette.

This time, she actually smokes it. She hopes that it will make sitting on a chair seem more elevated than just sitting on a chair. Takes one puff like she's posing for a painting. *Woman Smoking and Drinking While Having Some Thoughts*, she'd call it.

But when she blows the smoke out into the salty air, she starts coughing so hard, it burns her lungs.

"Shit," she says. Not a good feeling. "Ugh. This is truly awful."

Yet she takes another puff, because when she imagined her death, she imagined herself smoking. She imagined it would work like a metronome keeping the time. Keeping her steady. Because she has nothing to keep her steady. No dinner to eat, no music to enjoy, no luggage to unpack, no husband to call, no book to finish, no counters to clean, no hormone shots to inject, no vacations to research, no future life to organize into spreadsheets. There is no more time left and so there is weirdly no urgency for anything.

She smokes the rest of the cigarette slowly. She does not want to feel rushed. She does not want to go out frantic and through a window like

Septimus in *Mrs. Dalloway*, a scene that upset her so much, it became the only book in graduate school that she never finished reading.

Her stomach growls. She hopes she doesn't get too hungry to kill herself. She takes another sip of the chocolate wine. At least the wine is partly chocolate, she thinks. At least I have this balcony. She watches the waves in the distance start to gather, but they never get large enough to break. Sort of like the jazz from the reception below—the notes rising and falling and rising and falling but never coming to an end.

She leans over the edge to get a better look at the reception. She's curious, she admits. She's always loved a wedding, will watch any TV show or read any book to the end if it promises a wedding. That's how she got through those long novels in graduate school, reading hundreds of pages just to watch people get married.

She scans for the bride but sees only High Bun and Neck Pillow, picking up long-stemmed drinks from a tray. The Jims standing under some fairy lights, arguing with faces of men who want to kill each other, and it surprises her when they break into laughter.

At least I'm on the top floor, she thinks—up on the balcony from where she can stare and pass judgment without being noticed, like the seagulls that circle high above. From here, she can see it all, even what it will be like to be dead, because that is one of the few gifts that depression gives her: aerial vision. She already knows what the world will look like without her, because last August, she sat at home while everyone returned to their offices, their routines, their roles—and she knows the bride will be able to do this, too. The bride may gasp at the news of Phoebe's suicide, but then she'll take a walk down the beach to calm herself. She will feel the breeze blow her hair back. She will be grateful for the sun. For her champagne. She will laugh and lean on her groom's shoulder, beautiful hair falling into her face, and Phoebe will be forgotten by sunset.

"Just get on with it," Phoebe tells herself.

But then there is a knock on the door, as if someone heard her. She puts the cigarette out quickly, closes the balcony door, and the feeling of hiding her cigarette is strangely familiar. It makes her hope that her husband is at the door, though of course he's not. He doesn't even know where she is.

"Are you seriously smoking?" the bride asks.

The bride walks into the room as if it is her own. The bride's dress is bloodless now—another white one, but gauzier and with dramatic fluttery sleeves.

"Sure, yes, please do come in," Phoebe says.

The bride's hand is wrapped in gauze, and Phoebe wonders who wrapped it. Gary, the groom with the barely receding hairline? Her loving mother? Is the bride the kind of woman who has a loving mother? Yes, Phoebe decides. Phoebe has become good over the years at detecting who has a loving mother and who does not, because Phoebe believes a loving mother gives a person a kind of confidence to exist that Phoebe never quite had. Phoebe could never burst into someone else's room and give orders like it's her own.

"You can't smoke," the bride says.

The bride talks louder than she needs to, the way actors on the stage are present but locked and preserved behind the fourth wall, and for the first time, Phoebe wonders what the bride actually does for a living. Is she an actress? Or maybe she is an airline attendant, good at announcing things to forty-seven passengers.

"Actually, it's one of the few things left that I can do," Phoebe says.

As if to prove this, Phoebe walks back out to the balcony.

"Actually, no," the bride says, following her. "This is a nonsmoking room."

"Good thing I'm out here on the balcony, then."

"How did *you* get a real balcony, by the way?" the bride asks, like this is the real betrayal. "My balcony is just like, the suggestion of a balcony."

She pauses to study the view.

"I mean, you can see the whole ocean from here! Why on earth wouldn't Pauline put me in this room? I specifically requested a shoreline room."

"Well, a shoreline room presumably faces . . . the shoreline."

"But I thought shoreline meant . . . that you could see the shore."

"Shoreline refers to the line where the ocean meets the land."

Phoebe waits for Lila to blush, but she doesn't get embarrassed. She just gets angrier.

"Who on earth would want a shoreline room then?" Lila asks. "Why would they even advertise a shoreline view like it's something special? If I wanted to look at houses, I'd just stay home and look out my own window at houses. You know?"

Phoebe lights another cigarette, hoping the smoke will make the bride leave. But she doesn't budge.

"The balcony is part of the room, by the way," the bride says. "So you can't actually smoke on it."

Phoebe feels the sudden urge to argue. She has a contrarian impulse that stirred within her during class or at a party when anybody had the audacity to talk in absolutes. She never acted on it, though, because she never wanted to be accused of talking in absolutes. Those people were her least favorite.

But what does she care now? Might as well go out showing the world what she got from all those years of studying.

"The word *balcony* is borrowed from Italian *balcone*," Phoebe says. "Derived from medieval Italian *balco*, which originally meant 'scaffold.' And that comes from a Proto-Germanic word *balkô*, which probably meant something like 'beam.'"

The bride stands there, confused.

"So, taken all together, we know that the word *balcony* originally referred to the beam or structure that holds up the balcony." Phoebe releases a long, slow exhale of smoke before her final conclusion. "That's how far outside the room it is. The balcony is not even the balcony."

"Who *are* you?" the bride asks.

The bride sounds genuinely impressed, and Phoebe will admit that she has not lost the capacity to enjoy this kind of moment. Knowledge is power, all her teachers told her as a kid, which is why she spent the best part of her youth in quiet corners of libraries, reading books as quickly as she could. She wanted to be stronger, bigger. She knew that she would never be taller than her father, never be bigger or stronger, and that this was the only way to one day see beyond her father's house.

"I'm a Victorianist," Phoebe says.

"Huh?"

"A nineteenth centuryist," Phoebe rephrases, thinking it might make more sense to the bride.

"I still don't know what that means," the bride says.

"I research nineteenth-century literature."

"And people pay you for this?"

"Not well."

"And the nineteenth century is really the 1800s?"

"Right."

"I always have the hardest time with that."

"A lot of my students do."

"But I'm twenty-eight. I work at an art gallery," the bride says. "I should know that."

Phoebe is surprised enough by this new information to want to ask her first question of the bride.

"Are you a curator?" Phoebe asks.

"That's my mother," the bride says. "I'm her assistant. But one day, I'm supposed to be the curator."

Lila waits as if Phoebe should ask follow-up questions, but Phoebe doesn't want to know anything more.

"Though honestly, after I get married, I think I'm going to quit," the bride says. "I'm just not very good at it."

She confesses to getting Bs all the way through her art history degree in college.

"I never understood why my mother was so obsessed with art. I studied it for four years, and honestly, I get it even less now. Like seriously, what's the point of it?"

Again, the bride looks at Phoebe and waits.

"Are you asking me?" Phoebe asks.

"Have you never been in a conversation before?"

"It's been a while, actually."

"I can tell."

"And to be honest, I'm not sure I get the point, either."

When Phoebe left for graduate school, she had very clear and

beautiful ideas about art, how art is what elevates us, art is the magnificence wrung from the ugly dish towel of existence. Art helps us feel
alive. And this had been true for Phoebe—Phoebe used to read books
and feel astounded. She used to walk around galleries, inspired by the
beautiful human urge to create. But that was years ago. Now she can't
stand the sight of her books. Can't bear the thought of reading hundreds of pages just to watch Jane Eyre get married again.

"Well, that's a relief to hear," the bride says, like they're old cousins
again. "Nobody ever admits that. Everyone at the gallery walks around
like, Oh, my, look at this white canvas. Look at what this painter has
done with all this white space. He has chosen not to paint it! He has
defied the conventions of painting by not actually painting! Isn't that
bold? Doesn't that make you want to pay thousands of dollars for it?
And some of the people are like, Yes, yes, it does, actually."

Phoebe can feel how easy it would be to slip into this casual conversation about the false promises of art. She can feel herself wanting
to rant about literature and how it didn't end up saving her in the end,
but the sun is starting to set. Phoebe is halfway done with her second
cigarette. She looks back at the pills on the nightstand.

"What did you come in here for again?" Phoebe asks.

The bride seems offended by the directness of the question.

"I came to tell you to stop smoking," the bride says with that edge to
her voice again. "And to warn you that if you don't change your mind
about . . ."

But she can't say the words.

"Killing myself?" Phoebe says.

"Yes. Then I am going to tell the front desk."

"They can't make a paying guest leave because the guest is sad."
Phoebe is amused by the thought. "'I am so sorry, but we've all had a
vote, and we've come to the conclusion that you are too sad to be here.'"

"You're not sad, you're *suicidal*," the bride says. "You should leave
the hotel and seek help immediately."

"Tried that."

After her husband left, Phoebe tried so many things. She applied to
forty-two teaching jobs. She took a virtual painting class. She purchased a

brand-new bike with cute handlebars like her virtual therapist suggested. Go have real experiences, the virtual therapist commanded. Go read real books on your condition. So she read real books on depression. Books by real, depressed people. She journaled in real journals. She downloaded a meditation app. Ate bananas for breakfast every day. Started Lexapro, then stopped, because it didn't make her feel any better, just made it impossible to orgasm. And that was the only time she felt relief from herself—in those few moments when she could make herself come, thinking of her husband being a terrible man.

But orgasming didn't save her, because after, she was still herself. She sobbed. She signed up for online dating sites, exchanged texts with a man who called himself Transatlantic and talked a lot about his job in biotech. But then Transatlantic met someone else, someone in real life, he explained, and she deleted her profile, turned on the TV, and basically never shut it off.

"Then at least wait until the wedding week is over!" the bride demands.

"I'm not rescheduling," Phoebe says. "This is not a dentist appointment."

"I seriously don't get it. What's the rush? You're going to be dead forever, you know. You might as well wait a week."

Because if she doesn't do it tonight, Phoebe knows she will lose the feeling. She knows this is the kind of thing that requires a certain feeling. And if she loses that feeling, she will have to wake up tomorrow and go home. She will have to clean up the crumbs on the counter. She will have to bury Harry. Then, she will have to drive to school in her gray blouse and watch her husband get coffee every morning with another woman.

"It's not like you're going to live for much longer," the bride says. "Might as well wait it out."

"Do you know something about my medical history that I don't?" Phoebe asks.

"You're middle-aged, obviously. And you smoke. And drink. I'd give you like, twenty years, tops."

"That's really encouraging. Thanks."

"My father was perfectly healthy, used to run every other day and take these giant green vitamins from Switzerland, and he didn't even make it to seventy."

"Maybe it was the vitamins that killed him," Phoebe says.

"It was colon cancer."

Phoebe knows she is supposed to say "I'm sorry for your loss." But she can't feel sorry for anyone else right now. So she doesn't say anything.

"How does it not scare you?" the bride asks. "I'm literally terrified of dying. All I worried about for the last two years was catching Covid and dying before I could have my wedding."

"Well, that explains it! I already had my wedding," Phoebe says. "It seems I'm cleared to go."

"But what if you go to Hell?"

"There's no such thing as Hell," Phoebe says.

"How do you know that?"

"I don't know. It's just what I believe," Phoebe says. One of the few things Nietzsche wrote that she agreed with in graduate school. "Seems more plausible that Hell is some revenge fantasy concocted by unhappy people so they could punish all the happy people in their minds."

"I wish I could believe that," Lila says. "I always worry so much about going to Hell."

"Who did you murder?"

"Nobody," Lila says. "But don't you think I'm just like, a little too rich? All we ever did in Catholic school was talk about how impossible it was for rich people like me to get into Heaven. And then they had us write this paper on Dante's *Inferno*, which I actually got an A on, but for years, I had nightmares about being stuck in his different versions of Hell. It got so bad, I started seeing the guidance counselor about it."

She said her dread of Hell was extra annoying, because despite going to a Catholic boarding school, her parents didn't raise her to have any particular religion. Her parents couldn't decide which one. Yes, she went to Portsmouth Abbey but only because that's where her Catholic father went to school. And her mother was from a family of Protestants who dated back to the *Mayflower* and whenever Lila came home for the holidays, her mother whispered things about the Catholics being full of shit.

"And I was like, Hey thanks, this isn't confusing at all," Lila says.

The nightmares went on for years.

"They were really creepy, too. Like once I was stuck running around a racetrack getting beaten with my own leg. Another time I was turned into the oak tree outside my father's house and I bled every time my mother plucked one of my leaves."

Phoebe releases the smoke so slowly in the air, it's almost beautiful. She is getting good, she thinks.

"That's what happens to the suicides in Dante," Lila clarifies. "Except it's not my mother plucking the leaves, obviously. It's like, a bunch of random harpies."

"So I've read," Phoebe says.

"Then how can you take that risk? I'm not saying Dante is right. But I mean, what if Dante is right?"

Phoebe learned trying to explain her feelings to her husband that you can't explain this kind of darkness to someone who has never felt it. And the bride is very much like her husband. Phoebe can tell by the way she dresses, everything so tailored to her body. Up close, Phoebe can see that the romantic tangle of braids is actually a calculated system with the exact same number of braids on each side of her head. She is like a character from an Austen novel, sometimes disappointed in the sequence of events, but never psychically destroyed by them. Never paralyzed by existential horror. Always able to find relief from a long walk through the countryside or the busyness of the day. And that's how Phoebe had been, too, during graduate school and most of her marriage. She couldn't understand why someone like Tom wanted to die. But Mia is so beautiful? But Tom's a doctor? But they have a baby? Phoebe could only think practically about such a thing then, just like the bride now.

So Phoebe tries her best to speak the bride's language.

"The point is, this hotel is very expensive," Phoebe says. "I can't afford to stay here and wait all week."

"Problem solved," the bride says. "I'll pay."

"No," Phoebe refuses.

"Why not?"

"I don't even know you. And that's too much money."

"Do you want to know how much I've already spent on this wedding?" The bride looks excited, like she has been dying to tell someone all day.

"No." The more Phoebe learns about the wedding, the harder this will become.

"A million dollars," she says, and then turns toward the ocean view like she might cry. "That's what my father gave me when he got sick. Told me it was his dying wish to see his only daughter get married before he died. But then before we could have it, he died. And then there was a global pandemic for two years. So the least you could do is not die, too."

Phoebe can hear in her voice that she is about to cry. Now more than ever it is important to sound forceful.

"My death has nothing to do with you," Phoebe says.

"Of course it does! It's going to happen here, during my opening reception!"

The bride starts to slowly breathe in, then counts to four as she breathes out. Watching her, Phoebe feels an old impulse, a tenderness, the kind of thing she felt when a student sat in her office on the brink of tears. She was being presented with a choice: She could remain silent and pretend she didn't notice the despair because she had to get to class in five minutes and unpacking despair usually took longer than that. Or she could soften her voice and ask one more question, like, "What is this really about? Are you okay?" And that's when the student would burst into a teary tale of their entire life story. Phoebe would be late to class, but the student would feel better, and so would she.

But the bride is not her student. Phoebe has no responsibility to care or even pretend to care. She will not ask questions about her dead father. She will not concern herself with the wedding. She will not reschedule her suicide.

"Do you know how much I spent on just tonight alone?" the bride asks.

Phoebe watches the cigarette burn between her fingers, a long nose of ash growing with each silent second. Phoebe will wait this out.

"Fifty thousand dollars," she says. "Yep, that's right. Fifty thousand dollars."

But Phoebe must not look too impressed, because the bride continues.

"I special-ordered rare orchids from Borneo for the centerpieces. I took a calligraphy class so I could learn how to handwrite every single table card. I had each cocktail glass hand-sprayed in guanciale fat. I flew in the same jazz band that played at Prince William's wedding. And do you know how long it took to figure out who played at Prince William's wedding? How many hours I spent on message boards?"

"You didn't hire a wedding planner to do that?" Phoebe asks, genuinely shocked.

"You think I'd trust a wedding planner with my dead father's money?" Lila asks.

"I mean, yeah?"

"This money was the last thing my father ever gave me in this life. I wasn't about to give thirty-three percent of it away to some wedding planner who suggested it might be nice to parachute into my own reception. No. I wanted my father to be proud of how I spent it, and I know he would be. I know this is going to be the most beautiful fucking wedding, and if I wake up to your corpse being rolled into the lobby tomorrow morning, you should know I'll never recover from something like that."

"Neither will I," Phoebe says.

"Stop doing that!" Lila says.

The bride starts to actually cry, and it's weirdly satisfying and horrifying to watch. Like watching a beautiful building be demolished.

"How can you joke about this?" the bride asks through her tears.

Phoebe doesn't know. But after her husband left, her first impulse was to joke about it. She spent days making phone calls to friends from grad school that she hadn't spoken to in years, saying, "Well, I never really liked the guy anyway," in a high-pitched voice that didn't sound like hers, because she wanted to impress people the way she had been impressed when she read what Edith Wharton said after seeing the names "Mr. and Mrs. Wharton" written in a guest book at a hotel she had never visited.

"Apparently I *have* been here before," Wharton said.

But her friends laughed uneasily. Her friends had been at her wedding, had seen how in love Phoebe had been. "It's okay to be sad that your husband left you," one of them said, and it made Phoebe feel stupid for trying to joke about it—joking was all she had left.

"Just get out," Phoebe says in a stern voice.

"You can't tell me to get out," the bride says. "This is my wedding hotel. *You* get out!"

Phoebe doesn't know how some girls grow up to become women like the bride, or like Mia, who treat everything, even this nineteenth-century mansion, even Phoebe's husband, as their inheritance. Phoebe had been raised to feel sorry for everything—sorry for being born, sorry for almost drowning, sorry for getting an A-minus on my exam, sorry for not bearing children, sorry for not getting to the last three slides of the PowerPoint, everybody. Sometimes, Phoebe sent her class apology emails after lectures when she didn't finish on time. Because she was a good professor. A good woman. But where is the line? When did Phoebe being good become Phoebe being nothing?

She doesn't know. But she does know this.

"I paid eight hundred and thirty-six dollars to stay in this room for one single night!" Phoebe yells. "This is *my* fucking room!"

The bride looks stunned, as if nobody has ever shouted at her this loudly before. In the bride's silence, Phoebe waits for some bad, foolish feeling to come, but she feels so exhilarated she wishes she had yelled at Mia like this. At her husband after he told her about the affair—but she couldn't yell then. She was still trying so hard to be her best self, to stay reasonable, to save the marriage, to ask the right questions, gather all the information, as if understanding could help her solve the problem. But it didn't matter how much he told her—she never understood. She was sick with information, sick with all the things she never said or did.

"Get *out*!" Phoebe screams.

"Fine," the bride says. "Whatever. What do I care? Just *die.*"

"I *will!*"

Phoebe came here to die and so she will die.

But then the bride says "*Good*" so angrily, she bares her teeth just enough for Phoebe to see it again: the food.

Phoebe can't believe it's still there. Phoebe figured one of her friends would have told her by now. But maybe the bride is the kind of woman who doesn't have friends like that, friends who are honest even when it's embarrassing. Maybe that is why she is here in Phoebe's room instead of down at her reception sipping on a fat-washed cocktail.

"Have a nice time in Hell," the bride adds.

The cigarette ash falls on Phoebe's leg. She is surprised by the burn. It feels like something awful being set in motion. The world gone bad. The bride will be sent down to her reception with food in her teeth and Phoebe will die.

But not yet.

"Wait," Phoebe says, because she cannot send a woman out to her wedding with food stuck in her teeth. Whatever the bride might think, Phoebe is not a monster.

"You have something in your teeth."

The bride's face falls. "But I haven't eaten since this morning."

The bride walks to the bathroom mirror, which is as tall as the room itself. She picks at her teeth as she says, "I've seriously been going around all day with food in my teeth and nobody said a word?"

"Maybe nobody noticed."

"Oh, trust me, the people here notice everything."

She leans closer to the mirror, picks harder.

"Gary's mother has noticed that my dress tonight is 'very young,' which is code for her saying I look like a godless whore. And Marla, my future sister-in-law, has noticed how expensive this hotel is, though she won't ever say it. She'll just list off the price of every single item on the menu until we all want to scream."

Lila backs away from the mirror. "Do you have any floss?"

"I seem to have forgotten the floss."

Lila looks around the bathroom. "They're supposed to have everything here."

Phoebe helps her search through the contents of the most beautiful wicker basket she has ever seen, but there is only ginseng lotion. Hibiscus bath salts. Thyme bodywash. By the time she looks up, the bride is at the phone.

"Can you bring floss to the Roaring Twenties?" the bride says. "Yes, that's fine. I'll wait. Thank you."

"Why are you having him bring it here?" Phoebe asks when she hangs up.

"Let's wait on the balcony" is all the bride says, like they are a team now and their only job is to restore Lila's teeth to their perfect condition. But when Phoebe doesn't budge, she adds, "I think you can hold off on eternity for thirty minutes. Oh, hey, there's the bird watching kit I bought for everybody."

She picks up a pair of binoculars from the desk and ignores the pamphlet about North Atlantic birds.

"Thirty minutes?" Phoebe asks, but she follows the bride out to the balcony. "How long does it take to bring up some floss?"

"Carlson has to go to CVS to buy it. Apparently they don't have any."

"So he's going to *CVS* to get it?"

"It's literally his job."

"Is it?"

Lila shrugs and crosses her legs. "I'm Lila, by the way."

It sounds funny to hear Lila introduce herself so formally after all this, and Phoebe must be smirking because Lila says, "Is there something amusing about my name?"

"No," Phoebe says. "It's a beautiful name."

It was a name Phoebe had wanted for herself when she was younger. Phoebe had read too many Sweet Valley High books, in which the most beautiful girl at the school was named Lila. One of the first beauty icons with brown hair that Phoebe had encountered—until Lyla from *Friday Night Lights*, who had long brown hair so thick, it made Phoebe want to move south and join a football team.

"It's a nickname. My name is actually Delilah," Lila says. "My mother named me after her favorite artist. And not even like a classically famous artist. Just some woman who lives in Bushwick and makes millions painting abstractions of babies eating womb-shaped fruit."

Phoebe pours herself a little bit more of the wine, then offers the bottle to the bride. Why not? They have thirty minutes. And it's her wine.

"This *is* better than I thought it would be," the bride says, taking a sip. She leans over the edge to see the reception in full swing below. "Wow, you can really see the whole thing from up here."

The bride looks through the binoculars and starts announcing names like she's spotting wild animals at the zoo.

"There's Nat and Suz," Lila says. "Marla. My mother. Jim. Uncle Jim."

Phoebe can feel the bride still wanting her to ask questions, and she does find herself wondering.

"How many people in your family are named Jim?" Phoebe asks.

"The Jims are in Gary's family," she says. "Gary's father, uncle, and Gary's dead wife's brother."

"Oh. Gary was married before?"

"Yeah. They had a daughter. Then his wife died of cancer. Weird, right?"

"I don't know. Was she supposed to be immortal?"

"I mean, it's weird that his dead wife's brother is *here* as his best man. Gary insisted on Jim. He kept being like, Lila, come on, the man is my brother."

She says it's true that they're really close.

"They watched a woman die together, and now they're like, bonded for life, I guess," she says. "Jim comes over like every Saturday, even though that's Gary's one day off, and we spend it watching Jim cut up monkfish at the kitchen table while he brags about himself. He's like, Oh, I've just been at home building my seaplane, even though I know for a fact he doesn't have any of the parts. And did you know his great-uncle used to be in the Mob?"

"How deep was his uncle in the Mob?"

"That's really not the point," Lila says.

"What's the point?"

"The point is, I don't get why Jim has to be around all of the time. They'd never be friends if Gary didn't marry his sister."

She explains that her fiancé, Gary, is this handsome doctor who lives in Tiverton and spends his one day off running science experiments in the garden with his daughter, and Jim is an engineer who can't keep a girlfriend longer than a month so he is always kind of hitting on everyone.

"Even me," she says. "He like, bought me a skirt for my birthday. I mean, isn't that weird?"

"I don't know. Did you need a skirt?"

"That's exactly what Gary asked, and I was like, It doesn't even matter if I needed a skirt! Why would my fiancé's brother-in-law buy me a skirt for my birthday? It's not even a normal skirt."

"What's a normal skirt?"

"Whatever kind of skirt you can buy a woman and it wouldn't be weird."

"I don't think that skirt exists."

"This was some kind of professional skirt. The kind you'd buy at Macy's or something to wear with a matching jacket. And when I showed Gary, he was just like, Yeah, I don't think Jim understands how to buy presents for women."

Phoebe likes how Lila does Gary's voice, too. Lila, it seems, is good at voices.

"He was like, Lila, this is a man who used to buy his own sister tampons in bulk whenever they were on sale at Costco."

"That's kind of nice, actually," Phoebe says. Phoebe's father mostly pretended her period didn't exist, and so Phoebe pretended it didn't exist. She felt criminal throwing a tampon in the trash, like she was throwing out a bloody carcass, because her father didn't think to keep the can lined, so she often flushed them down the toilet. When the toilet backed up once a year, she knew it was her fault but watched her father with the plunger and said nothing.

"Gary thought so, too," she says. "Gary is such a doctor. He like, truly only sees the good in everybody."

"That is . . . not my experience with doctors."

"Well, maybe he's just got this blind spot when it comes to Jim. It's like, Wendy died and Jim did their dishes for a year straight, and took his daughter to school when Gary didn't have the strength, and now Jim is a forever hero. And so is Wendy. That's the dead wife."

The words *dead wife* land hard at Phoebe's feet.

"Might I suggest alternate phrasing?" Phoebe asks.

"There's seriously no other way to describe her," she says. "You can't use her name. Anytime her name is spoken, somebody is required to have a complete mental breakdown. Sometimes it's his daughter. Often, it's me. But still."

Lila clutches the wine bottle, looks back down at her party.

"We'll all be having a nice time sitting at the beach or something, and out of nowhere, Jim will just be like, Remember when Wendy tried to make a kite out of beer cans?"

"Is that possible?"

"Apparently, it didn't fly," Lila says. "And fine, I get it. In his eyes, I'm his dead sister's replacement and he always wants me to remember that. But this is my wedding week. And I can't stop having this horrible feeling that somehow Jim is going to ruin it. I mean, if you don't beat him to it."

Then Lila scans the reception with the binoculars again like she's looking for Jim. When she finds him, she narrows her eyes with alarm.

"Oh my God, is Jim seriously hitting on my *mother*?"

She hands the binoculars to Phoebe.

"Which one is your mother?" Phoebe asks.

"The one who looks like she's just about to go on *Dancing with the Stars*."

"Can you be more specific?"

"That's actually very specific," Lila says. But then she points to a woman in a yellow dress.

Even with the binoculars, Phoebe can't see much beyond a man and a woman talking with drinks in their hands. Every so often, Jim leans in, puts his hand on her mother's shoulder. But it doesn't look especially flirtatious. More familial.

"They look like they're just, you know, talking," Phoebe says.

"Oh, there is no just talking with my mother," Lila says. "With her, it's like always this intense spewing of information, like here is the last book on Gaudi that I just read and now I am going to tell you all about it verbatim. And my father used to just sit there and take it for thirty years, until he finally exploded and told us that he hated modern art. He actually confessed that to us on his deathbed. Isn't that awful?"

"Wait, what?" Phoebe asks. "Your father confessed on his deathbed that he didn't like modern art?"

"That's right," Lila says. "My father called from the hospital and asked to be put on speaker, and we were all gathered around, because we never knew which call was going to be his last, and he was like, My darlings, every man must come to terms with his true nature at the end of his life, and it is time I do the same, and my mother was like, Are you sure that's a good idea, Henry? And my father was just like, I have always despised modern art, particularly the Cubists and everything that followed."

Her father blamed Picasso, especially, for bringing dignity to the whole movement away from painting as representation.

"And maybe in some families this wouldn't seem like a big confession, but my parents' marriage had basically been built on the fact that they were these great, benevolent supporters of contemporary art," Lila says. "My father bought my mother her first painting."

Buying art together was how they fell in love. They made a name for themselves building one of the country's most important collections of contemporary artists. They gave a five-hundred-thousand-dollar grant to the NEA each year. All of this helped make sense of the millions her father made in waste management. Helped give meaning to the landfills of trash her father owned across the country.

"So to find out that he only did all this just to impress my mother in the beginning," Lila says. "Insert a montage of monologues from my mother about how her mother was right, how she never should have married a much older man who was literally in the business of trash, and how dare that man call anything a waste, let alone *Cubism*, and she knows now she really should have married her cousin's cousin Gregory Lancaster like her mother had suggested, because the joke's on her. Gregory is still alive."

Phoebe looks through the binoculars and watches Jim walk away. She waits to see if anything comes over Lila's mother's face. She wonders if it's hard to be at this wedding alone after her husband's death. Is she worried about who she is going to talk to next? How long she'll have to stand there alone?

"And so now my mother is convinced that I'm making a mistake marrying Gary, just like her," Lila says.

"How do you know?"

"She tells me! When she's really loaded at two in the afternoon, she just says these things. She's like, Lila, you don't have to get married just because your father's dying wish was to see you get married. What does it matter? He's already dead! And then she goes off about how I might want to think twice about marrying an older man in waste management like she did."

"I thought Gary was a doctor?"

"My father owned landfills. Gary is a gastroenterologist. Totally different jobs, but my mother is just like, Like I said, they're both in waste management. Two men, on a mission to help the country deal with their shit."

Lila is quiet for a moment, like she is considering something deeply, perhaps the entire trajectory of her life.

"Can you imagine having a mother who talks to you like that?"

"My mother is dead," Phoebe says.

"Oh. Well, you're lucky then. My mother, she just monologues," Lila says, as if she were not doing the same exact thing right now. "Which is absolutely why she is not getting a speech at this wedding. I kept telling her, Mom, the mother of the bride doesn't even get a speech, and she was like, Yes, and why do we think that is, Lila? Why do you think the men have always wanted the mother of the bride to be silent?"

The bride takes another sip.

"And I'm like, It's not about men! It's about you! Why would I trust you with a speech? You're just going to get loaded and stand up there and talk about how Gary is too old for me or something!"

Phoebe wonders how long Lila could go on without a response. Again, she wonders if this is the difference between growing up with and without a mother. Having a mother helps you believe that everybody wants to hear every little thing you think. Having a mother helps you speak without thinking. It allows you to trust in your most awful self, to yell and scream and cry, knowing that your mother will still love you by the end of it. In her teens, Phoebe was regularly astonished by how awful her friends were to their mothers, and the mothers just took it, because the mothers knew that sometimes they were awful, too. The mothers had made their own mistakes.

But Phoebe's mother sat high up on the fireplace mantel, in a gilded frame, like a martyred saint. Under her gaze, Phoebe was careful never to make any mistakes. Phoebe was quiet and obedient, never talking too fast or too loudly, because she never wanted to be a burden to her father. She had felt this way in her marriage, too—careful never to cry too hard or tell meandering stories at dinner. Careful always to wear nice pajamas to bed. Careful never to lose control. Even at the end, when she learned about the affair, she stayed so calm that her husband was confused. "You're being so nice about this," Matt said.

But Lila talks without end, without clear transitions from topic to topic, assuming that Phoebe, a total stranger who has already announced multiple times that she wants to die, is interested in hearing every detail about her personal life. Phoebe can't tell if it's the most appalling or most impressive display she's ever witnessed.

Either way, Phoebe *is* interested.

"How much older than you is Gary?" Phoebe asks.

"Only eleven and a half years," the bride says. "He's forty, but you can barely tell."

"Oh," Phoebe says, genuinely not impressed. "That's not bad. I've seen much worse."

"Like what?" The bride looks hopeful.

"Like this seventy-five-year-old historian at my university had an affair with the twenty-six-year-old admin."

"Jesus. That's just weird."

"Especially since she wasn't even trying to get her PhD," Phoebe says. It feels good to talk about her old life so casually like that. As if it were all just funny subject material to share in conversation with Lila. "I mean, we could never figure out why she was doing it exactly. Like what would this admin with no aspirations in higher ed gain from dating a married geriatric academic?"

"Maybe she was in love," the bride says. "Not everything is a pathology, you know. I was like, Mom, not everything is about Dad dying! I didn't even know Dad was dying when I met Gary. Gary just randomly came to our art gallery looking for some paintings to fill up his new house, and then two days later, I took my dad to his GI because we were expecting bad news, and I was shocked to see that Gary was the doctor. I mean, truly a wild coincidence. Gary and I both knew it had to mean something."

But her mother was not convinced.

"My mother is like, We all knew on some level that your father was going to die. And I'm like, Well yeah, I've always known that someday my father will die. But maybe, just maybe, it's possible that Gary and I love each other? I mean, why does everything have to be about my father one day dying? And my mother is like, I didn't make the rules, sweetheart. Take it up with Freud."

The bride sighs.

"We should have just gotten married right after he proposed," Lila says. "My father was actually doing really well then, responding to the treatments the way Gary said he would. But we had just gone into lockdown, and so we kept postponing the wedding, thinking the lockdown would end at any moment. And then my dad got so much worse and after he was hospitalized, it didn't feel right to celebrate anything. I mean, he hardly made any sense at the end. He was so high on morphine, it became unbearable to take his phone calls. We'd put him on speaker and be like, Hi, Dad, but then there would be nothing but this long dramatic pause until finally, he was like . . . Herbbbbballll Essences!"

Phoebe is confused. "Herbal Essences?"

"I don't know," the bride says. "That's what he said. It made no sense. It was just . . . silence . . . and then Herbbballlllll Essences! And I was like, Okay, Dad. What *about* Herbal Essences? But he hung up. And then he died. And those were literally my father's last words to me."

Phoebe looks at Lila and Lila looks at Phoebe. The sadness of the story is so stark, her voice so monotone when she delivered it, they erupt into a laughter so intense it surprises Phoebe. Every time they are about to calm down, the bride says, "Herrbbbballll Essences!" and Phoebe starts laughing all over again. It makes her feel high.

"Stop," Phoebe says. "I can't breathe."

"Isn't that your goal?" the bride asks.

The snipe makes it feel serious between them again. Phoebe can't remember the last time she laughed like that. Maybe that time with her husband in the Ozarks when they found the *Sax for Lovers* CD? But that was so long ago. And they didn't even really laugh—they smiled and joked and then had sex. But they had never, Phoebe thought, really laughed.

Phoebe looks down at the reception, sees waiters in white shirts passing out tiny dots of food. Women in cocktail dresses eating olives off toothpicks. People already on their second drink. Phoebe wonders why Lila is so worried about her million-dollar wedding being ruined yet doesn't seem concerned to be missing the start of it.

"It's actually Gary's sister, Marla, who is the worst about it all," the bride says.

"The worst about what?"

"Our age gap."

"I thought we were talking about your dad."

"I am tired of talking about my dad. My dad is *dead*. It's been a year and a half and it is time to finally accept that, even if my mother cannot."

"Okay, so Marla."

"Marla keeps making this big deal about me being super young whenever we're together. Like earlier today in the lobby, she was like, Wait, what do twenty-eight-year-olds know again? I forget. And she doesn't even think this is rude. She acts like it's just professional curiosity, like she's just getting to know twenty-eight-year-olds as a species."

"Is she an anthropologist?"

"She's a lawyer, or well, she was until she became the mayor of her town. And now she acts like she's the most moral human being to have ever walked the earth. Meanwhile, she's the one who will probably have to resign for having an affair with a federal judge. And do I say a word about it? No."

Now Phoebe is really interested. She is curious about affairs, as if any affair can teach her something about her husband's.

"Why did she have an affair with a federal judge?"

"She must have a fetish for judges, because that is exactly what her husband is, too," Lila says. "Except he's just like, a regular judge. But honestly, I don't know much more than that. Gary doesn't like to talk about his sister's sex life, understandably, and the rest of the family doesn't know about it. And she never talks to me about it, obviously. We're not close. But I do know that her children and husband barely speak to her right now, which is why they probably aren't coming to the wedding. And serves her right. Because she fucked up her life, for real. And sometimes, I just want to be like, What do *you* know, Marla? Do you know anything? Because even twenty-eight-year-olds know that being the mayor and then having an affair with a federal judge is definitely a terrible idea."

"Did you say that to her?"

"No! I'd never say that to Marla. You can't really say anything to Marla. She's very defensive."

There's a knock on the door, and Lila rushes to open it.

"Your floss," Carlson says, and presents it on a regal brass platter like it's a meal. It looks so small on the plate, it makes Phoebe want to laugh again. But the humor is lost on Lila.

"Thank you, Carlson," Lila says.

Lila starts flossing while Phoebe tips him.

"I feel so much better now," Lila says after, like all the problems are gone now that the body has been restored to perfection. She picks up the brush from the wicker basket. She combs her feathery bangs back into place. She puts a cold washcloth to the back of her neck. She is so quiet, so steady, it almost feels holy, like watching a nun prepare herself for the Lord.

"I guess I should get back down there," the bride says, as if now she doesn't even want to go. Now, she just wants to stay here and drink wine that is really chocolate and talk shit about her entire family with Phoebe. Phoebe almost wants that, too. Phoebe hasn't sat and talked like this with another woman in so long. But Lila puts her hand on the doorknob.

"What can you do?" Lila asks.

"Excuse me?"

"It's what my father said to me after we got his diagnosis. I couldn't stop crying about it, and he was like, Lila, is there one thing you feel capable of doing right now instead of crying? And there always was."

"What was it?" Phoebe asks.

"I would take a very long bath," the bride says.

After the bride leaves, Phoebe feels surprisingly lonely in the big room. The way she did after she shut off the TV at home. All of those characters distracting her from the reality of her own life—the monologuing mother and the dying father and the sleazy brother-in-law and the kind doctor and the groom's sister—gone.

That's when the darkness returns. That's when she is returned to herself, and she hates always having to return to herself, to live alone inside her nonviable body. It reminds her why she is here, what she came to do, but something feels off now. The sun is too low in the sky, and she is thinking about all the wrong things, like, Will Marla have to resign? Is Lila really just marrying her father? And is that what Phoebe did, too?

No. She will not think of her father or her husband. She has spent too much of her life thinking of them.

Phoebe pours herself the last of the wine. She just wants to stop thinking. She opens the bottle of painkillers, and the smell of fish is nauseating. She forgot the pills were tuna-flavored. But she will not veer from her plan. She will not prove her therapist right, who once told her that she'd never kill herself.

"You're not really the type," he said, and she had been so floored by his statement that she'd refused to see him for three weeks.

"That's a wildly inappropriate thing to say," she said when she returned, and he agreed.

"This is good, we're making progress, I'm happy to hear you being openly critical of me," he said.

But his comment had wounded her, had confirmed her worst fears about herself: She didn't even have the guts to kill herself. She was not the bold type. She was not like Mia, who cut her hair short over the pandemic, who finished her third book with the word *Bitch* in the title, who had the audacity to not only fuck someone else's husband, but to start a new life with him. Mia was a Modernist, liked experiments, bold forms, poems that made no fucking sense. If Mia wanted to kill herself, she would put the stones in her pocket and walk into the water like Virginia Woolf.

But Phoebe did not want to die outdoors. She did not want to be cold. She did not want to battle mosquitoes. She did not want to sink to the depths of the murky, endless sea. She liked knowable, comfortable things. She liked cozy reading nooks. Books that always ended the same way, characters in novels who were easily recognizable by their outfits. Beds with elaborate canopies that protected her from the world, and maybe that is the problem. Maybe this bed is too beautiful. It makes her feel grateful to be so far away from her own.

She is not tired, either. She feels very alert. Very aware of the bride's perfume. She can still smell it in the air, though she can't identify it. She can see the bride's lipstick on the rim of the wine bottle, a mauve red that Phoebe imagines she picked out one year ago just for this week. She knows too much about the bride already. Her real name— Delilah.

But she shouldn't think of Lila, either. She shouldn't think at all. Bob was right—she thinks too much. She thinks and thinks and thinks until she gets so tired of thinking, she never properly finishes whatever she started. She never turned the dissertation into a book; rarely finished a lecture on time; couldn't decide when to start having children until it was too late. And now here she is, doing the same thing, trying so hard to make sure her suicide is a masterpiece, something the critics might applaud for years to come, when really, she should just do it. Be fearless for once in her life, like Mia. Like Woolf. Open the bottle and swallow all the pills with one quick gulp of water, which is exactly what she does.

And then it is done. For a moment, she feels proud of herself. She did it. But as soon as she sits back on the bed and closes her eyes, she starts thinking again. Will the pills be enough? How different are cat doses from human doses?

Then there's a knock on the door.

"Jesus," Phoebe says.

She fully expects it to be the bride again, but it's Pauline.

"Your coconut pillow," Pauline says. This time, the pillow looks comically large for the brass tray.

"Oh," Phoebe says. "The pillow."

"Can I help you with anything else? Can I book any complimentary spa treatments for you tomorrow, to make up for our lack of room service tonight?"

Pauline sounds so eager to help that Phoebe is tempted. Maybe Pauline would go down to CVS and get her more pills?

"No, thank you," Phoebe says. "But you're very nice to offer that."

"People here are always saying that," Pauline says. "But the truth is, I'm not really that nice. I'm just from the Midwest!"

"So am I," Phoebe says, and continues to stand in the doorway, though she's not sure why. Phoebe doesn't really want to be talking to Pauline as she drops dead, but there's also something very familiar to Phoebe about Pauline. Reminds her of home.

"No kidding!" Pauline says, then explains how she just graduated from Kansas State with a degree in hospitality and is astounded to have gotten this job right away. "I seriously just applied to be a waiter here. But they called and asked me if I would be the property manager! They told me I had to wear coastal business casual, and I honestly had to google it."

Pauline laughs like this is a great joke between the two of them, and Phoebe looks at her tight body-con black dress with an overly formal boat neckline. Normally, Phoebe wouldn't say anything, but she feels bad for Pauline, a girl who showed up to her new life in the wrong dress. She wants to help, as if this could be her last act of kindness on earth.

"That's not quite right," Phoebe says gently.

"No?" Pauline asks, looking down at her outfit.

"The boat neck is a little formal."

"I thought the boat neck was like, relaxed and boaty."

"Try more blues. And whites. And loose linens."

"Oh my God, thank you for actually being honest. This job is extremely important to me, and while I am doing my best to learn, it's all happening so fast. I'm actually not sure I'm even qualified? But anyway. Please let me know whatever I can do to enhance your stay."

Phoebe feels a sudden wave of exhaustion come over her.

"Thanks," Phoebe says.

She closes the door. The pills are working. What's done is done. And Pauline cannot help. Pauline is not her mother. Pauline is just a recent grad with a degree in hospitality.

Phoebe rests her head on the coconut pillow, which looks like a normal pillow and feels like a normal pillow but smells undeniably like coconut. Phoebe is mystified. She presses her nose deeper into the pillow but can't figure out where the coconut is located. It seems to be permeated throughout the pillow, part of the pillow's constitution. Like Pauline has woven the coconut fibers into the thread herself. And maybe it's the pills, maybe it's the image of Pauline weaving, but Phoebe starts to feel funny again.

Phoebe Stone, professor and scholar, found dead on an artisanal coconut pillow at the Cornwall Inn.

No. She can't die on a coconut pillow. She goes back to the balcony to hear the music. The jazz is soft but lively. She picks up the binoculars to get a look at the band, but in the dark, she can't see much. In the dark, each musician looks exactly like his instrument. Like they must curl themselves around their instruments when they go to sleep each night, and the image makes her want to cry. It makes her think about how beautiful the world can be. How long have these men been practicing just to come together and create this perfect harmony?

The bride emerges—that's what she looks like again down on the patio. No longer Lila with the dead father and passive-aggressive mother, but the beautiful bride with her white fluttery dress perfectly suited for cliffside cocktails. She takes a glass from a waiter, and then searches for someone. She looks eager. Quick to move, quick to laugh and say hello. She kisses a few people on the cheek, then leans into a tall man Phoebe assumes must be the groom because she rests her head on his shoulder. Phoebe can't make out his features, but she can see his age—there is a lack of urgency in his movements. A sense that there is no real rush to do anything, like he could stand right there with his arm around his fiancée all night and be fine about it.

They kiss. They look, from a distance, like they are very much in love, and how weird it is to be dying on a balcony while two people are down below, being in love. How weird to think that once Phoebe was the same bride, leaning her head on her husband's shoulder, and now she is here, moments from death.

How does this happen?

The question makes Phoebe dizzy. She lies down on the bed and that's when the jazz stops.

"Good evening, everyone," a woman says into a microphone. "For those of you who don't know me, I'm Patricia, the mother of the bride. And before this party gets away from us, I thought I'd give a little speech."

Phoebe feels herself suddenly get tense, as if she were down there in the audience. This can't be good, she thinks, and it's not. Patricia begins by saying how unfair it is that the mother of the bride does not have a properly designated time to give a speech at any point throughout the wedding and that she had to specifically carve out this time for herself.

"On a Tuesday," she says, and the crowd laughs. "But anyway, before I'm raked offstage, let me just say something about my daughter, Lila. As many of you may know, Lila was not an especially humorous or playful child. Most mothers might have been disappointed by this, but I will confess, I was impressed. Lila was never trying to be funny like the other children, never running around like some tiny unpaid performer."

It's a troubling start. Lila was right; her mother does not sound like a very good mother, not that Phoebe understands what that is. Phoebe was raised by a father whose most complicated relationship was to televised sports. But Phoebe spent a lifetime studying mothers, paying close attention to them when they showed up in movies, and the best mothers were always the ones who died young. The ones who lived had to make pancakes a lot and wear a long braid and show up whenever nobody expected with large bags of multicolored taffy, laughing at everything the children said, until the moment they must get serious. Dispense a kind of hard truth that the child won't appreciate until long after the mother is dead.

"Time and time again I tried to engage Lila in creative play, but no, Lila wouldn't stand for it. I would point to the ducks at the pond and say, Lila, what secrets do you think the ducks are trying to tell us? And Lila would turn to me with a face more serious than Churchill and say, 'How would I know? They don't speak English.' God, this made me laugh. So I said, 'Oh, do the ducks speak Spanish?' And again, Lila said, 'How would I know? I don't speak Spanish!'"

The crowd laughs, and Phoebe wonders if Lila is laughing. She wonders if this story has pleased her or mortally wounded her in some way. If this story has confirmed all her worst fears about herself, about her mother, or if there was actually something sweet communicated here that only Lila can understand. Phoebe doubts it but hopes so. Phoebe hopes that the mother will somehow turn it around soon, dig herself out of this hole, repackage Lila's lack of imagination as her best quality, not to mention the reason she is so perfectly suited for the groom— Phoebe's favorite part of any wedding speech.

But Phoebe will never know what happens—by the time Lila's mother is finished talking, Phoebe will be dead. Phoebe will not get to know how the speech ends—or how anything ends. And Phoebe does not like this. Phoebe always finishes a book or a movie, even a bad one. "Don't you want to know if they get married?" she asked, when Matt suggested they turn it off. But Matt did not need to know. Matt said, "This is a terrible movie. Of course they're going to get married." And Matt could do that—turn off the TV, quit a marriage—right in the middle of the climactic scene.

She feels knocked over by another wave of fatigue. The sudden sleepiness scares her. It feels too much like being too drunk. Or like that time she almost drowned in the river when she was fishing with her father, the last time he ever brought her. Phoebe had been leaning too close to the edge of the boat, and then she was in the water, and how terrifyingly fast the water moved her to places she didn't recognize. After, her father found her curled up in a shallow eddy where the river spit her out, shouting, "What were you doing so close to the edge like that? You could have died!"

She knows that's what he would be shouting now if he were here, watching her be so careless with her life again. "What are you doing so close to the edge like that?" he'd shout. And maybe her mother would be with him, and maybe she would be furious, too, shouting something directly into the microphone.

"She's truly one of a kind," the mother says. "She's the reason I get up every morning. The reason I don't have my own life anymore!"

The crowd laughs loudly, and Phoebe opens her eyes. What *is* she doing?

She is about to die, she knows, and the mother is about to do it— make the end circle back to the beginning, make the worst thing about Lila be the best thing about Lila. Because the mother must do this. The mother can't end it here—she can't just insult her own daughter's imagination in front of all these people and then take a bow. Phoebe can't bear it, thinking of Lila getting ready this afternoon, laying out her dress, putting on her lipstick, combing her hair, feeling so beautiful, only to wind up with her fists clenched under the table, trying not to cry.

"Now, honey, come stand up here with me," the mother says. "Come on, get up here!"

Yes, Phoebe thinks. Get up get up get up. Because Phoebe doesn't want to die. No, Phoebe just wants to hear the rest of the speech. She realizes it with such sudden certainty it feels like the only thing that she has ever known to be true about herself.

So she gets up.

She doesn't call 911. She doesn't yell down for Gary the doctor. She doesn't want to ruin the wedding. And these are just pills for cats. And how many did she take? Ten? Eleven?

She runs to the bathroom, because that's what people do in movies about this moment. She hopes they are medically accurate. She sticks her finger down her throat and throws up chocolate wine and bile until there is no more chocolate wine left, only a raw burning.

After, she is too tired to move. She just sits there, listening to the end of the speech in the really beautiful bathroom. White marble all the way to the ceiling. Calacatta, the kind with gold veining that Phoebe had dreamed of getting for their kitchen. She presses her face against it. She wants to feel like a sick child for a few moments longer, head pressed to the cool floor, listening to the mother's voice as if it were her own mother's voice.

"Lila, you are a grown woman now, something I have been realizing each day you work for me at the gallery. And it's impressive. I mean, this woman can sell a piece of art like her father could sell a piece of trash—and I mean that as a compliment. She's organized. In this way, she is very much her father's daughter; rest in peace, my late husband, Henry. She keeps a damn good spreadsheet. And trust me, that's a skill most artists do not have. Most of them are living far away in their imagination, always pretending to be something they're not, painting like Picasso one day or Rembrandt the next! They're delusional! They're never going to make it in this business! But my daughter will, and do you know why? My daughter has only ever been interested in being herself, for better or worse. That's what makes her one of a kind. And when Gary came to the gallery that day and asked about one of our paintings, she thankfully did not do what I carefully trained her to do. She did not describe the way William Withers juxtaposed the hyperrealism of the garden with the cubist representation of the woman. She said nothing about the way Withers masterfully navigated the tension between the white space of the canvas and his subject. That's what she should have done—that's what the painting was all about. I should know—it was a painting of me! But no. My daughter was all business. My daughter saw what only my daughter would see and said, 'This painting is three by five feet, would look great over a mantel or high up on the wall in the bathroom, and can easily be taken home yourself in any standard-sized crossover SUV.'"

The crowd laughs.

"And Gary bought it. I mean, he literally bought it! I knew in that moment he must be a real easy mark—"

The wedding people laugh again.

"Or that he must have really fallen for my daughter."

Everyone claps. And that's how Phoebe falls asleep—on the bathroom floor with the balcony door wide open so she can listen to all the impromptu speeches that the mother inspired. All the others who were not given a designated time to speak, like Gary's cousin Roy, a former sniper who flew all the way from Kennebunkport to suggest inappropriate things about a secret tattoo that Gary might have on his thigh. Suz, one of Lila's best friends from Portsmouth Abbey, who had nothing else to say other than that she loves loves loves Lila so so so much and thinks Gary is so so so wonderful. And finally, the father of the groom, who concludes the night with his gravelly Boston accent. He thanks everybody for coming to the reception, says they should all look out for tonight's dinner bill in the mail.

"Just kidding," the father says. "You all know I'm not paying for this."

Everybody laughs.

"More seriously, Lila and Gary, we're so thrilled to be celebrating with you this week. Let's all raise a glass to the happy couple."

WEDNESDAY

Sailing

When Phoebe wakes, it takes a moment to remember who and where she is. But then she sees the tassel lamps. She smells the coconut pillow.

"I am alive," she says out loud, just to make sure.

Outside, the patio is quiet. The party is over. And the pillow smells so much of coconut, it actually makes it difficult to get back to sleep. So does the giant alarm clock, keeping time quite dramatically. It's three a.m. The grief hour, according to Phoebe's therapist. The demon hour, according to medieval peasants. The hour that you wake up when you have excess cortisol in your body, according to a doctor Phoebe once saw.

Whatever it is, it's the hour that Phoebe often wakes up.

The bride is right. Phoebe has been to enough weddings to know that the bride is always right. Phoebe has to do a thing. She has to get up and do any single thing because she knows the feeling that will come if she lets herself sit in the empty shame of three in the morning, especially after trying to kill herself.

Normally, she would just sit in bed and ask herself questions that made her feel like garbage, like, What kind of psycho tries to kill herself? And, What is her husband doing at this exact moment? Was he sleeping? Was he having sex with Mia this very second? Was he still at a bar somewhere, getting free drinks because people always liked to give him free things for some reason? Then she would probably pull up Mia's Instagram page, even though it made her feel like shit. Because it made her feel like shit. There Mia always was, in bright lipstick, saying, Look at my big red lips. Look at us on our autumnal weekend. Look at this pie that I made for July Fourth and look at my baby taking a tiny baby bite of this pie, isn't she such a baby.

But luckily, Phoebe's phone is dead. She decides never to look at her phone again. She doesn't see the point in staying alive only to do all the same things that made her want to die.

So Phoebe thinks: What is one thing I can do right now instead?

Lila's question surprised Phoebe, and she's not sure if that's because she didn't expect insightful questions from someone wearing so much self-tanner or if it's because she spent the last few years overwhelmed by all the things she could not do, the papers she could not grade, the conversations she could not bear to have, the baby she could not create, the awards she'd never win, the marriage she could not fix.

It's time, she knows, to imagine the things she can do.

Right now, it's not much. Her body feels worn out and weary. But she can brush her teeth. She can use mouthwash. She can drink a bottle of water. Then she can take a very long bath in the beautiful soaking tub.

But when she turns on the faucet, she realizes she can't actually take a bath. There's no drain stopper.

But that's fine, she thinks. Even better. She can go down to the hotel's hot tub and look at the ocean instead.

She undresses to her underwear. Black lace, the fanciest she owns, because she had refused to die in bad underwear. She wraps herself in the giant fluffy robe, the kind she's seen at hotels before but for some reason has never once thought about wearing. Yet now it seems like it was put there by God just so she could feel soft in this moment.

She reaches for the door handle and looks down at her wedding ring. She takes it off, puts it on the black marble tray in the bathroom, and decides never to wear it again.

DOWNSTAIRS, SHE WALKS through the empty lobby. She passes the built-in oak bookcase and for the first time notices something very wrong with the books. They are all turned backward so only their pages show. It creates a monochromatic scheme—a trend she saw once on an HGTV show. Madness. She was offended by it then and is more offended by it now in real life.

She pulls out one of the books.

Sonnets by Shakespeare.

She looks back at the front desk to see if Pauline is watching, but it's Carlson.

"Hello, Phoebe," Carlson says.

It must be a house rule to say hello to each guest, to learn their name, the way it is also a house rule never to set any house rules. Never question what the guest is doing. The guest is paying too much money to be questioned. Make the guest feel the hotel is their home, even at three-thirty in the morning when the wedding people at the bar demand one more Manhattan. She sees the bartender pour them with the energy of a man who just woke up.

"Hello," she says.

She puts the book back on the shelf so that the spine is showing. Then she walks out to the hot tub, proud to have saved Shakespeare.

PHOEBE THINKS YOU can tell a lot about a hotel by its hot tub, the way she could tell a lot about her husband by looking at his fingernails when she first met him in the computer lab. She could see that he clipped them short, all the same length. He was not a nail-biter. If he had fixations, they had nothing to do with his hands.

And this hot tub—if it has flaws, she cannot see them. It sits right on the edge of the deck, like nothing separates it from the ocean in the distance.

She steps into the tub and feels her whole body warm. She sits with her back against the jets. It doesn't really feel like a massage, but she pretends it's a massage. She closes her eyes. Lila is right. Water helps. It feels good to be warm. Good to have a body. She dangles her arms out and lets them float. She sits like that for a long time in a sleepy haze. When she finally opens her eyes to look up at the stars, she sees a man stepping into the tub.

"Hello," the man says.

There really is no getting away from the wedding people here. And this one—he looks directly at her as he gets in. Normally, this would be enough human interaction to make her leave a hot tub, but she's electrified by the direct eye contact. It's nice to be seen in this moment. Nice not to fear the sight of other people. She is the only person she is afraid of now—she is the only one here who just tried to kill her.

"Hello," she says.

The man has a long, angular face, softened at the edges by a beard. He is handsome in the way Phoebe always imagined coastal New Englanders to be. A kind of beauty that's been weathered by wind and water, like he's been out sailing every day of his life for a little too long. And maybe he has been. Maybe that's why he's wrinkled around the eyes or why he slowly sits down in the tub with a long sigh.

"I didn't think anyone would be here at four in the morning," the man says.

"Neither did I."

"Well, don't worry," he says. "I promise I won't make you talk to me."

"That's too bad," she says. "I was actually hoping you would talk to me."

He seems surprised by her frankness.

"Really? You aren't tired of talking yet?" he asks. "All I've been doing at this wedding is just talking to people and then talking to more people."

"What have you been talking about?"

"How was your flight?" he says. "What do you think of the hotel? What shows did you watch during the pandemic? How did you better yourself with all that free time?"

"Well?" she asks. "How did you?"

The man strokes his chin as if he's thinking hard. "Mostly, I just grew this quarantine beard."

"It's a better beard than that," she says. "Very trendy."

"Oh, come on! Don't say that," he says. "Beards can*not* be trendy. People have *always* had beards."

"Have they?"

"Jesus had a beard," the man says. "Darwin had a beard. Marx had a beard."

"Yeah, but not the way people have beards now."

"How do people have beards now?"

"People now have . . . ironic beards."

"And what did Darwin have?" he asks. "A sincere beard?"

"My best guess," she says, "is that Darwin's beard was a product of Victorian notions of masculinity and naturalist beliefs, all coming together . . ."

"On the bottom of his chin . . ."

"To form Darwin's beard."

"Right," he says. "Right. Okay, well, very good. Thank you for this peer review of my beard. I'll certainly incorporate your feedback."

She laughs. Who is this man? Is he an academic? Is he flirting? Is she flirting? It's been so long, Phoebe can't remember the difference between having fun and flirting. Maybe there is no difference. She lifts up her feet, lets her legs float in the water.

"What about you?" he asks. "How did you better yourself during lockdown?"

She could lie, give him the answers he's likely been hearing all day, the things she told her colleagues when she got back on campus yesterday. Oh, I wrote a ton during the pandemic. The book is really coming along!

But that is how it happens, she realizes. One moment of pretending to be great leads to the next moment of pretending to be great, and ten years later, she realizes she's spent her entire life just pretending to be great.

"I drank a lot," she says.

"Did it help?" he asks.

"It helped me not care about the fact that I basically stopped changing my clothes," she says. "Or that my dissertation was actually a piece of shit."

She waits for him to break eye contact, to look at his phone, find some excuse to get out of this conversation. But he keeps looking at her, so she continues.

"And my advisor kept emailing me being like, Who cares if it's a piece of shit! Everybody's dissertation is a piece of shit. That's what dissertations *are*."

He laughs. "Are you in grad school?"

"I'm a professor."

"I didn't know we had a professor in the family." He looks at her like he's trying to figure something out. "You don't look familiar. Are you in the Winthrop family?"

"No."

"The Rossi family?"

"I'm not actually here for the wedding."

He looks confused. "I thought Lila said everyone was supposed to be here for the wedding. I distinctly remember that being a very big deal to her."

"Well, I'm not."

"So you're on vacation and you get surprised by a wedding?"

"I'm not here on vacation."

"This is becoming very mysterious."

"I came here to kill myself," she blurts out.

This is the gift random strangers can give you, Phoebe is realizing—the freedom to say or be anything around them. Because who cares? He doesn't know her, will never know her. He will list all kinds of reasons why she shouldn't die, and she will tell him that she is not planning to die anymore, and then they will get out of the hot tub and carry on with their lives and never think about each other again.

But all he says is "Shit," like she stepped in a puddle of mud. It makes what she said sound small and fixable. Like something he understood.

"Perhaps I should have added that I decided not to," she says.

"That's actually a pretty crucial detail," he says. Then he adds, "I shouldn't joke like that. I'm sorry."

"No, please. Joke," she says. "It's the only part of this that could ever be any fun."

"May I ask how you were going to do it?"

"Professor Stone, with the cat painkillers, in the Roaring Twenties," she says.

"Cat painkillers? That's a little . . ."

"Cliché?"

"No," he laughs. "Ineffective. Who uses cat painkillers?"

"Apparently people who are not setting themselves up for success."

"So, you came all this way to kill yourself with some cat's painkillers—"

"I mean, it wasn't just some cat. It was *my* cat."

"—and get surprised by a fucking wedding?"

"Yeah," she says. "That's why I couldn't do it. That and the lack of room service."

"Personally, I never kill myself unless there's room service," he says.

She laughs—it feels like a cloud slipping out her mouth, floating up to the sky.

"And the air conditioner," she says, "smelled weird."

"Say no more."

Suddenly, it all seems so ridiculous to her. So funny.

"I'm sorry you've been in that much pain," he says. "I know what that can feel like."

She stares at him. Now she's the one surprised by his honesty. "Have you ever . . . tried?"

"Not exactly," he says. "But I came close. A few years ago, I used to think about it a lot."

"And now you don't?"

"Now I don't."

"How did you stop?"

"Honestly, I think I just waited. That, and I watched *Breaking Bad* every night for a month."

"The therapeutic cures of drug deals gone awry."

"You joke, but by the end of it, I felt actual relief that I was not Walter White. Like, at least I didn't shoot myself with my own machine gun after being hunted by my own brother-in-law."

"Hey, spoiler," she says.

He laughs. "It's been ten years! Come on."

Then they just sit there in silence, heads rested back against the tub, and enjoy the warmth, as if they've shared something vital. As if they are no longer alone with themselves or their secrets. She looks up at the sky, and his foot brushes against her leg.

"Sorry," he says, very quickly, but she likes it. She feels a flutter of something she hasn't felt in a long time. She has just been touched after hours by a man who is not her husband, and yes, it was just an accidental foot tap, but it felt unbelievable to her. Maybe because she is supposed to be dead by now or maybe because she is supposed to be her husband's wife. Or maybe she just wants to fuck him?

"Do you have any other secrets?" she asks.

"Of course."

"Tell me one."

"I don't even know you," he says.

"Isn't it better that way?" she asks.

He considers this. "Once in college, I became addicted to my girl-friend's romance novels. We started reading one together as a joke, but then I actually got hooked. I mean, I got completely addicted. Read them for months. So there you have it."

"That's not that embarrassing. What's wrong with that?"

"Clearly there is something very wrong with that," he says. "A twenty-one-year-old boy in his dorm reading *Confessions of a Victorian Virgin*?"

"I don't know," she says. "I've always been weirdly impressed by people who read four hundred pages just to have a single orgasm. That's a lot of work. Watching a video would have been astronomically easier."

"Thanks for the support, but I have a feeling my time might have been better spent actually finishing *Moby-Dick* or something."

"*Moby-Dick* is porn, too," she says.

"*Moby-Dick* is not porn."

"It's ship porn!" she says. "The total fantasy of being a man on a ship, having a wild adventure. But instead of it ending with a woman having a triple orgasm, it ends with a . . ."

"Hey, no spoilers!"

"Giant whale . . ."

"Having a triple orgasm?"

"Exactly. Then it smashes into the ship and basically everyone dies."

"Ugh, I knew it," he says, and they laugh. She spreads her arms out and trails her fingers along the warm water, looks up at the moon. Life is unbelievable, she thinks. Last night, she was about to die alone in her hotel room and now she is here, in a hot tub, flirting with a man she would have deemed "too attractive" before. She would have seen him

out at a bar and dismissed him because he was beautiful. And how ridiculous is that? That she made rules about not being attracted to people
who were too attractive for the same reason her husband refused to hire
a philosopher with an agent. "I mean, we have to ask ourselves, Is someone that famous going to want to teach our Intro to Ethics course?" he
asked her. "I think not." And she agreed, because this is often what she
wondered when she met men. Is someone that handsome going to want
to wipe up the spills on the counter? Hold our daughter's hair when she
vomits with the flu? Listen to me talk at length about the ideological
underpinnings of the Victorian beard trend?

No. She couldn't imagine it. She could only imagine beautiful people
doing beautiful things. But right now, she feels equally beautiful. More
beautiful. She is alive. Enchanted. I have fingers, she thinks, and brings
them to the surface of the water. Look at these magical fucking fingers.

"So what's your specialty, Professor?" he says. "Your field? Not sure
how you say it."

"My field is Victorian literature," she says. "Novels, mostly. The marriage plots. The Jane Eyres."

"The book about the orphan girl?" he asks. "Or am I thinking of
Annie?"

"They're both orphans."

"So your field is . . . orphans?"

"Yes," she jokes. "I specialize in . . . orphans."

She tells him she was always drawn to their stories.

"Were you . . . an orphan?" he asks.

"No. But I always wanted to be one."

"Who doesn't?" he says. "Orphans, they're living the life."

"I mean, my mother died when I was born."

"Okay. So you were halfway to the dream."

"But my father raised me."

"I'm so sorry to hear that."

"Yes, a real tragedy." She laughs. "No. He was a good man. I loved
him. But he also was so depressed about my mother being dead that
much of the time it was like he was hardly there at all. So I think I

convinced myself that I functionally had no parents, yet was still bound by the rules of my father."

"An orphan without all the perks."

"Lonely with no street cred."

"Strange the things we convince ourselves as kids," he says. "I always wanted to get the shit kicked out of me when I was younger."

"Why?"

"Boys were always getting the shit kicked out of them in movies, and it just seemed like a rite of passage. Like I couldn't grow up and be a real man until someone deviated the hell out of my septum or something."

"That's what all the real men say."

"Unfortunately, it never happened," he says. "A notorious people pleaser."

He grows quiet. He leans back.

"Did you just get tired of talking?" she asks.

"No," he says. "I just got actually tired. This doesn't really feel like talking."

"What does it feel like?"

"Just feels like being here," he says. "It's relaxing."

Then he looks at her, like he is somewhat astonished by her presence. Like maybe he doesn't quite believe in this moment, the way she can't quite believe it. She wants to reach out, touch him. She wants to believe that something even more amazing can happen next. She feels certain that this moment, and moments like this, are what she stayed alive for.

"I know what you mean," she says.

But at a certain point, a person can no longer be in a hot tub anymore, no matter how much they want to be. It's just too hot. The body can't take it. She stands up and remembers that she is only in her black lingerie.

The man looks away. "Sorry."

"Don't be sorry," she says. "I mean, I'm the one in my underwear. I should be sorry."

But she's not. She doesn't even reach for her robe. She just continues standing there. Because why should underwear be more embarrassing than a bathing suit?

"To be honest, I never really understood the logic of it," she says. "I mean, underwear covers the same exact parts of my body, and yet because it's made out of different fabric, it's suddenly inappropriate?"

"I've wondered that myself before," he says. "But it does seem categorically different somehow."

"Well," Phoebe says.

She could invite him up to her room. And why not? Her marriage is over. He's not wearing a wedding ring. And they have a connection. Phoebe is certain of it, because it has been so long since Phoebe has felt connected to anybody, even herself. Their connection is the most obvious thing—the only thing she can feel at the moment.

But Phoebe hesitates. The old Phoebe never made the first move. Not even with her husband after years of marriage—she always waited for him to initiate. She was always too embarrassed to admit that she ever wanted anything, as if there was something humiliating about being a person with desires. But what would it feel like to be different? To be totally honest about what she wants?

"I want to fuck you," she says to the man.

"Oh," the man says. He sits up straighter in the tub, no longer relaxed. "I really wasn't expecting you to say that."

"I wasn't, either," Phoebe says. "Just figured in the spirit of total honesty—"

"In the spirit of total honesty, I should tell you that I—"

"You're with someone," she interrupts, because there is the old Phoebe, rushing back to save her. The old Phoebe who assumes she knows all the terrible things that people are thinking, so she says them first, as if this somehow protects her from the truth. "Of course."

But he doesn't seem offended or embarrassed by what she said. He doesn't say anything for a moment. He just watches her with curiosity, like she's some kind of rare deer spotted in the woods that will vanish if he makes another sound. And suddenly, the old Phoebe seems like the fool. So defensive, so afraid, so silly in the face of this very honest moment of two people just wanting each other.

"I am," he finally says.

She nods, ties her robe closed.

"Well, I sincerely hope someone beats the shit out of you this week," Phoebe says.

"Thanks," he laughs. "Me too."

She smiles the whole way to the elevator. Her heart pounds wildly as she stands there. She feels alive. She feels so real. Like she could do just about anything, so she starts to turn around more books on the shelf. *The House of Mirth. Huckleberry Finn.* She doesn't stop until she pulls out *Mrs. Dalloway*, by Virginia Woolf.

She holds *Mrs. Dalloway* in her hand as if it is a message from the universe, even though the old Phoebe doesn't believe in messages from the universe. It's just a book that belongs to the hotel. It's just a book they probably got when they ordered books in bulk from some used bookstore. But it's also the last book she never finished.

She puts it under her arm, gets in the elevator, and that's how it becomes hers.

UPSTAIRS, SHE THROWS out the cigarettes. She opens the minibar, which the room literature insists is a "beverage cooler." She pulls out a guava hibiscus kombucha.

"Don't eat from the minibar," her husband always said.

But she doesn't care if she gets ripped off. She wants to get ripped off. She has chosen this overpriced hotel just to be ripped off. She feels giddy as she cracks open the can. Then she opens Lila's gift bag and takes out the Oreos that are not Oreos because they are made from love and not trans fats. She holds up a not-Oreo in her palm and then eats an entire sleeve, like her husband used to. Until his affair, Oreos were the one thing her husband couldn't keep under control.

"They're just so damn good," he would say. "I don't know how anybody stops eating them."

And they were. She bites into one and thinks, Even not-Oreos are so damn good.

She opens *Mrs. Dalloway*. She doesn't want to think of her husband anymore. She has already thought about her husband so many times, and she has never once finished *Mrs. Dalloway*. She always told herself it was because she didn't care for Woolf's style, the circular sentences, the never-ending thoughts punctuated with semicolons; like this; and this; and then this.

"If you ever want to learn how to use a semicolon, don't go to Woolf," she used to tell her students.

If she were being honest, though, Phoebe would have admitted that she didn't care about Mrs. Dalloway's inner life. Mrs. Dalloway was too old, too unhappy, too married, already beyond the years of life that interested Phoebe at the time. And she hated Septimus for the same reasons—he was back from the war, threatening suicide, and after he jumped out the window, she felt betrayed by the book, betrayed by Woolf and all the other great authors who killed themselves. It was too horrible to know that getting married wasn't enough. That creating their masterpieces hadn't been enough, that going to World War II hadn't been enough, that being a valedictorian of both her high school and then her college wasn't enough—her father was still depressed. Still alone, always just sitting on his chair watching Vietnam War movies.

That's how she found him when she returned from St. Louis after her first year of graduate school—dead on his chair. She assumed it was suicide, because that's what she had always worried about, but then she saw the cereal bowl spilled all over his potbelly and she looked away. A stroke, she thought. Or maybe a heart attack. And when she looked at him again, the sadness was blinding.

She went back to school, and the darkness was all she could see for days. She was alone. Truly alone. She would walk around the Forest Park gardens and notice only the fungus on the leaves. The whiskey smell of Bob's breath in the hallway. And Nancy, the department administrator, who ate tuna for lunch every day of her life and then got cancer and then quietly died offstage and was replaced by someone with the same exact haircut.

So she read the novels about slow, incremental improvement, about sisters who were also good friends, women who were too witty for the sincerity of their landscapes, women who were above marriage and its conventions and, yet, got to be beautiful and experience the joys of it anyway. She devoted her career to these books because she needed them. She didn't care that most of the other graduate students thought this was boring. These stories were like little bibles to her, teaching her how to be normal, how to dream, how to believe that happiness and a new family would arrive in a single moment, on a single page, like the sudden crescendo of a symphony. She needed to believe these people were out there looking for her, these good and moral people with big estates and bigger hearts who would fall madly in love with just how alone she was, because wasn't life fucking hard enough?

But now she needs something else. Now she rests her head on the coconut pillow and begins to read *Mrs. Dalloway*. Now she knows what it feels like to be beyond the traditional plot points of a life, to sit on a chair in an empty room feeling like there is nothing more than this solemn march forward. Yet, there must be something else. She is suddenly gripped with such curiosity it feels primal. She needs to know: After the war, after the marriage, after the suicide—what happens next?

Before they fell in love, Phoebe and her husband sat next to each other in the graduate computer lab for two months, not talking to each other. They were both busy trying to finish their dissertations before their sixth year ended, both gifted with some ungodly ability to focus relentlessly on a task, even on the hottest St. Louis afternoons when thunderstorms split open the sky above. They typed and typed and typed, and probably would have gone on like this forever if the power had not gone out.

"Shit," Phoebe said.

The room shut down like a body that had died. For a moment, it was too quiet.

"I can't remember the last time I hit Save," Phoebe said.

Matt walked over to her immediately, like an emergency responder.

"It'll be okay," he said. "It's fine. There's always a way to recover the document."

She had been reworking a chapter all morning, pages she no longer had to rework, according to Bob, who was just starting to become very concerned about what he called her unproductive perfectionism. "Just finish by May," Bob said, and now it was April.

"We'll get it back," Matt said with the certainty of a boat captain. Phoebe didn't yet know where Matt was from, didn't yet know he had a very devoted mother who put up a real Christmas tree every year. But she could feel it.

"I hope so," Phoebe said, relaxing.

Bob walked in, picked up papers at the printer, and said, "Oh, good! These printed in the nick of time." Then he looked at Phoebe with the glassy look of a man who hadn't been outside all day, and said, "Oh, hi Phoebe, I didn't recognize you for a moment. You don't look all Virginia Woolfish today."

Phoebe looked down. Did she normally look Virginia Woolfish? She was confused. She had never thought of herself that way before.

"Oh," was all she said. "Yeah."

Her advisor left and the room was quiet until she said, "Was that a compliment or an insult?"

"I guess it depends," Matt said. "Was Virginia Woolf . . . hot?"

Phoebe laughed. "I mean, I never think of any historical figure as hot. They're just these bodiless, dusty, sepia-toned entities."

Matt agreed. "Even the US presidents, the ones who are famous for being hot presidents, like JFK, aren't really what we'd call hot."

They sat there and talked about the US presidents, saying things like, "I mean, Lincoln had nice bone structure, I think," and "What? Lincoln was famously ugly." They debated whether Nietzsche would be hot if one of his aunts had shaved his mustache, but it was too hard to say, too impossible to imagine the man's face without that mustache, so Matt finally said, "Hey, want a beer?"

Matt and his friends kept beers upstairs in their departmental fridge because you could do that kind of thing in Philosophy, where the new admin was everybody's best friend. They sat in the eerie purple light of the storm and talked about how nice it was not to be writing, and how did every waking moment become about our dissertations?

"When my parents call, my mom is always like, But are you doing anything fun for the summer? And I'm like, Well, I've been thinking a lot about Platonic forms."

Phoebe laughed. She felt like she was skipping school, not like she had ever done that before.

"Same," she said. "I mean, my father. He didn't really get it, either."

She told him that her father didn't understand why she read so much. It had worried him, something he told her during her first Thanksgiving break from graduate school. She had spent it reading instead of going out with her friends or on dates with men. And yes, sometimes she read too much. Sometimes, she read books instead of living a life, but didn't that just mean that her life was about reading books? And couldn't that be a life the way his life was all about floating on a river? Every night, she watched her father put on gear and wordlessly get in the boat and try to hook the same fish he'd fished for years and he never thought this was strange at all. But he looked at her reading *Emma* and said, "Go outside, live a little."

"Power's back," Matt said.

She wished for a tornado to tear through the quad and keep them hidden in the basement for so long, they'd be forced to start a new life together. But the room was lit up now, the computers were alive again, and Matt said, "Okay, let's see the damage."

She pulled up the Word document. The morning's work was gone.

"Is that really bad?" Matt said.

"Yes," she said. "Very bad."

She had two weeks to finish her dissertation. And she didn't have a tenure-track job lined up for the fall like Matt—a stroke of luck, he told her, a retirement at the right time, but Phoebe knew it was more than that. Phoebe knew everybody in the philosophy department must truly love Matt, the way she could already feel herself start to love him. He was the boat captain in every room, who made you feel like everything was going to be okay. He would run the internship program and he would help figure out why nobody cared about philosophy anymore and he would publish a book to much acclaim—a book so popular, he actually made money off it.

But Phoebe wasn't beloved by her department. She wasn't hated, but she wasn't a star—she didn't have any real publications like many of her colleagues, because she was always in the computer lab, just trying to finish her dissertation.

But it had been worth it, Phoebe thought—to lose the morning's work in exchange for his company. And maybe this was what her father had been talking about. Maybe this is the life he had wanted for her.

"I'm impressed by your calm," Matt said. "If I lost this morning's work, I'd be under the table right now, crying and drinking gin."

"Well, there's no gin, so . . ." Phoebe said.

"Oh, there's gin. Every academic building statistically has at least one bottle of gin."

"Let's go find it."

"First, work," Matt said. "Gin, later."

They went back to work, but she couldn't focus. The energy of the room had shifted. She wanted to sit there and drink gin with this man. She wanted to know: What did Virginia Woolf look like again?

She pulled up her photo online and realized that she never properly looked at the woman before. Yes, she saw her square photo on the back of books her colleagues were reading, but that afternoon, she could see Woolf in a new way, the way she could suddenly see herself—through Matt's eyes. And through the eyes of a man falling in love, she could see how spirited Woolf had been, how beautiful she was at the right angle. Phoebe had always felt this way about herself. Pretty, but only at certain angles.

"Okay, I give up," Matt said. "All I'm doing over here is googling photos of Virginia Woolf."

"Me too," she confessed.

"Well, let me just say this," Matt said. "Bob was definitely giving you a compliment."

She smiled in the privacy behind her computer.

AFTER THEY BOTH finished their dissertations, they spent the summer together, not working. There were long nights at the bowling alley. They listened to the drum circles on Delmar. They took long drives along the Mississippi. Had barbecue at beaver-trapping festivals. She started reading *Mrs. Dalloway* and fell in love with that, too. She would text Matt her favorite lines without any explanation and he understood.

But nothing is so strange when one is in love (and what was this except being in love?) as the complete indifference of other people, she wrote.

It's like today when I was at the gas station filling up my tank, Matt texted back. *I thought, So I still have to do chores?*

But then Septimus killed himself and the fall semester began. She put down *Mrs. Dalloway* for good, and Matt moved into his new office. She started teaching her first class as an adjunct, while applying to jobs all over again. Each time they said goodbye before one of her interviews, it was upsetting—felt like practice for the real thing. She called him from the hotels, which made her feel like a kid in high school, trying to learn everything about Matt over the phone. Tell me more about your mother, about your father, about the little dog you held in your arms as it bled out in the street, and do you like chocolate or citrus desserts, do you like lakes or oceans, cats or dogs, and why does the world always make us choose?

"People love creating false binaries," Matt said. "It's clarifying."

In November, she was offered her first job—a tenure-track position at a college in Wisconsin. She looked up the town online, researched it like a book, agonized about what to do. She knew it was an opportunity, but when she pictured herself there, she could only picture herself as her father, sitting on a chair in a dark room, entirely alone.

"It's your decision, of course," Matt said, and Phoebe was disappointed. She didn't want it to be her decision. She wanted him to decide—to be the captain.

She made no decision. She read drafts of Matt's new article, and it was easier to fix his work than her own. She made suggestions in the form of questions: Do you know the shape of your argument? When you close your eyes, can you see it?

"Let's go to the park," he said one afternoon.

Everyone they knew was going to the park. Everyone had been obsessed with the eclipse for two days now. Even their friends who didn't believe in things seemed to think it meant something. There was a metaphor in it. Somehow, it represented something. And she wanted to feel it, whatever it was, so she looked straight at the dark center that was once the sun. The red light was supposed to be blinding, but they were fine, protected. They were in love, not to mention wearing special glasses, holding hands in a park, surrounded by mansions built during the World's Fair. Phoebe thought it was all so beautiful.

"Hey," Matt whispered in her ear, "want to get married here?"

He whispered it so casually, it stunned Phoebe. The same way he said, Hey, let's have a beer. Like their marriage was a thing so natural, so organic, it grew all around them like grass.

At noon, Phoebe wakes to a loud knock on her door.

"I knew you wouldn't do it," Lila says. She walks in and stands in front of the bathroom mirror. "What do you think of this hat?"

The mother of the bride was right, Phoebe thinks. The bride has little imagination. Phoebe can't imagine being a person with so little curiosity about other people. Can't imagine walking into someone else's hotel room, someone who is openly suicidal, and not asking, "How are you?" She couldn't even start her therapy session on Zoom without asking her therapist, "How are you?" which made her very annoyed because wasn't she paying him just so she didn't have to consider the fact that he was a human being? But when she saw his face, he was so clearly another human being, and she began to wonder what it was like to sit on Zoom for nine hours a day listening to people like her talk about how they don't want to fuck their husbands anymore.

"Too much like a sailor's hat?" Lila asks.

"I guess it depends," Phoebe asks. "How much do you want to look like a sailor?"

"I don't really know," Lila says, like this is a big problem.

Yesterday, Lila's lack of concern would have seemed like more evidence for her aloneness. But this morning, Lila's indifference is a gift. Because Phoebe can't explain last night. She doesn't want to explain last night. It feels like a secret that she has with only the universe—and the man in the hot tub—a secret that will become a foundational memory she will carry with her everywhere she goes. Like the memory of meeting her husband, which was so life-affirming, it sustained her for a decade.

"We're going sailing," Lila says. "And Nat and Suz said it looked cute. But now I feel like I can't even trust them anymore."

Lila looks out at the ocean view, as if it is an old lover walking by.

"God, I fucking love your view," Lila says. She walks out to the balcony, sits down. Sighs. "I swear, you've become the only one I can trust here."

Phoebe joins her on the balcony, waits for Lila to speak, because Phoebe is sure any minute now, the bride will begin her monologue. But Lila doesn't say anything.

"Why can't you trust Nat and Suz?" Phoebe asks, like she knows them.

"They're supposed to be my best friends, but they just let me humiliate myself yesterday, walking around with food in my teeth," Lila says. "Then, after the reception, they were like, Such a perfect night! Such great speeches! Your mother was so so so wonderful! And I mean, just no. Did they *hear* my mother last night?"

"She turned it around at the end, I thought."

"No. Like, I'm sorry I don't speak to ducks," Lila says. "Jesus. My entire life this woman has been expecting things from me that I just don't think mothers should expect from their children. And she didn't even get the story right! Gary didn't buy the painting that first day we met at the gallery. He came again a week later to buy it. And she wasn't even there!"

Lila takes off the hat.

"And now I don't know what my friends mean when they tell me something is wonderful," she says. "That's the only word Suz and Nat have been able to use since they got here. Oh, Lila, Gary is so so so wonderful!"

"Is Gary not wonderful?"

"He's *Gary*."

"I don't follow."

"Christmas is wonderful. A vacation in Tuscany is wonderful. A kayak around the lake is wonderful. Those tiny soufflés that you have to order an hour in advance at restaurants are wonderful. But Garys are not wonderful. That's just not what they are meant to be."

Phoebe feels the professor come alive in her. The professor is always tempted to say something wise that will get the student to reflect on their own words—something like, If you don't think he's wonderful, maybe everybody else isn't the problem. Because isn't that what Lila is coming here for? The truth about her sailor hat?

"What are Garys supposed to be?" Phoebe asks.

But Lila doesn't answer. She suddenly looks confused, like maybe she has no idea what Garys were put on this earth to do.

"Ugh," she says, looking at her phone. "I have to go. Apparently there's something wrong with my mother's room."

Lila walks to the door but is stopped by the sight of Phoebe's unmade bed.

"If you're depressed, you should really try making your bed in the morning," Lila says. "It's supposed to make you happier. I read a study."

"Well, you should tell the researchers that you know a woman who made her bed every single day of her life for forty years and it didn't work."

"But maybe it did work. Maybe you would have killed yourself years earlier if you hadn't been making the bed. See? You never know."

"I invite you to make the bed then. This is your wedding week. You should have all the happiness that's available."

"No, I mean, it literally has to be your bed to get the happiness."

"Well, this isn't really my bed, so."

"Oh, and don't you love the coconut pillow? I thought they would be fun for everyone."

"It's very coconutty. Maybe too coconutty. Then again, I'm not sure how coconutty a pillow is supposed to be."

"It's the perfect ratio of coconut to pillow, I think. I simply cannot sleep without one anymore."

Phoebe feels a tiny headache start, the kind she gets when she waits too long to drink coffee.

"I need some coffee," Phoebe says, reaching for the pot.

"Oh, no. Don't," Lila says. "Even in a five-star hotel, the room coffee is shit. It's simply a rule of hotels. Let's order some. It's going to be a long day."

It is. Phoebe's first day back to life. Because if she is not going to die, she is going to have to live. She is going to have to book a plane ticket. Email Bob. Think of something wise and life-changing to say to Adam. Return to St. Louis. Bury Harry, which is already more than she can think about right now.

"Do you take your coffee black?" Lila picks up the phone.

"Cream," Phoebe says. "And sugar."

"Thank God. People who take their coffee black are always so smug about it, you know? Marla this morning was like, Oh no, no, I don't need things in my coffee. I like it just black, thanks. And it's like, Well, I'm sorry, excuse me, but I happen to be a human being and I like sugar."

Then she dials room service.

"Yes, I'd like to order coffee with cream and sugar," Lila says into the telephone. "Two eggs. And the Patriotic French Toast."

"Patriotic French Toast?" Phoebe asks when Lila hangs up. "What war did it serve in?"

"Maybe it's shaped like a flag or something," Lila says.

"Maybe it votes."

Lila gives a half laugh, like a horse caught by surprise. "For a suicidal person, you're kind of funny."

"Thanks."

Lila walks to the door but looks at Phoebe as though she's leaving behind a sad couch at Goodwill.

"So this is what is going to happen," Lila says. "You're going to eat your patriotic breakfast, and then join us in the lobby to sail at two."

"Why would I come sailing with you?"

"Because I want you to."

"Why would you want a random depressed woman on your sail-boat?"

"You honestly don't seem that depressed," she says. "And the captain said we need a certain number of bodies in the boat to keep it balanced. And most of the people here are apparently too hungover to be on a boat right now. And if you don't come, I'll have to ask my mother to come. So don't even bother telling me you have plans, because I know you were planning on being dead right now."

Yes, Phoebe is supposed to be dead. She is supposed to be a cold slab at the morgue right now, but instead she is going to eat Patriotic French Toast and go sailing. Because isn't that why she had chosen the Cornwall with Matt? To go sailing on an America's Cup winner? To feel the ocean breeze in her hair? To be the people who ordered ridiculous breakfasts to their rooms?

"But I have to check out at eleven," Phoebe says.

"No need," Lila says. "I already told you I would book the room for the week."

"And I told you not to."

"Well, I don't want any more randos coming in here. You're the only acceptable rando."

"I'll be sure to put that on my tombstone. Phoebe Stone: the only acceptable rando."

But Lila doesn't laugh. Instead, she lifts her eyebrows in alarm.

"I'm kidding," Phoebe says. "And besides, I don't have anything to wear sailing. All I have is that . . . dress."

They both look at the green dress that Phoebe left crumpled on the floor. The dress looks like a corpse, fallen where it was shot dead. Phoebe wonders if she'll ever be able to touch it again.

"I'll have this laundered," Lila says, picking up the dress. "For now, buy something in the gift shop. The stuff there isn't too awful."

"But I don't even have anything that will get me to the gift shop, other than this robe."

"I see."

They scan each other's bodies to have that moment that women often have with each other—will my clothes fit you? Do we have the same body? And the obvious answer is no. Lila has the spindle legs of a Shaker table. Meanwhile, Phoebe has the body of a woman who has been drinking gin and tonics in bed for a year.

"I'll get something from my mother's," Lila says.

Phoebe objects, but Lila cuts her off.

"It's fine. It makes her feel like a better woman every time she donates," Lila says. "This is actually a service you're doing for her."

"Well, in that case," Phoebe says, "okay."

This is exactly what Phoebe has always hated and loved about life—how unpredictable it is, how things can change in an instant. One moment she could be wondering what to make her husband for dinner and the next moment he could walk into the room and tell her he is in love with someone else. But it is also true that one day she can be alone in a room preparing to die, and the next, she can be preparing to be on a boat with beautiful strangers.

"I'll see you in the lobby at two."

THE PATRIOTIC FRENCH TOAST is not shaped like a flag. There is nothing at all patriotic about it. Phoebe is disappointed by this.

But she eats it anyway. She is very hungry, she realizes. She washes her face in the sink, then brushes her hair, and what a goddamned beautiful brush. Carved out of a solid piece of wood like a boat.

She takes a long shower, using all the products, so elegantly packaged she wants to eat them, too. She rubs what smells like a wooded forest all over her body. She hears another knock on the door but opens it to find only a bag of clothes that Lila left. She peers in. She sees something shiny.

"Jesus," Phoebe says.

But it feels exciting, actually, to put on some other woman's sequins for the day.

"Everybody, this is Phoebe," Lila says.

The group says a collective hello, like they are all in a cult. High Bun is the first to hug her.

"I'm Suz," High Bun says, though High Bun no longer sports a high bun. She now wears a long fishtail braid hanging casually over her right shoulder. Her hair is endless. There is something almost prehistoric about it. No wonder the bun was so high. "I'm Lila's friend from Portsmouth Abbey."

"Portsmouth Abbey?" Phoebe asks.

"Don't worry, we're not nuns," says Neck Pillow, who now has a tiny diamond necklace resting at the center of her throat. "Just Catholic boarding school survivors. Hi, I'm Nat."

No one else hugs Phoebe, but each wedding person continues to introduce themselves by stating their relation to the bride or groom. The groom's sister, Marla. The groom's daughter, whose name is Mel but prefers to be called Juice.

"Right," Lila says. "I keep forgetting you want to be called Juice. And why is that again?"

Lila waits with a smile, as if she's giving Juice the chance to tell a really funny story about herself. But the groom's daughter just stands there, fiddling with a small green plastic circle in her hand. Her aunt is the one who speaks.

"We just always have," Marla says with a cool tone, smoothing the dark hair that frames her face. She has gray splints on both her wrists. She takes a sip of her black coffee.

"Yeah, like since the dawn of time," Juice says, with a learned coolness that sounds years older than eleven, which is what Phoebe guesses she is. Her outfit seems years older, too—big black combat boots, a cropped top that sits just below her navel. It looks uncanny against her childlike features—the baby fat, the missing canine tooth she must have recently lost.

Phoebe waits for Lila to say something snarky back, but Lila is flattened into silence by their tones. By their jokes, if that's what they even are. Lila puts her arm around her future stepdaughter, and when Juice slinks away, Lila looks at Phoebe like, See? And Phoebe does see. Phoebe feels suddenly protective of Lila, who already seems different around the wedding people. Quieter, more subdued. She does not talk at length about all of her family members at once. She is polite, gracious, cheery to a fault, and Phoebe remembers feeling pressure to be the same way at her own wedding. She feels glad she can say things when Lila cannot.

"Like on the sixth day, God created the oceans, and on the seventh day, people started calling you Juice?" Phoebe asks.

"That's very funny, yes," Marla says, without laughing. "That's exactly how it happened."

"I'm pretty sure God created the oceans on the second day, though," Lila says.

"Yeah, they were definitely, like, a priority," Neck Pillow says, and the women laugh.

But Marla ignores them.

"And who are you again?" Marla looks at Phoebe's outfit, as if the outfit will answer, though Phoebe has no idea what she communicates with this oversize sequined sweater, leggings made from some plastic faux-leather fabric that Phoebe avoided buying for nearly twenty years of her adult life, and sandals with a fake sunflower wedged between the toes that she bought from the gift shop.

"I'm Phoebe," she says. It feels surreal to introduce herself to the wedding people. They can hear her now. "I was asked to be a body on the boat."

The women laugh.

"Phoebe and I met at my mother's gallery," Lila says.

Phoebe is surprised by how coolly and quickly the lie comes out of Lila's mouth. It seems unnecessary to Phoebe. But as soon as she hears it, Marla's face lights up with interest.

"Oh, interesting, you work at the gallery?" Marla asks.

"No. I'm a professor," Phoebe says.

"Phoebe just came in one day to look," Lila says. "And we hit it off!"

"That's how you met Gary!" High Bun says.

"Yes, we all know the story," Marla says.

But that doesn't stop Lila from telling it, because it seems that nobody, not even Lila, can get over the coincidence of it all.

"When Gary came into the gallery, I had no idea he was my father's doctor," Lila says. "At the time, I just thought he was this guy."

"Wasn't Jim there, too?" Marla says. "You always leave Jim out of the story."

"Jim is not the point of the story," High Bun says.

"Jim was just there for Gary," Lila says. "Jim didn't actually come to see the art."

Gary was the one who cared about art, who was transfixed by the painting of her mother and just stared at it for what felt like ten minutes. Finally, Lila went over, and he had all these questions. Was this acrylic? Did Lila know the artist? Were they local? No—he was a painter who lived in New York. William Withers.

"I can't believe Gary had no idea that the painting was of your own mother," Neck Pillow says.

"How could he?" Lila asks. "We didn't know each other yet."

"But of all the paintings to be moved by," High Bun says.

"Wasn't it a nude?" Marla asks. "You always leave that part of the story out, too."

"Wait, it was a nude?" High Bun asks.

"You definitely never told us that part," Neck Pillow says.

Lila blushes. "Just a partial. And it's a little abstract, so it's like, she's not even really a person. She's more like a bunch of cubist nude color squares."

"Color squares with breasts," Marla says.

Neck Pillow and High Bun lean on each other as they laugh.

"Oh God, I bet your mother *loves* that part of the story," Neck Pillow says.

"It honestly was really more about the garden behind her," Lila says.

"Well," Phoebe says. "That's a really lovely story."

But then it gets quiet. Nobody seems to have anything more to say about the nude painting, not even High Bun and Neck Pillow, who stand on either side of the bride like soldiers. Phoebe doesn't know what she expected from these wedding people, but she expected conversation. They've been so loud from afar, so chatty on the patio last night. And Lila, so forceful in the room with Phoebe, now trying her best to be polite.

"Well, I guess we should go get the car," Lila says.

"I thought we were waiting for the car?" Marla asks.

"No. We were just . . . talking," Lila says.

As they walk out of the lobby, the men in burgundy rise. High Bun asks one of them to get the car, and then the women stand there in another long silence. Everybody looks at their phone or does whatever they can to pretend like the silence is totally normal, until Marla looks around, concerned.

"Where are Gary and Jim, anyway?" Marla asks.

"They're meeting us at the wharf with your dad," Lila explains.

"Oh," Marla says. She is visibly disappointed by the answer, as if she had not realized she'd have to spend the morning driving with Lila and not her brother. Or maybe she's just one of those people who look perpetually disappointed, with hair annihilated by a straightener, dyed so black that it makes her look like a grown-up version of Wednesday Addams. Her brown sweater, too stiff and formal for a day on a boat. And then there are the wrist splints, which Lila keeps periodically looking at, until Marla notices and finally says something about having a combination of carpal tunnel and tennis elbow.

"I don't even really like tennis! Just something to do with other women, you know? I mean, there's like no other sport you can just casually play with other women," Marla says. "How sad!"

"I don't think anyone should play sports," High Bun says. She is anti-sport now. A nurse–turned–physical trainer during Covid who has officially grown weary of all competition. Now High Bun specializes in yoga and nostril-breathing and calming down her system. "Competition is not good for the body or the soul. That's my gospel. It keeps us in trauma. Keeps us inflamed. That's probably what's going on with your hands. You're all inflamed. Do you take vitamin C?"

"I'm not inflamed," Marla insists. "I'm injured."

"I had bad carpal tunnel once," Neck Pillow says. She explains that she's a musician. A harpist for the Detroit Symphony. "It was a total disaster. I couldn't work for months."

"You're a harpist?" Phoebe asks.

"Nat is going to play for us at the clambake tonight, and she's amazing," Lila says to the group. "She's an experimental harpist."

Marla finally laughs. "An experimental harpist? Oh, that's not a joke. I'm sorry, I thought you were joking. I truly didn't know experimental harpists existed."

"There aren't many," Lila says. "Nat sort of pioneered the style, isn't that right?"

"You could say that," Neck Pillow says.

"How interesting," Marla says.

It is very easy to imagine Marla playing tennis or speaking in a courtroom or standing behind a podium running for mayoral office, less easy to imagine her in a hotel room, fucking a federal judge. But as they stand there in a new silence, Phoebe tries to imagine Marla giggling in lace lingerie, spread over the bed, the way she has imagined Mia laid out for Matt so many times.

"God, look at these cobblestones!" High Bun says.

Phoebe is starting to realize that this is a wedding like all others—here are people who came from very different corners of the bride's life, only to gather in a room and have no idea what to say to one another.

"Lila got us a vintage convertible for the week," High Bun says.

"Suz rented it," Lila says.

"But it was Lila's idea." High Bun smiles and pets her braid.

"Only Lila would have thought of something like that," Marla says, and it's unclear whether this is a compliment or an insult. Marla looks back down at her phone, and Phoebe wonders what it was about the federal judge that was so irresistible. Why was Marla willing to give up her whole life?

"The car is here!" Neck Pillow says.

The man in burgundy pulls up the vintage convertible.

"What a beautiful car!" High Bun says.

"How are we all going to fit in it, though?" Marla asks.

"We'll squeeze in it, no problem!" High Bun says. "We've put more people in a car than this."

"Remember my wedding on the Vineyard?" Neck Pillow asks. "We fit seven people in that car!"

"I'm sitting in the front," Marla says. "I get carsick in the back."

"I'll drive," the bride says.

"You're the bride!" High Bun says. "You shouldn't have to drive."

It's the bride's big week. The bride should be rendered helpless, given drinks, fluffed and complimented at every turn, put out like a kitchen fire, appeased like an angry toddler, prodded like a doll, then driven by a well-dressed stranger to the altar of her new life.

"But I want to drive," Lila says. "That's why I *got* the convertible."

Nobody, not even Marla, challenges the bride. If the bride wants to drive, the bride gets to drive.

But when Lila gets in the car, she can't. "Why did you ask for a stick shift?"

"I didn't," High Bun says. "I asked for their fanciest, most vintage-y convertible."

"Well, of course it's a stick shift," Marla says. "It's a car from like, 1940 or something."

"Well, I didn't know that," High Bun says.

"Does this mean that nobody here knows how to drive this car?" Marla asks.

Lila looks lost at the steering wheel.

"I can drive it," Phoebe says from the back. "For the most part."

"For the most part?" Marla says.

"I mean, I knew how to do it once upon a time," Phoebe says. "My father taught me."

"That sounds good enough to me." Lila gets out of the car and looks at Juice squished in the back seat.

"Mel, would you be more comfortable sitting on my lap?" Lila asks.

"No," Juice says. "And I told you I wanted to be called *Juice*."

"Right. Sorry," Lila says. She climbs in the back, and High Bun and Neck Pillow do a little dance to welcome her. In the driver's seat, Phoebe puts her hand on the gear shift, her foot on the clutch. It's been years, but it's a kind of muscle memory from childhood that she'll never forget, driving up the road in her father's Saab, learning how to change gears as he said, "Easy, now, easy."

"Onward," Marla says, tapping the dashboard.

"Where am I going?" Phoebe asks.

"Bowen's Wharf," Marla says. "Waze will know."

"I don't have a phone with me," Phoebe says.

The women are mystified. "Seriously?"

"I'll pull it up," Marla says, and hands Phoebe her phone.

As they drive, this is what they can all agree on: Newport is beautiful. The women in the back seat keep saying, Wow. Look at that mansion. And that one. And that one. And isn't that the Vanderbilts'? Aren't they all the Vanderbilts'?

"Who are the Vanderbilts?" Juice asks, but nobody answers, because the air is too crisp, the trees are too green. The people so rich-looking. The roads so roadlike.

"They were one of the richest families in Newport," Phoebe finally says, following the directions and trying to ignore the messages that silently pop up on Marla's phone from somebody named Robert.

I am thinking about your sweaty cunt, Robert writes.

Phoebe flinches. She wonders if it's the judge. She looks over at Marla, but Marla seems to have no idea what's happening to her phone, her gaze steady on everything outside the car—the high boxwoods, the crepe myrtles.

"*That's* the Vanderbilts'," Marla says, pointing to the Breakers.

"I can't believe that's where you're having your wedding!" High Bun says.

"I know. It's amazing. Especially because they *never* host private events," Lila says.

"Why did they let you, then?" Marla asks.

"My mother is on the board of the Preservation Society," Lila admits. "She gave a very large donation."

"Gary did tell you that our mother will never recognize your marriage unless you do it in a church, right?" Marla asks.

"Wait, what?" Lila asks. "Are you joking?"

High Bun leans over and turns up the music. Alicia Keys. She sings loudly, and changes the words to "Now we're in New-pooorrrt!!! These streets will make you feel poo-ooorr!"

"And rich people will juddddge you!" Neck Pillow sings.

"Let's hear it for Newpooort, Newpooort, Newpooort!" Lila adds.

The three Portsmouth Abbey girls laugh hard at their song, and for the first time since Phoebe met them, she feels the shared history, the fact that High Bun and Neck Pillow are really Suz and Nat. Lila's best friends from high school, curling their hair before parties and doing Tae Bo workouts in the mornings and making blueberry muffins on Sunday afternoons and menstruating at the same exact time and being so proud.

"I can't believe we're here!" Suz shouts and Nat adds, "Woot, woot, bitches!"

"What?" Marla says, turning around. "I can't hear you over the music!"

"I just said, Woot, woot bitches!" Nat says.

"Hoot hoot?" Marla asks, then looks to Juice for help, but Juice is silent and humiliated against the door. She just shrugs, returns her gaze to her green toy.

I want to slam it with my hard cock, Robert writes.

"Turn right," Waze orders.

At some point, Marla suggests putting the top up so they can all hear each other better, but Lila says that defeats the point of renting a convertible.

"We already have cars with tops," Lila says.

Suz agrees immediately. "That's true. All my cars do have tops."

Phoebe heads down Ocean Drive and everyone squeals, hands in the air. Phoebe is quiet but is glad to be in motion. The wind makes talking almost impossible. Though Suz keeps trying anyway. Suz shouts something about convertibles being fun. And Phoebe can feel it, too. Some kind of satisfaction feeling the car sticking to the road as she rounds the curb a little faster. She never drove her father's car like this.

"Jesus, slow down!" Marla says.

"I'm going the speed limit," Phoebe says.

The child is in the back, entirely silent, traumatized. Her face looks comical in the rearview mirror—exactly the same when in motion and not in motion. Sort of like a dog. Phoebe wonders when the child will speak, what she might possibly report from the depths of her consciousness. Juice reminds Phoebe of herself when she was younger, always silent in the car. Silence is her communication.

"No, go faster!" Lila cries. "I love it. I just love it."

But when they approach downtown, they hit traffic. A long line of red taillights in front of them. Phoebe can't see the end of it. She slows down, and the car keeps lurching just enough to make them jostle. She is not very good at being in first gear, but nobody complains.

"I can't believe we're actually here!" Suz says.

The nurse, despite all she has seen these past two years being a nurse, lives in a constant state of disbelief about the most ordinary things.

"I feel like we've been planning this forever," Nat says.

"We seriously have!" Suz says.

But Lila is concerned they are going to be late to the boat. "Does Waze say how long the traffic will be?"

"Twenty minutes," Phoebe says.

"Guess this is what happens when you plan a destination wedding," Marla says.

"This isn't a destination wedding," Suz says. "They *live* here."

"Anywhere farther than thirty minutes in Rhode Island is a destination wedding," Marla insists.

"We *were* actually thinking of doing a destination wedding in Germany, until Covid," Lila says.

"Why Germany?" Nat asks.

"They got engaged there!" Suz says.

"I only vaguely sort of remember that," Nat says.

"Ooohh, tell the story!" Suz says to Lila, clapping her hands. "Tell the story."

"We've heard the story," Marla says.

"Well, I don't know it," Nat says.

"Neither do I," Phoebe says.

So Lila tells the story.

"Six months after we met, Gary and I decided to take a big trip to Europe because my father was doing really well," Lila says, leaning forward. She sounds very excited to tell the story, and Nat and Suz are excited to hear the story, and Phoebe imagines they could probably listen to it a thousand times the way that her father could watch Vietnam War movies over and over again. Bridesmaids need the same kinds of stories soldiers do, stories that justify why they do what they do. Why they are willing to sacrifice who they are and a good night's sleep for the noble cause of defending democracy and Lila and Gary's love.

"Germany was our last stop," Lila says. "We went to the Black Forest to see the Walt Disney Castle."

"Oh, wow, you actually went to the Mad King's Castle?" Phoebe asks. "I've always wanted to go there."

"No, I said, the *Walt Disney Castle*," Lila clarifies.

"I know, but it's also called the Mad King's Castle," Phoebe says. "Or, the Neuschwanstein Castle."

"Well, I don't know what it's really called," Lila says. "We just called it the Walt Disney Castle because Gary told me it was the castle that Disney used as a model for Sleeping Beauty's. And Gary knows that I love all things Disney. So he planned to rent a car, drive us to the castle, and then propose outside the front doors. But we had been driving this stupid shitty rental thing that wouldn't go above like sixty, and we were going to be late and miss the last tour of the day. So Gary stopped at a BMW rental place on the side of the Autobahn and picked up a new car that could go super fast."

"There's no speed limit on the Autobahn," Lila adds. "It was exhilarating."

Phoebe can see them so clearly. Gary, whoever he is, with his only-faintly-receding hairline blowing back in the wind, and Lila, her mouth big and full, laughing, eyes toward the sky.

"And when we got to the castle, he proposed," Lila says with a smile. "I was actually really surprised. We had only been dating six months."

"That's so romantic," Suz says

"He really is so wonderful," Nat says.

But something isn't sitting right with Marla. "Why is it also called the Mad King's Castle?"

In the rearview mirror, Phoebe sees Lila's eyes roll and Juice's flicker up in interest.

"Because people thought the king who built it was insane," Phoebe says.

"But why?"

"Because he built the castle using all his money, even though he had already built two other castles. He went into debt building this elaborate third castle just for himself, and so there were rumors that the king must be going mad."

"Was he?" Marla asks.

"Eventually they found him drowned in the pond outside the castle."

"He was murdered outside the Disney castle?" Lila asks.

"Actually, they suspect he killed himself," Phoebe says, and meets eyes with Lila in the mirror.

"Of *course* he did," Lila says, and leans back, defeated.

So Phoebe adds, "But not in front of the Disney castle. It was actually at one of his other castles."

"Well, that's good then," Suz says, and like a loyal bridesmaid, she won't let them linger on the Mad King's suicide. "He went to Cornell, right?"

"The Mad King?" Marla asks.

"Gary!"

"Yale," Lila says.

"He must be really smart," Suz says.

"He is," Lila says. "So smart."

"He's not *that* smart," Marla says. "You know how many idiots get into Yale every day?"

Phoebe is irritated by Marla's desire to ruin everything, even though Phoebe was the one ready to ruin Lila's wedding last night. But there is something awful about doing it right in front of Lila's face, in the middle of the afternoon.

"So wait, what's your point?" Phoebe asks.

"My point is, Gary is not this Yale doctor hero. Sometimes Lila talks about him like he's this god," Marla says. "But I'll have you all know that once, Gary lit our house on fire."

"He lit your house on fire?" Lila asks. "How did I not know that?"

"He doesn't lead with that," Marla says. "Burned the entire kitchen down by accident and we had to live in a Marriott for a month. Best month of my life, to be honest. But don't tell my brother that."

The sun feels very hot above Phoebe. Marla starts covering herself with sunscreen.

I'm stroking it right now, Robert writes. *Where are you?*

Phoebe feels a twinge of delight, thinking about how embarrassed Marla will be at some point later when she realizes that Phoebe saw the messages.

"I really think we should put the top up," Marla says.

"But it's a convertible," Suz says. "We got the convertible so that we could put the top down."

"I've already had skin cancer and survived, twice, thanks. I don't feel like dying because I got stuck in traffic," Marla says.

"You've had skin cancer twice?" Nat says. "Holy shit."

"Okay," Lila says. "Fine. Let's put the top up."

In the enclosed car, in traffic, everything feels too quiet. There is something wrong here. People who are supposed to be bonding are not bonding.

"There's never any traffic in *The Gilded Age*," Suz says.

"My wife is obsessed with that show," Nat says. "But I think it's a bore."

But Suz doesn't care. Suz will watch anything when the Little Worm is sitting quietly on her lap. "I literally watched seven hours of *Wife Swap* the other day because she had stopped crying and I didn't want to move the Little Worm and get the remote."

"The Little Worm?" Phoebe asks.

"That's what Suz calls her child," Nat says. "And why I, for one, am now no longer sure I want a child."

"This whole time the Little Worm has been your *child*?" Marla asks.

"I should check on her, actually." Suz reaches for her bag.

"How far are we?" Lila asks again.

According to Waze, they are only a tenth of a mile away from the wharf.

"I bet it's a beautiful fucking wharf," Suz says.

"If we ever get there," Marla says.

"Of course we'll get there," Nat says.

"Waze says twenty minutes," Phoebe says.

"But it's right there?" Lila says. "How can that take twenty minutes?"

Suz looks up from her phone. "Shit. The Little Worm is sick."

"Oh, no," Lila says, but nobody in the car asks with what.

THEY SIT IN traffic for so long, Phoebe learns that each woman specializes in something. Suz, the trainer, specializes in celebrities. Nat, the musician, specializes in nontraditional plucking instruments like quarters and paper clips. And Marla, the lawyer, specializes in sexual harassment. She hears cases about whether something is or is not sexual harassment, and the women are intrigued.

"I didn't know someone actually decided that," Suz says.

"What did you think happened?" Marla asks.

"I don't know, I guess I never thought about it."

Then everyone starts wanting to know if they have been legally sexually harassed or not. Even Phoebe.

"On Monday, the Americanist in my department looked at me at the printer and said, 'Woweeee! Nice dress!'" Phoebe says. "Is that sexual harassment?"

"If you think you are being sexually harassed, you are," Marla says.

Phoebe didn't think it was harassment at the time, because the Americanist was so old, in that abyss of age just beyond sex, but also because she agreed with him. Yes, the dress was nice. That's why she bought it. That's why she wore it. That's what she wanted her husband to think! She wanted him to look at her and say, Woweeee, nice dress!

"So why would I be offended when the Americanist finally said it?" Phoebe asks.

"Of course the Americanist was the one who said it," Marla says.

"What's an Americanist?" Suz asks.

"What do you *do*?" Nat asks.

"I'm a professor," Phoebe says.

"A nineteenth centuryist," Lila says, sounding proud.

"My point is, Phoebe," Marla continues, as if she were actually providing legal counsel, "if you weren't offended, you weren't sexually harassed. That's how the law works."

"That doesn't sound like the law," Suz says.

"The law is partially subjective," Marla says. "Would *you* have complimented the *Americanist's* outfit?"

"No," Phoebe says. "Never. But mostly because the Americanist just wears the same thing every day. Dockers and some blue shirt. I mean. What do you even say about that?"

"I have a lot to stay about that," Lila says.

All the women laugh. Phoebe picks up speed. They lower the top again. Suz turns up the music. Katy Perry. "Teenage Dream." "I hate this song," Marla says, and they all agree that yes, they kind of hate this song, yet listen to it anyway. They finally get to the sign that says WEL-COME TO BOWEN'S WHARF. Everybody on the street looks like they're on vacation. Khakis and Nantucket reds. Soft baseball caps. Maybe they are all on vacation, or maybe this is just how you dress if you live in Newport. Phoebe parks.

"Lila! I can't believe you're getting married!" Suz shouts.

AT THE WHARF, all the men are dressed in polo shirts and khaki shorts except for one: the man from the hot tub. He stands there in his jeans and windbreaker with keys in his hand. It's weird to see him dressed, in daylight, out in the open. He is no longer a man in a hot tub. He is taller than she expected and looks very prepared to get on a boat.

"Gary!" Lila shouts.

He kisses Lila, and everyone claps like they did on the patio last night. He pulls away, smiling, until he sees Phoebe.

"Hello," he says, giving her a puzzled look.

He's the *groom*? The man in the hot tub is Gary? Even though he stands by Lila's side, she can't picture it. She can't see him speeding in a BMW on his way to the Disney castle. She can only imagine him in the hot tub, so resigned, so solitary, so unconnected to anything else in the universe except for Phoebe and his beard.

But maybe that's the trick night performs. Darkens everybody, highlights the nothingness around them. Maybe in the dark, everyone seems more alone than they are. Because he is clearly not alone. He is holding Lila's hand. He is putting his arm around his daughter. He is standing tall in front of a handsome sailboat.

"Hello," Phoebe says.

She suddenly doesn't know what else to say. The tension between them feels so palpable to Phoebe, so embarrassing, but nobody else seems to notice. Marla starts slathering Juice in sunscreen. Suz starts asking one of the men if he got the orders to stock the boat with Lila's favorite drink, which she keeps calling a Vacation in a Cup.

"Phoebe is a good friend," Lila says to Gary.

"Is that so?" Gary asks.

If Phoebe is being honest, she has no idea if she and Lila are friends. No idea what it means to be a friend. She's forgotten what it's supposed to feel like. Mia was the last good friend she made in her adult life. So what does Phoebe know?

"And here I thought I met all your friends," Gary adds.

"Well, here's one more," Phoebe says, and sticks out her hand.

"The more the merrier," Gary says, and shakes it.

He isn't going to acknowledge it, and so it is confirmed. Had everything been normal between them, he would have acknowledged that they already met. He would have said, Oh, how funny, I met Phoebe in the hot tub! But he doesn't say anything like that, which makes Phoebe feel like their meeting was remarkable. Like when Phoebe used to say, "Mia is so beautiful" to her husband, and he would say,

"Yes, Mia is a good laugh," when what he really meant to say was: I want to fuck Mia.

"We already—" Phoebe is in the middle of saying when Juice screams.

"My dog is dead!" Juice shouts. She immediately starts crying, and Phoebe is shocked to see her transform from sullen teen into crying child in a matter of seconds.

"Oh, sweetheart," Gary says.

Gary kneels down to become Juice's size. In that one swift motion, Gary is no longer the man in the hot tub. He is no longer the groom. He is just a dad wearing white sneakers. Probably orthopedic. Phoebe can see their years of history, the way Gary must have held Juice after Wendy's funeral. The meals he made her in the lonely afternoons. And is that what made him want to die? Losing his wife?

But then Gary stands up, puts his arm around Lila, and becomes the groom again, addressing his crowd.

"Don't worry," he says. "It's just a virtual dog."

"It's not *just* a virtual dog!" Juice shouts. She holds up the green plastic circle for all to see. "My mom gave her to me. Her name is Human Princess."

The people are silenced either by the mention of the dead wife or the fact that the dog's name is Human Princess. Lila does not speak. Marla does not speak. Not even Suz speaks. Nobody knows what to say to the crying child about the dead mother, except for Gary's father.

"I told you to get the girl a real dog," Gary's father says, but this is not the right thing to say.

"*Dad*," Gary warns at the same time that Juice shouts, "It's real to me!"

Phoebe can see the wedding people blankly stare at Juice the same way her therapist stared at her when she told him Harry was sick—as if he wanted to care, but he just couldn't, because who cares? It's a cat. "And I *know* it's just a cat," Phoebe went on. "But Harry was with us that whole time we were married. Harry was there for us. And now he's just going to slowly die?" And yet she could see that the therapist didn't understand the horror of this.

"How did Human Princess die?" Phoebe asks.

Phoebe is starting to wonder if this is why she is here, to fill the silences between the wedding people that they don't know how to fill, to ask the questions nobody can bring themselves to ask. Phoebe has nothing to lose here. She is not part of this family. She is not part of anything anymore. She is free in a way none of them are, so she kneels down and looks directly at the girl, as if it's her from many years ago.

"Lung cancer," Juice says.

"Since when do virtual dogs get cancer?" Gary's father whispers loud enough to hear.

"Apparently, Dad, it happens."

"Are you sure you didn't drop it in the water, though?" Marla asks.

"No!" Juice says. "She just was in my hand and then she . . . died of cancer."

"My cat died of cancer, too," Phoebe says. What she would have given to have Matt there with her when she found Harry—to have anybody with her yesterday morning helping her figure out what to do. She extends her hand to Juice. "Come on. We'll have a funeral for her on the boat."

Juice nods. Suz and Nat look horrified. Lila just looks out at the water.

Suz takes a deep breath, puts on a smile, claps her hands, and says, "Well, I don't know about you guys, but I'm ready for a Vacation in a Cup."

"Let's get on this boat!" the other man shouts. He leans forward to shake Phoebe's hand. "I'm Jim, Gary's brother-in-law."

"Phoebe," she says.

Jim holds her hand for a moment too long—like maybe he's checking for a ring, and maybe Lila is right. Maybe Jim really is always hitting on everyone. Even Phoebe.

"Very nice to meet you," Jim says.

"You, too," Phoebe says.

Jim lets go and takes a sip out of a bottle called Muscle Milk. Lila smooths out her shirt and adjusts her sunglasses.

"Okay," the bride says, taking the groom's hand. "Let's get on this boat."

They all sit against the sides of the narrow sailboat. The captain tells them not to lean too far back. "The boat will tip," he says.

"Seriously?" Marla asks.

"Just kidding," the captain says. "Though not really. There is, of course, a tipping point."

Marla gives the captain a look, like a captain has no right to joke about tipping while they are trapped in open water, but Lila looks unconcerned. Lila sits perched on the boat like she's sitting in her own living room—upright, poised, with the confidence of a woman who has systematically removed all of her body hair. Nothing bad can happen to a woman like that during her wedding week, not even in the middle of the ocean.

"So how about those Vacations in a Cup?" Lila asks, and Nat immediately opens the cooler.

"It's Vacation in a *Cups*," Marla says.

"Excuse me?" Lila asks.

"The plural is actually Vacation in a *Cups*," Marla repeats.

"That's how people have always said it," the groom says with a smile, and Phoebe can recognize what Gary is doing because it's what Phoebe does. He is trying to de-escalate the situation, trying to tease Marla's comment into sounding funny. But Lila does not laugh.

"How do you know how the drink is pronounced?" Lila asks Marla, as if she is genuinely curious. "It's a drink I made up."

Before Marla can answer, Suz starts telling everyone the story of how Lila created the cocktail in their dorm one night and changed their lives for the better.

"Before that, we were always drinking stolen church wine," Suz says.

"You stole sacramental wine?" Jim asks, looking at Lila like he's both surprised and proud.

"For the record, I was never comfortable with it," Lila says.

"Well, you certainly drank enough of it to get sick," Nat says.

"It was . . . not award-winning wine," Lila says.

Jim pretends to be a parishioner pausing before the Eucharist. "Excuse me, Father, is this a pinot?"

Everyone laughs, including Lila. Gary smiles, takes her hand.

"The last time we drank the sacramental wine, Lila vomited all night," Nat says.

"The whole time she kept asking, Do you think we're going to Hell, you guys?"

"After that, I swore I'd never drink again," Lila says. "Unless the drink tasted like a vacation in a cup.'"

"And voilà, the Vacations in a Cup were born," Nat says.

They spent many months during high school perfecting the recipe. And it's clear that this is where the women want the conversation to stay—on the things they used to do together, the special, funny moments that had once bonded them.

"Right," Marla says. "But if the singular is a Vacation in a Cup, then the plural has to be Vacation in a Cups."

"That just sounds really dumb, though," Suz says.

"Yeah," Nat agrees.

"It's not many vacations in one single cup, is it?" Marla says. "It's a single vacation. Spread out in each individual cup."

A heavy silence falls over the group. They are hardly away from land, and everybody already seems to have had enough of Marla. Lila just sits there, made speechless by her future sister-in-law, twice in one afternoon.

"Let's drop it, Marla," Gary says.

Gary says it with the weary tone of a brother who has been saying, "Let's drop it, Marla," his entire life. He puts his hand on Lila's back and the gesture surprises Phoebe, even though it shouldn't. There is nothing surprising here; they are a classic older man and younger woman combo. Gary is the stage and Lila is the song. Or maybe it's more like, Gary is the house and Lila is the chandelier. Blond and dazzling in the way that suggests she's never bought a loaf of bread at the store. And Gary, so handsome and sturdy, a man who is always bringing bread home from the store.

And yet, when she looks at Gary, she can only see the man in the hot tub, the man who once wanted to die. The man who read romance novels in college. She can feel that invisible wire between them, until Gary pulls Lila onto his lap and holds her close, as if he's protecting her from his overbearing sister.

"For instance, you wouldn't say, Please pass me some Sexes on the Beach," Marla continues. "That just sounds gross."

Nat and Suz look at each other and raise eyebrows, like there is nothing left to do at this point but ostracize the disturbance. Phoebe can tell that this is how they got through high school together, searching for each other's eyes in the classroom, doubling over with laughter about a teacher who was more embarrassing than they were. But Lila doesn't join in. She can't openly mock her future sister-in-law, the future aunt to her children, the person who will be at her Christmas dinner table for all time.

Instead, Lila looks at Phoebe for help.

"Well, what is it?" Lila asks Phoebe. Then she turns to Gary. "Phoebe actually knows everything. She's an English professor."

How funny it feels to be looked at by all the wedding people. All these strangers who can see her. They are waiting on her to speak. To say something that will settle the moment, return them to normalcy, neutralize Marla. Phoebe is moved to be called upon like this. For too long, she had felt stuck in the depths of her house, in the void of her depression, where she was not actually real. Where nothing was real. As if she had slipped out of the known world without anybody noticing, except for Harry, who would follow her around all day, up the stairs, down the stairs, into the bathroom where he would sit with his serious face and watch. When she found him dead two days ago, she felt certain it was all over for her.

But now here she is, in daylight, on a boat, with the wedding people.

"Well?" Gary says. "How do you say it, Professor?"

He looks over at her for the first real time since they got on the boat, probably because the rest of them are also looking at her now. It has become safe to stare, safe to rest his eyes on her. She wants to savor this feeling. Package it, drink it later when she needs it, when she is back at home in the dark of her bedroom tomorrow, feeling like a piece of shit.

"It's Vacations in a Cup," Phoebe says. "You have to pluralize the head noun, not the modifier."

"But no one would ever say Sexes on the Beach," Marla protests.

"Right, but that's because 'sex' isn't really a count noun and so it sounds unnatural to pluralize it."

"A count noun?" Suz asks. "Huh?"

"I just mean we don't say 'We had two sexes,'" Phoebe clarifies. "We say 'We had sex twice.'"

"Speak for yourself," Jim says. "I had two sexes last night."

Everybody laughs, except Marla, who looks half-irritated, half-impressed. "Did you study languages or something?" she asks.

"In college," Phoebe says. "I thought I wanted to be a philologist."

"But you're not currently a philologist," Marla says.

"No. But I also know that language is determined naturally by the people who speak it," Phoebe adds, for Marla's benefit. "That's how we wind up with different languages. People in different regions make it their own. So, in theory, you can pronounce the drink however you want and ten years from now, it'll be correct."

"So it sounds like you're saying there's no right answer?" Gary asks.

"Spoken like a true English professor," Phoebe says.

Everybody laughs.

"Well, now that we know the drink's entire etymology, can we just drink one already?" Nat asks.

Suz pours everyone drinks, and it feels like the party has really begun. But Marla leans back against the boat, turns on her phone, and looks horrified.

"Oh, God," Marla says.

Has she seen the sexts from Robert?

Phoebe waits for Marla to explain, but nobody from the group asks her to. Gary and Jim talk to Gary's father. Juice quietly holds her dead virtual dog and looks out at the water. And Lila, Nat, and Suz seem set on ignoring Marla now. They are deep in giggly conversation about their past, the stolen church wine, the things they used to confess to priests, how attracted Suz used to be to Jesus, that time Nat told Father

Leon she was gay—and it's a place where the rest of them can't go. Especially not Marla.

"Everything okay?" Phoebe finally asks her.

"I just realized my car registration is expired," Marla says.

Phoebe wonders if she's lying, but then Marla pulls out her wallet, starts typing things furiously into her phone. This is too much for Gary to ignore.

"Are you really reregistering your car while we're sailing?" Gary asks.

"It's a literal *crime* to drive an unregistered car," Marla says.

"But you're not driving a car right now. Do it when we get back on shore."

"I'm a lawyer, Gary. I need to stay on the right side of the law. And I'm getting shockingly amazing service here in the middle of the sea."

Gary looks down at his Vacation in a Cup. So does Phoebe. When she peeks, she meets Gary's eyes. Gary raises his eyebrows and then they both smile. A big release that makes Phoebe feel giddy. Phoebe can't help it—Marla is too much. But Phoebe doesn't want to laugh at another woman for being too much, not even Marla. So she takes a big sip and she will admit: the drink is so fucking good. Because it's so fucking terrible. Like Kraft mac & cheese. Like a Dunkin' donut. The kinds of things Phoebe could never properly enjoy before, because she was too worried about her body, about sugar levels, about fructose. Even when she was drunk, she would binge by eating a bowl of flax berry cereal that would always make her shit at eight in the morning, give or take a few minutes.

"What's actually in this drink?" Phoebe asks. She sits back against the side of the boat and the wind picks up her hair. "It's so good."

"A vacation," Gary says.

"Right," Phoebe says. "But what kind of vacation? Like a beachfront condo in St. Thomas?"

Gary takes another sip as if he's a sommelier. "I'm getting more, RV visiting Civil War battlefields in the South for three days."

Phoebe takes another sip. "Really? I don't taste any battlefields."

"No?" Gary says. "You clearly don't have a complex palette. Or a father who once dragged you to all the Civil War battlefields as a child."

She laughs. He laughs. Jim just watches them talk as if the conversation is too weird to join.

"No, he was more of the we-already-live-in-a-tiny-fishing-cabin-on-a-river-so-we-don't-ever-have-to-go-on-vacation kind of a father," Phoebe clarifies.

"Oh, I didn't know about that father," Gary says.

There are some people in this world who remind you of exactly how you like to speak. She hasn't met a person like this in a long time, not since she met her husband, which was why it was so painful when she started to forget how to speak to her husband. When she looked at him, she was too often reminded of what not to say, what never to mention, like ovulation, or depression, or anything that might carry a hint of sadness. Perhaps that's why she didn't tell him that Harry died. She didn't want to give him any more proof of her unlovability, of her failure. Perhaps that's why she just put a blanket over Harry and ran away, too.

"That father is out there," Phoebe says. "Well, not technically anymore. He's dead."

"Oh, I'm sorry," Gary says. "So you're a real orphan now."

She blushes. The conversation.

"And surprise, surprise, being an orphan doesn't feel like I imagined," Phoebe says.

"The perks are even better than you thought?" Gary asks.

"What the hell are you guys talking about?" Jim asks.

They all laugh.

"Phoebe used to dream of being an orphan," Gary explains.

"Gary wants someone to beat the crap out of him," Phoebe adds.

"I'll have you know this explains nothing," Jim says.

Phoebe takes another sip of her drink. "Oh, okay, I think I am tasting the battlefields now."

"See?" Gary says. "It's like just the tiniest note at the very end."

Jim gives up on them and turns to Juice. "So how are you doing, my beautiful niece?"

Marla puts down her phone with a deep sigh.

"You on the right side of the law now?" Gary asks Marla, putting his hand around her neck, giving her a faux massage. It looks like an apology for being short earlier. "Don't want any fugitives on this boat."

"I know you're making fun of me, so I refuse to answer that," Marla says.

Sitting side by side, Phoebe can see that Marla and Gary look very similar. They both have dark brown hair, dark eyes. Long, angular faces they have inherited from their father, whose face is so long, he looks somewhat like a pelican at the bow. But Gary is a little soft where Marla is hard. Phoebe wonders if this is what losing his wife has done to him. If it has rounded out his edges. Or maybe it's just the beers over the years that Marla likely refused, filling out his shoulders and his face.

"You think you'll get to an age where your brother stops making fun of you, but no," Marla says to Phoebe, "it will never happen. I'm forty-two and I am ready to accept this now."

Then she offers a long list of all the things Gary did over the years to ruin her life, and yet, Gary is still the Golden Boy in their father's eyes.

"No," Gary says. "Roy is the Golden Boy."

"Is Roy your brother?" Phoebe asks.

"Cousin," Marla says.

"You talking about Roy?" Gary's father shouts through the wind.

"See?" Gary says. "It's like catnip to him. He can't get enough of Roy."

"Roy's a goddamned hero," Gary's father says to Phoebe. "The only hero we have in the Smith family."

"Every time," Gary and Marla say in unison and then laugh. Laughing changes Marla's entire face. She becomes soft like Gary.

"What did Roy do?" Phoebe asks.

"He was a sniper in Iraq," Gary's father says.

"Then Roy wrote a memoir about it," Gary says.

"And someone turned it into a movie," Marla adds.

"Phenomenal film," Gary's father declares to Phoebe. "Jude Law."

"It wasn't Jude Law," Marla corrects. "Jude Law is like fifty now."

"You're thinking of that movie where Jude Law played a Russian sniper," Gary adds.

"I know who Jude Law is," Gary's father says.

"Okay, fine, whatever. The point is, Dad watches it at least once a year and then immediately calls us to say that Roy is the only true hero in the family," Gary says.

"I mean, I went to law school for you, Dad!" Marla says.

"I thought you went to be a feminist?" Gary's father asks.

She elbows him. "That, too," Marla says. "But honestly, what was the point of going to law school if your dad doesn't respect it?"

"Oh, stop it. You're the goddamned mayor!" Gary's father says. "Of course I'm proud of you."

Marla sips on her drink.

"Anyway, that's Roy," Gary says, and they all laugh.

"Roy got really wasted last night, huh?" Marla says.

"Speaking of," Jim says, and hands Gary a beer, because yes, yes, there are only so many Vacations in a Cup he can have, and then the two men start telling everybody about the actual vacation they went on before the pandemic.

"A cross-country road trip we all took together after," Jim says and then trails off. He takes a sip of beer and then a sip of Muscle Milk.

"We went camping in the Wind River Range out in Wyoming," Gary says.

"Taught this one how to fish, huh?" Jim says, and elbows Juice. "And remember when that bunny got eaten right in front of us?"

Juice nods. "A hawk just picked it up right in front of us."

"It was gruesome," Jim says.

Phoebe can feel Jim trying to impress them all with his stories of adventure and battle and death. She scans his face for evidence of his sister. Was Wendy a brunette, too? Did she have the same big oval eyes? The same aggressive stance, always leaning forward a little too much when she talked? Jim has the energy of someone who should be an investment banker or a car dealer or a wedding singer, someone who is out there in the world, but this is probably because Phoebe is a reader, always expecting people's careers to match their personalities exactly. In real life, Jim is an engineer.

"In my free time," Jim tells Phoebe, "I'm building a seaplane."

"That's impressive you know how to do that," Phoebe says.

"He doesn't actually," Gary says.

"You build it," Jim says. "That's how you learn. And actually, you become certified, too. In the state of Rhode Island, you build a plane and voilà, you're a certified plane mechanic."

"But how do you know it's a *good* plane?" Phoebe asks.

"Oh. You don't," Jim says. "Not until you're up there."

"But then it's too late," Phoebe says.

"That's right," Jim says.

They all laugh, and Lila finally looks over. For a second, Phoebe feels like she's in class and she's gotten in trouble. But for what?

"Jim, are you talking about that plane you haven't even bought parts for yet?" Lila asks, and the group falls silent.

"Well, now I'm fucking not," Jim says, and everyone laughs again.

Marla leans back against the side of the boat, satisfied now that she's on the right side of the law. The boat tips in her direction, and her drink spills all over her shirt.

"Shit," Marla says, and Suz comes over to refresh her cup.

"So you're a professor?" Jim asks Phoebe.

Phoebe can feel Lila and Gary both watching them now, as if a match is being made, like maybe this was Lila and Gary's plan: for Jim to meet someone at this wedding, finally settle down.

"I am," Phoebe says, even though it feels less true as they get deeper out to sea. She feels very far from her old life out here on the ocean with the wedding people. She hasn't checked her email in one full day. Her students are supposed to be reading something for tomorrow's class— Shelley—but Phoebe already knows she will not be reading Shelley tonight. She will not make it back in time for class, and yet she feels no guilt. Only relief. Only the good feeling of the steady wind on her cheek. The sweet drink in her cup. The knowledge that she has finally done something she never thought she could do—she has made it out of the dark bedroom of her life. She is *here*.

"That's cool," Jim says. "Very cool. Wasn't much of an English guy myself."

He finishes the last of his Muscle Milk, and Juice says, "You know that's not really milk."

"I know," Jim says. "It says right here, This Product Contains No Milk."

"Then why do you drink it?"

"Because I don't want it to be milk," Jim says.

"That makes no sense," Juice says.

The captain takes them to Fort Adams, to an old lighthouse, and as they circle around it, Jim asks more questions as if he really wants to get to know Phoebe. What do you teach? What are the students like? Does it feel good up there, knowing everything? She can feel him advancing toward her, like he knows they are destined to fuck, the two unmatched partners on the boat. She can feel everyone watching out of the corner of their eyes, hoping it'll happen, as if they are on a TV show.

It's a relief when Juice finally taps Phoebe's shoulder.

"Can we do it now?" Juice asks, holding up the virtual dog so Phoebe can see.

Phoebe looks at Gary, even though it's clear that Juice is asking Phoebe and nobody else. Phoebe remembers this feeling, too. How going over to her next-door neighbor's house and eating dinner there was somehow easier than sitting in her own kitchen with her family, because Mr. and Mrs. Blank would ask her questions about her book report, about her concert recital, and she could say anything in response because the Blanks didn't matter to Phoebe at all—they were just neighbors and she didn't need their love, yet somehow got it because of this. She could even ask them about her own mother, what she used to be like, what she used to sound like, and when Mr. Blank cleared his throat before he answered, she didn't feel that tense knot in the middle of her chest every time her father did.

"Yes," Phoebe says.

"What do we do?"

Anything would be better than what Phoebe did. She should have buried him. Harry deserved a grave. He had been *Harry*, she would have said over his tiny tombstone, our little psychiatrist who never solved one problem.

"First, it's customary to say something about the deceased," Phoebe says. "Something you love. What did you love about Human Princess?"

Juice says something about Human Princess always being there for her in her pocket, the dog always being such a good dog, something she could hold whenever she was nervous during school presentations or at night. Phoebe can see Gary leaning toward them, trying to hear what his daughter is saying, but her voice is too quiet. The wind too loud.

"And now do other people say something about Human Princess?" Juice asks.

Phoebe thinks it's amazing how easily children ask questions. They don't think there's anything wrong with it. They know that they don't know everything, and it's a little jarring to Phoebe, a woman who spent her entire career pretending that she had been born knowing everything. Bob had suggested it, said it can be precarious for a female scholar to be caught asking too many questions, and so she sat at happy hour with her colleagues, and she nodded her head, and listened to them talk about the Protestant Reformation or the printing press in early America and how their students lacked a basic understanding of history, and when the conversation got too dark, too depressing, too angry (which it always did by the end of happy hour), her husband would say, "But honestly, I think my students teach me so much more than I could ever teach them." Phoebe raised her eyebrows, waited for him to catch himself on the bullshit, because that was just something they said on their teaching statements in order to not sound like assholes, no?

But now she understands what he meant. There are so many things Phoebe doesn't know anymore. Things children know that Phoebe has forgotten, like how to look at a green plastic circle and see a beloved dog.

That's how she got in trouble, Phoebe thinks. When she was alone, she stopped seeing the meaning in things. She stopped writing in her journal, stopped making elaborate meals, stopped combing her hair, let Harry just stay there on the basement floor, because what did it really matter? What did anything matter when she was alone?

But everyone on the boat is so quiet, staring at the green little dog, it starts to feel like a real funeral.

"May I hold her?" Jim asks.

Juice gives him the dog, and Jim talks directly to it.

"You know, Human Princess, I remember when my sister bought you," Jim says. "She was so excited that I remember thinking, Wow, that's real love, you know? When you get that excited by the thought of making someone else happy. So thank you for making my niece happy."

"Dad?" Juice asks. "Your turn."

Gary looks startled. But he comes forward. He takes the dog in his hands. He is quiet for a moment.

"Jim is right. We were very excited to bring you home to Juice," Gary says. "We knew you'd be a great dog and you were. Thank you for keeping my daughter company all these years. Thank you for being here when—"

Then Gary pauses, looks down, as if he's about to cry. Phoebe looks over at Lila, who is unreadable in this moment, with her head down, her hands in her lap like she's at church—though Phoebe already knows Lila well enough to imagine what she'll say later.

Jim pats Gary on the back. Eventually, Gary composes himself. Chokes out the final few words.

"Anyway. We really appreciate that, little fella. Rest in peace."

Gary wraps the dog up in a napkin like it's a soldier. Hands Human Princess to Phoebe, which makes her feel like the girl's mother, who should have some words, too.

"Thank you," Phoebe says to Juice's dog, but also to Harry.

Thank you for keeping us company. Thank you for being the only witness to our marriage. Thank you for always waiting for us in the mornings outside our bedroom door, and especially that night you sat outside the shower, keeping careful watch. Because Harry always knew when something was wrong. And something was very wrong—Phoebe was ten weeks pregnant and she was bleeding. Look at the blood, she kept saying—and Matt brought her to the shower, put his hands between her legs, as if to catch it. Or maybe to just to feel it. To be a part of it. After, Harry followed them silently to the bed, and Matt curled around Phoebe, and Phoebe curled around Harry.

"I really loved you," Phoebe says, because now that the horror of it is over, Phoebe can feel the good part—this love for her little family, the one she had and the one she never will have. It is so strong, it makes her sob momentarily in her hands. Nobody says a thing, except Juice.

"Did you like, know my dog?" Juice asks.

Phoebe laughs. They all laugh. Phoebe wipes her tears and looks up to see Gary returning her gaze, smiling.

"No," Phoebe says. "I didn't know your dog."

Phoebe didn't know the dog. Didn't know her mother. Didn't know her daughter. Didn't even know if it would have been a daughter, but she imagined the girl so many times, how they would read plays aloud in the open field behind their house, because there would be an open field. Phoebe would make sure of it. They would take the girl out to the field, and teach her how to dance, how to skip. They would find frogs. They would go camping. They would tell stories at night and in the morning, too, and Phoebe would show the girl how to write the story down, bind the pages together with yarn, as her father had once showed her. She wanted to give that same feeling to her child. She wanted to teach her child how to create, how to make a lot of applesauce from scratch and harvest strawberries and when the child would fall asleep, Matt would make them strawberry cocktails and they would curl up and watch a terribly wonderful awful movie that they'd seen a million times, like *Terminator* or *Dune* or all the Austen adaptations.

This vision of her family sustained her through her entire marriage, through all five rounds of IVF. When she injected the drugs into her belly fat, she thought of the girl, her little fingers plucking the straw-berries. She pictured these fingers so often, and so vividly, at a certain point, she couldn't imagine them not existing.

But they won't. They never will.

"Now we let her go," Phoebe says.

"Should I just throw her in the water?" Juice asks.

"Maybe lightly toss," Phoebe suggests.

"Goodbye, Human Princess," Juice says, and as she holds the dead dog above the water, Phoebe thinks, Goodbye, Harry. She hears it inside her head like the final lines of Ophelia in *Hamlet*: Goodbye Harry. Goodbye daughter. Goodbye mother. Goodbye father. Goodbye hus-band. Goodbye, goodbye.

But before Juice releases the dog, Marla shouts, "You can't actually drop it in the ocean! That's littering."

"It's not littering, it's my *dog*, Aunt Marla."

"It's plastic," Marla says. "It'll take millions of years to decompose."

"*Decompose*?" Juice cries.

"We do ask that you keep all your belongings inside the boat," the captain says softly.

Juice looks at Phoebe as if she is making a choice about who to be, and Phoebe makes a choice, too.

"Go ahead," Phoebe says, because fuck it. If she is going to live, she's going to live differently this time. "Let's have our funeral."

Juice drops the dog in the ocean. When it's immediately swallowed up by the white foam of the water, Juice actually laughs a little. It's the glee of a child who has done something she shouldn't, and Phoebe feels it, too, which is why she waits to get scolded by someone.

But the captain doesn't scold. He starts doing something to the sails. The others have restarted their conversations. The funeral is over. They skid along the water, while the adults return to being wedding people on a boat. They drink like nothing happened. But something did happen. Phoebe can feel it as Juice leans into her. And Gary must feel it, too, she thinks, because he looks wistful, like he knows he just watched something important happen in his daughter's life but is not sure what to do now.

"Hey, how about some ice cream?" Lila says, coming over to be a part of it all. She hands Juice a little sandwich from the cooler.

But Juice doesn't want it. She holds it up to the light because she's suspicious of even that. "This isn't really ice cream, you know."

"What do you mean, it's not ice cream?" Gary asks.

"These things don't melt. It's not real food."

"Well, you don't have to eat it, I guess," Lila says. "I just thought you might be hungry."

"Well, I'm not."

Gary gives Lila an apologetic look, and Juice puts the ice cream sandwich down on the seat next to her. Juice opens her phone and calms herself by reading the Wikipedia page for the Cornwall Inn. Lila returns to her friends on the other side of the boat, and Gary follows his bride. Phoebe can feel Juice's whole body relax against her as she reads aloud.

"So the hotel was built in 1844," Juice says to Phoebe. "By a man named Albert Schuyler. He built it for his mistress."

Gary slides his arm around Lila, and the two of them kiss.

"Hey ho!" Jim shouts, and everybody cheers.

Phoebe is ready to believe in them as a couple. She waits to hear what it sounds like when Gary and Lila talk directly to each other. She wants to understand what makes them laugh. How they flirt. She is ready to accept things as they are. But after they kiss, they are entirely public-facing, embracing their guests, telling stories to them, and not each other. And every so often, Gary looks back at Juice and Phoebe like he wants to say something. Eventually, he does.

"Juice, please throw the sandwich away if you aren't going to eat it," Gary says. "It's melting on this man's boat."

"It's not actually melting, though!" Juice says. "See?"

Juice is sort of right. It doesn't really melt. It still keeps its shape, which Phoebe admits is disturbing. But her father is not impressed. The father can only see litter. "Throw it out," he says.

"Fine!" Juice yells.

Juice throws the sandwich overboard, and Marla says, "See? I knew this would happen. Littering is a slippery slope," and Gary says, "Drop it, Marla," and then looks at Juice like he's about to punish her but doesn't. He returns to his bride, and Juice looks out at the water like she's contemplating something damning about her father, or Lila, or her life in general, but Phoebe knows she's just trying to keep herself from crying. Phoebe knows this move. She watches Juice pick up her phone again.

"Do you think he really loved his mistress?" Juice asks.

"Excuse me?" Phoebe asks.

"Albert Schuyler."

"I suppose he must have," Phoebe says. "You don't make buildings for people who are just sort of okay."

But it's a different kind of love, Phoebe knows. The wife is the reason the man becomes the architect. The mistress is the reason the architect keeps building. The blueprints of his dreams that he may never realize, so he keeps it in his drawer.

"Good point," Juice says. "Though to be honest, I could never love anyone named Albert."

"Alberts are people, too," Phoebe says.

Juice cracks up. She repeats the line to herself, "Alberts are people, too."

Juice continues reading to Phoebe about the hotel in hushed tones, like she's telling a secret story after bedtime, and Phoebe is surprised to find herself genuinely interested, though she doesn't know why she's surprised, since this is exactly the kind of thing that she likes to think about.

By the time they are almost back to the wharf, everybody seems drunk and happy again. Gary and Lila are laughing at something Nat is saying. Marla and Jim are deep in conversation with Marla's father about Roy. And Juice is really leaning on Phoebe now like she's a bookend. As the people prepare to get off the boat, Phoebe closes her eyes. She doesn't want to move. Like when Harry was on her lap and he was so cute, Phoebe wouldn't even take a sip of coffee. Phoebe doesn't want to ruin the moment.

But then they are docked, and Phoebe looks up at the wharf, at all the people and the houses and the new life that waits behind it.

"That was so fun," Lila announces as she stands up.

"So fun," Suz agrees.

Nat holds up her camera. "Kiss!"

And so they kiss.

Back at the hotel, Pauline stands behind the front desk in a navy linen dress. She has the expression of a woman who has been fielding requests that are impossible to field all day long, yet when she sees the wedding people, she gives a cheerful, "Hello! Welcome back! How was your sail?"

"Phenomenal," Lila says. "Oh, that reminds me. I need to talk to you about my mattress."

Lila turns to Pauline, and the group scatters. Nat and Suz are off to get their nails done. Marla and Juice require naps. Jim heads to the bar with Gary's father to meet Uncle Jim. And Gary and Phoebe wait for the elevator in silence, listening to Lila explain to Pauline that the mattress is not soft enough.

"Not as soft as I was hoping," Lila says.

Phoebe wonders if this is how Lila operates. Lila is upset about the funeral on the boat, but she can't say anything about that, so she complains about the mattress to Pauline, because that's where Pauline stands most of the day, waiting for complaints. Pauline is ready to fix any problem, which is why Phoebe is not surprised to see that Pauline has already restored the books on the shelf to their original positions, pages facing out.

"Is there anything you can do?" Lila asks.

"I'm just not sure there is anything we can do about the actual mattress," Pauline says. "I mean, they're brand-new mattresses."

"Unfortunately, those brand-new mattresses are not very comfortable," Lila says.

Gary looks down at his feet like he's embarrassed, but then again, what does Phoebe know about Gary really? Gary could like this about Lila. Many men do—it took her a long time to realize that. Some men like the fuss. Some men like being told what to do, because then they never have to make any decisions, never have to think. It was probably very helpful when Lila told him where to hang the nude painting, probably for the same reasons that Phoebe always liked watching Matt roll up his belt into a neat and tidy ball. She liked watching his hand sweep the gutter clean. It's arousing to see someone passionately take care of all the problems. Especially for someone like Phoebe, the perpetual passenger of the relationship, according to her therapist—the one who always asked, "Where do you want to go to dinner?" hoping the other person knew where they wanted to go.

But then Gary reaches out and makes a decision. He turns a book around just like she had.

Great Expectations.

Gary holds up his fist. "Free the books," he says, and Phoebe laughs. She is surprised. Maybe she doesn't know Gary at all. Maybe Gary makes decisions like that all the time. And why is she always trying to reduce people, squeeze them into these knowable, tiny boxes where there is room for only one or two personality traits? Gary is the stage and Lila is the song, she thinks. But then she thinks: Nobody is ever like anything all of the time. Because one day, Phoebe woke up and decided to kill herself, and that is not what the perpetual passenger of life does. The perpetual passenger of life just continues sitting in bed.

"Free the books," Phoebe says.

Phoebe turns a book around, too. They continue on like that, freeing the books, while Pauline tries to appease Lila.

"The mattresses may take some time to, you know, break in," Pauline says.

"Don't mattresses famously get worse over time?"

"Well, I just don't know what we can do about the mattresses, to be honest. They are, unfortunately, already here."

"What about a topper?" Lila asks.

"A topper?" Pauline says. "Yes. That's what we'll do. We'll get you a topper."

Pauline says the word *topper* as if it's foreign, and Phoebe imagines she is writing down on a little pad, *What's a topper?* Either way, Pauline sounds relieved.

By the time Lila returns, Gary and Phoebe have freed two shelves of books.

"What are you doing to the décor?" Lila asks. She looks at them like she's stumbled upon a bank robbery.

"They're books, not décor," Phoebe says.

Phoebe doesn't have too many beliefs, but this is one of them.

"Are you going to tell me that books have souls now or something?" Lila asks.

The elevator doors open.

"I am going to tell you that they are books," Phoebe says. "They're meant to be read. That's what books are."

"Okay, Siddhartha," Lila says, then pauses, as if she caught herself being too much like the Lila that she is around Phoebe. "Pauline says she'll get me a topper. Do you want one, too?"

"No," Gary says. "I need a firm mattress."

"Right," Lila says. "Your back. How is it?"

"It's, you know, still my back," he says, and chuckles softly to himself. Then they ride in silence until Lila says, "Why is this elevator so slow?"

"It's from 1922," Phoebe says, reading the plaque.

"But why wouldn't they have renovated it when they redid the hotel?"

"Beats me," Gary says, and then they are at the top.

"Well, that was fun," Lila says. "A fun day."

"Absolutely," Gary says. "Very fun. A great idea."

But Phoebe hates the word *fun*. Phoebe thinks that if people could just stop using the word *fun*, stop expecting everything to be fun, everything could be fun again. She was exhausted by her husband's insistence that everything should be fun. He never used to speak like that, when things were actually fun, but at the very end, when nothing was fun, he would say, "Let's go for drinks, it'll be fun." "Let's go hiking, it'll be fun." And wasn't that why she suggested they go to the Cornwall in the first place? "Let's do something fun for spring break," he had said.

"So Vivian, my maid of honor, will be flying in from Chicago tonight," Lila says. "She's my best friend from college. She's amazing. I know you're both going to love her."

"I'm sure we will," Gary says.

Then Lila lists off other good things that will happen today: "The reception will start at seven on the patio. Nat will be playing the harp with an award-winning cellist who served in Iraq and learned to play cello as part of his PTSD treatment, and maybe it would be good to tell Roy that."

"I'll let him know," Gary says.

The doors open.

"Oh, good," the mother of the bride says, kissing Gary and Lila on the cheek. "You're back."

She looks like the kind of woman Phoebe might see at a very high-end flea market. Flowy linen that matches the color of her hair. She gives Phoebe a kiss on the cheek.

"My sweater looks good on you," the mother says, and pulls away to get a look at her.

Phoebe forgot she wasn't wearing her own clothes, though how she could forget about sequins on her shoulders and a sunflower wedged between her toes, she's not sure.

"Mom," Lila says. "This is Phoebe."

"So you're the woman from Missouri who didn't bring a sweater to the ocean."

Phoebe smiles and shrugs. "First-timer."

"I didn't realize there were people still like that! Well, you certainly need this sweater more than I do."

Up close, the mother of the bride has a strong jaw, like it's been strengthened over the years from staring blankly at the ocean. She smells faintly of booze, though what kind Phoebe cannot tell.

"Do be kind to it," the mother says. "It was the last gift your father ever bought me, you know."

"Oh," Phoebe says, horrified. "You know what? I'll take it off."

"Don't be silly," the mother says, waving her hand. She gives Phoebe a look that suggests she is not, at this point in her life, ever getting anything back. "Enjoy it. It's yours."

"Mom," Lila says, looking at her mother's door. "Why are there a bunch of statues lined up outside your door?"

"Oh, Carlson is going to remove them," she says. "This hotel is very lovely, but the art in the room is just *terrible*. So morbid."

She picks up one of the statues. "Who would put a sculpture of this dead bird in an old woman's room?"

They all study the bird sculpture. Lila looks disturbed by it but says, "I don't think that bird is dead."

"Is it sleeping?" Phoebe asks.

"I bet it's just sleeping," Gary says.

"Since when do birds sleep with their necks all crooked like that?" the mother asks. She points to the other birds against the wall. "Look at them all. They look like they've been assassinated."

"Well, yeah, when you line them up against the wall like that, it's creepy," Lila says.

Phoebe takes a closer look. "Ravens actually sleep like that."

"Of course you know things about the sleeping habits of ravens," Lila says.

"They tuck their heads into their chests," Phoebe adds.

"Well, that doesn't seem very comfortable for them," the mother says.

"And why is everybody messing with the hotel's décor?" Lila asks. "The Cornwall hired award-winning designers to plan out every detail of this place. You can't just move things around."

"Carlson said I can do what I like," the mother says.

Lila looks at Gary and Phoebe. "Go on without me."

Lila starts to bring the bird sculptures back inside her mother's room as Gary and Phoebe walk down the hall. They don't say a word until they turn the corner.

"How *do* you know things about the sleeping habits of ravens?" Gary asks.

"At some point, every lit professor has to spend a full day researching ravens," Phoebe says. "They're everywhere. Writers can't resist a raven. You know, symbols of death and grief and the underworld and all that jazz."

"Oh, yeah, love that jazz," Gary says. "Poe, right? That was the raven poem?"

"Nevermore, nevermore."

"God, I haven't read that since high school," he says. "I remember liking it, but now I don't remember why."

"It's very emo," she says. "Most of my students tend to respond to it for that reason. Brokenhearted man never gets over dead wife."

She says it without thinking, but he doesn't seem rocked by her words.

"I'm just impressed they care about the middle-aged longings of a grieving widower, to be honest," Gary says.

"My students tend to love characters who sentence themselves to never-ending grief," Phoebe says. "It seems noble to young people, I think."

"Little do they know the truly heroic thing is somehow . . . taking a shower and getting yourself to the grocery store."

They laugh.

"I just want to say thanks for helping Juice with her dog," Gary says, still sounding caught up in some emotion from earlier that day. "I know it probably seemed weird, making such a fuss over a little toy, but she got the dog from her mother just before she died."

"Oh, trust me, I get it," Phoebe says. "I could tell it wasn't just any dog."

He said that even as Juice got too old for it, she checked on Human Princess every day. She still announced her major achievements at breakfast, like, "The Human Princess is eating," or "The Human Princess has not been tucked in," and he and his wife would laugh so hard they'd cry.

"I told her I'd get her a new one after the wedding," Gary says. "But that's crazy, right? I mean, even as I said it, I didn't believe myself. We probably won't get her a new one. I mean, she's going to be twelve soon. And my dad's probably right, it's probably best we get her a real dog, no?"

"Probably," she says. "But then again, real dogs require real work. You can't just drop them in the ocean when they die."

She and Matt debated for years about how much work a dog would be and would it be worth it. Sometimes, she thought just getting a dog would have been easier than endlessly debating about whether to get a dog.

"But maybe it's a good thing you can't just drop them in the ocean?" he asks.

They both seem to feel confused for a moment, thinking about

Human Princess falling to the floor of the ocean, not being fed, not being tucked into its virtual bed, when Gary's Uncle Jim and Aunt Gina come out of their room.

"Gary, the man of the hour," Uncle Jim says, and pats Gary on the back.

"How are you two doing?" Gary asks, in what sounds like his doctor voice. He turns it on very quickly—smooth, controlled, friendly without being overbearing.

"Oh, just terrible," Aunt Gina says. "Your uncle slipped on the floor yesterday and hurt his ankle, then played a terrible round this morning."

"Just terrible," Uncle Jim says.

Some days Uncle Jim does great. Some days Uncle Jim stinks.

"Lost my swing," he says.

"You'll get it back," Aunt Gina says. "You always do."

"I'm not *worried*, Gina," Uncle Jim says. "I know I'll get it back. Jesus."

Then Uncle Jim leans in and says, "Hey, son, we have a question for you. It's about your Aunt Gina's bowels."

"It's terrible," Aunt Gina says. "I haven't gone since Friday. Travel always does this to me."

"You just came from Cranston," Gary says. "It's only thirty minutes away."

"Just the *idea* of traveling gets me," Aunt Gina says.

"I can come by later," Gary says, and pats his uncle on the back. "But you know I can't give you actual medical advice, right? I'm not your doctor."

"Oh, stop it," Uncle Jim says. "You're our nephew. Of course you can. What's the point of my nephew being a shit doctor if we can't get some free medical advice?"

When they walk away, it takes only one look from Gary to make Phoebe burst into laughter. Everything is light between them again, like earlier on the boat. Like last night in the hot tub.

"You must get that a lot, don't you?" Phoebe asks.

"Let's just say that I know the shape and size and color of the shits of about fifty percent of the inhabitants in any given room," Gary says.

They laugh. She knows she should head into her room now. She knows they have been talking for too long. But she is not quite ready to leave yet. She doesn't want to go back to being entirely alone in her room again.

"Hey, I'm sorry I was so forward in the hot tub last night," Phoebe says. "Had I known."

"Please don't apologize," he says. "I should have told you I was the groom."

"Yeah, why didn't you tell me you were the groom?"

"I don't normally go around introducing myself as a groom."

"You might need to start. You made me think you were . . ."

"What?"

"A regular person in a hot tub."

"You made me think you were a regular person, too. But apparently you're Lila's friend from the art gallery?"

"I'm not," Phoebe says. "I mean, I guess I became her friend, like literally last night. Or maybe this morning. I'm not sure. But we didn't meet at an art gallery."

"Why would Lila say you met at the gallery then?" Gary looks concerned, as if Phoebe is going to say something that might reveal the true character of his future wife. And Phoebe doesn't know why Lila lied to them all but suspected it had something to do with how Marla's face lit up when she mentioned the gallery. Or how embarrassing it would be to explain to everyone how Phoebe and Lila really met.

"Better to lie than tell everyone on the boat that I'm the crazy suicidal woman she met in the elevator yesterday," Phoebe says.

"You're not crazy," Gary says. "Please don't say that. That's truly all I ask."

She nods. She won't. "But I could have been—"

"No, you were great," he says. "You were so . . ."

Gary thinks for a moment, not like he is hesitating, but like he is trying to find the most accurate word.

"So what?" she asks.

She is surprised that she genuinely wants to know. She has always been so afraid to know things about herself—so afraid of reading the truth in course evaluations, or seeing her large nose in a photograph, or listening to her therapist draw unbearably accurate conclusions about her. "Have you always been this critical of yourself?" he asked her. And yes. Yes. She has. "I'm literally a critic," she reminded her therapist, and he laughed. And where did she learn this? How did she become so good at identifying flaws? At seeing only the fungus on the trees?

"Alive," Gary says. "You struck me as a person who was fully alive. It was inspiring, actually."

Maybe it should be embarrassing to talk like this, to be so sincere in the middle of a hotel hallway at five in the evening, but Gary doesn't seem embarrassed about it. Maybe one becomes comfortable with sincerity when they listen to people talk about their own shit with the utmost seriousness. He spends his days in a small room where people can only ever live or die. He is the one trusted with telling people the absolute truth about their assholes. Not to mention, their fates. Whereas Phoebe was trained in the depressive school of her father, and then the snark of graduate school, taught to poke holes in everyone's arguments, to see the fatal flaws in papers, and it had been exciting for a short period of time. "For Matthews to claim that *Jane Eyre* is or is not a feminist text is to misunderstand what feminism is," Phoebe wrote in her one published paper. She had been proud when it came out, but then for months after, she had a sour taste in her mouth, like she had put something rotten out into the world, and every time she worked on her book, she felt like she was just waiting for a critic to point out the ways it was spoiled. Who cares how many times Jane Eyre goes walking? How can Stone claim the natural world is both a domestic space and a public space at the same time? And how does the freedom Eyre experiences on those walks with Rochester not contradict Stone's earlier claim that Jane is "trapped in the 'unnatural' world of a man's making"? That's usually when Phoebe stopped working on her book and picked up her cigarette.

Phoebe prefers this new way of talking. And maybe this is just one of the really nice things about getting older. Maybe this is the part of her life when she gets to start saying what she means, for better or worse. Because no amount of truth can be worse than the feeling she got after years of hiding from it.

"Thank you for saying that," Phoebe says.

"Will we see you at the . . . reception then?" Gary says, so awkwardly that it feels like it's the end of a date. And how easy it would all be if it were the end of a date. How nice it would feel to lean forward and kiss him.

But it's not a date. Lila is coming down the hall. Lila belongs to Gary and Gary belongs to Lila, and Phoebe belongs to no one.

"No," Phoebe says. "Like I said, I'm really not a part of the wedding."

"Take care then," Gary says. He gives her a long hard look, like he knows this will be the last time they ever see each other.

"Bye," she says.

IN THE ROOM, Phoebe feels disappointed to return to the facts of her own life, to the night she will spend in the Roaring Twenties all alone. Not to mention, the life she will spend alone. And why does she do this? Why does she have a nice day with people, feel connected to them, and then, when alone, think only about the possible horrors of her isolation ahead?

"You catastrophize," her therapist said to her once. "Depressive realism."

She knows that. Yet her thoughts still have power over her anyway. They make her feel pinned to the checkered rug, to her solitary existence.

She thinks she should probably call a new therapist. But she still has this feeling that she is outside of time. She is supposed to be dead, and she's not—it helps every time she remembers she's living in some kind of bonus afterlife where she has a view of the ocean and a man named Carlson who shows up at sunset to "turn down" the room.

"Turn down?" Phoebe asks.

"Get you ready for the night," Carlson says.

"That's a service you provide here?"

Phoebe imagines Carlson pulling down her sheets, tucking her in like her father once had. Telling Phoebe sweet things about the universe like her husband used to. Petting her head as she drifts off into a sleep with no dreams.

"Yes," Carlson says. "We are so sorry to have suspended it for the reception last night."

Phoebe watches Carlson turn down the room. Lower the shades. Turn on the lights, fluff the coconut pillow. Pull the bedsheet down.

It is nice, this ritual. She likes that there is a specific phrase for it, this turning down of the room, this recognition that night is something we must prepare for. Because the night is hard.

Usually the worst time of day for Phoebe, when the depression surfaces like a cyst. Her therapist suggested that maybe it was body-related, maybe she just had a sugar deficiency, and maybe she would be happier if she ate six snacks a day. But she started to eat six snacks a day and the sun would begin to set and she would look at her husband's shoes still by the door and she sobbed so loudly in the empty kitchen that it scared her. She would crawl into bed and think of all the different women she could have become. All the different ways better women end their days. How did Mia end her day?

She didn't know why the end of each day always felt like such a test, but it did. It felt like a rehearsal for the end of life, which did not bode well for her, because Phoebe often did it with a drink in her hand, watching endless episodes of some period drama. Phoebe turned on all the lights at home and then her TV and lowered the woofer because the sounds of the British rifles were too realistic.

"Anything else you need?" Carlson asks.

It is nice the way everyone here keeps asking this, even if it's just their job. Each time feels like another chance to practice asking for what she needs, something that used to be so difficult for Phoebe. I need to go on that vacation in March, she should have said. I need you to tell me that you love me more often right now, she should have said. But it had felt humiliating. Because her husband needed nothing—he was always so busy, so totally fine, always walking out the door with a million papers in his hand.

But Carlson waits, gives Phoebe time to think, looks at her as if he really wants to help, and maybe he does.

"I need a phone charger," Phoebe says.

"Sure thing," he says. "Anything else?"

"And a drain stopper for the tub."

"Absolutely," Carlson says. "I'll be right back."

"You're not going to CVS, right?" she asks.

He laughs. "No. Just downstairs."

She likes his Southern drawl and wonders if, like Pauline, he sounds nicer than he is. Though she suspects this is true of most people, especially herself. Because Phoebe was not nice. No—Phoebe was just trying very hard to be liked, even by Mia and her husband, even after the affair. She behaved like she was a very nice woman in an Ibsen play, waiting for the audience to clap or turn on her at any moment. To declare her a terrible woman or a great woman. But in her fantasies, she didn't think nice things. She always wished bad things for them both.

"Here you go," Carlson says when he returns, and presents the drain stopper and the phone charger on the brass platter. This time, she actually laughs.

"These brass platters are funny," Phoebe says.

"We have to do it," he says, and smiles.

"Where are you from?"

"Georgia, but I'm coming up from South Carolina," he says. He works at their resort down there. He's just here to offer some help as they get settled again after Covid. "We're short-staffed."

"Well, thank you for your service," she says, and it's so overly formal, it makes him laugh.

He does a grand bow. "You're welcome, my dear. Now you enjoy your evening."

How does one enjoy an evening?

She charges her phone. She puts on the fluffy robe. She fills the Victorian tub. She lets out her hair. Combs it with the softest brush she has ever felt as the sky turns pink.

She steps in the warm water one foot at a time. She opens *Mrs. Dalloway*. She makes it to Septimus's suicide and then she reads on until the water gets cold. She turns on the hot water again and begins to wash. She picks up the shower head, and washing is less romantic than it appears it would be in a tub with vintage brass hardware. She goes to wet her hair and sprays water all over the floor by accident.

"Shit," she says.

Eventually she gives up trying to bathe beautifully in this tub. She gives up trying to feel like she's in a painting. She doesn't have to be beautiful in this moment. She doesn't have to be anything, ever. Her husband is not watching. Her father is not watching. Nobody was ever really watching, except Phoebe. Phoebe was the only person waiting in the dark to condemn herself for every single thing when the day was over.

"Can you take a different approach?" her therapist asked her. "Can you sometimes just try to love what you hate about yourself?"

She didn't understand this question at the time. She didn't understand how she could love herself. She didn't understand what people even meant when they said they loved themselves. She honestly didn't believe them. How could you love yourself? How could you love yourself when you know every single horrible thing you've ever thought? When you end most nights fantasizing about your husband fucking his mistress against the wall? And sometimes, Phoebe is in the fantasy, too. Phoebe is there to watch, to tell her husband he must do it harder and harder and harder.

"It's sick," Phoebe told her therapist.

"Why does it have to be sick?" he asks. "Why can't it just be you, wanting to be a part of it?"

"Okay, so it's sick *and* pathetic," Phoebe said.

"It's not pathetic to want things, Phoebe," he said. "It's good."

"It's not good to want that."

But now she can understand what he was trying to tell her. It *is* good to want things, even the humiliating things. Even the things you aren't supposed to want, like Gary, the groom. Because every time she thinks of sitting in that hot tub with Gary, she feels so lucky to be alive. She can't believe she almost missed the chance to meet him. She can't believe she almost threw her body away. This beautiful body, she thinks, and runs her fingers over the soft fuzz of hair that has grown on her legs. The scar on her knee. Her breasts, sticking out of the water like two smooth and ancient rocks in the ocean. And it turns her on a little, just looking at her breasts, so she starts to touch herself. She always thought it was a myth, all these water orgasms women were having in movies, but she can feel herself get close, feel her whole body begin to shake, when the door opens.

"Phoebe!" Lila shouts as she walks in.

"Jesus," Phoebe says, sitting up so fast, water spills over the edges. She is flushed from the hot water, the heat of being caught. But Lila only notices the soaked phone on the ground.

"You can put that in dry rice and it'll be fine," Lila says. "I'm sure Pauline can get you some from the kitchen. Want me to call?"

"No," Phoebe says.

Phoebe is not worried about the phone. Phoebe is more worried about how Lila got in here. But Lila just starts talking.

"God, I don't know *how* Gary is related to Marla," Lila says. "Could you believe Marla today? Honestly, the Vacation in a Cup thing. I don't even know why I bother being so nice to her. And Juice, too. It's like they hate me! They probably do hate me. And fine, I get it. I'm really fucking rich. I know it's annoying. But I'm not rude to people. I'm not a bitch like Marla! And I know I'm not supposed to call another woman that, but what am I supposed to do if she's just a bitch?"

Phoebe stares in disbelief as Lila sits down on the tiny black bathroom chair, which suddenly looks like it was put there just so Lila could sit on it and call people bitches.

"She was even worse at the cocktail party tonight," Lila says. "I coughed, because I got some vodka down the wrong pipe, and Marla looked at me and was like, I'm sorry, but you just can't cough like that in public anymore. And I said nothing, of course. Because she's going to be my sister-in-law. I am going to have to spend the rest of the week with her. I mean, the rest of my life, technically. Though we don't have to spend *every* holiday together. Like, we get Halloween to ourselves, right?"

THE WEDDING PEOPLE   *163*

The tub is cold again. Phoebe turns on the hot water, but it's too hot and burns Phoebe's fingers. This is how it happens. She just lets people around her do what they want. She doesn't call them on their shit. She pretends like she has no needs, like it's just fine to walk into her room when she was in the middle of trying to have an orgasm.

"How did you get in here?" Phoebe asks.

"I have a key," Lila says.

"You have a key?"

"Yeah, I got a key when I booked the room for the week," Lila says.

"Okay," Phoebe says. "But that doesn't mean you can just walk in on me while I'm in the middle of taking a bath."

"Oh, I don't mind you being naked," Lila says, staring directly at Phoebe's breasts. "I lived in a dorm room all my life. Seeing a naked woman is basically like seeing wallpaper."

"That wasn't my point, either," Phoebe says.

"Then what's the point?"

"The point is, I was about to have an orgasm!"

"In the water? That actually works?"

"Now we'll never know, will we?"

"And my life is not perfect. Have you even been listening to a word I've been saying?"

"I have, yes," Phoebe says. "You have a sister-in-law who doesn't want to get Covid. A mother who is not dead and in attendance at your wedding. Not to mention a fiancé who is really wonderful."

"Oh my God, not you, too," Lila says. "You sound like Nat and Suz."

"Nat and Suz are right," Phoebe says. "He's wonderful."

"What do you think is so wonderful about him?"

"Don't you already know what's wonderful about him?"

"Of course I know. But it's more interesting to hear what you think is wonderful."

Lila waits.

"Please?"

"He's sincere," Phoebe says, because if Lila wants honesty, she will get honesty. "He seems to accept that people are, well, human."

"Okay," Lila says, clearly unsatisfied. "But what else?"

"He's smart. But he's curious, too. A lifelong learner type."

"A lifelong learner?"

"He's engaged with the world. Like he's on a mission to know it better. And he's funny, but not in-your-face funny. Just in that dry kind of way that's hard to notice at first, because he looks more friendly than funny, but once you do, you can't stop seeing it."

"But do you think he's attractive?" Lila asks.

"You want to know if I think your fiancé is attractive?"

"I'm curious what you see."

"Yes, I think he's attractive," Phoebe says, and it feels good to admit it out loud. Especially to Lila. "Very attractive, actually."

This seems to please Lila, but then she looks momentarily doubtful. "Even with the beard?"

"The beard is maybe the best part."

"But it's *gray*."

"A sexy kind of gray."

"Gray is not sexy."

"It's like just a touch of gray," Phoebe says. "Just enough to make him seem wizened."

"That sounds way too close to wizard."

"They're actually not etymologically related."

"Sometimes he does look like a wizard, though."

"He does not look like a wizard," Phoebe says. "He looks like a man with a beard."

"Every man with a beard looks a little like a wizard."

"Trust me, Gary seriously has the most ideal hair situation for a man his age."

"That's what I *used* to think," Lila says. "But then he grew his beard and it came out all gray. I think if he just shaves the beard, it might be better."

"I'm not sure it's ever that simple."

"That sounds cryptic."

"Not cryptic."

"Yes cryptic. Are you mad at me or something?"

"No, I'm not mad at you," Phoebe says, but then remembers she is trying to be honest. "I'm annoyed."

"With *me*? Why?"

"Because I was trying to take a bath!" Phoebe says. "And you just waltz in without even knocking, then sit down and bitch about your sister-in-law and your fiancé's sexy gray beard and your million-dollar wedding to a naked and suicidal and divorced woman in a tub, and you think that's really how I want to spend my bath? You think that's fair to do to me?"

Lila looks hurt or confused or both. But Phoebe doesn't care.

"And you do, I think!" Phoebe says. "You really think you can just walk around, spewing your inner monologue onto everything, but you can't. You have to respect people. You have to knock on their doors before walking into their bedroom. Nobody cares that you're the fucking bride. It doesn't give you a license to just watch people bathe. You're not God. You're just another fucking woman, put here on earth like the rest of us."

"But I did knock on your door," Lila says. "You didn't answer."

"If a person doesn't answer, that means you don't come in."

"Well, excuse me, but I was worried you might be dead!"

"Oh," Phoebe says.

It honestly didn't occur to Phoebe that Lila might still be worried about her, since Lila never seems particularly worried about anything but her wedding. Yet Phoebe is softened by the thought. Lila was worried she might be dead. Of course. That's what happens when you tell people you're suicidal. They worry about you. They worry about you so much, it makes them angry, too.

"You really want to talk about fair?" Lila asks. "You think it's okay to tell someone that you want to die, then kick them out of the room, and then act like it's not going to affect them in any way whatsoever? I'm not a monster, Phoebe. I would care if a woman died at my wedding. I have feelings. But everybody thinks that just because I'm like really fucking blond or something, I don't have feelings, but you know what? My hair is not even blond!"

"It's not?" Phoebe asks. "It's impressively natural seeming."

"Well, it's brown, just like my father's! And my grandfather's! We're Italian!"

"You are?"

"Like, a quarter! My dad's dad was Italian," she says. "My name is actually Lila Rossi-Winthrop, a hyphen that my parents fought over their entire lives. My father was so proud to be Italian, never really forgave my mother for not taking his name, even though he's a total hypocrite. Because when I grew out my dark hair in college, do you know what my father said? He said, I liked you better as a blonde. And so now I am here, with super blond hair, because not even my own father likes my real hair. Which is really just his hair. The man gave it to me, then acts like it's my fault for growing it!"

Lila stands up.

"Everybody in my life is always telling me I can be anyone I want, but then whenever I do one thing they don't like, they act like I've ruined myself," Lila says. "And so I come up here, because you're the only person at this wedding who doesn't seem to give a shit what I do."

None of what Lila says is a surprise to Phoebe, yet it's a surprise to hear Lila say it. Phoebe looks at Lila, a bride still in her white silk reception dress. It has cherries on the trim. It makes her look a few years younger than she is. It must have taken her hours to get ready for the reception, carefully considering each decision, and yet, she is not even at the reception. It makes Phoebe feel suddenly tender toward Lila, like Lila is the old Phoebe now. Lila is the one hiding in the library or in the dark of her room because she feels most comfortable there.

"That's really why you're here?" Phoebe asks.

"Yes," she says. "And also because my maid of honor, Vivian, just called to say she's not coming. I was upset."

They laugh.

"Shit," Phoebe says.

"Her son has Covid."

"Double shit."

"But does she need to really *be* there if he has Covid? Like, can't Max take care of the kid for once?" Lila wonders. "Max is seriously the worst, by the way. I mean, he's the best in the worst kind of way."

"You lost me."

"He researches endangered jaguars or something. They like, fell in love on some research trip trying to save the last living jaguar in South America. But now that they have a kid, she is always at home, while he's traveling the world counting up all the jaguars, I guess. Needless to say it's very . . . annoying. For Viv, I mean. Viv is always stuck taking care of the kid."

"Maybe she's not stuck. Maybe she likes it."

"Nobody likes *that*."

"Some people like it."

"I try to like it," Lila confesses. "But most nights, Gary doesn't make it home in time from work and it's always just me and Mel at dinner. Sometimes, it's okay. Sometimes we just watch a movie or something. But sometimes, when I make her sit at the table, it's excruciating."

And she doesn't know if this is Juice's fault or her own.

"She hardly ever speaks to me," Lila says. "And I never know what to say to her. I ask her about school, about her friends, about why she wants to be called *Juice* now. But she's just like, It's none of your business, which means that it has something to do with her mom, but she won't say it. She's just like, Because my name is *Juice* now, and so I'm supposed to just start calling her Juice?"

She sighs.

"I don't know. Maybe I'm just not very good at being around children. My mother was right. I didn't even know how to be a child when I was a child. And sometimes I wonder if the people who say they love being around children are lying. It's like people who claim to like raisins. They just want to be people who like raisins."

"I like raisins."

"Well, of course you like raisins."

"My hands are like raisins," Phoebe says, holding up her pruned fingertips.

"You should probably get out of the tub," Lila says.

"But I haven't even washed my hair yet. To be honest, it's actually really hard to bathe in this thing. I've decided it's one of those things that looks more romantic than it is."

"Like chocolate," Lila says.

"And cross-country skiing in the forest."

"And paddleboats. I loathe paddleboats."

The thing she is starting to love about Lila is this: She begins to shampoo Phoebe's hair without a word and continues her angry chatter in such fixed tones, it becomes soothing to Phoebe.

"Do you think it's weird that you're the only one I can tell all this stuff to?" Lila asks.

"I wouldn't say weird," Phoebe says. "But maybe it's a little sad."

"It is sad," Lila admits. "It's really sad. And how did that happen? How did I end up becoming a person who has nobody?"

"You have Gary."

"But I can't be honest with Gary," she says. "I can't tell him that I'm not sure I really like his daughter. That I pretty much hate his sister. That I'm sick and tired of hearing about his dead wife."

"What about Nat and Suz? You could tell them."

"Not really."

Lila admits she does not do the best job of keeping in touch with her friends when they are no longer right in front of her face. She has no idea what's going on in their lives, really. She knows that Viv is somewhat responsible for repopulating the Atlanta Zoo with the giant panda. She knows that Nat is married to the third violin in the Detroit Symphony. And she knows that Suz has a baby, and she thinks it's weird how she calls the baby a little worm, but also maybe it's cute. The point is—Lila doesn't know. She wishes she could ask, but they don't ask each other real things like that anymore.

"When my father died, none of them called," Lila says.

They just sent texts. Heart emojis. They said, *We're here for you, Lila,* and Suz sent a picture of the Little Worm like she was the moral support. And it weirdly made Lila feel like she couldn't call them. All she wanted to do was sob in their arms like she had once in high school. But the time for that seemed to be over.

"Ever since I arrived here, I've had this feeling that we're just pretending to still be friends. Reenacting the friendship the way it used to be, when we were actually close," Lila says.

That was how Phoebe felt at the end of her marriage. They reen-
acted the beginning—went on date nights, invited each other to things.
Matt was always saying, Sure, yes, come to happy hour. But she could
feel how he didn't really care if she came. Her presence had somehow
become irrelevant to her own husband, and how are people supposed
to tolerate that kind of pain? How are you supposed to go from being
the center of someone's world to being irrelevant? To sobbing in your
best friend's arms unthinkingly to being afraid to call them after your
father dies? Phoebe doesn't know. She, too, was caught unprepared by
that kind of loss.

"That's sort of how it is with everyone here," Lila says. "Like I'm pretending. Acting out this idea of what we once were or what we could be."

Phoebe wants to ask what she pretends to be with Gary. But it
doesn't seem right. She's in a fragile state. It feels like one small pull of
the thread, and Lila will unravel. And Lila surely has to go back out to
her cocktail party. It's only eight.

"When does the pretending stop?" Lila asks.

"I'd like to say whenever you want it to," Phoebe says, but she knows
this isn't true. It's harder than that. "But I think it stops when you get
fed up."

"Fed up with what?"

"Yourself," Phoebe says.

"But how long does that take?" Lila asks, as if she's at the doctor,
writing down notes.

"It took me forty years."

"Well, that's not promising. Forty is so far away."

"I mean, it doesn't have to happen at *exactly* forty."

But Lila puts her face in her hands. "Ugh. I can't believe I have no
maid of honor."

"Maybe Pauline will do it."

Lila doesn't smile. She doesn't seem to like the joke. "Will you do it?"

"I'm not in the wedding."

"I'm the bride. I get to decide who's in the wedding. It's like being
the president of your very own country. So ta-da, now you're in the
wedding."

"But I don't even know you," Phoebe says, and as soon as she says it, Phoebe regrets saying it. She knows it's no longer true.

"You already know me better than most people at this wedding," Lila says. "Except for maybe my high school guidance counselor."

"Why did you invite your high school guidance counselor, by the way?"

"Is that weird?"

"It's a little weird."

"Well, he's local. And he was really very kind to me when I was a kid," she says. "A better mother to me than my own mother. Even gave me his sweater once when I got my period on his office chair."

"Even stranger."

"You think so?"

"I think he probably got the invitation and was like, Wait, what? The girl who menstruated on my chair?"

Lila laughs loudly and looks truly happy for a second.

"He probably did," she says. "Because actually it is a little weird. I finally had a chance to talk to him, and he was so familiar and unfamiliar at the same time, halfway through the convo, I was like, Wait, who are you? Why did I *invite* you?"

She laughs again and it's good to hear Lila make fun of herself. But Phoebe is starting to understand that on some nights, Lila is probably the loneliest girl in the world, just like Phoebe. And maybe they are all lonely. Maybe this is just what it means to be a person. To constantly reckon with being a single being in one body. Maybe everybody sits up at night and creates arguments in their head for why they are the loneliest person in the world. Lila has no maid of honor and Phoebe has never been a maid of honor. It has always been a mark of shame for her, that no woman in this world was willing to claim her.

"Anyway. It's not even like you have to do that much," Lila says. "Viv already planned everything. You'll see tomorrow, it's all in the binder. You just kind of have to like, read the binder and then stand there and do what Viv would have done."

"You do remember that I came to this hotel to kill myself," Phoebe says.

Saying it aloud makes her feel very far away from that woman who put on her green dress and came here to die—to think of someone being in that much pain. To think of herself walking in here like she had no other option. Phoebe wants to hug that woman, not hurt her.

Her therapist was right. She won't kill herself. She is not the type. She has always known this about herself but somehow forgot. Somehow, everything felt so dark back at home, and only now that she is here can Phoebe look back and see just how dark. At the time, the darkness felt like life. Phoebe was too familiar with it, the way she was too familiar with her own house. She could walk to the bathroom in the middle of the night, no problem—she knew the knobs on every door, could feel the walls of her house like they were the walls of her own body. To be stuck inside her house was to be stuck inside herself and all the choices she made over the years.

"I'll do it," Phoebe says. Saying it aloud feels like grabbing on to something.

"Yes!" Lila says. She claps her hands and Phoebe starts to feel a tiny bit excited. Phoebe does not have to go back—not yet. "Tomorrow morning, you can join us for the bridal brunch in the conservatory."

A ridiculous sentence if Phoebe ever heard one. But she's cheered by the thought.

"Only if you get this shampoo out of my hair," Phoebe says.

Lila holds the shower head above Phoebe. The water is warm down her back. Phoebe sinks deeper into the tub.

"Have you tried the back scrubber?" Lila asks.

"There's no back scrubber."

"They didn't give you a back scrubber?"

"I don't need a back scrubber."

"How else were you planning on scrubbing your back?"

"Do I need to scrub my back?"

"Have you never washed your back before?"

"Maybe not?"

The only time she ever washed her back was when she showered with her husband. At the start of their relationship. Their first trip to the Ozarks, in the little B&B, how they would wash each other. She remembers the feeling of him spreading the soap over her back, his hands sliding down her spine.

"Head back," the bride says.

Just submit, Phoebe thinks. Put your head back and close your eyes and let the water rush down your body. Let the bride wash the shampoo out of your hair if that's what the bride wants to do. You're the maid of honor now.

BY THE TIME Phoebe turns her phone on, it is dark outside. She sits on the balcony and listens to all the messages come in at once. A familiar ding, yet the phone feels foreign in her hand, like some object pulled from an archaeological dig, filled with messages that no longer have anything to do with her.

Bob asking why she took off in the middle of her Intro to Lit class.

Her student Sam who wants her to know that she didn't come to class today because her grandmother had a bloody nose and her bloody nose got all over *Leaves of Grass* and she thinks it's probably a biohazard to bring the book into a public space now, though she knows how Dr. Stone feels about students who do not bring their books, but the syllabus doesn't mention what to do if the book is covered in actual human blood? This is what Sam needs to know. *Thanks!*, she wrote.

And then Bob again.

Are you okay? Bob wrote. Because Bob is not a total jerk. Bob is wondering where she is. Does she need a medical leave of absence? Does he need to get another adjunct to cover the semester for her? Will she be back?

And then there are the texts from her husband. They start on late Tuesday, just before midnight.

Phoebe, her husband texted. *It might be weird to say this, but it felt equally weird not to have wished you a good start to the semester when I saw you today in the office. So, I guess what I am trying to say is, I hope your classes went well today.*

But by this morning, he was concerned.

Hate to bug you again, but Bob emailed and is wondering where you are. I told him I don't know. Are you okay?

And now he is very concerned.

Phoebe, I know I don't have a right to ask, but if you could please let me know if you're okay, I'd really appreciate that. I'm very worried about you.

Now he's worried? She is stunned by his sudden concern. Because why wasn't he worried two years ago when he left? Or on her birthday last May, when she woke up and the first sound out of her mouth was a sob that had sounded so much like an animal dying in the woods it spooked Phoebe into silence?

She doesn't respond. Maybe I'll never respond again, she thinks.

But she should write to Bob. She types and deletes a few responses.

~~I am going to be back in a week, after I finish taking care of my dying grandmother's estate.~~

~~I am researching 19th-century estates on the East Coast for my book, which I am going to seek publication for in 2023. (Did you know Edith Wharton lived in Newport?) My research might take all semester.~~

But none of this is true. Writing these emails makes her feel like her students lying their way out of something. And she is lying—she has no idea what she will do after the wedding. She can't imagine going back now. But she also can't imagine not going back.

I will need someone to cover my classes this week, she writes to Bob. *I am very sorry for taking off without any notice, and I'll write as soon as I can when I have more information about what I am going to do regarding the rest of the semester. Thank you for understanding.*

She uses the flashlight on her phone to finish Mrs. Dalloway. But when she's done, she doesn't go inside. She wants to stay and look up at the stars. At home, she would never sit out in the dark alone. But nighttime in a hotel is a different thing. At night, a hotel comes alive. The fairy lights in the garden start to sparkle. The experimental harpist and cellist begin to play. The wedding people sprawl out of the parlor and assemble on the patio. They are still partying. The wedding people are always partying. It feels like what they are sent here by God to do.

To have loose ties around their white collared shirts and to laugh very hard while slamming the tables with their palms.

She read something once about how the cello is soothing because it mirrors something about our physiology. Phoebe can't remember what exactly. But it does soothe her. So do the sounds of doors closing, opening, closing, opening. The sink running next door. The roll of laughter so steady and constant, rising and falling like waves. The constant motion of the world. The whole place is designed to keep her from descending into despair. On every wall, there is evidence that somebody has thought about her stay here. The little candles on the tables below. The torches that come on automatically at dusk.

It is so easy to hate Mrs. Dalloway for worrying so much about her stupid party, the way it's so easy to hate the bride, she thinks. But in the end, everybody goes to the party and that's the point. It's Mrs. Dalloway who brings them all together in a modern world full of railroads and wars and illnesses that are always tearing people apart. If the problem is loneliness, then in this way, and maybe in only this way, Mrs. Dalloway is the hero for giving everybody a place to be.

THURSDAY

❧

The Bachelorette Party

Phoebe wakes at sunrise with an urgency to touch the ocean. It's time. She puts on Lila's mother's sweater again (must get new clothes today, she decides) and heads downstairs to the Cliff Walk.

On the way out, she's surprised to spot Gary and Lila in the conservatory—they are being photographed under two giant ferns. It feels too early for something like that, to be dressed so formally before the ocean mist has evaporated, but there they are, leaning into each other. They look like well-dressed cartoons. Something about Lila's pants looking too clean or Gary's blazer too checked.

Phoebe pours herself some coffee as they pose. She thinks Lila looks beautiful in her silk tube top, though Phoebe imagines Lila does not call it a tube top. She can hear Lila in her head saying, Tube tops are for teens in the nineties at the mall, Phoebe. Strapless blouses are for women about to get married.

"If you can just put your hand *there*," the photographer suggests to Gary, so Gary puts his hand there. Moves the hair off her shoulder. Yes, yes, like that. Lean back into him. And Lila does, but her face is too stiff, the way people's faces look when their abs are slightly clenched.

Lila sees her. She waves and Gary nods. Phoebe nods back, then slips out of the room. There is something embarrassing about watching a couple take photos like this. Watching a couple try to be a couple, even though they are a couple.

On the Cliff Walk, there are no people out yet. Just someone's yellow dog milling around the Forty Steps entrance, though she doesn't see anyone connected to the dog. She starts to walk faster, which tricks the dog into thinking it's a competition, and that's how she starts racing this random dog on the Cliff Walk.

I will get a dog, she thinks. No offense to Harry. But the dog will go walking with her in the morning. The dog will keep her out in the world. And it feels amazing to just decide something like that, like, I will get a dog.

The dog slows to a happy trot two steps ahead of her. Together, they pass signs telling them to stay on the path, but there are thin dirt trails made by those who did not listen, like this dog, who starts walking down to the rocks.

HIGH RISK OF INJURY, the sign warns, complete with a helpful picture of a man falling off to his death. Yet Phoebe follows, because people, like dogs and the fisherman down below, will do anything to get closer to the water.

"Hey, hey!" the fisherman says as soon as he sees the dog. The dog barks. "Thanks for bringing him to me."

The fisherman is smiling, like she did the dog a great service. When he looks at her, his headlight blasts her in her eyes.

"Sorry," he says, fumbling with the thing. "I sometimes forget I've got this thing on my head."

"It's okay," she says.

He turns back to the water, and she sits down on a rock, even though he has not asked for her company. But she decides that's how some people are (she decides that she likes deciding things now that she is forty and alone, *that's how some people are*). Some people don't ask for what they need. Some people are like religious children that way, mistaking suffering with goodness. Her father acted like being lonely was a good workout, something that would pay off in the end, and sometimes it didn't, but when he was fishing, it did: He always filled his bucket, dropping in each fish unceremoniously, saying to Phoebe, "Don't get excited, folks. Just a trash fish."

She always liked that her father did this—said "folks" when it was just her, as if Phoebe was a grand audience. Yet Phoebe stood there stoically as instructed, like she was just a girl who liked being a good girl, and good girls did not like killing things. Good girls liked the breeze through their long hair and the flush on a man's face when he smacked the fish against a rock. Killed it instantly. Threw it in the bucket.

The waves build in the distance and crash against the rocks, and she can't look away. Phoebe feels grateful, like she has achieved something monumental just by sitting here at sea level, even though from down here on the rocks, the ocean is terrifying. It's the closest embodiment to what eternity might look like. She can't see the end of it or the bottom of it. She can't see the darkness of its expanse, but she knows there are creatures who have to live in it. Who think it's normal. She reaches out her hand and she touches it.

Her phone dings.

Please tell me you're okay and that I shouldn't call the police, Matt texts.

This is how her husband shows affection. Like her father, who was most comfortable showing love by announcing the ways he thought Phoebe might die—you're going to trip on these socks and break your neck! You could slip on some black ice and drive right off the road! He was always worried about protecting Phoebe from herself. Like when Phoebe was pregnant, Matt looked at the two lines on the stick and said, "It's too early to get excited, isn't it?" and she agreed, but when she started bleeding ten weeks later, she hated herself for agreeing, for not getting excited when she had the chance.

So she doesn't respond to her husband. He doesn't deserve a response, she thinks. He deserves to suffer like she did, to spiral out of control. Because that was the problem. He never lost control. Neither did she.

"Hey, hey!" the fisherman shouts, and starts pulling on his line. "I got one!"

He looks over at Phoebe, so excited. He needs Phoebe to see the fish. And Phoebe wants to see. But by the time she gets to him, he's lost it.

"Shit," he says. "Mind holding this for me? I bet he took the bait."

"Happy to," she says.

He bends down to get more squid from his bucket. Phoebe feels the heavy pull of the water. Much stronger than the pull of the river. It takes strength to hold the rod still, to not be scared as the water breaks against the rocks and pools around her feet. She imagines it's easy to get wiped out by a wave here.

But the man acts like standing here on the slippery rocks is just business. Holds up some fresh squid and tells her to reel in the hook. But she starts to feel little nibbles, the small bites of something alive in the water.

"I think I got something," she says, and pulls the rod up sharply to set the hook. "Got it!"

She reels it in, slowly until the fish is dangling above the water. It's so jarring—this fish yanked from its dark watery world, plunged into an entirely new one, where the most ordinary things like light and air are shocking. The fish shakes wildly on the end of the line, the force of his will to live so enormous. He is like Virginia Woolf's moth, fluttering its wings—all struggle, all life.

"It's beautiful," she says.

"Agh," the fisherman says. "Just a sea robin. Nobody buys those."

She takes the fish off the hook, looks at its big ugly mouth, and throws it back into the sea. Wipes her hands on her leggings and gives the rod back to the fisherman.

"You've got a lucky touch," he says. "Want to do another?"

"I need to get going," she says.

She wants to see Edith Wharton's house before the bridal brunch. She says goodbye, pats the dog on the head, climbs back up the rocks. On the way, Phoebe slips, falls, scrapes her knee, but does not slide into the water like the little man on the warning sign.

"She always had the feeling that it was very, very dangerous to live even one day," Woolf wrote.

And it's true. How easy to be dead. How lucky to be alive, even for just one day. Charlotte Brontë's father understood this—the man had lost every single one of his children except for Charlotte, which is why he repeatedly turned down her final suitor. He worried marriage and the childbirth that followed marriage would kill her. And one year later, it did.

But Phoebe has made it out alive. She is back up on the path. Nothing has destroyed Phoebe. She feels very aware of this as she continues walking.

She was never much of a walker, never really understood the point of walking just to walk, which made her feel like a bad Victorianist sometimes. She didn't take walks like Jane Eyre or wander the moors like the Brontës, though she always imagined she might if she had a moor at her disposal.

And now she does. An ocean is like a moor, she thinks. It's an open watery horizon, and she walks along its edge until she reaches Land's End. Edith Wharton's house. Not that it's really Wharton's house anymore. The new owners are some random people from Connecticut, which is all she can gather from her phone.

She tries to get a better look, scrambles over some rocks, and she's not an ardent enough Wharton fan for this to feel like a holy pilgrimage, mostly because her books ended in too much tragedy, a Romeo and Juliet–style fatal miscommunication that Phoebe respected yet hated. But she loved everything up to that point. The parties, the clothing, the conversations. She loved Wharton's sense of humor. Her careful eye. She loved Lily Bart and was devastated when she killed herself at the end.

But Wharton hadn't published any of her books while she lived in this house. At Land's End, she had been unknown, an unhappy married woman. She had not yet become the real Edith Wharton. Not yet divorced. Not yet a novelist. Not yet a war correspondent in France. She wonders how terrifying it felt, not to know any of this about herself, to sit out on this big lawn, looking at the sea, feeling like she was at the very end of it all. She wonders what it was that made her realize there was somewhere else to go.

THE WALK BACK feels longer, but she likes feeling her legs strain as she passes mansion after mansion on her left. She is suddenly curious about what she has not yet become, and is proud of herself when she returns to the Forty Steps. And maybe that's who she will become—a woman who enjoys a good walk alone.

Phoebe, I'm at the house and it truly looks like you were abducted in the middle of making breakfast. Where are you? Did you bring Harry with you?

It's unsettling to think that after all this time he is actually at the house. He is back among their things, walking up and down the stairs. But he is too late in arriving. Like a party guest you hate for showing up when you are throwing out all the uneaten food.

I just found Harry in the basement under a blanket. I presume you know that Harry is dead?

"Yes, I know Harry is dead," she says to her phone. "So fuck you, you fucking fuck."

She feels the urge to throw her phone off the cliff, to get him away from her, like his texts might grow more powerful the longer she keeps them in her hand.

"Uh-oh," a man says.

She turns to see Gary standing there in his jogging clothes. Phoebe is disarmed.

"Is this the moment when the protagonist throws her phone into the ocean to symbolize how she's ready to live a new life?" he asks.

"Yes," Phoebe says. "And in the next scene, you can find me waiting in line at the Apple store to buy a new phone, like, immediately."

"Like just hours of you shopping for a phone and making small decisions about how to set it up?"

"That's basically how the movie ends."

"Very experimental."

"A commentary."

"Somebody give this woman an Oscar," he says, facing the ocean like it's the audience.

"Thank you, thank you," Phoebe says. She feels light and funny again.

"Lila sent me to come get you," Gary says. "Your absence at the bridal brunch has been noticed."

"Oh," Phoebe says. "I didn't realize how long I was out here."

Gary must be wondering why she was invited to the bridal brunch if she's not really part of the wedding. But he doesn't ask.

Her phone starts vibrating, and they both stare at it like it's the fish, exhausting itself until it dies.

"Everything okay?" Gary asks.

"It's my husband calling," Phoebe says. "My ex-husband, I mean. I have to practice saying that."

"Good luck," he says. "I still have trouble saying 'my dead wife.'"

"There have to be better options."

"Nothing else sounds much better," he says. "My deceased wife?"

"Too formal," Phoebe says.

"My late wife?"

"Too old-fashioned."

"My first wife."

"Asshole."

"My departed spouse."

"Okay, now you just sound like you murdered her. You're right. I see your problem."

"There is always the option of just calling her Wendy," he says. "But it feels wrong to do it around Lila. It feels . . . rude somehow."

Which is a real shame, he says, because he always liked the name Wendy. So did Juice, who said "Wendy" even before she said "Mama," maybe something to do with how many times Juice watched *Peter Pan*, he wasn't sure.

"Wendy was disappointed by it, she was like, what am I, her co-worker?" Gary says. "But after she died, I was glad that from the very beginning she could see her mother as a person."

"That's a nice way to think about it," Phoebe says. "Can I ask how Juice got the nickname?"

"It's something Wendy used to call her," Gary says. He explains that Juice had so much energy as a toddler, zipping back and forth across the room, with this incredible strength. Wendy would always laugh about her being juiced up.

"We stopped calling her that a long time ago, but after Wendy died, Juice started asking to be called that again," Gary says. Then, as if he fears he has been rude for talking so much about his family, he asks, "Do you have kids?"

"No," Phoebe says. "I mean, I tried."

She tells him about all the trying. About IVF. About how that might have been when the depression started. It was hard to say. Hard to work backward and see the beginning. All those appointments and by the end, Matt didn't want to come.

"Matt?"

"My ex-husband," she says. "He never wanted to come. He said he was okay doing IVF but then would look at the medications in the fridge and say, This is all so expensive. And it was. But I also know it was his way of telling me he wanted it to happen naturally. He wanted the child to light up inside me like a firefly. He wanted it to be so obvious, so natural, that no doubt had any room to creep in."

But they had appointments. Phoebe had polyps. She had operations.

"Then the egg-stractions," she says.

"Egg-stractions?"

"Technically, they're called retrievals. But they should be called Egg-stractions, right? I mean, come on. It's just sitting right there."

The Eggstraction, she joked with her husband. Sounds like a horror story someone should write.

"But Matt wouldn't joke about it with me. He was just like, Oh God, who would read that story?"

"A lot of people would."

The hotel is visible now. The bridal brunch is waiting inside. Phoebe takes small, slow steps.

"Here we go," Gary says.

"Not ready to talk to people again?"

"It's just been a lot of family," Gary says. "I'm supposed to be having coffee with them right now, but there are only so many times I can listen to Marla list off the price of various houses in the neighborhood."

"Marla's pretty funny," Phoebe says.

"She really is," Gary says. "Even though I know she can be a lot for people."

"A lot can be okay. It can be good. It's better than nothing."

It's what Phoebe longed for in the silence of her house growing up. Her father was not a loud person, and neither was she, but she wanted to be. She longed for a lot of noise in the kitchen, for clanging pots, for the sounds of people laughing by the fire.

"I used to dream of having one of those big families in nineteenth-century British novels," Phoebe says.

"I thought you dreamed of being an orphan?"

"Well, if I couldn't be an orphan, then I wanted a big messy family," she says. "Like in *Pride and Prejudice* or something."

"I'll just nod and pretend I read it, too."

"It's one of those books that are about the big family, and what the big family is up to, and how the big family changes over time, and all the little ways the members of the big family irritate each other but also love each other."

"I see," Gary says. "So I'll just pretend that I'm a character in an Austen novel I've never read, and all will be well."

"Totally healthy," Phoebe says.

He holds open the hotel door like a butler. "The ladies await, Maid of Honor."

She blushes. So Lila told him.

"GARY, YOU'RE LATE for your Bourbon Bubbler," Lila says as soon as they walk into the conservatory.

"What's a Bourbon Bubbler?" Nat asks.

"And how do we get one?" Suz asks.

"Sorry," Lila says. "It's a massage for men only."

"How can a massage be only for men?" Marla asks.

"That's like when they tried to market wine just for bros," Nat says. "As if there are some grapes that are manlier than other grapes."

"Wine for bros," Juice repeats, and laughs.

"I for one can only feel okay about being rubbed down if it's done with literal poison," Gary says, and the women laugh.

"Are you ready for some very relaxing poison, bro?" Juice asks, pretending to be a masseuse.

"Oh come on. It's a classic bourbon sugar scrub," Lila says. "People have been doing it for . . . years."

Lila kisses Gary goodbye. Every kiss they have in public seems grander than the last—designed to produce applause. Phoebe feels her stomach lurch. Maybe she's hungry. Maybe she needs a big breakfast, like the kind she used to order for herself when hungover. Phoebe sits down at the table of women, looks at the menu, while the bride tries to order a coffee.

"That's all I am trying to do here," Lila says to the waiter. He wears a name tag that says, RYUN, DRINK CONCIERGE.

"Oh, we have free coffee in the samovar," Ryun says.

"What's a samovar?" Juice asks.

Phoebe imagines that when Ryun is not being asked, What's a samovar, he's spending a lot of time trying to explain why his name is spelled with a *U* and not an *A*.

"It's that jug of coffee over there," Ryun says, pointing to a table.

"Right, but I don't want free coffee from the samovar," Lila says. She points to the menu. "I want *this* coffee."

"But it's the same coffee," Ryun says, smiling. "The only difference is that this coffee is just six dollars more."

"Look, I am just trying to order the coffee that's on the menu here. Can you please give me that coffee?"

Juice and Marla give each other eyes across the table. Ryun nods.

"Right, okay, I understand," he says, and then goes to get a cup of coffee out of the samovar. When he brings it over to Lila, the cup wobbles violently on the saucer.

"Thank you," Lila says.

Lila is the only one at the table not embarrassed.

"Here is your binder, Maid of Honor," Lila says.

Being maid of honor comes with a schedule of events and a list of duties, some already crossed out, like "Research old restaurant that Oprah loves," "Book the water spa," and some duties yet to be crossed out: "Buy compostable dick-themed flatware," "Confirm tarot reading, 7 p.m.," and "Confirm Sex Woman, 5 p.m."

"Confirm Sex Woman?" Phoebe asks.

"What's a Sex Woman?" Juice asks.

"Nobody knows, sweetheart," Marla says.

"I'm not *supposed* to know," Lila says, closing the binder. "Today is supposed to be a surprise."

"I bet she's one of those women who show up with toys and things, and, like, teaches us how to have sex," Suz says.

"Do you not know how to have sex, bro?" Juice asks Lila.

"Mel, please don't call me bro," Lila says.

"Bro, please don't call me Mel."

"But Mel is a beautiful name," Lila says. "And Juice is actually the nickname of a professional football player who was famously tried for murder."

Marla looks at Lila accusingly, and Juice asks, "Wait, what?"

"It's true," Marla says, with an apologetic look. "O. J. Simpson."

"Then why did my mom call me that?" Juice asks.

"I honestly can't remember," Marla confesses.

Juice is not pleased. She looks at Lila like it's her fault that her nickname is forever ruined now. She sits back and crosses her arms in defeat.

"So what's good here?" Phoebe asks, closing the binder.

"I highly suggest the squash toast," Lila says.

"What happened to avocado toast?" Phoebe asks.

"That's over now," Lila says.

"So soon? I just started understanding the appeal."

"Too late. Squash toast is like, the next generation," Lila says.

"Avocado toast was a total scam," Marla says. "And squash toast is even more of a scam."

"How can it be a scam?" Lila asks. "The menu says how much it costs."

"Yeah, twenty-two dollars! It's somehow even more expensive than avocado toast, despite the fact that gourds are historically the cheapest vegetable known to mankind."

"What are gourds?" Juice asks.

"Squash," Phoebe says.

"Why don't people just say 'squash' then?" Juice asks.

The Drink Concierge returns.

"I'll have the gourd toast," Juice says, but the Drink Concierge doesn't break character.

"Anyone else?" he asks.

"Same," Phoebe says.

Phoebe doesn't give a shit how much it costs. Phoebe is hungry. Phoebe is still buzzing from the walk. Phoebe wants to feed her body.

"Cheers," she says when she finally takes a bite.

But Phoebe knows that if she were really at this wedding the way Marla is really at this wedding, if she were the Phoebe of ten years ago, she would be making a mental bill in her head, too, tallying up everything, trying to create some big argument about how wasteful it all is.

But now she is counting other things.

"In just this room alone, there are ten doors," Phoebe says, and she loves this about historic houses, though nobody else looks astonished.

"Is this supposed to be the start of a game or something?" Suz asks.

Juice rips a sugar pack in half over her coffee.

"Juice!" Marla says, when half of it gets on the table. "You just got sugar everywhere."

"It's fine," Juice says. "I'll lick it up like I'm a priest."

"I'm sorry," Phoebe says. "You're going to have to explain that one."

"Grandma said that when the priest spills the wine, he has to lick it off the floor," Juice says. "Because it's literally Jesus. And if you don't, then Jesus will just sit there on the linoleum for the rest of time."

"Wait, seriously?" Nat asks, and Juice nods, then licks the sugar off the table.

Lila turns her gaze to Phoebe.

"You know what open-toed shoes are?" Lila asks.

"Is this a maid of honor test?" Phoebe asks.

"I certainly hope not. You know, right?"

"I refuse to dignify that with a response."

"See?" Lila says to Juice, who is still licking up the sugar. "That's what I told Mel. I mean, Juice. Everybody knows what open-toed shoes are."

Juice pulls away from the table with sudden coolness. "Well, sorry, I don't."

"Phoebe is going to take you to get open-toed shoes today."

"Was that in the binder?" Phoebe asks.

It's not really what she imagined for the day. She imagined getting a massage. She imagined lying by the pool.

"You both need shoes," Lila says. "You can take the vintage car."

Lila looks at Juice for some expression of excitement, but there is only disdain.

"The one we took yesterday?" Juice asks. "I hate that car."

"It's a beautiful car," Lila says.

"It's embarrassing," Juice says. "People just look at you while you drive."

"That's the point," Lila says.

"Why do you want people to just look at you all the time?"

Lila opens her mouth to respond, but Phoebe stands up as a way to finish the argument.

"Let's do it," Phoebe says. "Juice, I'll meet you in the lobby at noon."

"You should get some dresses while you're out," Lila says, and no one asks why Phoebe is the maid of honor and yet has brought no dresses for the week. They are three days into the wedding now, ready to accept whatever reality the bride dictates. "One for every night. Go down to Bellevue. That's where they have the best stuff."

More wedding people arrive, and the bride is bombarded. She shrieks as she stands up. She hugs them and then introduces each one to the bridal party. Her cousin, a skier who almost made it to the Olympics. Her uncle, who wears a full linen suit. And then her grandmother, who calls herself "Bootsie" and then introduces the man next to her as "my guy." She is old, just on the cusp of ancient, and she looks around at the room like she's never stayed in a hotel in her life.

"I don't understand why you couldn't have the wedding at home," Bootsie says. "Like Jackie."

"We talked about this, Grandmother," Lila says, kissing her on the cheek. "This isn't Jackie's wedding. We do things differently now."

"But the Breakers is very gaudy. A poor man's imitation of a European castle," Bootsie says.

Lila looks at My Guy. "Can you help Grandmother get settled in the St. Georges room?"

They watch Bootsie go, and Phoebe whispers, "Who is Jackie?"

"Jackie Kennedy."

IN THE ROARING TWENTIES, Phoebe opens the maid of honor binder and feels like her old self, about to embark on a series of tasks. She finds herself wanting to make today perfect for Lila. She starts by calling the number for the Sex Woman.

"Hello?" a woman answers.

Phoebe was hoping she would answer by introducing herself the way many businesses do.

"Hi, are you the . . ." Phoebe begins. "I am calling to confirm your visit to Lila Rossi-Winthrop's bachelorette party tonight at five p.m.?"

"Rossi-Winthrop?" the Sex Woman says. "Will you hold please?"

For a Sex Woman, she seems very formal. She types a lot of information into the system and makes no attempt to fill the silence with conversation.

"Okay, that's right. Five p.m.," she says. "And will there be a projector?"

"Do you require one?" Phoebe asks.

"Historically, yes," the Sex Woman says.

AT THE FRONT desk, while Phoebe waits for Juice, she asks Pauline where she might find compostable dick-themed flatware in this town.

"Oh!" Pauline says, and if she thinks this is a weird question, she doesn't show it. "Does that exist? I don't know if that exists. But if it does, it would be at a place called Coastal Intimates down in the Navy district. I can get you a driver?"

"No, I'll be taking the vintage car," Phoebe says. "Oh, and we'll need a projector at five p.m. sharp in the billiards room for the bachelorette party."

"Of course, absolutely!" Pauline says, like this is the most sensible request in the world.

Phoebe turns around to see Juice waiting by the double doors. She looks out of place standing in front of the velvet drapes in her big black combat boots. Like a girl from the future, lost in time.

"Hey," Phoebe says.

But Juice just waves. She has gone quiet again like she did on the drive to the wharf. Phoebe doesn't know if this is because this is the first time they are alone without her family or if this is just something that happens to Juice in the bright hot sun of the afternoon.

"Your car is ready," the man in burgundy says.

Phoebe drives fast, but not so fast that it would scare Juice. Juice seems to relax into the speed, reads something off her phone, and the silence is fine with Phoebe. A relief, really. Phoebe hates having to perform happiness in front of other people's children. This is probably why Phoebe has been told many times that she is not particularly maternal, but she thinks what people mean by this is that she does not act like a mother on TV, who is often loud, always trying to hug someone, doesn't really matter who.

But Phoebe is not a hugger. Her father was not a hugger. He gave a small pat on the back whenever he wanted to say "I love you." He did not oohh and ahh over Phoebe, and so Phoebe did not oohh or ahh over other people's children.

But this did not mean she didn't enjoy kids. She just didn't feel the need to try so hard with them, like her husband always did. She suspected kids didn't really like it when adults tried too hard, mostly because Phoebe never liked that as a child. Then again, the first time her husband picked up Mia's new baby, he swung her around like she was an airplane, and she seemed to really like it.

"Does she eat any real food yet?" he asked Mia.

It had been their last Thanksgiving together, three months before the affair started. Mia and Tom had come over with their new baby because Matt didn't have a big family, either. The people at the university are my family, he always said. And that made sense for him. He was wedded to them for life.

"Today is going to be her first day of real food, actually," Mia said.

"Wow," Matt said. Phoebe's husband looked genuinely thrilled by this, but Phoebe didn't know how to look genuinely thrilled. She mostly just felt fat from her most recent IVF cycle. "She's going to expect a Thanksgiving dinner every day from now on."

"Right," Mia said. "She'll have the most complicated palate at preschool. Like, I'm sorry, but where is the turkey jus?"

They laughed, and even though the affair hadn't started yet, Phoebe already felt outside of something they shared. They were different somehow—they were the ones making jokes over the turkey. They were the ones debating whether the Waldorf school would be good for the child, and Phoebe was the one just trying to hang on. Trying to smile. Phoebe was becoming like Tom. She looked to Tom in solidarity, but Tom was assessing the turkey.

"Are these the giblets?" Tom asked.

Phoebe felt like she was in a dream, watching Mia and her husband and the Waldorf Child continue on so merrily with Thanksgiving dinner. Tom asking why the turkey was flipped upside down, and Matt saying, "It's the only way you can make it."

Her husband was full of advice like that. He knew how to best do everything, and Tom seemed interested in being like this, too. Tom asked him a lot of questions while Mia had her breast out, and Phoebe didn't remember if it was rude to look at the breast or rude not to look.

Phoebe tried to say something nice about the Waldorf Child. She imagined what some other woman would say. Another mother.

"Oh, how cute, look at those little killer whales on the baby's onesie," she said.

"I think we say orcas now," Mia said.

And normally, Phoebe could have looked to her husband in this moment and laughed. I think we say orcas now, Phoebe imagined them saying. But nobody met her eye. She was left alone with her scolding. It was not a joke, just a fact. Parents say orcas, not killer whales. Ho hum. Then they ate the meal and she continued to notice how none of them really looked her in the eye. When they told stories, they bypassed Phoebe, as if she were not part of the conversation. Did it have something to do with her hair? It was a taupe wall that blended in with the taupe wall. The table roared. Her husband laughed, head back, and looked at the Waldorf Child with such tenderness. It occurred to her that if her husband didn't leave her, she would probably have to leave him. Looking at him look at a child that way.

When they left, Phoebe didn't feel relieved. She felt nervous, as if they took real life with them. The extra pie. The Waldorf Child. The whole life. She started to clean up, hoping it would return her to herself.

"I like children," Phoebe said, and why did she feel the need to say this? "It's just boring to make them the center of attention all the time. It's like bringing a new toy to dinner and only looking at the new toy and only talking about the new toy and expecting everybody else to care about it."

Her husband didn't say anything at first. Just washed the turkey plate. "I thought it was fun."

Was this the moment he fell out of love with her and in love with Mia? Was that what he was trying to tell her in the kitchen? Stop being so negative. Just be fun. Just say orcas.

It wasn't until after Valentine's Day when the actual affair began. But Phoebe knew something had shifted after Thanksgiving, because they stopped touching in the kitchen when they walked by each other. They stopped having sex, and Phoebe was scared by how easy it became to live without sex with her husband. She got spooked by the fact that she preferred some other version of her husband, the one she created in her fantasies. She thought of this husband when she masturbated in the mornings. She got lightheaded. She felt empty, but in a clean kind of way. Not having sex sometimes felt like giving up meat or pasta. Sometimes, she felt absurdly proud of herself.

But after three months of this, she sometimes missed her real husband so much, she walked over to him at the couch, kissed him on the mouth.

"It's a simple prompt," he said, while grading papers. It was February, only a few weeks into the spring semester, and he was already very annoyed by them. It wasn't like him. "Analyze the crow metaphor. But they keep getting it wrong. They keep describing the crow as some harbinger of death, even though nothing about the passage suggests death. But they expect crows to be harbingers of death, so they can't see that the author is trying to say something about how crows are actually very curious and social creatures! That's what I want to write on their papers—Do you see the words on the page? Do you even know what a crow is?"

By lunch, her husband was still so angry about the crows that he had to take a break to eat lunch. Then he decided to go grade on campus because he had to finish up some committee work there. He and Mia had been tasked to pick the art for the humanities center hallway, and he needed to go look at the paintings that had been delivered.

Even though it was planned, it felt like a miracle seeing Mia in the hallway—that's what he told Phoebe in their first conversation about the affair. He said he had been grading papers at home and feeling so depressed about everything—about his life, about their marriage, about his students and the crows—and when they were done talking about the paintings, he didn't want to go home. He asked Mia if she wanted a drink, and Phoebe wonders if he said it the way he once said it to her— Hey, want a beer?

By then, it was whiskey, though. Her husband was off beer. He was a grown man, a professor, and drank amber liquids only while they talked about their lives—about Tom's depression, about Phoebe's depression, about how easy it was to become depressed by someone else's depression. And then when the drink was over, it started to rain, which he said felt like a reason to stay put and have another, because neither of them wanted to walk across campus in the rain. And then her husband had the thought, What if I never have to go home again? It truly never occurred to him, but once it did, he couldn't stop thinking it. He could just never go home. He could start a new life. Take the hands of the woman before him and say, "I love you."

He said it just came out, like a sneeze he could not help. Once he said it, he understood it to be entirely true. He could see a whole future with Mia and the Waldorf Child. Mia said "I love you" back right away.

Neither of them knew it until that moment. He said that falling in love with Mia was like being a frog sitting in water that was slowly coming to a boil, and Phoebe said, "I take it that's not the romantic metaphor you use when talking with her about it?" and he said, "I just mean it was slow, okay, so slow I didn't realize it," and she said, "But isn't the frog in boiling water a myth? A frog wouldn't jump out of boiling water, it would just *die*." She was hoping he might riff on this with her, that together they would unpack the metaphor until it had no meaning.

"I love her," he said again.

"You love that she has a baby," Phoebe said.

"Not everything is about that, Phoebe."

He said it wasn't about sex, either, which he seemed to think would make her feel better but only made her feel worse. They had only slept together once before the pandemic started, and it had been a mistake. He should have waited, he knew. He should have talked to Phoebe about what he was feeling for Mia. But then it was the pandemic, and he didn't know what to do. It was always Matt and Phoebe stuck in their home all summer, Mia and Tom in theirs. He thought he could wait until the pandemic was over, but at a certain point, lying to Phoebe made Matt feel too awful. Sneaking out to call Mia was just wrong. By the end of that summer, he knew he would have to make a decision about how he wanted to live. And so, in August, he did.

"She brought me to life again," Matt told Phoebe. "I can't help it. I need to see this through."

For months after he left, it made her want to vomit thinking of another woman making her husband feel alive. Phoebe had been so jealous—but not just of Mia. Her husband felt alive again. She couldn't even imagine it.

PHOEBE FEELS A tiny thrill as the car hugs the curve of the country. To feel alive on this beautiful road, to be at the border of sea and land. To be here, driving this beautiful car on this beautiful day.

"Lila is such a bitch," Juice says.

Juice doesn't say it until Phoebe starts looking for parking, as if Phoebe's ability to ride in complete silence, her insistence on not making Juice talk, has impressed her into actual speech.

"Why do you say that?" Phoebe asks. She has long practiced this art of keeping an even tone with students, making her questions sound like statements.

"Aren't you going to scold me for calling your best friend a bitch?" Juice asks.

"No," Phoebe says.

Juice looks confused, as if she's never met this kind of adult. The one who doesn't give a shit. And this is one of the great things about not having kids, Phoebe realizes. She truly doesn't have to give a shit. She doesn't have to worry about Juice's development and whether or not the phone is reprogramming her brain, even though of course it is. She is not Juice's mother, not even a professor anymore, no longer standing in front of the classroom in a completely appropriate blouse and a skirt that shows a little knee, but of course not too much knee. She is free now in a way that people like Gary or Mia never will be. She can wear her skirt however high she wants. She can speak to Juice as if she's just another person in the car, because that's what she is.

"But I want to know why you would say that," Phoebe says. "If you're going to call someone a bitch, you should have a pretty good reason."

"Honestly, I bet she was just born that way."

"So like one of those babies that emerges from the womb as a total bitch?"

"Exactly," Juice says.

"Lila slid out, and the doctors were like, Congratulations, Mom and Dad, it's . . . a bitch!"

"Yes!" Juice laughs. Once she gets the joke, she can't stop. "Surprise! It's a giant bitch!"

"Would you like to swaddle your giant bitch?" Phoebe asks, and this sends Juice over the edge.

They get out of the car. They walk down Bellevue Avenue and Juice stops in front of an art gallery.

"Ugh," she says. "I wish my dad never walked into this gallery."

The Winthrop Gallery of International Art. The door is locked, the lights are off, but through the window, Phoebe can see big canvasses and shiny frames in the dark. She tries to imagine Gary walking in there, Lila at the desk.

"Wait, is that a Hudson River School painting?" Phoebe asks.

Juice shrugs. "What's a Hudson River School?"

They enter the boutique next door because Phoebe spots shoes against the back wall.

"I seriously don't get it," Juice says. "I already have shoes!"

Phoebe looks at Juice's combat boots. "Not open-toed ones."

"What's the difference?"

"Boots don't reveal your toes."

"Yeah, because my toes are actually kind of *private*."

"Not for much longer, I'm afraid," Phoebe says. "At this wedding, there are public toes only."

"Has anyone ever asked themselves . . . why? Why do we want to see other people's toes so much?"

"Juice," Phoebe says. "Let me make your life a lot simpler. You always need the shoes that the bride wants you to have."

"But why? I'm tired of doing everything she wants."

"It's just one of those rules."

"One of what rules?"

"Like, nobody can make fun of your father but you. Don't eat a giant cake before running. And always buy the shoes that the bride wants you to buy."

Juice looks impressed. "What other rules do you know?"

"Too many," Phoebe says.

PHOEBE HELPS JUICE pick out gold shoes that she doesn't completely hate more than life itself, and Phoebe gets a black pair for herself. She tries them on and they look so good, she feels proud of her feet.

"What do you think?" Phoebe asks, stretching out her leg.

"It looks like a foot," Juice says. "With a shoe on it."

"But do you like it?"

"You sound like Lila," Juice says. "Lila's obsessed with her feet."

"What do you mean, she's obsessed with her feet?"

"During the pandemic she spent hours watching TV and soaking her feet in this pedicure machine she bought. And it was *my* pedicure machine. I mean, she gave it to me for my birthday. And she was like, Yeah, but you never use it. And I was like, Well yeah, why would I use that? I mean, who cares what someone's feet look like? It's like she has no idea that we're all just going to die someday."

Juice leans over to unbuckle her shoe.

"Is that what you said?" Phoebe asks.

"Once," Juice says.

"Harsh."

"Well, it's not normal. She's obsessed with the way she looks. It literally takes her hours to figure out what to wear . . . to the bathroom. It's such a waste of time."

It's a similar kind of thing Phoebe used to tell herself in graduate school when everybody showed up to class looking like they had spent all morning turning themselves into a postmodern painting. It made her feel better about just wearing jeans. But Phoebe no longer believes this is the whole truth.

"A woman is asked out as much for her clothes as for herself," Phoebe says. "It's a line from an Edith Wharton novel."

A line that struck Phoebe as very true, even though her students always thought it sounded shallow. So does Juice.

"Well, that's just sad," Juice says. "You shouldn't ask someone out because of their clothes."

"I think Wharton meant something more than that," Phoebe says. "I think she wants us to think about the secret things people reveal through their clothing choices. Like when we admire someone's dress or jacket, we're really admiring something else."

"Like their body?" Juice asks. "Like how much money they have?"

And yes, yes. But no.

"Clearly you've never fallen in love with a man because he wore the same leather belt every day," Phoebe says.

Juice laughs. "Wait, you fell in love with a man because of his belt?"

"My ex-husband wore it on our first date," Phoebe says. "I remember admiring how the leather was smooth and tan, and then I kept noticing him wear it again and again."

It was a good belt, Matt told her when she finally asked about it, said he bought it when he was eighteen, and that he hoped to keep it until he died. And she could see it all, how this man would care for this one belt his whole life, how he would walk the perimeter of their house each night, making sure the doors were locked and the cups were in perfect order in the cabinet.

"Did he?" Juice asks.

"Yes," Phoebe says.

"Then why aren't you still married?"

"He had an affair."

"Oh. Like Albert Schuyler?"

"Like Albert Schuyler."

"Did he build his mistress a building, too?"

Phoebe chuckles. It feels good to finally laugh about it for real.

"Not quite," she says.

"So you were wrong about the belt," Juice says. "He didn't take care of you forever."

"No," Phoebe says. "But I was not wrong about the belt."

Phoebe remembers the last night she spent with her husband, watching him undress for bed, rolling up the belt into a little ball. Here was a man who took care of everything, she thought. A man who folded his laundry with the precision of a dressmaker. So why couldn't he take care of this, too? Why did she believe that somehow he could always save her, like her womb was a cupboard with cups in all the wrong places? A place her husband would rearrange, if only he could get to it.

"The belt revealed what we both wanted him to be," Phoebe says. "But we can't always be what we want every second. And that's okay. That's just life, you know?"

Juice picks up her boots and stares at them like they look different to her now.

"What do you want your boots to say about you?" Phoebe asks.

When Juice doesn't say anything, Phoebe worries she's lost her, that this might be too much for the kid, the way she used to worry about losing her students when they fell silent in class. Because their silence during the pandemic was excruciating. Their silence sounded like proof that they hated her, proof that they couldn't wait to leave, too.

But Phoebe had not always felt that way about teaching. When she first started, she loved it so much, she often felt bad for the parents of her students who didn't get to know their children in the way Phoebe sometimes did. Because a professor was in a unique position to open students up. They seemed inclined to trust that when Phoebe asked a question, it was leading somewhere worthwhile. It was nice, Phoebe thought, how often they went with her. How they trusted her to be a good professor, and she trusted them to be good students who sat in silence not because they hated her but because they were thinking.

So she decides to trust in Juice's silence. She does not retract her question or apologize for it. She just waits, until finally, Juice speaks.

"I guess I want people to know that I don't care what my feet look like," Juice says. "That I'm not like Lila at all."

"What are you like?"

"Like my mom."

"What was she like?"

"Really fun," Juice says. "We used to paint a lot together. She used to let me use my hands and feet and walk all over the canvas like a monkey. And once we all built this mini-sculpture of our house out of pancakes. And after we ate it all, my mom was like, Uh-oh, where are we going to live? We laughed so hard. And sometimes I feel like my dad doesn't even remember that day. It's like he's totally forgotten her."

"He hasn't forgotten her," Phoebe says. "Trust me."

"But how do you know?"

"Because he talked to me about her just this morning."

"Really?" Juice says.

"Really," Phoebe says. "And you can tell your dad these things, you know. You don't have to rely on your boots to do all the talking for you."

"Well, that's good," Juice says. "Because they're actually getting kind of sweaty. It's really hot out."

Phoebe laughs, picks a pair of Tevas off the shelf, and holds them up. "What about these?"

AT THE OTHER boutiques, Phoebe tries on dresses that hug her body. She stands in the three-way mirror of the dressing room and admires herself in a plum-colored floor-length dress. It feels good to be wearing a form-fitting dress, to see the outline of her body again.

"What do you think?" Phoebe asks Juice. She steps out of the dressing room.

"I don't know why you keep asking me that," Juice says. "I don't know what looks good on people."

Phoebe can feel Juice's embarrassment at being asked. She can feel it because Phoebe used to be embarrassed like that. That's why Phoebe was a terrible shopper—always too burdened by thoughts of future embarrassment, so she never bought anything that could potentially be considered excessive, like a dress with puffed sleeves or three drinks at a bar.

"First gut reaction."

"You look like Miss Scarlet from *Clue*," Juice says.

"Is Miss Scarlet hot?"

Juice laughs. "Oh my God, nobody from *Clue* is hot. That's so not what *Clue* is about, Phoebe."

Phoebe laughs. It feels good to hear Juice say her name.

"I'm buying it," Phoebe says.

It's an epic shopping trip. Phoebe needs practically everything. Before they are done, Phoebe has picked up five other dresses, new clothes for the week, makeup, two bathing suits, and anything else she thinks she might need while here, including a comically large sun hat that seems more like something the wedding people would wear.

"This hat should have its own police escort," Phoebe says to Juice, but Juice is by the register now and only the woman behind the desk hears her.

"You picked the prettiest one in the store," she says.

Phoebe feels guilty, because picking it up had only been a joke. The clerk stares at her with such admiring eyes, until Phoebe feels pressured into purchasing it, and outside the store, when Phoebe puts on the giant sun hat, Juice says, "Oh my God. It's so big. It's so embarrassing."

But Juice says it with a smile, like now, in the anonymity of the street, now with Phoebe's guidance, it's good to be so embarrassing. It's funny.

People on the street step out of the way to avoid brushing Phoebe's brim with their shoulders, and when they do, Juice and Phoebe look at each other and crack up.

"Make way!" Phoebe shouts, and they walk down the cobblestone.

"Clear the streets!" Juice yells.

When it begins to rain, Phoebe says, "Look, we don't even need an umbrella. You can just get under the hat."

Phoebe pulls her in close.

"I'd never carry an umbrella anyway," Juice says.

"Why not?"

"It's so embarrassing."

"To carry an umbrella?"

"It's . . . humiliating."

Phoebe is fascinated by Juice's relentless embarrassment. Phoebe wants to know everything about it, study it like a book. She is used to being around college students who are usually a bit more okay being embarrassed.

"It's humiliating to not be rained on?"

"It's humiliating to be so . . . prepared."

After, they buy lunch from a café that asks if they want collagen shots in their lattes. Phoebe likes the way the barista talks, how her voice is much louder than she expects it to be. Phoebe takes a sip of the warm coffee, and as they pass the art gallery on the way to the car, Phoebe can feel Juice's sourness return.

"I seriously just don't get why anybody cares about their car," Juice says, opening the car door. "It's just a hunk of metal."

"Some people might say that your dog was just a piece of plastic," Phoebe says.

"It's different."

"You're right. It is different," Phoebe says, "because you loved that piece of plastic."

"Yeah, fine, I loved a piece of plastic. So what!"

"Exactly!" Phoebe says. "So what? Love your piece of plastic. And let other people love their hunk of metal."

"Fine," Juice says, but she does not sound satisfied. Phoebe is not letting her do the one thing she wants to do, which is talk shit about her future stepmother.

"But I can't really talk about my mom with my dad," Juice says. "Because Lila is always there. And Lila won't let us."

"Has she ever told you not to talk about her?"

"She just gets this look on her face. And it's like we all know that if we talk about her she's going to get upset."

"She probably will get upset."

"But why? She's my *mom*. And when Lila gets upset, it's like all of a sudden, I'm not allowed to have a mom anymore. We have to pretend she never existed. My dad does, too. He's so weird around her. Like she's this queen or something. He'll like, put out a glass of white wine when she gets out of the shower, like her shower was oh so traumatic."

"That's actually nice."

"He never did that stuff with my mom."

"Maybe he became nicer after she died."

"Well, *I* didn't."

"Clearly not," Phoebe says, and Juice laughs.

"I want to be nice," Juice says. "It's just that we have nothing in common."

"You both enjoy air. And food."

"Okay, yeah fine, we both like breathing. But we don't have anything important in common."

"You're right. Air is so not important."

"Who needs air? I, personally, hate air."

Phoebe puts the keys in the ignition.

"I mean, I guess we both love all things Disney," Juice says.

"That's something," Phoebe says, and starts the car. "That's something."

For the rest of the ride, Juice asks to be quizzed on the things she knows, like the country's capitals. She has a test next week. But she also just thinks it's fun. She likes maps. She likes knowing where things are. She likes using Waze and pointing out things on the street, like the most impressive mansions. They drive out of the historic district, and Phoebe looks for a parking space that's not right in front of the sex shop. She parks two stores down in front of an animal shelter.

"Oh my God, it's fate," Juice says. "Can I get a dog?"

"That's a question for your father," Phoebe says.

"But he always says no. Lila hates dogs."

"Nobody hates dogs."

"I just want to go look."

"Trust me, there's no just looking when you're at a shelter," Phoebe says.

"But I'm ready for more than a piece of plastic."

"Okay, fine. You have ten minutes to go adore nonplastic animals."

"Aren't you coming with me?"

Phoebe is not ready for it, can't bear to see all those little animals with their noses pressed against the cages.

"I need to run this last errand. I'll meet you back at the car."

Juice claps her hands and goes alone into the shelter, while Phoebe looks down at her phone. She finally listens to the voicemail from her husband.

I don't know what you know about Harry, or where you are, but I thought I should tell you that I buried him in the backyard. Please call me back, Phoebe.

His voice—it sounds just like him, though she doesn't know why this should be surprising. It makes her cry, thinking of her husband getting the shovel, probably her father's old one that she keeps in the garage. She wonders where he buried him. By the stone near the pine?

But she doesn't call him back. She has no responsibility to make her husband feel better about anything at this point. He is her ex-husband, she repeats. Ex-husband. And she is a maid of honor. She wipes her tears, drops her phone into the purse, and walks into the sex shop.

PHOEBE HAS PASSED sex shops hundreds of times on the St. Louis highways but has never actually stopped in one. It never even occurred to her to enter, the way it never occurred to her to stop at a church. She was a married woman who never watched porn, never orgasmed theatrically, never saw a need for props. She didn't like anything too weird, she told Matt.

So she is surprised by how not weird it is inside, set up like any other store, except where the blouses should be, there are silicone vaginas. Chains on the wall. Panties everywhere.

"Can I help you?" the saleswoman asks.

"I'm looking for dick-themed flatware," Phoebe says, slightly embarrassed at first. It helps that the saleswoman is not. She looks as bored as she might working at Kohl's.

"We have straws shaped liked dicks," the woman says. "And those silicone vaginas that I guess you could like, use as a bowl or something?"

"Are the dick straws compostable?" Phoebe asks.

"No. But I think they're recyclable."

"I need compostable."

"The only thing we have that is close to being compostable is the edible underwear in the back. I mean, assuming you eat it all. Zero waste."

The whole exchange is so businesslike, Phoebe wishes she could go back and speak the same way when in bed with her husband. She wishes she could have had the courage to ask for what she wanted, even if it sounded weird. Because she is starting to suspect that she actually likes weird things. That everybody likes weird things, which is why sex shops are open in the middle of a Thursday afternoon.

She picks up the plastic penis straws and wonders if with Mia, for whatever reason, Matt can be weird. If that is why he needs her. If that is what made him feel alive again. And for the first time, the thought doesn't fill her with horror but with hope. Maybe one day she will find someone and together they will be weird.

She pays for the penis straws, as well as a few strappy red thongs simply because she imagines it's impossible not to feel sexy while wearing them.

OUTSIDE, JUICE IS not in the car. Phoebe pauses in front of the shelter, looks through the window to see Juice on a chair holding a small yellow dog. Juice looks so happy, and Phoebe decides to go in. She wants to be a part of it. It's okay, the therapist said, to want to be a part of it.

"Oh my God, Phoebe, you should come hold him!" Juice says.

So Phoebe picks up the dog. Feels the animal's soft fluffy paws. "What's your name?"

"Unfortunately, it's Frank," Juice says. "But you can change that, right?"

"Me?" Phoebe asks like this is crazy, even though she can already imagine it. This is Frank, her new dog. They'll go on long walks together. They'll go clamming in the mornings when nobody is awake. "I can't buy a dog. The hotel doesn't allow them."

"Well, someone has to buy Frank," Juice says. She points to a smaller beagle in a cage. "I've already decided I'm going to get that one."

The entire ride home, Juice tries to come up with new names for Phoebe's dog. But when they walk back into the hotel, Phoebe breaks the news.

"I don't know, Juice," she says. "I think I like the name Frank."

Before Phoebe leaves for the bachelorette party, she returns Lila's mother's outfit. She knocks on the door of the Raven.

"Thank you for letting me borrow your clothes," Phoebe says, and hands her the bag.

Patricia stands there with a cocktail in one hand, surprised, as if she truly said goodbye to the outfit in her mind and can't comprehend how it is here, back from the dead.

"Just put them there," Patricia says, pointing to the marble table where the raven sculptures sit, like that is where all the dead things must go. Phoebe puts the bag down next to the ravens, all of them turned around so they are facing the wall, like they're in trouble.

It only takes one quick glance around the room to see that the ravens are everywhere, one painted just above the bed, one sitting under the lampshade on the nightstand. Next to it, Phoebe sees two books, *How to Be Your Own Best Friend* and *We Die Alone*.

Patricia turns back to where she had been sitting, which feels like a sign that Phoebe should go, but Phoebe feels compelled to stay. Maybe this woman will die alone, but she shouldn't have to drink alone.

"May I join you for a drink?" Phoebe asks.

"You want to join *me* for a drink?" Patricia looks equally confused and delighted, like she just witnessed a sudden snowfall. "Usually Lila's friends can't get away from me fast enough. They think poor old widows are the plague."

Patricia pulls out a glass for Phoebe and opens the beverage cooler.

"I went to your gallery today," Phoebe says. "I mean, I looked in the window."

"Thirty years we've been building that collection," Patricia says.

"It must be impressive."

"At first it was just living artists. And then, as we got older, and some of those living artists, well, died, we started to branch out into dead ones. That really opened things up for us."

Now they host a huge collection of the Hudson River School paintings, not to mention one Warhol.

"You have a Warhol?"

"I should donate it to the hotel, honestly, give them something worthy to hang on the walls," she says, then looks to the painting above her bed. "Tell me, Professor, this is a death painting, is it not?"

Phoebe looks at the image of a raven perched on a dried-up orange slice.

"That is undeniably a death painting," Phoebe says.

"*Thank* you," Patricia says. "Finally, someone with a little sense. Lila refuses to acknowledge it, no surprise there. And I understand the hotel is trying to achieve some level of authenticity here, bringing in the Victorian macabre, but must they hang it right over an old woman's bed? It's hard enough getting to sleep without the bird of death watching me."

Patricia holds up a yellow bottle.

"I wasn't sure about this spicy margarita elderberry hibiscus concoction," Patricia says. "I'm quite suspicious of any cocktail with such a long name. But it's delicious."

Patricia pours her a glass.

"I'm sure Lila has told you all kinds of things about my drinking in the afternoon, even though I keep explaining to her that my doctor was the one who suggested I start day-drinking. I simply can't drink at night anymore. Just two glasses of wine at dinner, and I'll never fall asleep."

Phoebe takes the glass and sips.

"It's good," Phoebe says. "Spicy."

But Patricia is not listening.

"And honestly, what else does the girl expect me to do up here all day? She tells me I can't bring a date to my own daughter's wedding. Tells me I can't give a speech. I can't drink in the afternoons. Can't come to the bachelorette party. She expects me to just sit up here with nothing to do. I'm like Rapunzel. Except nobody wants to abduct me. And my hair hasn't grown past my ears since Bush Senior was our president."

Phoebe laughs.

"Tell me, friend of Lila's I know almost nothing about. How did I not know you before this week?"

"I'm not local," Phoebe says.

"But to never have even heard of you," Patricia says. "Lila's closest friend in the world, and I don't hear a peep? *This* is what it's been like, Pamela."

"Phoebe, actually."

"See? I don't even know your goddamned name. Ever since her father died, Lila keeps herself so buttoned up, so closed off to me. She used to tell me things. We used to be what you might call friends before her father got sick. Not that I believe in the whole mothers-and-daughters-being-best-friends thing. That's, frankly, unnatural. But I do miss her. The real Lila, the one who used to sit in my bed and talk my ear off. Do you know what a talker Lila really is?"

"I do, actually," Phoebe says.

"God, as a little girl, she was even worse. Total stream of consciousness. Like living with a little Salinger novel. When she lost her teeth, I heard every gruesome detail. When she got her period, I was the first one she told. Besides her guidance counselor, but that couldn't be helped. The whole thing happened on his chair, which is a little odd, I'm now realizing."

Patricia takes a sip.

"Wait, Lila wasn't molested by her high school guidance counselor, was she?" Patricia asks. "Is that why he's *here*?"

"Oh no. She wasn't. If she was, I doubt he'd be *here*, you know?"

"What a relief," Patricia says. "It's not easy having a daughter who's always been attracted to much older men. That girl fell in love with her sixty-year-old piano teacher when she was nine. I'm the only mother I know who had to force her own child to quit piano. And you don't have to tell me, I know it was all my fault. I, as Lila said so recently, set the tone."

"Was Henry a lot older than you?" Phoebe asks.

"Fifteen years," Patricia says. "I was twenty-six when I met him. God, such a little baby. I had no idea what I was doing, except driving my mother slowly insane. That was clear. After we got engaged, she said to me, No daughter of Paul Winthrop is marrying a Catholic who calls himself the Trash King of Rhode Island."

"That's what Henry called himself?"

"It was the name of his business. It's what everyone in Newport called Henry back then, after he started making his fortune. But my mother didn't understand. She kept asking me if he was in the Mob, and I kept telling her he was only pretending to be in the Mob. That was his entire advertising strategy, and it worked, and did my mother care that he basically built a million-dollar business in under three years?" Patricia says. "No. My mother is a true snob, and trust me, she'd take that as a compliment. She prides herself on being a snob, on telling everyone how embarrassing it was that JFK's family wore tails to the reception while Jackie's family knew to arrive in linen. But I was a kid in the sixties, you know. I didn't want to be snob. I didn't want to sit around with my mother and gossip about who didn't wear linen. I wanted to wear bell-bottoms. I wanted to be *American*. One of the people. I wanted to go to Woodstock and marry a handsome entrepreneur who seemed to have come out of the dust fields of Ohio in a cowboy hat just to save me from my horrible snobbish family. But my mother, she was not wrong about everything."

"What do you mean?"

"She kept telling me, Patricia, do not marry this man thinking he can save you from who you really are," Patricia says. "You're a Winthrop. A terrible snob, just like me. And one day, you'll wake up and you'll see the Trash King of Rhode Island for what he really is. And she was right. I did."

"What was he?"

"A mortal!" she says. "A mere human being! When the first doctor gave him three months to live, I was so shocked, I started to laugh hysterically right there in the office. I couldn't understand. My big strong Henry? I actually said, But this is the Trash King of Rhode Island! And so Lila barred me from going to the next doctor's appointment.

"God, I worshipped Henry in the beginning," she says, and smiles. "He was so exciting. A man of business, building an empire. He bought me my first painting, you know? And we'd go on these long boozy dates, and I'd listen to him talk about his landfills at dinner like he was talking about Leonardo's *Gran Cavallo*. I had no chance, really. The younger woman never has a chance. She's always doomed to worship, right from the start."

"I don't think Lila worships Gary like that, though," Phoebe says. "I really don't get that vibe."

"You should have seen when she came home from that doctor's appointment with Gary. Her eyes were glowing, Pamela."

"Phoebe."

"I'm sorry, once I decide on a name in my head, it might as well be your name," Patricia says. "It was like the girl was on drugs. She went on, telling me all about this wonderful doctor who was going to save Henry, all we needed was a little optimism like Gary. But I was under no such illusion. I knew the first doctor had been right. I knew Henry was dying. I would try to tell her that, get her ready, but she wouldn't listen. She had Gary and his second opinion."

Patricia sighs.

"She's always been like that, though," Patricia says.

"Like what?"

"Every man she dates, she thinks they're going to solve all her problems, make her this better woman, the one she ought to be. The woman she doesn't know how to make herself be. But she never got engaged to any of them. She never took it *this* far. This is just ridiculous, and it's all Henry's fault."

"Why?"

"He told her that his only dying wish was to see his little girl get married before he died. And what do you know, but a week later, they're engaged!"

"You don't think they love each other?"

"My daughter doesn't fully love people yet," Patricia says. "Not the way she will."

"What do you mean?" Phoebe asks.

"I mean she loves Gary the way that I love this cocktail. The way that I have come to love a foam body pillow. The way I loved Henry at the start, when I thought love was about getting something from people. I fell in love with what Henry gave me. And he gave me so much. He truly did. But loving someone like that doesn't make you a better woman. Only losing them does."

She wonders if this is what it's like to have a mother, to sit together, drinking in the afternoon, listening to her meandering stories about what it means to truly love. Phoebe feels like she's watching a woman write her posthumous autobiography aloud, like Patricia is the dead version of herself whose saving grace is somehow knowing everything.

"How did losing Henry make you better?" Phoebe asks.

"Henry quickly deteriorated after the first diagnosis, and I couldn't stop having this horrible feeling like I was dying, too."

At night, she stared at her sagging breasts and her blue veins and the thin skin over her hands and wondered what happened to her. How did her skin become so thin? How had she come to own so many paintings by dead artists? How had she wound up on the board of the Preservation Society? How had she come to be a woman who put on lip liner just like her mother? She had once been so young, so beautiful that an artist from her gallery asked to paint her, and why didn't she say yes?

"I had been too embarrassed then," she says. "Simply put, I thought I was fat. And I didn't think it was tasteful for a married woman to do something like that. My mother was right. I was a terrible snob. But what a shame. Because now I see that I was too young and beautiful then not to be naked all of the time."

When Patricia realized that's exactly how she would feel when she was ninety—that she was too young and beautiful at sixty not to have been naked all of the time—she reached out to the artist.

"It had been decades," Patricia says. "But I just called William like no time had passed and said, I'm ready to pose for you. God, that's what impresses me now the most. How I just did that. It felt like the boldest thing I had ever done, somehow scarier than even getting married.

"William and I didn't have an affair," she adds. "Even though I know that's what Lila must think. I just wanted him to paint me. I needed him to document my body as it was at that precise moment. Of course, I didn't realize that he had turned into a Cubist over the last thirty years. But that's beside the point. The point was to be standing there in the garden, knowing he was considering me, every muscle, every vein. To be fully seen like that. To be fully myself in front of someone else and not ashamed one bit. To feel proud, actually. *That* saved me. But let me be clear. Not from myself."

"What do you mean?" Phoebe asks.

"I didn't want to be saved from myself. Nobody does! All we want is permission to stand there naked and be our damned selves."

This sounds true to Phoebe. This sounds like exactly what she wants, what she has secretly always wanted. To read books when she wanted to read books. To be sad when she was sad. To be scared when she was scared. To be angry when she was angry. To be boring when she felt boring.

"Of course, Lila was horribly embarrassed by the painting," Patricia says. "She wouldn't talk to me for weeks after I brought it to the gallery. She was hysterical, kept saying, Dad is sick and you strip naked for another man? So I said, Honey, your father *loves* Cubism."

She laughs to herself.

"Of course now I know it took Henry his entire life to admit the truth about who he was, too," Patricia says. "I hope it doesn't take Lila that long."

She turns to Phoebe.

"Is she horribly embarrassed of me?" Patricia asks. "What a humiliating question for a mother to ask."

"She's angry at you."

Patricia nods again. "She's been angry at me ever since Henry got sick."

"And you've been angry at her."

The comment takes Patricia by surprise, as if she hadn't quite been able to admit this aloud yet.

"When Lila gave away the painting to Gary for free, what a slap in the face that was. Never mind that a William Withers painting goes for at least twenty thousand at auction these days. That painting was priceless to me. It wasn't even for sale, and she knew it. She said, Yes, you kept saying it was literally priceless, so I gave it away for free."

Patricia sighs.

"It's not easy being angry at your own creation. It's like being angry at yourself."

She worries it's her fault and that by giving Lila everything, they have given her nothing. They have stripped her of the most important thing: actual human desire. Her life has no urgency. There are no stakes.

"The girl spills a bottle of red wine on the brand-new couch, and we just get a new one. It is as simple as that. Everything is replaceable. The windows in the bedroom, the Barbies whose heads popped off sometimes for no reason I could understand, replaceable. Her world is a world of one million Barbies; a world of cartoons, where Daffy Duck can get baked into a cake or fall out of a tree and never bleed. Her father was the first thing she ever truly lost, and so what else does she do but try to immediately replace him with a man who works in corporeal waste management."

She finishes off her cocktail.

"Anyway. Nothing can be done now. The past is like the *Gran Cavallo* and you can't fix the *Gran Cavallo*, right? I mean, sure, who doesn't fantasize about drawing in the rest of the horse, and maybe the sky around the horse. But what would the painting be worth then? Absolutely nothing. So it is what it is. Imperfect, unfinished, forever. We just have to move on, call it a masterpiece, even if it's not, and start working on a new goddamned painting."

"I suppose I didn't realize that's what it would feel like getting older," Phoebe confesses. She always imagined getting older as a narrowing street that got darker as you walked. A concretization of your personality and all the things that made you who you were. "But it's not, is it?"

Patricia shakes her head.

"Pamela, it is *all* about moving on. Saying goodbye to whoever you thought you were, whoever you thought you would be. Let me demonstrate."

She gets up, opens the bag of clothes. Holds up her sweater to the light.

"Henry was always trying to make me a sequins gal, but now that he's gone, I can finally admit, I am not a sequins gal. So, goodbye."

She drops the shirt in Phoebe's lap.

"In full disclosure, I'm not a sequins gal, either," Phoebe says. "I mean, it was fun for a day."

"It was fun for a life," Patricia says. "But now I wear linen and drink in the afternoon, and so be it. Because when did afternoons get so long? I mean, Christ, let's just get on with the evening, shall we?"

The bachelorette party begins with a "water journey" at a nearby spa.

"I just wish they wouldn't call it a water journey," Marla says, standing in the changing room. "Then I could actually enjoy it."

"Shh," Suz says, and points to a sign on the door demanding that they whisper at all times. Not just for other guests, but for themselves. This is proving to be tricky for Marla and Lila, though.

"This is sort of like the hot springs in Baden-Baden, except not," Lila says.

"Shouldn't we be allowed to have our phones if this is our own personal journey?" Marla asks.

Phoebe waits for Lila to respond but then remembers that Lila almost never speaks directly to Marla, just stands there and lets Marla say whatever she wants.

"You can't heal and sext at the same time," Phoebe says. Phoebe meant this as a joke, but Suz takes it literally.

"Marla, oh my God, you *sext*?" Suz asks.

"Don't we all sext?" Nat asks.

"Do we?" Lila asks, looking off-balance in her tiny body and giant fake veil.

"Shh," Marla says and gives Phoebe a look. But Phoebe has no time for it.

"Okay, so the woman at check-in told me we're allowed to go in naked since this is a private event," Phoebe whispers.

"Why would we want to be naked?" Marla asks.

"Why wouldn't we want to be naked?" Suz whispers.

While the women debate in loud and hushed tones, Phoebe just takes off her clothes. She quotes Patricia without quoting Patricia.

"We're too young not to be naked all of the time," Phoebe says, and the women all disrobe, except for Marla.

"Marla, come on," Suz insists as they enter the pool area. "If you're not naked, that somehow makes us more naked."

"You can't be more or less naked than naked," Marla says.

"So, those over there are the cold pools," Phoebe whispers. "Fifty-five degrees."

"Sounds painful," Marla says.

"Apparently," Phoebe says, reading from the literature, "cold pools help with inflammation, boost your immune system, cure your depression—"

"Fix your relationship with your mother-in-law," Suz adds.

"And sometimes go grocery shopping for you," Nat adds.

The women all separate into different tubs, each going on their own journey. Or maybe they just want an excuse to have some time alone. Marla goes to the hottest pool, and Phoebe gets in the cold one simply because it's the one that promises to cure depression, though she knows that's not how depression works. There is no quick fix, and sometimes trying to fix it only made it worse. Going to yoga three times a week only confirmed that she was truly a lost cause since not even yoga could make her feel better. But what else can a person do except keep trying? And the cold pool is easy enough. All she has to do is sit in it and be cold. Success, she thinks, as her toes start to go numb. She can feel herself start to relax, until Lila joins her.

"Gary's mother cornered me for the third time this morning and asked why God has not yet made an appearance at this wedding," Lila whispers as soon as she gets in. "I was like, Oh no, I completely forgot to invite him."

Lila says it hasn't been easy being so annoyed with a woman who has the beginnings of dementia.

"It feels truly evil to get mad at her," Lila says. "But how many times do I have to explain that I'm godless? That I can't get married at a church, because what church? I don't have a church!"

She said she doesn't believe in anything, except money. And what's so bad about that? Money keeps the mansions upright on Bellevue, does it not? Money makes art, does it not? Money makes the world handicapped accessible, does it not? Did God do that? Maybe. If God made money.

"But Gary's mother thinks that the marriage will be invalid unless I do it at a church. And who knew Gary's family was *that* Catholic? Like, Marla and Gary never talk about God. They must be traumatized or something."

Phoebe looks at her. "You're paying a lot of money to relax right now. I suggest you try."

"I've never been very comfortable relaxing," Lila says. But then she slips a little farther into the water. "What do we do, just like, sit here? It's so cold. Marla's right. I don't get it."

"Take a breath," Phoebe says.

The pool is so cold, the shock of it hasn't worn off yet. But Phoebe likes the shock—likes how it reminds her she's alive.

"Oh, remind me to tell you about my dream later," Lila says. "It was about Jim. And it was *awful*."

"Take another breath," Phoebe says, and so Lila takes a deep breath. She leans her head back. She doesn't seem to care that the hem of her fake veil sits in the water. Soon, the whole room quiets down, and it feels nice again. There is only the sound of water, dripping from each woman as they get out of a pool and into another. There is, finally, peace. Quiet unity among them as they silently pass each other until their journeys are complete.

By THE TIME they return to the hotel, Phoebe feels truly relaxed. So does Lila, whose face looks lost in some dream. When she is stopped by Jim in the lobby, it takes her a long moment to figure out what he's saying.

"We have a problem," Jim says. He has the red face of a man who has either been drinking all day or golfing all day or both. "Somebody fucked the vintage car in the parking lot."

Nobody understands what this means, especially not the bride.

"Somebody fucked it up?" Lila asks.

"No. Somebody fucked it."

The other women give Lila a little wave goodbye like this is none of their business. Suz mouths, *Shower*, before they all take off, but Lila doesn't notice.

"I hear the words you are saying, Jim, but I truly don't understand," Lila says.

"I truly don't know how else to say it, Lila. That's what happened. The vintage car was . . . fucked."

Lila stands there as if he just tossed a bucket of red paint on her.

"Right," Phoebe interjects. "But I think our confusion is . . . what does that mean exactly?"

"Somebody literally stuck their dick in the tailpipe and ya know."

"Ya *know*?" Lila asks.

"Ya know," Jim says.

"Why would anyone do that to my *wedding* car?"

"Why would anyone do that to any car?" Jim asks.

"*How* does someone do that?" Phoebe is genuinely curious. She's having trouble visualizing it, when Gary walks in with his golf clubs. Lila goes to him at once.

"Somebody fucked our car, Gary," Lila says.

"Excuse me?" Gary asks.

He sets down the clubs, and a man in burgundy takes them away.

"Tell him, Jim," Lila says, as if she had been there when it happened, as if now in front of Gary who knows nothing, Jim and Lila are the couple, the bearers of bad news, telling Gary what happened.

"Well, I was putting my clubs back into my car, and I saw the car just sitting there in the sunlight, and I thought, God, now that's a beautiful vehicle," Jim says.

"Jim, you don't need to set the scene," Lila says.

"I literally said one sentence," Jim says.

"Well, it was a run-on," Lila says. "Just get to the point."

"I would already be at the point, if you hadn't interrupted."

"Okay, so just tell me what happened," Gary says.

"So I was just standing there, looking at the car, admiring it, and then this guy just came into focus, standing right behind the car, with his thing in the tailpipe, and you know, it's been a long day, I thought I was hallucinating for a second. But then I yelled at him to get the hell out of here, and he bolted."

Gary doesn't look horrified, but Phoebe is learning that Gary never reacts wildly to any situation. It seems important to him, as a doctor, as the only parent, to be presented with a problem and immediately go on a search for a solution. Like okay, yes, the car was fucked, but luckily he had prepared for this.

"We should tell the front desk," Gary says.

"What's the front desk going to do?" Jim asks.

"Call the police!" Lila says.

"And say what, Help, someone fucked my car?" Jim asks.

"I'm sorry, but I just don't think you can *fuck* a car," Phoebe says. She will die on this hill. "It's a car. It can't be fucked the way . . . a lawn mower can't be fucked because it's a lawn mower and not a living being."

But Lila is not persuaded. She sits down on the velvet couch. Another thing ruined, just when she was starting to relax. She presses her fingers to her temples. Gary sits down next to her.

"I'm sort of having a panic attack," Lila says.

"A real one? Or a figurative one?" Gary asks.

"A real one, Gary."

But she doesn't move or do anything at all. She just stoically shifts the hair out of her eyes. Reframes the veil around her face. The world's classiest panic attack.

"What can I do?" Gary asks.

"I need you to ask Pauline for a different car," Lila says.

"A new car?" Jim asks. "Why? That car is perfect."

"The car has been *fucked*, Jim!" Lila says, but it's Gary who flinches. "I can't take that thing to our wedding, knowing what happened to it."

"I mean, technically, the car is kind of the victim here," Jim says.

"*I* am the victim here," Lila says sternly.

Nobody speaks. Jim looks at Gary with raised eyebrows. But Gary doesn't return the expression. Doesn't say a word. Just puts his arm around her like he did when Juice melted down on the wharf.

"Okay," Gary says. "I'll take care of it."

"Good." Lila adjusts her veil again, as if this will transform her back into the relaxed and happy bride who had not yet walked into the lobby. "I need to go get dressed for my bachelorette party."

Lila walks away into the elevator. Jim and Gary and Phoebe all look at one another.

"Jim, why did you tell her that?" Gary asks.

"Because it happened!"

"Lila doesn't need to know every single thing that goes wrong."

"She's not a child."

"I know she's not a child," Gary says. "She's an adult who is now stressed out for no reason. Like she would have even known?"

"She'd find out eventually."

"How? No. She really wouldn't have."

"It'll be fine," Jim says. "I'll handle it."

"No, I'll handle it," Gary says.

"Fine, I'll go back outside. See if I can find this pervert."

Jim leaves Gary and Phoebe alone in the lobby. The groom and the maid of honor, left to handle the situation, and it gives Phoebe the feeling that they are Lila's parents now.

"I honestly still don't get it, though," Phoebe says. "Is the tailpipe even the right size for that?"

"I guess it depends on the guy."

"I guess he'd have to have like . . . used his hand first and then go into it?"

"Because you can't like, use it as a . . ."

"No."

"Shit."

They laugh. Lila's grandmother walks in.

"Gary," Bootsie says, and she hands him a Tupperware container full of clear liquid.

For a second, Gary looks horrified, like it might be a urine sample.

"It's a gimlet," Bootsie says. "Can you make sure this gets to the Breakers for the reception?"

"Of course," Gary says. "But that's days away, Bootsie. And you know they can make you a gimlet at the wedding."

"I make it a rule not to trust anything that comes out of the Breakers," she says. "And nobody makes it like my guy. He's only had forty years of practice. And who are you, my dear?"

"I'm Phoebe," she says. "The maid of honor."

Lila's grandmother accepts this. Funny how people just believe you are who you say you are, Phoebe thinks. She's not sure why she never realized this power that she had before. But it's true. She is the maid of honor. She puts her hand on Gary's shoulder and says, "I'll handle it," and Gary mouths, *Thank you.*

"Excuse me," Phoebe says to Pauline at the front desk. "It seems that the bride will need a new car."

"Is there something wrong with it?" Pauline asks.

She can see Jim's problem: "Made love" is too weird. "Had sex with" doesn't capture the spirit of the crime.

"Someone fucked it," Phoebe says.

Pauline does not even blink, not even when one of her fake eyelashes falls off. She just continues to stand there, as if she is in the middle of training herself never to have another reaction again.

"That's . . . highly unusual. We are very sorry for that. We will . . . make a note of it. None of our cars have ever . . . We'll arrange for a new one right away. Oh, and please tell the bride that the Commodore's Punch Bowl tonight is on me."

Phoebe leaves and wonders how long Pauline will wait before she reaches out to pick up her eyelashes.

UPSTAIRS, PHOEBE TAKES a long shower to wash off the oils from the spa. Water—she can't get enough of it this week. She is sure that she could live forever if she could always be in this shower. She turns off all the lights and scrubs herself with something called Oat Milk Soap for Human Beings. It works. She sits on the watery floor and feels more like a human being than she has in years.

She puts on her dress and then applies the makeup she bought earlier. She used to feel some kind of professorial obligation to despise the stuff, but if she is being honest with herself, she likes putting on makeup. She missed it during the pandemic. It's a nice ritual, and if you do anything enough, that's what it becomes. A ritual that has the power to make you feel something. She spreads the bold red stick across her lips, and she feels suddenly awake, ready for the evening.

DOWNSTAIRS AT THE bar, the women are clumped around Lila. They look bright against the dark-blue drapes, their cocktail dresses like different lollipops. But when Phoebe joins them, the mood is heavy.

"Do you think it had something to do with how beautiful the car was?" Suz asks.

"Like that's why a person chooses to fuck some cars over others?" Nat wonders.

The women don't know. None of them can begin to understand the psychology of car-fucking, except for Marla.

"That's not how it works," Marla says. "It has nothing to do with how hot the car is."

"Can we not talk about the car?" Lila asks, with a new edge to her voice. She sounds like the Lila that Phoebe first met in the elevator.

"Let's get some cocktails and bring them upstairs for the Sex Woman," Phoebe says.

"Where's the Drink Concierge?" Lila asks.

Suz gets a text, which is a public event for all of them, because she insists on keeping the phone face up on the table at all times.

"Ugh. I don't know why my husband keeps texting me every little detail about the Little Worm's shit," Suz says. "Like he thinks I must know, right now, about what color it is. I'm at a bachelorette party!"

But it doesn't feel like one until Ryun arrives with five glasses of the Commodore's Punch. Lila looks relieved. She sips her cocktail, while Marla asks Ryun, "What's the difference between a Drink Concierge and a bartender?" and "Why the *u*?"

"Guess my parents thought it'd be more original," Ryun says.

"Ugh. Why does everybody need to be so original these days?" Lila asks.

"Just wanted me to be special, I suppose."

"But that's the worst part!" Lila says. "Why were they so afraid that you *wouldn't* be special? Why couldn't you just be an ordinary baby?"

Ryun shrugs. He doesn't know. "Turns out the joke's on them because I'm not very special."

Ryun is a surfer. Works here to support his lifestyle.

"I have literally no other ambition than that," he says. He doesn't even want to be a professional surfer. He is realistic. He knows that's no life. He just wants to . . . do it.

"Well, good for you," Lila says. "Don't make anything of yourself. My mother wanted me to be special, too. She expects me to be her grand masterpiece. And she's not even a painter!"

Ryun laughs, looks at her in her big fake veil and glittering sash. "You seem pretty special."

Lila's cheeks flush like she is already drunk, and maybe she is. "Thanks."

Marla gives Ryun a death stare for flirting with the bride. Phoebe holds up her glass.

"A toast to the bride," Phoebe says, and Lila smiles. "Now let's go see the Sex Woman."

THE SEX WOMAN is already in the billiards room when they arrive.

"You're late," she says.

She stands behind a giant projector in a taupe suit and a low ponytail. She reminds Phoebe of her old self in the classroom, secretly angry at all the late students but trying desperately not to seem so. Maybe this is why Phoebe apologizes.

"Very, very sorry," Phoebe says.

They sit down on the teal couch with their drinks. Lila gives them all a big smile, like she is better now. Ready to have some fun.

"Good evening, ladies," the Sex Woman says. "And who is the special bride tonight?"

Lila raises her hand and the women cheer.

"Well, congratulations," the Sex Woman says. "As you likely know, I'm a former colleague of Viv's. We worked together not long ago while I was at the Atlanta Zoo."

They all nod like they knew this.

"But ever since the pandemic, I've obviously made a bit of a career shift. Turns out there's more money in bachelorette parties than the nonprofit sector," she jokes, and everyone laughs. "But more seriously, in case Viv didn't tell you, let me introduce myself. I am the world's foremost international mating expert for the *Ailuropoda melanoleuca*, otherwise known as the giant panda. I have been the chief consultant to three national zoos. I have appeared on two different PBS conservation specials and have personally participated in the sexual intercourse of at least four pandas across the world."

Nat and Suz laugh. Marla looks at Phoebe and nods her head, as if she's genuinely impressed by the Sex Woman's credentials. But Lila looks confused, whispers, "Is this Viv's idea of a joke?" and they shrug. Phoebe suspects that if they were in grade school, this is when they would break into uncontrollable laughter. But they don't. They are adult women. It does not feel right to make fun of any woman standing before them, not to mention pandas. It feels more like she's at an academic conference and should raise her hand, inquire about the pandas. But it's Marla who does it.

"You participated in panda sex?" Marla asks. "What does that mean?"

"Good question," the Sex Woman says. She pulls up the first slide. "This is Mei Mei."

She points to a sad photograph of a panda holding a single stalk of bamboo.

"I helped Mei Mei make love for the first time, probably one of the biggest achievements on my CV to date. For seven years, Mei Mei showed no interest in mating with the other pandas at the Atlanta Zoo. Our research suggests this is largely due to being in a state of captivity. In captivity, the giant panda has forgotten how to have sex. By trying to protect the pandas, we have nearly killed them."

More photos of pandas in separate rooms. Pandas looking forlorn.

"This is actually very upsetting," Suz whispers.

Phoebe is concerned, too. Phoebe wonders when she will break character, morph into the opposite of herself, rip out her low ponytail, pass out vibrators for each of them, like the stripper cop who arrives at the bachelor party angry and ready to make arrests, just before she removes her pants.

But maybe this is not a character? Maybe she's truly just here to talk about pandas. Maybe Viv was a terrible maid of honor. Phoebe should have asked the Sex Woman on the phone what it meant to be a Sex Woman. But it's too late now. Lila is staring at the Sex Woman like this is the worst kind of Sex Woman out there: the boring kind.

"During the pandemic, when we were all stuck at home every day, I realized that we, too, were in captivity. And just like Mei Mei, I, too, stopped wanting to have sex. And the only thing that carried me through this dark time was believing that there were other miserable and sexless folks out there who felt the same."

She started hosting Zoom sex workshops, sharing her research, her discoveries. Clips from her workshops went viral, and by the time the pandemic was over, she had helped millions of people around the world want sex again.

"What we've learned from studying pandas in captivity is that they are, essentially, trapped in paradise. There is too much leisure, too much comfort, too much bamboo. Too much ESPN, if you know what I mean."

Suz nods knowingly.

"The males stopped trying and the females no longer rubbed their anal glands over nearby trees like they did in the wild," the Sex Woman adds, and Suz stops nodding. "All their needs were met. There was no flirtation, no foreplay, no delicate dance, because through captivity, we eliminated almost all of the natural Darwinian factors in panda mating. What we know now, what we all know now, is that we can't just put two animals in a room and expect them to have sex. We can't even expect them to want it. So why do we expect this of ourselves?"

The Sex Woman, and her colleagues, spent years teaching the pandas how to remember to want it.

"We showed them videos of other pandas mating," the Sex Woman says. "Videos to stimulate them."

"Like panda porn?" Suz asks.

"Yes."

"Do pandas actually get turned on when they watch other pandas have sex?" Nat asks.

"Of course."

"That's kind of beautiful," Suz says and looks at the rest of the group. But Lila is unmoved.

"It's not beautiful," Lila insists. "It's porn, Suz."

"Yeah, but *panda* porn."

"Porn is not suddenly beautiful just because two bears are doing it," Lila says.

"Are there . . . like . . . panda storylines?" Marla asks.

"Two pandas, one a billiards champion and the other needs to learn," Nat says.

This was eerily close to a video Phoebe had caught Matt watching once. When she found him, she made it a point to join in on it, because he was so embarrassed to be caught. So they sat there and watched it and they critiqued the plot as if they were critiquing a television show—as if they didn't enjoy it at all. But at some point during the billiards game, they fell silent. They watched as the man went up behind the blonde and stroked her arm, put her on the table. And Matt reached out for Phoebe. They had good sex for the first time in months, but after, Matt never brought it up again. Neither did she.

"You joke, but for pandas, it's the matter of their continued survival," the Sex Woman says. "And for you as well, no?"

The women nod.

"So, bride-to-be, this brings me to you," the Sex Woman says.

"How in the world does this bring you to me?" Lila asks.

"Before you enter into your captivity, I mean, marriage," she says, and winks, "I am here to give you the skills you need to make sure you always want it with your husband. I want you to leave here knowing that you will have not just a good sex life but the longest, and the wettest, and the hottest sex with your man."

But first, she needs a little information.

"What's his name again?"

"Gary."

Then she asks Lila to describe her current sex life with Gary in one word.

"That's so personal," Lila says.

"That's what we're here to be, my bride," the Sex Woman says.

"Okay, well, wonderful," Lila admits.

"Wonderful!" the Sex Woman says, then asks the other women to do the same.

"Evolving," Nat says.

"Verbal," Marla says.

"Dead," Suz says.

"Germinating," Phoebe says.

"Now, I want you to think about the last time you got really turned on. See if you can locate what it was that got you so turned on. What made you really want to have sex? Not because your partner wanted to, and not because it had been weeks and you started to worry about how it had been weeks. But because you were overcome with desire. Because you didn't want to do anything else but fuck."

Then the Sex Woman passes out pieces of paper. They all write things down, and eventually, the Sex Woman says, "Let's start with the bride. What was the last thing that really turned you on about Gary?"

Lila blushes and looks at Marla. "I can't say with Marla here."

"I am very aware that Gary's a human being who has sex," Marla says. "In fact, I caught him once."

But Lila looks flustered. The difference between Lila inside Phoebe's hotel room and Lila outside Phoebe's hotel room is becoming jarring to Phoebe. Phoebe has become used to Lila's honesty, the storming in, the sitting down, the immediate confession about whatever it was that was making her unhappy. It made Phoebe feel like a priest or a therapist. But out here, around these women, Lila is private. Guarded. Like it's too difficult to be honest in front of Marla. Or maybe there is something about her sex life that she is terribly embarrassed about. But what is it?

"Oh, don't be a bore," Nat says. "This is *your* sex workshop, by the way."

"Okay, fine, he's a really good kisser," Lila says.

"Can you be more specific about that?" the Sex Woman asks. "Do you remember a specific kiss? Was there anything special about it? Was it passionate? Did he use tongue?"

"Like a regular amount of tongue."

But then her face gets red, like she's already admitted too much.

"Why don't I move on," the Sex Woman says, and turns to Suz, who talks at length about a man she met at her college reunion, a man who used to tease her, a man who knew her before the Little Worm. Then Nat says something about her wife, Laurel, gardening, the dirt on her face, the passion she had for doing something totally unnecessary.

"The last time I was really turned on, I was being choked," Marla says.

"Robert chokes you? I seriously cannot picture that," Lila says.

"*Not* Robert," Marla says, and then bursts out crying. "Robert would *never* choke me. Not even when I asked."

Robert is a man who uses bullet points on his Valentine's Day cards to explain the three reasons why he loves her, and they aren't even all that nice. He is a man who is pathologically incapable of complimenting her.

"And do you know what it's like to never be complimented by your own husband?" Marla asks. "I always thought it was because he was a judge. He was like, professionally neutral. But then we're at this work thing and I'm talking to this other judge, and he compliments my dress, like no big deal, and the next thing I know, we're at his house on the Chesapeake, watching the midterm primaries—"

They burst into laughter. "Hot," Suz says.

"I personally like to get choked while watching C-SPAN," Nat says.

"Samesies," Suz says. "But wait, how did he choke you?"

"He just reached out his hand and choked me."

"I seriously do not get the appeal," Lila says.

The Sex Woman reminds them all not to judge. "This is just about sharing," she says. "Keeping in touch with our desires."

She turns to Phoebe. "And what about you?"

"I was talking to a total stranger," Phoebe says. "It was the first time I really wanted to have sex after I got divorced."

"Wait, you're divorced?" Lila asks.

"How do you not know that?" Marla asks. "She's your maid of honor."

"Let's focus less on the divorce and more on what turned you on about this stranger?" the Sex Woman says.

"I don't know," Phoebe says. She thinks back to that night, that moment of sitting with him in the pink light of dawn. How when she told him she had come here to kill herself, he did not look away. "I liked that he made eye contact."

"Eye contact can be very sexy."

"He wasn't afraid of looking at me. He wasn't afraid of what I was saying. He wasn't afraid of the worst parts of me. And this made me feel like those parts were okay. Like I could say anything. Be anything."

The memory makes Phoebe smile, and the Sex Woman becomes curious. "What is making you smile right now?"

"I actually told him I wanted to fuck, and that should have been embarrassing, but it was really hot."

"Announcing our own desires," the Sex Woman says. "That can be very powerful. And now you know this about yourself. Now you know that when you are not in the mood, whenever you are starting to feel disconnected from yourself, you can ask yourself: What are you not being honest about?"

For the rest of the hour, the Sex Woman shows them short tutorials on how to touch themselves with various herbal lubricants, then concludes with a video of two pandas humping.

"May you all know such carnal bliss," the Sex Woman jokes, and the women laugh and clap. Then the Sex Woman unceremoniously dumps a bunch of sex toys on the coffee table. One of the dicks rolls onto the ground.

"A vibrator can be a memory tool," the Sex Woman says.

She tells them that, like the pandas, it's important to stay in communication with their desires. Important to recognize their kinks when they start to show themselves. Important to touch our bodies if we have forgotten what it feels like to be touched. Then she looks at her watch. In only this way, she is like a stripper. Loyal to the minute hand of the clock.

"My hour is up!" She shuts down the projector. "Now, who wants to buy a dick?"

The women laugh. They all reach out, and Phoebe picks up a purple one.

"I almost forgot!" the Sex Woman says. "The complimentary Cum Rags."

Suz holds one in her hand like it's cashmere. "Wow—such a good idea."

"So environmental," Nat says.

"WHY WOULD VIV hire *that* Sex Woman?" Lila asks at the restaurant.

"From what you used to tell us about Viv, it's *so* like Viv to hire her," Suz says.

They are having dinner at the White Horse Tavern. The oldest tavern in America, according to the menu. Dark green walls, high-back chairs, and thick wooden beams, yet food that is perfectly on trend. Shaved brussels sprouts and cabbage salads. Scallops in lemon herb sauce. Twin lobster tails on Phoebe's plate. The house wine sits on the table in clear jugs, like they are Romans. It's a little watered down and warm, but that seems to be the point.

"But we're like, *not* pandas," Lila says. "Like now when I have sex, all I'm going to think about is being a panda. I don't see how that's going to help anything."

"I thought she was great," Nat says. "You just didn't share anything, so she couldn't help you."

"Why do I need help?" Lila says. "Our sex life is good."

Everyone is getting bored of Lila's refusal to say anything real. Marla turns to Phoebe and says, "So why did you get divorced?"

"You can't just ask someone that," Nat says.

"It's okay," Phoebe says. "My husband had an affair."

"Asshole," they all say in unison, except Marla.

"And you couldn't forgive him?" Marla asks.

"He didn't even ask me to," Phoebe says.

"Are *you* going to get a divorce?" Suz asks Marla.

"I don't think we should be talking about divorce," Lila reminds them.

"Right," Suz says. "Okay. So, uh, what's the weirdest thing you've ever done in bed? Me first."

Then Suz admits that once she sort of liked it when this guy in college poured hot wax on her.

"I wasn't against it, but I wasn't really for it," Suz says.

Nat once pretended to be a nurse/tennis player in front of the camera for a college girlfriend, but only because it was her camera and she could delete the footage.

"A nurse and a tennis player at the same time?" Suz asks.

"A true theatrical challenge," Phoebe says.

They laugh.

"That's what she wanted," Nat says. "An athletic nurse. Someone who can both be sporty and save lives."

"What about you, Lila?" Nat asks.

"From the groom," the waiter says, and interrupts with a bottle of wine that Gary had handpicked and delivered for Lila's party. They all clap as the old man pours the wine into the glasses.

"Gary is so sweet," Suz says. "Marc would never do that."

"So?" Nat asks Lila. "What's the weirdest thing you've ever done?"

"I really don't feel comfortable saying with Marla here."

"Is it really that weird?" Nat asks.

"I'm not surprised," Suz says. "All doctors are weird in bed."

"All doctors are not weird in bed," Lila says. "You can't just say things like that."

"Trust me, I slept with a lot of doctors during med school," Suz says. "And they were all so bored of bodies, they always needed something extra."

"Gary is so not like that," Lila says.

"Then what is he like?" Suz asks.

"Just share with us," Nat says. "We're just trying to know you better. That's all."

"Okay, well," Lila says, seemingly touched. "Gary's just really sweet. The last time we had sex, Gary stopped halfway through to tell me that I looked so beautiful in the sunlight, I was like a Vermeer painting."

The table is silenced.

"That's not weird," Nat says.

"That's like, really beautiful," Suz says.

"It would seriously take Robert two decades of therapy to ever say something like that," Marla says.

"Well, I told you, we don't do anything weird!" Lila says.

"It's not even close to weird."

"Why does our sex have to be weird? It's not like it's more special the weirder it is. Can't I just have beautiful sex and be happy about it?"

"I don't know," Nat says. "*Can* you be happy about it?"

"What is that supposed to mean?" Lila asks.

"You just don't sound that happy about your beautiful sex," Nat says.

Lila looks at Phoebe like she's sending Phoebe a private message. Asking her with her eyes to end this conversation.

"Oh, I forgot!" Phoebe says.

Phoebe pulls out the pack of penis straws and puts them in the wine-glasses. But the glasses are too short, the straws too long, the dicks too heavy. They look perpetually at risk of falling out of the glasses. They look wrong, too neon and vulgar for this quiet rustic tavern. The waiter eyes them suspiciously when he clears the plates, but Lila looks pleased by them. Pleased that sex is just a stupid joke again among friends. She leans in and takes a sip from the dick.

"It's a real bachelorette party now," Lila says.

But Marla reminds them that Gary bought this Bordeaux. Went to an actual award-winning vineyard to research it and pick it out.

"I refuse to suck a fifty-year-old bottle of Bordeaux through a neon-green dick," Marla says. "This wine is meant to be savored."

"Suck it slowly then," Nat says, and everyone laughs.

"What would you think of men who drank beer out of plastic vaginas?" Marla asks.

"Can we not talk about sex?" Lila asks, as she takes a big sip from the tiny dick. "It's so . . . historic here. I feel we should be talking about like . . . something meaningful."

"Okay, like what?" Suz asks.

"Like Cubism," Lila says.

"You want to talk about Cubism?" Nat asks.

"What is Cubism?" Suz asks.

"It's honestly not all that interesting," Phoebe says.

"Oh good, of course Phoebe knows. Say something about Cubism," the bride demands.

They all look at her. Phoebe laughs a little. Cubism facts on demand.

"Well, it was an artistic and intellectual movement in the early twentieth century," Phoebe says. "They believed if you aren't seeing something from all sides, you aren't seeing it fully. Should I seriously go on?"

"God no," Suz says, but the bride nods.

BACK AT THE hotel, the bridesmaids meet in the blue parlor for the in-house tarot reader.

"I'm Thyme," says a woman sitting behind a glowing candle. Then she turns to the bride. "Would the bride like to go first?"

Lila nods, and Nat and Suz clap.

"Come with me," Thyme says.

Outside the parlor, the bridesmaids take a breath in the hallway. Then like in the spa, they all go on their separate journeys. Suz calls her husband. Nat goes to her room for a power nap. Marla looks at Phoebe and says, "Drink?"

As soon as they sit down, Marla wastes no time.

"Do you hate me because I had an affair like your ex-husband?" Marla looks at Phoebe as if she's waiting to be condemned.

Phoebe doesn't nod or shake her head. "I don't hate you. You're not my ex-husband. And honestly, I don't even hate him."

"That's a relief."

"To be honest, the only reason I'd hate you is that you aren't very kind to Lila."

Marla nods. "It's true."

"If you bothered getting to know her, you'd realize she's actually an interesting person," Phoebe says. "And a good friend."

"That's very hard to picture."

"You make her nervous," Phoebe says. "She's different around you."

"Look, I know she's your friend or whatever," Marla says. "But I don't have to like her just because she's marrying my brother. She's so spoiled. And ridiculous."

"Well, you're mean," Phoebe says. "And having an affair."

"See, you do hate me for it," Marla says. "And I don't blame you. I hate me for it. Some days, I just can't believe I did that to Robert."

"So why did you?"

"I felt like I would die if I didn't."

Twenty years of attending events together, twenty years of her husband looking at her in her dress and saying, "Not so shabby."

"So the judge had something that your husband didn't?" Phoebe asks.

But Marla doesn't see it that way. She can see now that it wasn't really about either of them.

"It was more about what *I* didn't have," Marla says. "According to our therapist, at least. The affair is the easy way out—the fantasy of believing someone else can give you what you don't know how to give yourself."

Phoebe imagines this is likely true about her husband.

"I think my husband fantasized about losing control," Phoebe says. Her husband, so tightly wound, like his belt. A man who would only eat Oreos in private. "He couldn't loosen up fully around me, and I don't know why."

"But that doesn't mean it's your fault," Marla says. "It's his fault. For not being able to do that. For not asking for whatever it was he needed from you."

"I am starting to see that, I guess," Phoebe says.

"I'm learning how to ask Robert for compliments. And he says he can't, so the therapist suggested we start sexting. Like some kind of gateway drug into real compliments. And now I'm on the path to forgiving Robert and Robert is on the path to forgiving me," Marla says. "That's how the therapist describes it. And when we get to the end of the path, I guess we're allowed to start having real sex again."

She's worried about how long this path will be.

"We've only been sexting since Tuesday and I've already run out of ways to describe my vagina," Marla says. "It's also very difficult sexting with one hand."

"Is it working?" Phoebe asks.

"Inconclusive," Marla says. "Mostly we just say filthy things to each other in between other very practical things, like, Suck my balls, dirty girl, and then, Did the guy come to check out the dishwasher leak?"

They laugh. "That's marriage," Phoebe says.

Phoebe thinks back to the failed sext she sent her husband, how scared she had been, how afraid. Phoebe feels such tenderness for that person who pressed Send.

"Do you regret it?" Phoebe asks.

"I regret hurting Robert," Marla says. "I regret lying. I regret that I'm going to have to resign. But even before the affair, the trust was already gone. We were fooling ourselves to think it wasn't. We had hurt each other in a million ways over the years, but then pretended like we hadn't. The affair just brought all of that to the surface. And now look at us! We're sexting! Look! My husband is telling me that he wants to pound my pussy as we speak!"

She holds up the phone.

"Progress," Marla says. "Maybe when he gets here, we can actually have sex. That's what I'm hoping for."

By the time it's Phoebe's turn to meet Thyme on the yellow couch, the candle is melted.

"It'll still work, even without the candle," Thyme says. Thyme picks up the cards. "Do you have a question for me?"

"Oh," Phoebe says. "I haven't really thought of one."

"We can do a general time period, if you like."

"No," Phoebe says. She wants to have a question. "I guess I've been wondering what to do."

"About what?"

"About anything. Like, where do I go from here? What's next?"

She hasn't yet let herself think about it—what happens after the wedding is over. Where does Phoebe go?

"Okay," Thyme says. She pulls the cards. "Oh, wow. So the two cards I thought might appear appeared. The children and the career card. The Ten of Pentacles—it's a card where she's very focused on the pentacles. There's no other focus. It's one thing or the other for you, it seems. Which means you have probably been facing a big decision. Does that seem right to you?"

"It does."

"The Empress is on her way out, so to me that reads as pregnancy is on the way out. This is tarot, okay, it's your life, only you know, but what I am seeing is that children are not happening for you right now."

Phoebe nods.

"But you have here the Hermit card. Your card. That's you."

"That doesn't sound good."

"That's a great sign, actually. I am really happy to see that, because that means that no matter what happens, you will always be here."

She feels embarrassed at how quickly this has moved her. She doesn't even believe it, and yet it's affecting her. Sort of like watching horror movies that you know are fake, and yet you pull the blanket over your eyes every time someone gets stabbed. It feels so real.

"I'm seeing the Hanged Man," Thyme says. "Your soulmate? He is hesitant. Or you are. One of you is stepping back. One of you is concerned. You've had a big conversation, it seems? Something has been decided?"

"Yes."

"Whatever it was, here is the Eight of Wands. That means moving. Travel. You are going to be moving. Not *Eat Pray Love*-style. No. I am sorry, you will not be going to India. I am not seeing India in your future. But you may do something else. Something smaller. You may . . . buy a small property. And this property, it has something to do with money. It is a lot of money or there's money in it. I'm not sure."

It is no small thing to hear this woman reimagine a future for her. It doesn't matter if it turns out to be true. It doesn't matter if it's bullshit. It doesn't matter that Thyme is actually, as she confesses at some point, an aspiring writer trying to sell historical fiction about the American Revolution. For so long, Phoebe could not imagine another possible future for herself, and she marvels at how easily this woman conjures up a new property for her. It is so obvious to Thyme that Phoebe is destined for greatness, and also a lot of money, and maybe a waterfront duplex, and as soon as she says it, Phoebe wants it to be true. That is how these things work. That is why people come.

Thyme turns another card.

"And what is this? Your King of Cups is here," Thyme says. "Your great love. Cups are love. And the king, well, he has, like, obviously the most of them. But this is in the future. This is not right now. The cups are moving toward you, but not here. Do not be impatient for it. Do you understand?"

"Yes."

She flips her last card. "And you! The Hermit. You keep coming up. This is so unusual. You are so present in this reading. It's like the cards are telling me that no matter what happens, you are here. I'm sorry I can't be more specific than that. That is all I can gather. You are here. Does that have any meaning to you?"

Phoebe begins to cry between her knees. "Yes."

IN THE UBER on the way to the Boom Boom Room, the women share what Thyme predicted for each of them.

Suz is going to have seven children.

Marla is going to do well in e-commerce someday.

"That's very specific," Phoebe says. "Why not regular commerce?"

"She kept saying, E-commerce! I see you marrying an e-vendor!" Marla says.

"So much hotter than regular vendors," Suz says.

"My wife and I are going to have a son," Nat says. "And then immediately go to Italy."

"I am going to come into property," Phoebe says.

But when it's Lila's turn to share, she says, "She was just way off."

"I thought you said she was amazing?" Marla asks.

"Did I?" Lila asks.

The tone is sharp, too serious. The sound of a day going bad. Maybe she has consumed too much alcohol for her size 4 body. Maybe it's heels on all this cobblestone. Phoebe can feel the blisters forming.

But then they enter the Boom Boom Room, and Lila says, "Let's dance!"

Nat and Suz shriek, as if nothing at all is wrong, and start dancing together in a way that reminds Phoebe of girls from her college. Phoebe never danced in college. Hardly danced at her own wedding. She and Matt, they weren't dancers. They took lessons, though, learned the steps, learned enough to do a foxtrot. But she never danced like these women, without thinking because they have danced together like this so many times before, in their dorm rooms, at parties, hands in the air. She wonders if this is what high school was like for them—Lila being upset, then Lila not being upset. Then, wild dancing.

"Come on!" Lila says to Phoebe.

And so Phoebe joins. Phoebe has no other option left but to join— she tried to opt out, tried to sit on the sidelines, tried to leave this world. But she is still here. So she walks into the group, and they celebrate her arrival, clap and twirl around her. She feels silly at first, but they make it so easy. They are generous with their enthusiasm. They give it all to Phoebe, hold her hands and bump her hips, and by the time the song is over, Phoebe feels so overwhelmed, so part of the group, she excuses herself to go to the bathroom. She looks in the mirror.

I am here, she thinks.

"Shots!" Lila exclaims when Phoebe returns.

But Marla doesn't understand. "What's the point of doing shots at this age?"

"I believe the point is to get drunk really fast," Phoebe says.

"Right. But why? Haven't we all been drunk before?"

"If you don't want to get drunk really fast, then I can't ever explain it to you," Nat says.

"Come on, Marla!" Lila says. "Be my sister."

Marla seems touched.

"Okay," Marla says, like, What the fuck, why not? I'll be a sister. Marla takes a shot. Then another. "Let's get drunk really fast."

"I can't believe I'm getting married!" Lila screams, and they all go back to the dance floor. Lila flips her hair, shows off moves learned from a childhood of dance recitals. She is the happy bride again, so girlish and excited with her friends, and it's good to see.

But then the night is over, and the Uber can't come for an hour. Too many people trying to get a cab at the same exact time. A man on the sidewalk chucks a glass at another man's face, and it explodes everywhere.

They walk home. It's a longer walk than Marla made it sound. By the time they reach their street, Lila takes off her veil. In the quiet space of night, with the courage of her drunkenness, she confesses that she knows Thyme was right about her.

"Right about what?" Suz asks.

"That I have no personality," Lila says.

"She *said* that to you?" Nat asks, like there is no graver insult.

"She said, 'My dear, you are a thousand different people orbiting around a pole,'" Lila says, in a French accent.

"She wasn't French, though," Marla says.

"Aren't we all that pole?" Suz says. "I feel like that pole sometimes."

Phoebe does, too. "Though sometimes I'm not sure there is even a pole."

They laugh. Lila looks lighter. Relieved. But Nat looks at them all, disgusted. "Seriously, what's wrong with you straight women?"

"This has nothing to do with us being straight," Lila says.

"Yeah, what does this have to do with us being straight?" Suz asks.

"I just spent my whole life trying to determine who I am and what I like so nobody does it for me," Nat says. "It's important to me. But it's like, none of you even bother to do that. You don't even bother to think about who you are and what you might actually like."

Nat is angry. Nat looks like she's been wanting to say this for years.

"Well yeah, like I just said," Lila says. "I have no idea who the fuck I am."

Lila is stunned into a kind of silence by her own confession. Nat, too. It makes Nat burst out laughing, like she's thrilled to have finally said what she's always wanted to say. She puts her arm around Lila.

"We'll figure it out," Nat says.

Then it is silence, the sound of cobblestones and heels, all the way back to the hotel.

IN THE LOBBY, Lila seems startled by the lights of the hotel, even though it is mostly soft candlelight. She leans on Phoebe for balance.

"Shit," Lila says. "I'm going to be sick."

Lila vomits in the plant pot near the stairs. She keeps her face at the trunk of the olive tree. She laughs. She says, "Who put *dirt* in this bowl?"

Softly, from behind the desk, Pauline says, "Me."

PHOEBE IS THE one who walks Lila back upstairs. The other women seem grateful. They seem very tired. Ready for bed. Six days is too long for any wedding.

But Phoebe is not tired of Lila. Phoebe is not tired of anybody. Phoebe feels like she has just returned from somewhere very far away. Phoebe is *here*.

"Ugh. My key is not working," Lila says. "It must be your key."

"Is your key not in your purse?" Phoebe asks.

"I don't know. I'm too drunk to find it. I'll just call Gary. I gave him an extra key."

Lila leaves a message on his phone asking for help. When she hangs up, Phoebe is about to suggest that she search through Lila's bag or go downstairs to get another key, but Lila slides the key into Phoebe's lock.

"Ugh. I can't get over this view," Lila says, opening the door.

"It's pitch-black."

Lila gets on Phoebe's bed. She leans back on a pillow like she is going to go right to sleep, so Phoebe takes off her shoes. There is blood on the back of Lila's heel.

"Ugh. I'm bleeding again," Lila says.

The blood darkens her mood.

"Nat is right," Lila says. "I never think about what I might actually like."

"What do you mean?"

"I mean, I just worry," Lila says. "I don't think about what I want, I just worry about what might happen to me and then figure out how to keep those things from happening. And when I think I know what I want, I don't even really know, because what I want is too . . . weird."

"I thought you said you didn't like anything weird."

"It's not like that kind of weird," she says. "It's awful weird."

"What is it?"

"I can't say it."

"Just say it."

"It's too scary."

"I told you I wanted to die. What could be scarier than that?"

Lila nods. "Okay. Fine. The last time I got really turned on, it was by Jim. Isn't that awful?"

"Not necessarily," Phoebe says. She takes off Lila's earrings. Her sash. Lila holds her hands up like a child.

"We had a bonfire at the beach last night after the reception," Lila says. "And Jim looked so good all night, oh my God, Phoebe. He sat next to me by the fire and he cracked a beer, and I was just looking at him, transfixed, and he like, caught me staring at him. He was like, What? And I don't know why, but we just laughed. We laughed so hard, Phoebe, I can't even explain it.

"And then I went to bed and I had this dream. I was in this big beach house. And Jim was there. But it's not really Jim. And I am leaving the kitchen to go meet my guidance counselor, weirdly, but Jim won't let me out of the house. Jim just stands there, blocking my way. He's like, No. You can't go meet your guidance counselor. And then he puts me up against the kitchen island and flips up my skirt and he says the dirtiest things to me . . . but it's like Jim's disgustingness is what turns me on. Isn't that awful?"

"No," Phoebe says.

"It's awful."

Phoebe tells her about her own fantasies, the ones of her ex-husband being awful to her.

"But you were thinking of your husband," she says. "I like, never think about having sex with Gary. Not even when I'm having sex with Gary. I think about Jim."

"Well, thinking of Jim doesn't have to mean anything," Phoebe says.

"It feels like it means something."

"It could mean that you want his approval. Maybe it's symbolic. Like, you want him to stand aside, give you permission, because of Wendy?"

"Oh my God, you sound like my mother now."

"It would make sense."

"What if I just . . . want to fuck him?" Lila asks. "Sometimes I want him so much I can't stand it."

"Then you want him."

"But I can't want him!" Lila says. "I'm Gary's Vermeer painting. And Gary is so wonderful. I know he is. He treats me so well. He's so smart. He's such a good dad. But sometimes I just hate him."

"You *hate* him?" Phoebe asks. "Why?"

"Because that day in his office, he put his hand on my shoulder, and he was like, This will all be okay. This new treatment can work. And the way he said it made me believe him. I really believed him. I *loved* him for it. I really did. But then my dad died. And it wasn't okay. It's still not okay. I mean, how could Gary just let my father *die*?"

The thought of her father makes her sob, and Phoebe holds her. Her body is frail, skinnier than it seems.

"And we never talked about it. We never talk about anything. We always just pretend like everything is fine," she says. "Like it was in the beginning. But it's not. Because sometimes, I just can't stand it when he touches me."

Lila explains that this is why she's always making sure they are busy doing amazing things.

"But then we're at the Louvre, and I was bored. I was bored in Spain. Bored in Florence. I just kept thinking, Wow, Lila, you're in Italy with your fiancé. Look at all those buildings. Look at those paintings. This old church. The cobblestones! And Gary was so fascinated, kept being like, Imagine the builders putting each one of these stones here by hand. But the whole time, I was honestly just like, I don't care. I mean, how does anyone really care about *stones*?"

She wipes her nose.

"Anyway. That's what being with Gary sometimes feels like."

"It's like trying to care about stones?"

"It's like having nothing to talk about anymore so you talk about stones," she says. "And I've never been good at caring about those things. My mother is right. I've never had any imagination. I'm practically dead inside. Sometimes, I feel like I have nothing real to say ever."

Phoebe shakes her head.

"No," Phoebe says. "That's not true. That's not even what your mother really thinks."

"No?"

"No," Phoebe says. "And I don't believe it, either."

Phoebe has sat with so many students who confessed similar things. Students who did not describe themselves as "readers," students who shrugged and were like, "Sorry, stories about women just aren't my thing," but then one day, something would click. One day, they were sitting down with her talking about how Rochester was such an asshole.

"It takes time," Phoebe says. "Gary is twelve years older than you. He's had a lot more time to . . . cultivate an interest in stones."

"But you care about stones."

"I'm twelve years older than you, too."

"Then maybe you should be with Gary."

"Why would you say that?" Phoebe asks, but Lila doesn't answer. So Phoebe looks at her. Like a soldier, Phoebe remembers her first responsibility to the bride. To always be honest. To say what nobody else at this wedding will say.

"Do you want to marry Gary?" Phoebe asks.

"I don't want to *not* marry Gary," Lila says. "I don't want to be alone."

"You can be married and be very alone," Phoebe says. "More alone than you are when you're, well, alone. Trust me."

Lila doesn't say anything but looks at Phoebe, waiting for her to go on.

"Your husband is not going to take care of you the way you think,"

Phoebe says. "Nobody can take care of you the way you need to take care of yourself. It's your job to take care of yourself like that."

"Did you read that on a pillow or something?" Lila asks, then grabs a pillow and puts it over her face, like she knows she's admitted too much, even to Phoebe. Because saying things out loud is the first step to them becoming real.

"It's a little long for a pillow," Phoebe says.

"This pillow is so coconutty," Lila says. "Ugh. I don't know what I'm even saying. I just don't know why it's so hard to be a person sometimes. It shouldn't be this hard. It makes no sense."

They wait in silence for a moment. And then, from underneath the pillow, a voice: "What if I *don't* want to marry Gary?"

Phoebe is careful to say nothing, because Phoebe is confused. On the eve of her own wedding night, Phoebe had no doubts. She wanted to marry Matt, wholly and purely. This is why it confuses her. She doesn't know what you're supposed to feel like. She doesn't know what ensures a happy marriage. She doesn't know if Lila's ambivalence toward Gary means that they are doomed or if ambivalence means there is room to grow, room to become sure over the years.

But this is clear: "I don't want to marry Gary," Lila says again.

Phoebe takes the pillow off her face, and this strikes Lila as so suddenly funny, she starts hysterically laughing. When she laughs, Phoebe can see what Lila must have been like as a little girl, when she was still called Delilah, sleeping in her mother's bed.

"Oh my God," Lila says. She stands up on the bed. She shouts it. "Phoebe! I don't want to marry Gary!"

"Okay," Phoebe says, and pulls her back down. "Just maybe don't shout it."

"But I need to tell him. I need everyone to know."

"In the morning."

Maybe it's the thought of morning or catching sight of her veil in the mirror, but she stops smiling.

"Ugh. This is not okay," Lila says. "He's going to be so upset. Everyone is. What am I going to *do*?"

"Nothing now. Tomorrow, we'll wake up and we'll tell everyone together."

"You'll be with me?"

"Of course," she says. "But for now just get some sleep."

"I am really glad you're here."

"Me too."

"And don't worry," Lila says. "I don't snore."

LILA DOES SNORE.

She snores so loudly, Phoebe can't sleep in the room. It reminds her too much of sleeping next to her husband, his loud vibrations taking over everything. Phoebe undresses in the dark corner, then wraps herself up in the fluffy robe.

She digs through Lila's purse until she finds the other room key, lets herself in to the bridal suite, which is not very bridal. It's called the Colonel. There are bright red floral curtains and red floral prints everywhere. A stuffy white carpet. A shoreline view that is somewhat ruined by a giant flagpole that cuts it in half. And a picture of a dead man on the wall who she assumes is the colonel.

She is surprised by how messy Lila is. She would have thought Lila to be aggressively organized. But her underwear is everywhere. Her life, spread out all over the room.

Phoebe starts to pick up some of Lila's dresses, so that the morning won't seem so overwhelming. It will be overwhelming enough, having to cancel this giant wedding. Having to tell everyone the truth. At least she can wake up to a clean floor.

But then she is startled by a knock on the door. She opens it.

"Oh," Gary says. "You're not Lila."

Phoebe tightens the belt of her robe.

"Lila fell asleep in my bed," Phoebe says. "Don't ask. We had a long night."

"We had a long night, too."

Gary sits down on the floral love seat. Phoebe gets this terrible feeling, the same feeling she got when she looked at her cat in those final weeks before he died. How horrible, Phoebe thinks, to not know the truth about your own life.

"Was it a good one at least?" Phoebe asks.

"A weird one," Gary says. "Let's just say that I'm not the twenty-eight-year-old groom Jim remembers me to be. And now I'm just . . . drunk."

Phoebe will not tell Gary what Lila confessed, of course. She would never. But not telling him makes her nervous. She doesn't like this feeling of being dishonest with Gary.

"Why was it so weird?" Phoebe asks.

"He threw me the same exact bachelor party," Gary says. "Brought us to the same exact cigar lounge. The same golf course. Bought me the same bottle of whiskey. I honestly don't know if it's because he was so drunk at the last one he didn't remember what we did. Or if he is just . . . trying to upset me."

"Why would he want to do that?"

"I don't know," Gary says. "I can't shake this feeling that he's mad at me."

"For what?"

"Moving on. Forgetting his sister."

"But you haven't forgotten his sister."

"But I think it's what Jim thinks."

Ever since Wendy's diagnosis, Jim was the best friend he had. He was truly there for all of them after. He did everything. He cooked, he cleaned. Cried with Gary at Wendy's grave, and they were brothers in that way. After, they went to Wyoming and shat side by side in the woods, then laughed hysterically with Juice into the night. But ever since he got engaged to Lila, it's been different.

"I can get married again," Gary says. "But he doesn't get a new sister. Nobody can ever make that better. And I can't explain it other than to say that sometimes, I feel like I'm betraying him."

"I doubt he thinks of it that way," Phoebe says.

"I promised to take care of his sister for the rest of her life."

"And . . . you did."

"But her life was supposed to be longer," he says. "I'm a fucking doctor."

"But wasn't it lung cancer? That's not even your specialization. Field? How do medical doctors say it?"

"Field," he says.

But he's too caught up in the emotion to joke.

"She complained about this cough, you know. And I kept telling her to go to the doctor, to be better when she cleaned her paints. I had known since art school that she needed to be more careful with that stuff. But I didn't want to nag. She hated when people told her what to do, especially me."

"That's not why she got cancer," Phoebe says. Maybe it's the fatigue, or maybe this kind of thinking is just too close to her own, but she gets irritated. "If that was true, then every painter would be dead at thirty-five. It's actually ridiculous to think any of this is your fault."

"It's not ridiculous," he says. "I advise people medically all the time."

"God, we're all so ridiculous! Why do we all think everything is our fault all the time?"

"Must be some evolutionary thing."

"Helps us survive somehow," Phoebe says. "Even as it destroys us."

"Yeah."

Phoebe aches for him. Gary is lost. Stuck somewhere between his first marriage and his second marriage.

"What was she like?" Phoebe asks. "Wendy."

"She was just this whirlwind of a person," he says. "We met in college. She was an art student, and I was premed. I used to walk by the open studios on my way back from the hospital. That's the first time I saw her, standing in front of this painting that was entirely red, and it was like she knew I didn't get it. 'It's thirty shades of red,' she said, and still I couldn't see it. Not until she started pointing them out to me. And I fucking loved this about her. She could always see things I couldn't. Seriously, all I could see was one giant blob of red. But then, a few days later, I saw all these different colors. And it was amazing."

"I think that might be the best description of falling in love that I've ever heard," Phoebe says.

They lived in Tiverton, in a beautiful old farmhouse that was featured in a small magazine about Tiverton. They had good friends, poets, writers, artists, actors, farmers who came over to drink beers in their backyard. Juice went to some private school in town where she bonded with other kids who thought it was fun to watch caterpillars build cocoons.

"We used to be fun. Once we stayed up and watched all three God-father movies in one night. We used to create themed drinks for, like, Presidents' Day. And it was perfect. It really was. But life is strange, always thinking this one thing is going to make you happy, because then you get it, and then maybe you're not as happy as you imagined you would be, because every day is still just every day. Like the happiness becomes so big, you have no choice but to live inside of it, until you can no longer see it or feel it. And so you start to fixate on something else—you want a child, and then the child is here, and that happiness is so big, it begins to feel like nothing. Like just the air around you."

Until it is gone, of course. Until you bury your wife or divorce your husband and then what? What do you do? Do you start all over again? Do you fixate on the new thing that you are sure is going to make you happy? How many times does a person do this over a lifetime? Is that just what life is?

"We had a whole life," he says. "And that whole life . . . is gone. It seems absurd that I'm supposed to just get over that."

"I don't know if you are," she says.

"But I have to," he says. "I can't go on like this."

"Like what?"

"There was this quiet that came after my wife died," he says. "This normal routine that developed that wasn't really life but was very much like life. I could get through the day if I just concentrated on these very menial tasks. I used to love nothing more than like, just peeling potatoes for dinner. I swear I could feel okay as long as I was just peeling those potatoes. But then you asked me in the hot tub when I started to feel better, and it's a hard thing to answer, because I'm actually not sure I'm better. I think I've just been stuck in that neutral place ever since. Where everything is . . . fine."

He says being here is weirder than he expected.

"Everyone keeps looking at me and saying, Congratulations, you must be so happy," he says.

"Why is that weird?"

"I'm not sure happy is a feeling for me anymore," he says. "Ever since Wendy died, I don't really think about what will make me happy. It's like I decided at some point that I can't ever be happy again, so I should just think about what will make other people happy."

She nods. She looks out at the fireworks.

"That's really why I went to Lila's art gallery that day," Gary says. "Because Jim really wanted to go. I said no, I was too bummed out. It was my wedding anniversary. But Jim kept pushing for it, and I wanted to make Jim happy. After all he did for us. I didn't get why Jim of all people wanted to go to an art gallery. I think he thought he was making me happy, giving me something to do on a sad day. But whatever. We went."

He walked around Lila's mother's gallery, annoyed with Jim, annoyed with himself. He knew the motions, the nodding of the head, the looking deeply at the colors to take in each one. But he couldn't feel it, couldn't feel anything, and he didn't know if this meant something was wrong with him or the paintings. It was always Wendy who was the art critic— the one who would deem them bad or good, whereas Gary always went by the price. If the painting was being sold for a hundred thousand dollars, it must be good.

"But the painting of Patricia had no price on it," he says. "It felt like an opportunity, a test. I stared at it for so long, thinking, Is this a good painting? Or bad?"

He had felt guilty when Lila came over and started talking like she expected him to take the painting home. Started describing where he could hang it, when it hadn't even occurred to him to buy it.

"And then Lila walks into my office a few days later," he says. "They had come to me for a second opinion. And it felt like such a coincidence, like we were being brought together for a reason. Lila was so hopeful that I became hopeful."

Hope is a powerful thing. He looked at the old man's pictures from

the colonoscopy, and he saw the mass, but it all looked potentially fixable to him.

"I know I save lives, but I also ruin lives. I say a few words and then
watch a person go from being one thing to another thing entirely. I
didn't understand that until a doctor did it to me and Wendy," he says.
"So I suggested one more round of chemo. I suggested this could work.
Or at least potentially extend his life by years. And they were so happy.
Man, I loved that feeling. It was such a high. I wanted more of it. I
wanted to make her happy again. So I went back to the gallery and actually bought the painting."

"At least, I tried to," he says. "But she insisted I take it for free. A gift
for taking care of her father."

It felt good to take the painting home. To put it in his bathroom, just
like Lila suggested. It felt like the first thing he had done since his wife
died. A small step back into the world, a nice gesture, a fight against the
entropy, something he could do to be human to another human. But
mostly it was a decision to say: I don't know if this is good or bad, but I
think this painting is meaningful.

"Because that's the point of art, isn't it?" Gary asks. "Artists look
at the world and see opportunities for creating meaning. Wendy was
always looking at her own suffering and trying to see something in it.
Even at the end, when she was dying. And I think that's why I've always
been jealous of artists. Every day, I look at a colon and I either see . . .
death or shit," Gary says. "I relied on Wendy to see other, more beautiful
things for me."

He leans back.

"Honestly, it's nice to hear you talk this way about art," Phoebe says.
"I've actually been a little down on art."

She tells him how lately she worries she always read books just for
the feelings they gave her in the end, and she's not sure how this is any
different from reading porn.

"Weren't you the one who told me you were impressed by those
people?" Gary asks. "Those people who will read four hundred pages
just to get off?"

"Oh, you mean like you?" she says, and he smiles.

"Well, I think it's amazing," Gary says. "How much work we'll do just to feel something. I don't think there is anything more human than that."

Phoebe agrees. She feels such tenderness for him, but she doesn't know how to say that, so she says, "I've missed talking like this."

She loves deep, winding conversations that go up and down, especially in the dead of night when everyone should be sleeping. She has forgotten the way conversations, really good ones, can change her—shape-shift her like a tree. Sometimes leave her bare, sometimes leave her fuller.

"I've missed talking like this, too," Gary says. "It's very easy to tell you things, you know. Is this the effect you have on everybody?"

"Historically, no," she says. "Often I've been known to make people more uncomfortable than they were *before* they started talking to me."

"I can't imagine it," he says. "I feel like I could tell you anything."

The honesty of his comment cuts right through her, and she can hardly bear it.

"You're drunk."

"It's not just that," he says, and looks hurt.

She should stand up. Go back to her room. But then she thinks of Lila standing on her bed, shouting, "I don't want to marry Gary." She thinks, this wedding is over. This man deserves to hear something true.

"I know," she says. "I feel it, too."

He scratches his beard, something he does, she notices, when he gets a little nervous. Once the wedding is called off, she thinks, Gary won't have to shave it. It's the first time Phoebe allows herself to fantasize about the wedding being called off. About a future where she can reach out and touch his face.

In some other version of this story, she would. And they would kiss. Then wake up and feel awful about it in the morning. But Phoebe knows too much to do that now. Phoebe has had too many awful mornings for a lifetime. So Phoebe just stands there, admiring his face, even the gray at the edges. Especially the gray. She didn't understand that this is what happens as you get older—that the same thing that repulsed her when she was young is the same exact thing that draws her near now.

There is something incredibly sexy to Phoebe about Gary's gray hairs, his exhaustion, his genuine confusion about life, and she's not sure she even understands why. She is drawn to the exhaustion of a lived life, to the man who has loved deeply and then lost suddenly and carries on. A man who has buried his wife and walked away and woke up to peel potatoes for dinner. A man who has lived through enough to appreciate the stones beneath his feet.

"So when did Lila tell you it was a naked painting of her mother?" Phoebe asks.

It's good to see him laugh.

"Three months," he says. "For three months I took a shower next to my naked future mother-in-law."

She takes his hand and squeezes it. Gary looks surprised by her touch, but not confused. Sort of the way he looked when she stood before him in the hot tub and told him she wanted to fuck. As if he wants it, too, but cannot bring himself to admit it.

"I should go back to my room," he says.

"Good night," she says.

Gary leaves, and Phoebe gets in Lila's bed. This time, she doesn't fantasize about her husband or Mia or the girlies at Joe's wine shop. She just thinks of Gary, how warm his hand felt, how the entire time she held it, he didn't look away.

FRIDAY

❦

The Blending of the Families

"You cleaned," Lila says, standing over Phoebe the next morning. "I'll try my best not to take that as an insult."

Lila drops her new room key on the nightstand. Phoebe sits up. She sees Lila's dresses, neatly hung in the corner of the room, and all at once, she remembers last night. The cleaning. The crying. The holding of Gary's hand. Lila, jumping on her bed, shouting about how she no longer wanted to marry Gary. But this morning, Lila seems as she always does just after she barges into a room.

"You didn't happen to stumble upon any Motrin during your cleaning spree?" Lila asks.

"Not feeling your best, I take it?"

"That's an understatement. This might be the worst hangover I ever had in my entire life. Worse than church wine."

Phoebe waits for Lila to say something else, to address her confessions from last night. But someone's at the door.

"You were supposed to meet us at nine in the lobby for surfing," Juice says, standing in the middle of the doorframe in nothing but a swimsuit and towel.

"Right," Lila says. "Surfing."

Lila closes her eyes like she's already tired from it.

"We're late," Juice says. "Dad's already down there, in the car."

"Give me a few minutes to turn back into a real human being and I'll be down," she says.

"You're coming, too, right, Phoebe?" Juice asks.

Phoebe feels the tug to join. But she also knows she needs to give them alone time. There are things that need to be sorted out.

"No, I don't know how to surf," Phoebe says.

"Nobody does!" Juice says. "They're going to teach us. It's a lesson."

"I'm going to sit this one out, kiddo," Phoebe says.

After Juice leaves, Lila won't quite meet Phoebe's eye. Phoebe waits, but Lila opens a bottle of Motrin.

"How does Motrin know where the headache is?" Lila asks. "I've never understood that."

"I think it just reduces pain all over the body. Head included."

Lila turns on the shower.

"You're taking a shower before surfing?" Phoebe asks.

"Oh no, there will be absolutely no surfing today."

"You just told Juice you'd surf?"

"I cannot surf, never will, won't put myself through the circus act of trying."

"Why did you plan a surfing morning as part of your wedding then?"

"Because it was the one thing Juice asked for," she says. "And I guess I thought by the time my wedding week arrived, I'd be the kind of person who wanted to go surfing."

Lila's makeup from last night is heavy below her eyes.

"I truly wish I was a person who liked to surf, but unfortunately, I have woken up to remember that I am just not that person."

Lila will never want to surf, for the same reasons she never wanted to play sports and she is ready to admit that. She wraps her hair in a towel, then mentions her uncle flying in from Santa Fe today and a facial at noon. But she says it with no enthusiasm. She sounds officially tired of her own wedding.

"I have no idea why I planned all these activities," Lila says. "Can you go surfing in my place? It's a three-person lesson."

But Phoebe is not ready to give up yet. "What am I supposed to tell them when you're not there?"

"Tell them that my stomach is upset, which is not a lie, by the way, and that I'll see them later at the Blending of the Families."

She says it like it's a cultural event, then turns on the TV.

"Aren't you going in the shower?" Phoebe asks.

"I always have the TV on while I shower."

Lila puts on the Food Network and raises the volume so she can hear Giada talk about bruschetta while she's bathing.

"Are we seriously not going to talk about last night?" Phoebe asks.

"Actually, I do have a question about last night," Lila says. "Did we eat cabbage?"

"Yes," Phoebe says.

"Ugh," Lila says. "I can't believe my maid of honor let me eat cabbage two days before my wedding. Cabbage destroys me."

"So the wedding is on."

"Of course it is," Lila says.

Perhaps this is when Phoebe should say, Actually, I can't go surfing. Actually, I shouldn't get any more involved in this wedding than I already have. Actually, I just came here to kill myself, and surfing is pretty much the opposite of killing myself. Surfing is an activity that belongs to other people. There is a whole group of things like this that live in a box in her mind—things like dancing to techno music and rafting through the Grand Canyon—things she decided were for people in California. People like Ryun. People like her mother before her mother died.

But she came all this way to see the ocean.

"Okay," Phoebe says. "Suit yourself."

Lila drops her robe. She steps into the shower. Giada toasts the bread. Phoebe stands up to leave. "Oh, while you're out there, get me some Gas-X," Lila yells, and Phoebe's sympathy from last night vanishes. This spoiled child, yelling out commands from inside her marble shower. Not even a thank-you.

ON THE BEACH, they are handed wet suits that look to be half the size of their bodies. Phoebe and Gary glance at each other with suspicion.

"And these are supposed to fit us?" Gary asks.

"Absolutely," Aspen, the instructor, says.

But Phoebe can't get her suit up past her thighs. Gary's gets stuck at the calf.

"This is ridiculous," Gary says, tugging at the fabric. "I'm supposed to get all the way in this thing?"

He hops on one foot while he tries to pull it up over his calf, then tips over like a rigid skyscraper.

"Shit." He laughs when he hits the ground.

Phoebe likes his loud balloon of a laugh. Likes it when he curses, too. It makes it easier to believe he was once a teenager. That he wasn't born a father. Or a fiancé. He's just Gary, trying to put some pants on.

"You okay?" Phoebe asks.

"Nobody tells you about this part, do they?" Gary says.

"No," Phoebe says. "In all the surfing movies, they always edit out all the montages of surfers just trying to put on their wet suits."

"That's the surfing movie I'll make one day," Gary says. "Just extremely hot people getting stuck with one leg in their suit and then falling over."

"I'd like to point out that you just called yourself hot."

"I hope you can excuse it knowing it was done only for the sake of continuing a joke."

"And we appreciate your sacrifice."

He looks down at the suit suctioned to his calves. She wonders where he got those calves. His father? Football in high school? Gym after work for twenty years? He didn't seem the type, but she's lived long enough by now to know it's foolish to ever be surprised by someone's secret hobbies.

"Well, it's a very dramatic scene, I admit," Phoebe says. "Will they be able to do it? Or will they just get stuck there, forever, on the sand?"

"It looks like it," Gary says. "I mean, there's no goddamned way."

Juice comes over, already in her wet suit. A pro. "What's wrong?" Juice asks.

"I can't get it over my calves, sweetheart," Gary says.

"I can't get it over my thighs," Phoebe says.

"Help us," Gary says.

"Ew," Juice says, and looks at the two of them. "This is weird."

Juice walks away to practice standing up on her surfboard. Phoebe pulls her suit up, slides her arms in the holes, and celebrates, while Gary lies there in defeat.

"Okay," Phoebe says. "It's basically just like wearing tights."

"I don't wear tights."

"You just got to shimmy this thing up slowly."

Phoebe kneels down to Gary's ankles. She pulls on the fabric, or whatever it is, gingerly.

"I think you just ripped some hairs out," he says.

"Surfing is pain, Gary."

"Surfing is already too hard."

She gets it over the mound of calf.

"Hooray," Gary says, pulling the rest up with ease. "Now I'm a wet suit person."

Phoebe zips him up in the back and Velcros it tight. The gesture is intimate, like putting a necklace on your wife's neck. He is so lovely, Phoebe thinks. He is so good, standing there, getting ready to surf with his daughter even though he is hungover and his back is shit. He is look-ing at Phoebe like maybe she is good for the same exact reason. Maybe they are a team. She gives him a tiny high five as though the big task of the day is over. It's friendly and sterilizes the moment between them.

"Ready to go," Aspen says, as she rubs sunscreen on her face. She announces it has some sand in it. "Exfoliator!"

Then she does some stretching and says, "Okay, take your boards." She shows them how to lie on it, bellies pressed against the board, legs centered for balance.

"Balance is everything," Aspen says.

The movement is like yoga, Phoebe thinks. She feels glad, suddenly, for all that yoga she tried doing on Zoom during the pandemic. She feels like maybe that wasn't a waste of time after all, if it allowed her to be present in this moment. And maybe that's it: You do things in the moment for the person you hope you might be two years from now. You don't kill yourself when you are sad because one day you might not be sad, and you might want to go surfing with a man you really like?

Phoebe uses her hands to push herself off the board into a plank, then jumps her feet up right in position. Gary looks at her with amazement.

"Very good," Aspen says.

They enter the ocean. Phoebe likes the cool shock of the water against her ankles. Phoebe sticks a finger in and tastes it. She's always been curious.

"It really is salty," she says.

"That's sort of its claim to fame," Gary says.

The waves are small, and Phoebe is grateful. Aspen sets up Juice first, pushes her when a wave comes, and she stands up on the board right away. Gary and Phoebe cheer even though Juice probably can't hear. It feels good to cheer. The cheering is in some way for the parents. It's good to celebrate the girl for doing a thing the girl has passionately wanted to do since . . . Lila and Gary got engaged. Even Aspen is smiling.

"Who's up next?" Aspen asks.

"Ladies first," Gary says.

Phoebe slides onto the board, feels Aspen take it from behind.

"Okay, paddle!" Aspen shouts, as the wave comes.

But Phoebe does not know what it means when Aspen screams paddle. Does she use her whole arms at the same time like long oars? Or is it more like swimming? Does she just use her hands? Aspen didn't say. For a minute, Phoebe feels foolish paddling, like a beached whale, but then the wave catches her, and she sees the water gliding over the board, over her hands, and she presses up just like she did on sand. She jumps and there she is, standing on the water. She can't believe it. "Oh my God!" she shouts to no one, to herself, to Gary and Juice. She is balanced. Steady.

But then she falls into the water.

It's been so long since she has fallen like that—she has never, she thinks, ever fallen like that. Totally and completely without any way of catching herself. Swirled up in the curl of the wave. And she loves everything about it, the cold water on her face, the ocean in her ears. It is life. It is up her nose and in her ears and she wants to swallow it all.

But it's very salty. She stands up and spits out the water.

"You, like, did it!" Juice says.

"I know!" Phoebe says.

They watch Gary as he tries to stand up on the board, and Phoebe can feel Juice silently rooting for her father. Phoebe roots for him, too, out loud, and is this what it's like, being part of a real family? Gary only gets halfway up, loses his balance immediately, then disappears into the water. He comes up nearby with a laugh.

"How was the ride?" Gary asks his daughter.

"Amazing," Juice says.

"I think your daughter just acquired a very expensive new hobby,"

Phoebe says, and Gary laughs. They watch Juice, who is already making her way back to Aspen beyond where the waves break.

"I'd need an entirely different body to be good at this thing," Gary says.

But they keep trying. It's just fun to try. It's fun when the goal is to just surf and not to feel happier. For the rest of the hour, they take turns with Aspen as she sets them up for the waves.

The waves get bigger as the hour passes. While she waits for her turn, Phoebe swims out a little deeper so she doesn't get toppled. She likes it. She likes the drama. The dark gray-green of the water when it's not lit up by the sun. Each time a wave builds, Phoebe feels a swell of fear, dunks her head under like Juice instructed, and rises with the water. She can feel how easy it would be to get carried out to sea, but she resists it. She swims back to Aspen. She takes another ride, and then another, and then another. Each time she falls, she's overwhelmed by the white foam, the sand in her ears. But she emerges.

They are all exhausted by the end of the hour. Phoebe is too tired to take off her wet suit, and when it gets stuck around her heel, she is the one who tips over this time. She laughs when she hits the ground. She feels like an overtired child playing in the sand. She feels like she could laugh hysterically or sob out of joy. She wants to stay on this sand forever, with Juice pulling at the leg of her suit, trying to tug it off. Each time Juice tugs, it makes them both laugh harder.

Eventually, Phoebe gets it off. She feels naked without it. Gary hands them towels. Sets out a blanket. The three of them fall asleep like that, the cool breeze drying them.

"I loved that," Juice says when they wake up.

Phoebe did, too. She still loves it. No matter what happens, she'll love it forever.

"Let's do it again tomorrow," Juice says.

"Never," Gary says and smiles.

AFTER, THEY GO to Flo's and eat fried clam strips. Gary and Phoebe get big waters. They toast to the day. They sit next to an elderly couple with matching fleeces and Phoebe likes how they order the same drink but one with a twist and one extra dirty. They say it like they have become proud of the minor differences left between them.

"I have to pee," Juice says.

"You don't have to tell us exactly what you're going to do in there," Gary says.

She laughs. She leaves Gary and Phoebe alone. The moment feels ripe with possibility and yet, at the same time, doomed. Gary's leg is resting slightly against Phoebe's, maybe by accident, maybe not. Maybe he's so tired, he doesn't even feel it.

"That was genuinely fun," Gary says.

"You sound surprised," Phoebe says.

"I am."

He looks at her like he's trying to tell her something he cannot say. Just say it, she thinks. But she can't say it now. She should have said it last night when she thought the wedding was off. Now she doesn't know if it would be cowardly or brave. She doesn't know if she is supposed to seize the moment or let the moment go.

"She's a great kid," Phoebe says.

"I'm lucky."

"It might not be all luck. It's possible you had some kind of hand in it."

"I suppose I was there for a few hours of her childhood."

"Oh my God," Juice says, coming back from the bathroom. Her hands are still wet from washing. "There was this sign in the bathroom that said 40 PEOPLE MAX IN THIS ROOM. Like why would forty people ever be in the bathroom? Like what would you even say to all forty people in a bathroom?"

"Hello?" Gary says.

Juice laughs. "Yeah! That's a good start. Hello, forty people."

"Why are we all in the bathroom?" Phoebe asks, pretending to be forty people.

"Whose idea was this, you guys?" Gary asks.

They laugh, and then Phoebe becomes embarrassed by the laughter. Or afraid of it. She's not sure. Whatever it is, it's too good. It connects them all. It draws them close. It's like a warm sweater that they all wear. Phoebe sits back, and she sips her water. She has never, in her life, felt totally at home around any restaurant table. Not even with her husband. She was often worried about what to say and did they have anything left to say and was there food in her teeth?

"Here you go," the waitress says and lays down the check.

Phoebe doesn't want to go. She wants to stay at this table with Gary's leg slightly brushed against hers and Juice reading off the back of the menu, which is really just a short story about how many times Flo's has been demolished by hurricanes.

"In 1938," Juice says. "In 1954. In 1960. In 1985. In 1991—"

"So . . . many times."

"Many, many times."

Phoebe imagines that rebuilding after each devastation must be a real chore, especially for a place like Flo's, which has knickknacks covering every inch of the walls. To rebuild each time with the same level of bursting, idiosyncratic personality—how do you do that? How do you remember where each rusty spoon was randomly nailed to the wall? How do you care where each bottle opener hangs when you put it up the fourth time? How do you act like this singular and quirky existence is entirely natural and will never be destroyed again?

"Let's get going, huh?" Gary says.

They get up and walk out the door. This is, Phoebe realizes, the one problem with falling in love with strangers. You don't get to keep them. She watches them spread out in their own directions as soon as they reach the parking lot.

It's a relief when Gary looks back and says, "Where to?"

At CVS, Juice proclaims her love for CVS. Literally everything in the world is here, she says. Anything you want! Juice buys herself a sleep mask with zebras on it. Then they follow Phoebe to the medicine aisle, even though Phoebe keeps saying, "I'll just meet you guys at the front in a minute."

"What else do we have to do?" Gary asks. "But follow you around like your helpers."

"Yeah, we're helpers," Juice says. "Paid by the hour. What do you need? I'll get it."

"Gas-X," Phoebe says.

Juice and Gary crack up so loudly, the employee at the counter looks over.

"We had cabbage," is all Phoebe says.

"Say no more," Gary says.

As they walk out, Phoebe looks up and sees them on the security TV for just a second. She is startled by the frankness of their image, the reality of seeing them on this ordinary trip to CVS, recorded by history, all together.

Lila does not stop by before the Blending of the Families the way Phoebe had expected. She thought Lila might have questions about her dress or complaints about Gary's mother, who has requested to say grace at the rehearsal dinner.

But at six, the hotel is emptied out, and Phoebe wonders if Lila is upset with her. If it's because she left the Gas-X at Lila's door without a bag. If she somehow knows about the joy Phoebe felt all day with Gary.

She suddenly feels guilty, but then reminds herself that it was Lila who told her to go. It was Lila who gave her the gift of today, and Phoebe is grateful. It's a day she'll remember for the rest of her life. It reminded her of a feeling she stopped believing she could have, a feeling she thought belonged only to other people. It makes her want to give something back to Lila, so she goes downstairs to the bar to work on her maid of honor speech.

But when she sits on the chair, opens a hotel notepad, she finds she's not sure how to begin. Not after her conversation last night with Lila. And then her conversation with Gary. Writing a maid of honor speech now feels like writing a lecture on a discipline she doesn't believe in.

It is becoming clear to Phoebe—they are not in love. Maybe they were in love, but now they are two people who are very confused. Very much wanting to be in love, because Lila doesn't want to be alone. Lila is a woman who experiences a problem, and then finds a man who is compelled to fix it. A man who becomes happy only because he can make her happy. But she is not happy—so what's the point of any of it?

Phoebe orders herself a beer from the Drink Concierge.

"Are you holding office hours, Professor?" Jim asks, sitting down before she answers. She closes her notebook.

"Mostly just drinking now," Phoebe says.

"That's too bad," Jim says. "I was hoping you could help me with my speech. Turns out, Miss Finnegan from the tenth grade wasn't wrong and I actually am a shit writer."

"A teacher said that to you?"

Jim looks at her notebook. "What did you write?"

"Are you seriously trying to cheat off my speech?"

He laughs. "Can't we think of this more like a brainstorming session? A writer's room?"

Jim looks at her like they are playing a game of chicken now. Because the stakes are high for the maid of honor and the best man. If they don't publicly believe in the couple's love, who will?

"I generally find office hours work best when we stay focused on the student's problem," Phoebe says.

"Fair enough," Jim says.

"So what's the problem?"

He says he could write a whole book about Gary, about what they've been through together.

"But I don't know this new Gary who's with Lila. I only know the Gary who was with my sister."

"Don't mention your sister," Phoebe says.

"Then what do I write?"

"Good writing is driven by a question," Phoebe says. "And the essay is the writer's best attempt at answering that question. So let's start there, with a question."

"But what's the question?"

"It's a wedding speech, so the question has to be, Why are these two people perfect for each other?"

"Why is anyone perfect for each other?"

"What do these two bring out in each other that is special, unique? That nobody else in the world can bring out?"

"That's two questions, not one," he says. "And how am I supposed to know that?"

"Isn't it obvious?"

"Is it?" He gives her that inquiring look again.

"Hasn't Gary ever said anything about why he loves Lila?"

"Has Lila ever said anything about why she loves Gary?"

In all their talking, Lila has mostly listed fears and complaints—his beard, his gray hair, his family.

"He's good to her," Phoebe says.

"But Gary is good to the cashiers at the grocery store," he says. "He's good to everyone."

Phoebe nods. Jim sits back in defeat. "This is a weird wedding, no?" Jim says.

"It is," Phoebe says.

"Do you know what we need? What every writer famously uses when they have writer's block. Drugs."

"I think that's just a myth." Phoebe tells him about the writers who were famously derailed by drugs. But Jim doesn't care. He was gifted a pound of edibles by one of Gary's cousins who bought more than he could bring back on the airplane.

"I've never used marijuana," Phoebe says.

"Spoken like someone who has never used marijuana," Jim says. "I'll have two weeds please."

Phoebe laughs.

"How have you never smoked weed?'

"I think it's as simple as nobody has ever offered it to me. It's like people can look at me and somehow tell that I don't want to do drugs."

"That was the first thing I noticed about you," Jim says.

In Jim's room, he gives her a quarter of his edible.

"Now what?" Phoebe asks.

"Now, we wait."

"How long does it take?" Phoebe looks at the bag.

"It won't say on the packaging."

"So we have no idea how much vitamin A we're getting."

Jim bursts out laughing. "You're funny."

"Will I get paranoid?" Phoebe asks.

"It sounds like you might already be paranoid."

"I am, I think, suddenly very paranoid about becoming paranoid."

"If you get me paranoid about you being paranoid about being paranoid . . ."

"Shit, it's happening. I really do feel something."

"Are you going to narrate the whole thing?"

"Is that a problem?"

"No, as long as you do it like a movie."

"In a world where a woman does drugs after a lifetime of not doing drugs," Phoebe says. "God, my mouth is dry. Is that normal?"

"Okay, let's set some ground rules so we can cut the paranoia before it takes over," Jim says. He looks her in the eyes, holds her hands. "Repeat after me. We're safe. We're grown-ass adults. We're not going anywhere tonight until we write these speeches."

"We're safe. We're grown-ass adults. We're not going anywhere tonight until we write these speeches."

"We stay right here in this room."

"No moving."

"No vehicles."

"No swimming."

"If we get hungry we can order food."

"There's nothing to be worried about," he says. "So take a deep breath. Relax. And let yourself go."

"Okay," she says. She sits down on the floor, lays out until she is fully stretched. "I'm gone."

"You're gone."

"Goodbye."

Saying goodbye makes them laugh.

"This is a weird wedding," Jim says.

"You already said that."

"Because it's that weird," he says. "Maybe it's just because it's the only wedding I've been to where I truly don't know anyone except my dead sister's family. And I can't even talk to them about the one thing we have in common because my brother-in-law is getting married to someone who refuses to acknowledge her existence."

"That does sound weird," Phoebe says.

"And that's not even the end of it," he says. He turns to her. "If I tell you something, will you put it in the vault?"

"What vault?"

"The one they keep at the Swiss fucking banks, the one you need blood samples to access."

She makes the sound effect of a door opening. "That's the opening of the Swiss vault."

"I liked Lila first," Jim says.

"What do you mean?"

"Before Gary met her, I worked a job on the street outside Lila's gallery. Kind of a random thing, brought in by the state to consult on the construction of this new sewer drain they were thinking of putting in, which meant I was always standing out there on her street, watching Lila go in and out. Girl took a lot of coffee breaks. Went in and out nearly thirty times a day, never once saying hello to me, but I could tell she was looking at me. I could tell we were locked on to each other and that I should say something. But I didn't know what to say. I didn't want to be one of those guys who hits on women just because they're walking on the street. And I couldn't just go in the gallery with my greasy hands and start talking about Monet, either. What the fuck do I know about Monet?"

"He was a French impressionist."

"Thanks, Professor. Would have been helpful to know then."

"So what did you do?"

"Nothing," he said. "And eventually Lila came out and called me on it. On my last day, she saw me packing up the truck and came right up to me and said, 'Are you seriously going to watch me walk by a thousand times and say nothing? How much coffee do you think I drink?' And I was done for basically at that moment. I was like, I'm working my way up to it, give me some time, and then she said, 'I'm out of time.' And I was like, Are you dying or something? And she said, If I were, wouldn't that be a very impolite question? And then she told me her father was the one dying and the doctor gave him three months to live and she burst into tears."

"In the middle of the street?"

"Yeah," he says, half laughing at the memory of it. "She just broke down right there in front of me."

"What did you do?"

"I held her," he says. "After my sister died, that's what helped me. People who just let me fucking cry. Like Gary. He didn't try to fix it or solve the problem. We both knew nothing could fix it. I just wanted to be sad, but not sad alone. And so I just held her, let her cry. And it was weird how it wasn't weird at all. I went home, and I couldn't stop thinking about it. How bold she was. How she just cried like that, in front of a total stranger. In front of me? She didn't even know me, I was just some dude on the street, but she trusted me, you know? It felt special. So the next weekend, I went back to see her with Gary. But I didn't tell Gary he was my wingman. I didn't think he'd come. Who wants to be someone else's wingman when they're depressed on their wedding anniversary? And I genuinely thought it'd be good for Gary to do something for a change. That kind of shit always cheered him up. He and Wendy went to galleries all the time. So two birds, you know?"

"Two birds."

"And then we're in the gallery, and Lila and I see each other right away but don't say anything. I'm just walking around the whole place, pretending to look at these paintings, and it's so hot, you know? Like we both know we're going to talk to each other, we both know that's why I came, we both know I don't give a shit about whatever painting Gary is looking at, I'm just secretly trying to figure out how I'm going to ask for her number. And when Lila finally came over, it felt like my chance."

"What did you say?"

"I said, 'So what's up with this naked woman?'"

"What did Lila say?"

"She laughed. She was like, To be honest, nobody really knows what's up with this naked woman."

"Sounds like Lila."

"Gary was embarrassed. Started asking her all these very appropriate questions, like who is the artist, and is this acrylic, blah blah blah, but I knew that for the first time in my life, I said the right thing somehow. At the right time. I made a woman laugh, at an art gallery no less."

"So, wait, what happened then?"

"She handed us her card, said to call if we changed our minds about buying the painting. I really thought she was giving it to me. But Gary was the one who took it. Slipped it right into his wallet, and we left. I was going to ask Gary for it a few days later. But then I'm at his house for Juice's birthday that Friday, and Gary says, 'You'll never believe who came into my office today. That woman from the art gallery.' Just a total fucking coincidence. He seemed really rocked by it. Said something about her father being sick, but he was optimistic. Thought he could give the man a few more years. Then asked me if I thought it was weird for him to go out with her, and I was just like, Gary, if I'm your ethics board, you're in trouble. And he laughed and they started dating and the rest is history.

"But man, I was disappointed," he says. "I know everyone thinks I'm a shithead, and maybe I was. But the pandemic really fucked with me. In a good way, maybe. It was just me, all of the time, in my apartment. Just me, and at a certain point, I thought I was going mad, you know?"

"I know."

"I could finally see why people got married and shit. Like, even if it doesn't last forever, I could see why it would still be worth it. I think I already felt it when I hugged Lila on the street that day. I just got this strange feeling. Like, This is the woman. This is your chance. She just walked right up to you on the street so fucking hold on to her."

"Why didn't you ever tell Gary that?"

"I hadn't heard Gary talk about another woman since my sister died. So I just . . . gave it to him. I felt for the guy," he says. "He was so amped up. Like it had to mean something. Like this was all proof that the universe was good again. I couldn't take that from him. And the truth was, I was still going through my shit. And I didn't really know Lila. How did I really know she was the one?"

"And now that you know her?"

He laughs. "Oh, she's something."

"What do you like about her?"

"She's just funny," he says. "You expect her to be this one thing, and sometimes she is, around everybody in the family, but if it's just us, she's different. She's honest. Sharp. Smart. Cuts right through me, calls me on my shit. Talks a million miles an hour."

It sounds like the way Lila is around Phoebe.

"They don't talk to each other that much," Jim says, turning to look at Phoebe. "You notice that?"

"I do."

They were always standing next to each other, talking to other people.

"Gary's different around her," he says. "Quiet. And I don't know. Maybe that's okay. Maybe he's happy. And if he's happy, I'm genuinely happy for him. I don't want the guy to be miserable forever."

"But . . ."

"But he doesn't seem happy. Not like he was with my sister."

"Maybe he's just different now."

"But he's not."

"What do you mean?"

"I thought the Gary I knew died with my sister that day," Jim says. "I didn't think I'd ever see him again. But then I saw you and him talking on the boat."

"Oh?"

"Yeah. He talks to you the same way he talked to my sister."

"How is that?"

"Like himself," Jim says. "It's been nice, watching. Nice to see him come out to play again. After all these years."

"Yeah," Phoebe admits. "I know what you mean."

They are quiet, and Jim gets confused.

"None of this really matters, though. I don't know why I get so excited about it in my head sometimes. They're getting married. *Fuck*. They're getting married. And I'm the best man. And do you know why we're giving our speeches at the rehearsal dinner and not the wedding? Because Lila said she doesn't trust me to do it at the actual wedding. I mean, that shit hurt. I thought if anything, Lila trusted me. And that just makes me feel like all of it was in my head. She doesn't want me. Probably never did."

When Phoebe says nothing, Jim looks at her.

"Right?" Jim asks.

They're playing chicken again. But all Phoebe will say is, "It's not as black and white as you'd think."

"So that means she wants me a little," Jim says, and smiles. "At least I can go down in my seaplane knowing that."

In their silence, Phoebe hears the sounds of people returning to their room. The Blending of the Families is over.

"Lila and Gary are back," Jim says.

Phoebe puts a finger to his mouth.

"Shh," she says. "This is research."

They pull out their notepads, pencils ready, and this makes them laugh again. But there is only the sound of Gary saying goodbye to Lila in her room. The murmurs of Lila's voice. Then the closing of a door. A faucet running. The sounds of a woman alone getting ready for bed. Brushing her teeth. Using the toilet. The steady routines of her night. Yet Phoebe feels rocked by the noise. She can feel each sound deep inside her head. She must be really high. She turns over on her side like she does in yoga class. Under the bed, she notices something. She pulls out a credit card folded in half.

"Jim," she says. "This folded-up credit card is from 1991."

"So?"

"Why would it be from *1991*? Isn't that weird?"

"Is it?"

"What do you think *happened* to this guy?"

"I think focusing on the credit card is a bad idea right now."

"But what is this credit card doing there, under the bed, folded up from thirty-one years ago? I mean, I can't think of any reasonable non-weird reason for it still being here."

Jim looks at her. "I think office hours are over."

"But I'm not ready to go home," she says. "I like it here."

"So don't," Jim says. "Stay here."

He says it so simply, it sounds possible to Phoebe. She will just stay here, on Jim's floor, listening to the sounds of Lila's quiet night.

"Is she crying?" Jim asks.

Phoebe listens for sobs, but she can't hear anything except the soft waves from outside the window.

"I think that's just the ocean," Phoebe says.

Phoebe stares at the ceiling and wonders what Lila thinks when she curls up in bed. Does she regret planning such a big wedding? Does she feel proud of her choices? Does she feel trapped in the spectacle of her own making? And how did weddings get like this? How did they get so big, come to be so important, that a woman couldn't see her way out of it? That a woman would sacrifice her entire life for it? These are big questions, Phoebe thinks, and good writing is always driven by a big question.

"I know what to write in my speech," she says.

BACK IN HER room, she writes her speech while eating the last of the Oreos that are Not Legally Oreos. And no, it's not her dissertation, but it's five whole pages, and afterward she feels victorious. She has completed a writing assignment for the first time in years, and it makes her feel like she can do anything.

I can go buy Frank the dog, she thinks. I can find a job here.

She searches for professor vacancies at nearby colleges and boarding schools. She searches for apartments to rent on Craigslist, even though she suspects Craigslist is just exclusively for murdering people now.

She finds a cute place on Mary Street with high ceilings where she could stay for a month. A condo on Thames where she could stay the entire year. But she is most intrigued by the ad for a mansion on Ocean Drive, owned by a man named Geoffrey. He is looking for something he calls a winter keeper to live there until May and keep it looking like a mansion through the winter. She has never heard of the phrase winter keeper before, but she likes it.

She messages all of them.

SATURDAY

✧

The Rehearsal Dinner

In the morning, Lila stops by on her way out to the flower vendor. She does not say anything about the blending of the families, just talks about a power outage and all the flowers that are melting in the fridge.

"Melting?" Phoebe asks.

But Lila doesn't explain. "I need you to take Gary to run some errands today, because a fun fact about Gary is that he can hardly walk right now."

"Why not?"

"He hurt his back again. This time from surfing. Thank God I didn't go. What a disaster. Imagine if I couldn't walk today? I don't know what Past Lila was thinking, planning a surfing morning before her wedding."

"I want to point out that it's only nine in the morning and you're already talking about yourself in the third person," Phoebe says, and Lila laughs.

"Lila is too busy today to be worried about that right now."

But Phoebe is worried—she's not sure she's ready for a full day with Gary. She's supposed to be letting go of him.

"Why doesn't Jim take Gary?" Phoebe asks.

"Because Gary has to try on his tux and go to the barber, and I just don't trust Jim. I feel certain that Jim would somehow send Gary back with a pink suit and a shaved head."

Phoebe wants to say something else but isn't sure what. Lila turns toward the door.

"You have your speech for tonight ready?" Lila asks.

"I do," Phoebe says.

"I can't wait."

Lila leaves, and Phoebe looks at the speech again.

"Oh no," she says. In the brutal light of morning, the speech is all wrong. It is way too honest. Nothing at all about Gary and Lila. Part op-ed, part long literary analysis, part sermon on the most extravagant, wasteful weddings in literature. "Every wedding, even a successful wedding, is a waste," Phoebe wrote, followed by a series of examples from literature that prove how the modern wedding has gotten totally out of control, how she blamed Queen Victoria for most of it, because prior to her big white dress, weddings in nineteenth-century literature were small affairs that happened in a sentence: "Reader, I married him." Then, a final and totally random concluding side point about how annoying it is when the female protagonist claims she never wants to get married, yet somehow gets to have the biggest wedding in town.

It seems I'll just be winging it, Phoebe thinks, and feels surprised at how excited she is by the challenge. She always gave her best lectures when she didn't plan them too much, when she was too busy to prep. If she planned too intensely, if she wrote it all beforehand, she got flustered halfway through, because they were always longer than she realized. She overdid it. She rarely trusted herself to be herself, even though the students liked it more when she looked at them, when she just stood there like a person and was honest about all the things she knew and all the things she didn't know.

GARY WAITS OUTSIDE the lobby in his car—a nonvintage, regular Hyundai. He is already in the passenger seat. Phoebe gets in to drive.

"I hear you're in pain," Phoebe says.

"So much pain," he says. "Do you want to hear all about it?"

"If it will make the pain go away, sure."

"It will make the pain feel . . . useful. Give us something to talk about, you know."

Phoebe rolls down her window. She wants to feel the ocean air.

"So, the pain," he says.

"Is it . . . painful?"

"Right. That's the word. Painful."

They laugh. They take off. He talks about his aches and pains, and then she talks about her aches and pains, and then they talk about how much more fun it is to talk about their aches and pains than their younger selves expected it would be.

"It honestly doesn't even feel like complaining," Gary says. "It's just like, valid subject material."

"I agree," she says. "How are we not supposed to talk about the slow decay of our bodies?"

"It's truly the most dramatic thing that will ever happen to us," he says. "It's basically like being on a sinking ship. Except you're never allowed to acknowledge that the ship is sinking."

"And then people roll their eyes every time you mention that the ship might be sinking," Phoebe says.

A car pulls up next to them at the light, blasting Kesha so loudly, it ends the conversation. They just sit there and wait, two faithful subjects of Kesha's universe.

"I truly cannot believe it when people drive by with their music that loud," Gary says after Phoebe takes a right.

"Maybe they think we like it," Phoebe says. "Sort of like when you're obsessed with a favorite song and you can't imagine anyone else not wanting to hear it a thousand times. They're probably just driving around thinking they're doing us a service, like, Everybodyyyy likes my music!!"

She sings that last part loudly, and Gary cracks up. He rolls down his window and repeats her song. "Everybodyyyyyy likes my music!"

This is her last day with Gary. She knows this. It deeply saddens her, and yet, at the same time, she is grateful for it. Excited, even. Determined to enjoy it, to want nothing from it but the day itself.

"I aspire to be them, in some way," Phoebe says.

"Really? I'm so embarrassed about my musical tastes, I don't even like turning the radio on when someone is in the car."

"What would you do if I asked you to turn on some music right now?"

"I would deflect the question and ask what you would like to listen to since you're the driver. Dealer's choice."

"Oh, so you'd make your anxiety seem like some noble self-sacrifice."

"Exactly."

She feels playful, like everything is a grand laugh. Even their aches and pains—just a joke between them. A thing to be shared. She turns left onto Bellevue Avenue, and if Phoebe forgets he is getting married tomorrow, and that her life is over, it is a beautiful drive.

They stop at the liquor store. "This should only take a minute," he says. "It's preordered."

They go inside and Gary moves to pick up the box but can't do it with his back. "Shit."

"I got this," Phoebe says. As she brings the box of booze to his car, it occurs to her that she is literally helping Gary and Lila get married with her own brute strength. But that is her job.

Back inside the car, her phone dings.

"It's Geoffrey!" Phoebe says. "Craigslist isn't just for murderers!!"

"Huh? Who is Geoffrey?"

"The mansion keeper," she says. She hands him the phone. "The winter guy. Hey, can you read this aloud?"

"In any particular accent?" he asks.

"You do accents?"

"Only around total strangers."

"What are my options?"

"New York," he says. "Boston. Rhode Island. I'm limited regionally."

"When in Rhode Island."

"Hi, Phoebe," he says, in a Rhode Island accent, which is just a more pronounced version of the way his mother talks. "Thank you for your interest in the Newcombe Mansion. I must say, I am keen to meet you, as I am very delighted to hear you have a PhD in nineteenth-century literature. As you know, the Newcombe Mansion was built in 1845 by a Civil War hero, Jonathan Newcombe, so this seems fortuitous. I hope I have the chance to meet an applicant with your level of expertise."

"Wait, a winter keeper?" Gary asks, in his regular voice. "What are winter keepers?"

"People who caretake mansions. In the winter, when the owners are at their real homes. Turns out it's a job in Newport."

"Newcombe is a twenty-room property," he reads again in his accent. "I would love to show you. I am available to meet you anytime this afternoon or tomorrow. I am hoping to have the matter settled before the end of the weekend."

"Holy shit!" she says. "Tell him I can meet him later after I drop you off."

"No, sorry," he says. "I'm coming with you to see this mansion."

"But we have to get your tux," she says.

"That can wait." He writes back to Geoffrey, and she puts the address in Waze.

"Wait, why don't you have a Rhode Island accent?" she asks. "Aren't you from Rhode Island?"

"I took a speech class at Yale, trained myself out of it."

"Wow," she says. "Traitor."

THE NEWCOMBE MANSION is guarded by tall iron gates that someone painted blue. The gates open as they approach.

"Naturally," Gary says.

Geoffrey waits for them in the front entrance. He is a small, Southern man wearing a light peach suit. He looks especially small next to the big house. The entrance is so formal, with giant gargoyles up on the roof, and when Phoebe says hello, she half expects Geoffrey to bow or curtsy. But he shakes her hand like any old American.

He welcomes her into the house and starts by telling her that this is a position exclusively for caretaking the interior.

"We have people for the grounds," he says. "But our main interior caretaker of ten years just unexpectedly resigned."

He asks what experience she has caretaking nineteenth-century mansions, and she tells him she has no experience, though researched many for her dissertation. She doesn't harp on the fact that most of them were fictional estates, often discussed primarily as metaphors for colonialism.

"In my line of work, I research historical buildings a lot," she says. "I have a chapter in my dissertation about Victorian domestic interiors. I study the way nineteenth-century novels portray domestic space as primarily female and the natural world as primarily male."

She tells him about the years she spent in the basement archives, and it feels good to talk about her research again. All those hours in grad school she spent cataloging the effects of each room on the characters in *Jane Eyre*—she would sit in the library and look up and before she knew it, it would be dark. She loved those early days, when she didn't know exactly what she was writing yet, when she was just on the cusp of figuring it out.

"Excellent," Geoffrey says. "Because this is a job about research. Let's say this fabric wallpaper from 1845 starts to tear. What do you do?"

"I don't know," Phoebe admits. "But I would research it until I found out."

Geoffrey laughs.

"Somehow, I believe you," he says. "Shall we?"

They turn to the door and Phoebe sees a face carved into the wood. "Is that Dante?"

"I'm really glad you know that," Geoffrey says.

HE TAKES THEM through the grand courtyard. He tells them about the owner, how he built this house for his daughter, Elizabeth.

"You can see Elizabeth's collection of Parisian art in the dining room," Geoffrey says. "She ended up marrying a French banker, who is featured here in this painting. But they didn't get along, and Elizabeth spent much of her time traveling the world, collecting the art and the vases you'll see everywhere in this house."

Then he gets a phone call.

"I need to take this," Geoffrey says. "Why don't you go through and look at the place on your own, let me know what you think?"

THEY WANDER THROUGH the house. Every doorway is framed with elaborate woodwork. Muses painted gold in each corner. The face of Cicero carved above the bathroom. And a tub made of marble so thick, it looks like a coffin. Phoebe runs her finger along the frame of the bathroom mirror.

"I think this is platinum leaf," she says.

"Platinum leaf?" Gary asks. "I didn't even know that existed."

They head into the bedroom, where Elizabeth's art collection continues.

"Do you think a woman who collects art like this is the happiest woman?" Phoebe asks. "Or the least happy?"

"The question presumes that we can be happy," Gary says.

"Can we not?"

"I think we talk about happiness all wrong. As if it's this fixed state we're going to reach. Like we'll just be able to live there, forever. But that's not my experience with happiness. For me, it comes and goes. It shows up and then disappears like a bubble."

"When was the last time you were really happy?" Phoebe asks Gary.

"The honest answer?" he says. "Right now."

She wants to ask why this is. Is it because he's getting married tomorrow? Or because of how it feels to be standing here in this mansion together? Phoebe feels strikingly happy, like this kind of connection between two people can fix everything. For just a moment, she fantasizes about them living here, together, roaming the halls, talking about Parisian paintings at breakfast.

"I think the collector's impulse is both beautiful and repugnant," she says.

To collect is to care more than most. But it is also to hoard. To take things out of the world and make them only yours.

"Art collections were basically like travel souvenirs for these people," Phoebe says. "Going to Paris and bringing back seven wall paintings."

They stare at Elizabeth's bed.

"Is this where you'd sleep?" he asks.

"I think this is where Elizabeth's ghost sleeps."

He laughs, and they look at the portrait of Elizabeth above the bed. She feels drawn to this woman. Maybe because she, too, lived alone in her own way, lived alone inside her marriage.

"I think you're right," Gary says, then he turns to her. "Can I see your phone, please?"

She hands it to him. She knows what he's going to do before he even does it.

"When you're living here, I want you to call me when you actually do see a ghost," Gary says, tapping in his number.

"What are you going to do about it?" she asks.

"Nothing," he says. "You're right. I'm famously ineffective against ghosts. Just ask Juice."

She laughs.

"But promise you'll call anyway?" he asks.

"I promise."

She looks down at the old wood floor, puts the phone in her pocket. It feels like she keeps something special in there now. The future, where she lives in this beautiful house and can call Gary when she needs to.

They walk into the next room.

"What do you think Geoffrey meant when he said, 'I believe you,' like that? Was that an insult?"

"I think, coming from Geoffrey, it's the highest praise of all."

"Is it something about my voice or my hair?" she asks.

"I think it's just your vibe," Gary says. "You come off as . . . very smart. Like you've studied everything and now have all the world's knowledge inside of you."

"Is that obnoxious?"

"It's the best."

When Geoffrey returns, he quickly apologizes, then says, "So what do you think?"

"It's wonderful," Phoebe says.

He takes her down the hall. "You can use the whole house as your own, but this would be your bedroom. We like to keep Elizabeth's as her own."

Her bedroom would be small, but she has always liked small bedrooms. Never liked the way her bed at home didn't fill up the room. Always felt like something was missing. But this bedroom is understated, a simple yellow-and-blue color palette. A cozy place to go when this house feels too big.

"Perfect," Phoebe says.

"The job would start in three weeks," he says. "But you could move in a few days before. Let me talk it over with my partner tonight, and we'll get back to you tomorrow."

Then, he takes them to the garden, a formal one with boxwoods carved into spirals. They walk up a small hill and sit on a tiny bench because from there, you can see the ocean.

WHEN THEY GET back in the car, Gary looks at his phone.

"Shit, I actually need to stop by the office to sign a few papers. Take care of things before I leave for the honeymoon. Do you mind?"

The honeymoon. In three days, Gary and Lila will be on a plane to St. Thomas. They will be married. They will be drinking champagne with rings on their fingers. And where will Phoebe be?

"On a Saturday?" Phoebe asks.

"We're open until noon."

Gary's office is in Tiverton. It looks like a house. Sits on the side of a beautiful coastal road, because most of the roads are beautiful here. On the edge of the country. It gives Phoebe this feeling like she is just about to fall off.

Inside, the receptionists see Gary and get excited. They have missed him, but they also want to know what the hell he is doing here.

"We're not supposed to see you until tomorrow at the wedding!" one of the receptionists says.

It is nice, she thinks, how he invited his whole staff to the wedding.

"I just couldn't stay away," Gary teases, and then goes into his office.

Phoebe waits on the chairs outside. She tries to imagine Lila and her father here doing the same, but it's hard to picture it. She listens to patients stand at the counter, casually spewing their tragic family histories aloud to the receptionist who asks about gaps in their medical history. Grandparents wiped out by lung cancer. A father who the daughter doesn't know. Many brothers and sisters, she adds.

"But I don't know those, either," the woman says, and she doesn't sound ashamed. It's just a fact. She has no family. Then she sits down, and Phoebe is impressed. Phoebe makes a note to start practicing that—not feeling ashamed of her family history but understanding it as just a fact.

On the wall, there are computer screens you can touch to learn more about your diagnosis. A playset in the corner for children. Seasonal decorations for every holiday. On the way out, Gary explains that there's no point in taking them down just to put them up. And they like having all the holidays with them at all times of the year.

"That's nice," Phoebe says. "Why not?"

"Exactly," Gary says.

This is Gary's life, she thinks.

AT THE TAILOR, the woman tells him he has the build of a football player. She tells him to spread his legs.

"Good, fits well," she says and looks at Phoebe. "What do you think?"

Does she think Phoebe is the fiancée? Gary looks at her, like he's waiting to hear what she thinks, too. And why? If she doesn't like it, is he going to ask for a new one? Is he not going to get married? No.

"Looks good," Phoebe says. "You look like . . . a groom."

Outside on the street, where honest communication is possible again, they don't speak. Here they are, alone together, headed to the car. Here they are, on the precipice of the rest of their lives.

"So if you become a winter keeper, that would mean you would move here and quit your job in St. Louis?" he asks.

"Yes," she says.

"You would just leave everything behind?"

"That's the plan."

He pauses like he is skeptical of this. "You won't miss it?"

"Of course I will," she says. "But even when I was there, I missed it. I missed everything all the time."

They get back in the car. She wonders if her feelings for Gary could be a new form of love, one she's never known before: love without expectation. Love that you are just happy enough to feel. Love that you don't try to own like a painting. But she doesn't know if that is a real thing. She hopes it is. She looks out at the parking lot all around them, like she's a kid going on an errand with her father, announcing whatever she sees.

"That's a creepy billboard," she says. "What's Mummy's Favorite Music? Why would that be a billboard?"

"I think it says, What Is *a* Mummy's Favorite Music? Not, What's Mummy's Favorite Music?"

They try to guess what kind of music a mummy might like.

"Baroque?"

"It would really matter when the mummy died."

"Synth-pop."

"A postmodern mummy."

She turns on the car.

"Ready?" he asks.

"Ready," she says.

But they continue to sit there for another moment, and it feels like the hot tub all over again, as if something is supposed to happen now, as if she should say a thing that will start her brand-new life, but what?

She can't destroy a wedding. This wedding is too big to fail. This wedding is like the revolution of the earth. It's going to happen whether Phoebe says anything or not. Whether anybody is in love or not. What right does she have to say anything?

"Where to?" she asks.

She needs to go back, needs to get out of this car before she says anything.

"To the barber," Gary says.

THEY GO TO this guy Nick that he used to see when he was a boy. It's out of the way but worth it, he says on the drive. Nick used to carve lightning bolts in the side of his head. Nick gave him his first buzz cut. Then a shave for his first wedding. But it's been years—Gary invested in self–hair cutting tools during Covid and never looked back. Yet here they are, pulling onto a side street, and Gary sounds excited, like they're traveling back in time.

"You got an appointment?" Nick says as soon as they walk in, but he doesn't turn his head from the man's hair he is clipping.

"You don't do appointments," Gary says.

"I do appointments now," Nick says. "Since Covid."

Gary looks at the line of men waiting on chairs and says he would have made one had he known.

"I've got some room on Monday," Nick says.

"Monday is too late. But thanks anyway, Nick."

"Too late? You off to fight the British or something?"

"Getting married," Gary says.

"Are you the lucky bride?"

"No," Phoebe says. "I'm just a friend."

Nick looks at the two of them like he doesn't quite believe it. Why else would she be here, watching him get a shave?

"For you, the groom, I'll make time," Nick says. "You'll just have to wait."

While they wait, they don't talk. They listen to the men on TV talk about the Celtics. Then the wind turbines going up on the coast. Then the hotly debated bike lanes in Providence. There is something routine about the silence, like sitting in a church pew where everybody knows not to talk, even the small boy who just kicks his legs. It's not until the last man is called to Nick's chair when Gary speaks.

"So you really won't miss teaching?" Gary asks, as if they had been in some long conversation about it.

"I'll miss some things about teaching," Phoebe says.

"Which things?"

"The moments of connecting with students," she says. "The moments when they really do learn something. The back-and-forth. The way it feels to have a really good class. I did love it when I first started."

"What won't you miss?"

"The pretending," she says. "I never realized how much pretending was involved."

"Pretending to be what?"

"Pretending to be excited. Pretending you haven't said the same exact joke over and over again. Pretending knowledge is some beautiful, fortuitous interweaving quilt of facts. Pretending that everything that happens can be strung along a satisfying, linear narrative."

"Is that what you said during your job interview?"

"I said something worse. I invoked Marx."

"Solid move. Everybody wants to hire a Marxist."

"I was pretty committed to pretending I was a Marxist then. I went on and on about how difficult it is to measure student progress, how there's no guarantee that they've learned anything, and how teachers, too, are alienated from their labor. We so rarely get to understand our effect on the students, yet we work anyway."

This is why she always needed research and writing.

"It was nice to create something," she says. She loved the thrill of discovery, of being able to look at the document at the end of the day and say, I did that. Like being a barber, she imagines. Getting to see the final creation. Trimming a man's hair just over the ears, then dusting him off. And when she stopped wanting to write, it was an actual loss. She can see this now, how she has been grieving that, too. The loss of her creativity.

"Bastards put in meters while we were all asleep during Covid," Nick says. He picks up change out of an old ash tray. "Got to feed this thing four times a day. When I'm back, you're up."

Then they're alone in the shop. They don't speak. It is only the sound of the TV that threatens to dull the moment, turn it into nothing.

"Are you pretending to be something right now?" Gary asks.

"Excuse me?"

She grows hot. She is pretending, yes. She is pretending to talk about pretending to be a Marxist when really she just wants to tell him that she thinks she might be in love with him, that she hasn't felt this connected to anybody ever, not even her husband, because she has never looked her husband in the eye and admitted she wanted to die, never actually showed her husband her full self. This whole week has bonded her to him and running errands with him does not help. Something about watching him sign papers at the office, watching him wait at the barber, watching him just be ordinary Gary.

But she had love once, great love, and that didn't end up mattering.

"I'm pretending not to be confused," Phoebe says. "How am I doing?"

"Excellent performance," he says. "You never seem confused."

"Well, I'm confused."

"What are you confused about?"

"Whether or not *you* are pretending to be something right now."

He pauses. "I'm pretending I don't want to say something to you right now. I'm pretending that it does not make me very nervous."

"Can I ask what's so scary about it?"

"I don't know how to phrase it. I don't know how to say it. I don't know what happens after I say it."

She gets the feeling that if this conversation continues, something irrevocable will happen.

"But unfortunately there's no one else I can tell," he says. "No one to talk to about it with . . . except you."

"Then talk to me about it."

"It's so easy with you," he says. "I don't understand it."

"What don't you understand?"

"I felt it when we talked that first night. I honestly cannot stop thinking about that first night in the tub. And trust me, I've tried. I have been trying to figure out why I can't stop thinking about you, because I am getting married tomorrow."

"Yes," she says. "You are getting married tomorrow."

"But I feel so drawn to you," he says. "I just want to be around you, Phoebe. Because when I'm around you, I feel good. I feel honest. I feel like myself. Like maybe I understand what life is again. I know what to say, finally, after years of never knowing what the hell to do or say. Do you know what I mean?"

Phoebe knows. She feels this way, too. Exactly. And she wants to tell him. It would feel so good to tell him.

"Is that crazy?" Gary asks. "You're looking at me like that's crazy."

"I don't think it's crazy. I think it's scary."

"It's scary," he says.

"It's very scary that you're saying this all to me the night before your wedding," she says. "I don't think you should be doing that."

"When else am I supposed to be doing it?" Gary asks. "If I don't do it now, when do I do it?"

The door dings. Nick is back.

"You got to use a fucking credit card now," Nick says. "So, the usual?"

"The usual," Gary says.

Gary gets up, slowly. Phoebe watches as Nick takes the clippers to the thick mass of Gary's beard. Phoebe watches Nick work, like a sculptor, who is trimming off layers of Gary, until he arrives at "the usual." It makes Phoebe nervous, seeing pieces of Gary fall off in giant clumps to the floor. After, Nick puts a towel over Gary's face and, for some reason, when he starts to shave him, Phoebe can't watch. Looks down at her magazine. She has always liked the sound of the razor against a man's stubble. Like the sound of a mason spreading mortar on a brick.

When he's nearly done, Phoebe looks up, and they lock eyes in the mirror. They stay like that for a moment, just looking at each other. Nick nicks him on the back of the neck. Phoebe instinctively leans forward as if to help with the blood. But Nick's got it.

"Happens all the time," Nick says, and puts a towel to his skin.

"I'm not sure I'd go around telling your clients that," Gary says, and the two men laugh.

"So you're still a wise ass," Nick says.

THE WHOLE WAY home, it's like driving with a different Gary.

"Is it weird?" Gary asks. "Do I have beard face?"

"What's beard face?"

"It's like glasses face. When you've only seen someone with glasses and they take them off, and all of a sudden, they're a different person."

"Maybe," she says. "I think it's more like when someone brings a dog to the groomer and the dog comes out looking like it's been robbed."

"Oh, gee, thanks. A dog that's been robbed. Totally the look I was going for."

They laugh. He looks at himself in the mirror, rubs his chin, like he can't get used to it.

"I do feel a little like I've been robbed," he says.

Maybe this is when one of them would have started up their

conversation from Nick's again, but Gary says, "Shit, I forgot about cash for the vendors. I'm sorry. One more thing."

"No problem," Phoebe says.

THEY CAN'T TAKE out enough cash at the first bank, so they drive to another bank, and at the second bank, Phoebe just waits in the car. She watches him disappear into the building, and then studies the strangers on the road. She sees families on vacation. Non-wedding people eating ice cream. Collagen shot lattes. People just shopping, carrying on. People who have no idea that Lila and Gary exist.

Amazing to think that just last week, Phoebe was one of those people, too. She had been so bold then, doing exactly what she wanted for maybe the first time in her life. She wants to feel that feeling again, the one she felt in the elevator, the one she felt in the tub, the feeling of standing up proudly in her lingerie, of owing Lila absolutely nothing, being loyal to nobody but herself. Because Phoebe knows what Lila cannot know yet: There is no reason to make decisions you don't want to make at twenty-eight. No reason to marry a man with gray sideburns if you hate the look of them. They are only going to get grayer.

Yes, Lila will be just fine, she thinks.

But then she sees Gary come out of the bank and put the money in his wallet, the wallet in his pocket, and something about this looks so final to Phoebe. He looks like such a groom, clean-shaven, putting money in his wallet to pay the vendors for his wedding. And Phoebe feels like the maid of honor again, with the box of booze heavy in the back seat.

She is loyal to Lila now. Loyal to the production that is this wedding—that's the truth of it.

When Gary gets back in the car, he says, "Should we finish our conversation?"

But Phoebe says no. "I honestly don't think there's anything left to say."

Phoebe just drives.

. . .

WHEN THEY STEP in the lobby, the hotel feels very empty. Like a stage just before the big performance. Everybody must be off doing their last-minute tasks before the rehearsal, getting dressed in their costumes.

Gary and Phoebe are quiet in the elevator, quiet as Gary carries his tux and Phoebe carries the box of liquor down the hallway. Gary says, "Do you mind holding this?" and gives her the tux as he gets his key. It feels so intimate, like they are opening the door to their home after a long day of errands.

But before they enter, there is Lila coming out of her room. Lila looks at Gary and then back at Phoebe. A flicker of realization—Phoebe is certain that she saw it. Certain that Lila knows. Women can feel these things. They know. Phoebe knew. Phoebe knew in that moment when she saw her husband laugh with Mia. Love is visible—it paints the air between two people a different color, and everyone can see it.

But all Lila says is, "Gary, oh my God, your face looks so different!"

"Good different?" Gary asks. "Or bad different?"

Bad different, Phoebe thinks. He is the clean-shaven groom ready for his ceremony. A man she will probably never get to know. By the time the beard starts to grow back, they will be strangers again.

"Good different, of course," Lila says.

Phoebe puts the booze down on the desk. Outside through the window, Phoebe can see Carlson setting up the chairs for the rehearsal dinner tonight. Phoebe feels a fog of grief, a sudden depression moving in like an afternoon storm. Like if she doesn't run now, it'll take her alive.

"I should go get ready," Phoebe says.

Lila gives Phoebe a big strong hug like she did the first day they met. Maybe Lila doesn't know. Maybe all Lila can feel right now is fear of what Lila doesn't want, all the bad things circling around her like a boa constrictor, closing in tight.

"Two things," Lila says. "It's just you and me driving to the wedding tomorrow. And can you make sure my mother doesn't get too drunk tonight? Apparently, she started drinking at two. Why does she do that?"

It's a rhetorical question, but Phoebe can't help herself.

"She can't drink at night," Phoebe says. "You'll understand, when you're older."

Lila's mother is sober by the time they get to the Breakers.

"Honestly, I'm ready for a nap," Patricia says to Phoebe.

In the Great Hall, the wedding people are all lined up in order of importance, as decided by Nancy, the events planner for the Preservation Society. First there is Gary's cousin Roy, the officiant for the wedding, likely the only family event at which he has been deemed the least important. Then the groom's parents. The flower girl, the ring bearer. The bridesmaids. The maid of honor. The mother of the bride and her grandmother. And, then, of course, the bride.

"Do not touch the walls. Do not touch the windows," Nancy says. "Do not touch anything here but your spouse! I find that's generally a good rule for life, and also the Breakers."

Everyone laughs.

"I'll be back," Nancy says. "And when I come back, be ready."

As soon as she leaves, people slacken. Marla walks over to introduce her son, Oliver, to Phoebe, because Phoebe is a professor of literature. Oliver gets excited about this in a way a twelve-year-old child normally does not.

"I've read all the Percy Jackson books," Oliver says. "My favorite by far is *The Titan's Curse*. Have you ever read it?"

"I'm afraid I haven't," Phoebe says.

Oliver looks disappointed but then runs off with Juice to see who can get closest to the walls without touching them.

Bootsie starts pointing out the things she finds most objectionable about the Breakers to Lila and Patricia, while Phoebe gets a phone call from her husband. She puts her phone on silent. She doesn't want to hear his voice tonight. Not here, in this Great Hall, which feels more like a courtyard. Not now, not tonight. Phoebe is already confused enough. She drops the phone back in her purse, and Marla pulls out hers.

"I sent my last sext to Robert before he got on the plane this morning," Marla whispers to Phoebe. "He hasn't responded since, and now I'm worried it's weird."

"Why would it be weird? Isn't he right there?" Phoebe asks, looking at a tall, thin man who has walked over to get the kids away from the walls.

"Yeah, that's why it's weird. I told him that my tiny little pussy is wet and waiting for him, and then we just greet each other at the Breakers with dry kisses on the cheek," Marla says. "I mean, shouldn't we be beyond this stage now? We've been married for fifteen years."

"Maybe it's the right place to be," Phoebe says. "If you're starting over, you're starting over."

Then Nancy returns and says, "Go, go, go!" as if they are kids entering a soccer field for the big game. When Phoebe walks past Nancy and through the door, she waits for a slap on the ass that never comes.

Outside, the sun is bright. She takes slow steps toward the pergola. She pauses in front of it, in front of Gary. She looks at Gary's face, but the sun is too bright behind him. She keeps her eyes low, focused on Jim's shiny shoes. She wonders if they were the same ones he wore to Wendy's funeral.

Phoebe walks to the left, completes the line of women that will stand at Lila's side. From there, she watches Lila walk slowly up the aisle in her white reception dress. Lila beams at Gary so brightly, it feels like the moment in the barbershop is long forgotten. It feels like all of the moments that came before this one are irrelevant. This is what the wedding ritual does to Phoebe—even just the rehearsing of it: Nothing can compete.

"Okay, then we'll cut the music and you stand here and look deeply into each other's eyes," Nancy says, and she turns to Roy. "Then you will say whatever meaningful thing it is you are going to say."

"And then we'll be married and hooray," Lila says.

They kiss, just for good measure.

It is over, and they walk out, one by one, each woman pairing up with a groomsman. Phoebe links arms with Jim. His arm feels good in hers. It is solid, the arm of a man who probably balances well on a ridgeline.

Maybe tonight I'll sleep with Jim, Phoebe thinks.

She's surprised by the thought. Jim feels more like a brother to her. But maybe they both need to redirect their desire. Have a night with each other. She's never had sex with a younger man before. Something about spending too much time around students. Their youth was appalling to her. How much they didn't know. How little they thought about the Battle of the Bulge.

But Jim is a good man. An engineer. He is building a seaplane.

"You ever finish that speech?" Phoebe asks him as they turn the corner back into the Great Hall where they started.

"I did, actually," Jim says, and he sounds proud.

BACK AT THE hotel, the patio has been transformed into a magical fairy-tale forest for the rehearsal dinner. Oak farmhouse tables, set up in rows, torches lining the border of the stone floor. White roses hanging from the balconies above. And right in the middle of it all stand Lila and Gary, staring at the giant painting of Patricia naked.

"Who brought this painting here?" Lila asks when Phoebe and Jim join them. "I did not ask for this to be brought here."

"It was your mother's idea," Gary says. "She wanted to surprise you. She knows how much it means to us."

"Right," Lila says, and nods slowly. "But there are *children* here."

"Technically only two," Jim says.

"Juice has seen this painting a million times," Gary says, confused.

"And Oliver seems . . . advanced," Phoebe says.

Phoebe looks at the painting of Patricia for the first time. There stands the cubist abstraction of a naked mother in the bright sun of a hyperrealistic garden. If the mother didn't look so fragmented, or if the garden didn't look so dead, it wouldn't work. But it does. It's beautiful. And sad. Beautiful because it's sad or sad because it's beautiful.

"I'll grab us a drink," Gary says to Lila.

When he walks away, Lila says, "I just don't understand why my mother must make even *my wedding* about her naked body."

Jim walks closer to the painting as if he might figure it out.

"Please do not get so close to my mother, Jim," Lila says.

He points to the book that Withers painted in Patricia's hand.

"Is the title of this book really *No One Gardens Alone*?" he asks.

"Wait, seriously?" Lila asks. She bursts out laughing. She looks closer at the painting. "I bought my mother that book for her birthday. I thought she might like, need a hobby or something."

Jim looks at her. "See? In that way, this painting actually is all about you."

"From one bullshitter to the next, that is some serious bullshit," Lila says.

He laughs.

"But thanks for trying," Lila says.

She stares at Jim tenderly, and Phoebe looks away as if she is witnessing a private moment she shouldn't. Something about the exchange, the meeting of their eyes. An uncanny moment when the universe is presenting the right order of things, or at least another possible order of things. If Lila's father had chosen a different doctor. If Jim hadn't brought Gary to the gallery that day.

But in this universe, she watches the two of them walk away from each other. Lila headed for her drink at the bar, Jim looping arms with Gary's mother. She wonders what will become of Jim, and worries that losing Lila might set him back another decade. Imagines he might become a man who finds it easier to build a seaplane before he builds a family. The kind of man who lives alone for so long, he ends up treating his own house like a country, carrying everything he needs as he walks the perimeter, his loud laugh the anthem the neighbors hear from afar. But maybe one day, he'll finally scrub the oil off his hands for the last time and think, Where did everybody go?

And Lila—where will she be by then? Ten years into marriage with Gary. Perhaps with two children. Already on her second sleeping pill in the upstairs bedroom. Starting to understand why her mother day drinks.

"So, WHAT DID it actually feel like to be a sniper?" Phoebe asks Roy by the appetizer table. Maybe she'll go for Roy instead, she thinks. Roy is the only man here seemingly not in love with someone else. And he is big, tall, like some action hero who is too large for every suit in the known world.

"It was phenomenal," Roy says.

"Phenomenal?" Phoebe says. "You mean in the traditional sense of the word?"

"What do you mean, in the traditional sense of the word?"

"Like when people back in the day used to say phenomenal to describe something celestial made visible."

"Huh?"

"Like a shooting star was phenomenal, because they believed it to be a sign from God."

Roy gives her a long look like maybe he understands what she's trying to say. But then he leans in and whispers, "Want to fuck?"

Perhaps it is not so strange of a request, two people at a wedding not their own. It happens in movies all the time. It probably happens to Roy all the time.

"Do people fuck you just because you ask?" Phoebe asks, genuinely curious.

"The ones who look me in the eye," he says. "In Iraq, the only women who look men directly in the eyes are prostitutes."

"That can't be true," Phoebe says.

"It is," he says.

He thought it was weird at first but then got used to it and thought it was amazing what you could get used to over time. He says it's really hard being back in the States.

"Women here have no problem looking you in the eye," he says. "Like you, right now. You're doing it. What does it *mean*?"

He says he can never tell who wants to fuck him and who is just being polite.

"That must be really hard," Phoebe says.

PHOEBE MAKES HER way back to Jim at the bar. She passes Nat and Suz in floral dresses down to their ankles. Marla and her husband, picking at the olives, trying to talk in real life. Then Gary and Lila, who have become unreachable during the height of cocktail hour. They stand near the door, greeting new people, holding drinks that match the sunset. When Lila laughs, Gary puts his hand on her back like he did on the boat. They already look married. She remembers her own wedding, how just making all those decisions together in some way married them. Each handshake was a way of saying, I do, I do, I do.

Phoebe orders a margarita. She wonders if she'll ever be able to drink gin and tonics again. She watches the bartender squeeze the lime.

"You finish *your* speech?" Jim asks.

"I did," Phoebe says. "And I learned never to write a speech after I've had two weeds."

Jim laughs so explosively, it seems like there's a good chance he might die before the end of it. Even Gary and Lila look over as he holds his chest. They all watch as it trickles out like exhaust from a tailpipe. But he survives. He puts his arm around Phoebe, and Gary looks over. They meet eyes, but then comes another wedding person to shake Gary's hand.

"You make me laugh," Jim says. "Sit next to me tonight."

"I think we have assigned seats," Phoebe says, picking up the card with her name on it. Phoebe feels proud to be at Table 1 for the first time in her life, assigned to the seat directly across from the bride and groom. Jim is seated beside her.

"It's fate," Jim says.

Lila picks up her glass, clinks a spoon against it. Gary raises a champagne flute.

"We can't tell you how grateful we've been for your support and your community this week," Gary says. "It's wonderful to be here, in this beautiful hotel, with you all."

When talking to his guests, it feels like the Gary who was sitting next to her in the barbershop is truly gone. This Gary is beardless and has nothing to do with Phoebe at all. But when Gary turns around to gesture at the magnificent ocean behind them, Phoebe sees it: the tiny spot of blood where the barber nicked him earlier.

"The dinner will be a five-course meal," Lila says. "With a palette cleanser in between. And then after, we'll go down to the beach to enjoy the fireworks and s'mores for the kids. So please enjoy and take your assigned seats."

As they all sit down, Gary's mother stands up.

"Let's hold hands and say grace," Gary's mother says.

Phoebe holds hands with Patricia, whose hand is as smooth and dry as a stone, and she worries about crushing it for some reason. On the other side is Jim.

"Bless us, O Lord, and these, Thy gifts, which we are about to receive from Thy bounty. Through Christ, our Lord," Gary's mother says. "Amen."

While half of the room does the sign of the cross, Juice reaches out for Jim's wine.

"Can I have a sip?" Juice asks.

"No," Jim says.

"But everyone else is drinking," Juice says.

"When you're older, you'll have time to drink more drinks than you'll ever want. Trust your uncle on this one."

Gary is just watching all of this, always a little stunned by Juice's attempts to get older. Or maybe he is just studying Jim, who is leaning into Phoebe now, very obviously, whispering something in her ear.

"What the fuck is a palette cleanser anyway?" Jim whispers.

"A lemon thing on a spoon," Phoebe says.

"Oh, right, that makes perfect sense."

Phoebe laughs, and in this space so close to Jim, it feels safe to return Gary's gaze. But Gary has already looked away, and it's so strange to Phoebe that humans have learned how to do that—how to look away just in time.

"But what if I die? Not everybody gets their time," Juice says.

"You will not die," Gary says.

"You don't know that," Juice says.

"Yes, I do," Gary says.

"Are you God?"

"He's an adult human," Jim says. "Statistically, most children in America live to see their own drinking age."

"How do you know that?"

"Because I'm an adult human! I know things," Jim says.

Every so often Marla and her husband talk to each other by asking Oliver to do something completely inappropriate, like publicly conjugate a Latin noun, which makes the table supremely uncomfortable, though everybody does a good job of not showing it.

"Your second course," the waiter says, and Gary's mother stands up.

"Let's hold hands and say grace," she says.

Lila looks at Phoebe, and Gary and Marla glance at each other, like they're not sure if it's the early signs of dementia or the late-stage Catholicism that is making her insist on saying grace before each course. But nobody stops her.

"Bless us, O Lord, and these, Thy gifts, which we are about to receive from Thy bounty," Gary's mother says.

Jim runs his finger alongside Phoebe's palm.

"Through Christ, our Lord. Amen."

After, Jim doesn't let go of her hand. Gary and Lila just stare at the two hands, while Phoebe tries to make jokey conversation about when and how often people should say grace in a five-course dinner.

"It's a good question," Jim says. "Which one is the real meal? Which one is the actual dinner for which we must be the most grateful, Professor Stone?"

"Sorry, I don't do philosophical inquiries," Phoebe says. "If you want to debate the categorical nature of a meal, you'll need my ex-husband for that. He's the philosopher."

They laugh and let go of each other.

"We don't need Socrates to tell us that this isn't a meal," Gary's father says. "This is just frou-frou soup. And why's it cold?"

"It's gazpacho," Lila says.

"Gazpacho?" Bootsie says. "Who is Spanish here?"

Gary hands Bootsie's Tupperware to the waiter. "Can you put this in a nice crystal?" he asks.

Then they eat in relative silence, which stretches too long. The clinking of spoons against bowls becomes unbearable, the acknowledgment that the families have nothing to say to one another, except for Phoebe and Jim.

"I can't believe I haven't asked you this yet," Jim says, "but where are you from again?"

"Missouri," Phoebe says. Phoebe is acutely aware that everyone is listening. "You?"

"Pawtucket, Rhode Island," Jim says. "The last place in America to make its own socks."

"What do you mean?" Phoebe asks.

"Factory closed, and now America doesn't make any of its own socks," Jim says.

"Nowhere in America?" Phoebe asks. She finds this both hard to believe and not at all surprising.

"I don't think that's true," Lila says. "Jim just likes to say that for some reason."

"Because it's unbelievable," Jim says. "What can we say about a superpower that doesn't make its own socks?"

"Something about frostbite," Phoebe says.

"Death traditionally starts in the feet," Gary finishes.

"That's a little morbid, Gary," Lila says.

The waiter puts down the next course. "Filet mignon."

They all wait to see if Gary's mother wants to say grace again, but she is already cutting into her meat. The platter of tiny steaks seems like a mistake next to the linen suits, the white lace trim of their lives. Some of the blood pools at the ridges of the serving plate, and Jim asks, "We're supposed to be doing the speeches after the fourth course, right?" But Lila shushes him.

"Let's just make sure we get through the meal first," Lila says.

Phoebe notices the lost button on Patricia's blouse. The yellow on Gary's mother's teeth. Oliver, who shows too much white of his eye when he speaks. Juice, who smells faintly of wet grass and booze. The food in Lila's teeth.

"Lila," Phoebe says, trying to get her attention.

But Lila is worried about the time. "Is the fourth course on its way?" she asks the waiter.

"Yes," he says.

Lila expresses concern about missing the scheduled fireworks at nine, and the waiter assures her he will put in an order to speed things along. And he does. The fish fillets arrive almost immediately, and Gary's mother stands up again.

"Jesus Christ," Patricia says. "Once is fine, expected. Three times, I can't. Enough God! Did God pay for this meal? Did God buy all these tiny steaks? No. I did."

"Actually, Dad did," Lila says.

"Yes! And we should be thanking Henry," Patricia says as she stands up.

"Does this family ever tire of talking about the Trash King?" Bootsie asks, and takes a sip of her gimlet.

"Thank you to the Trash King of Rhode Island," Patricia says to everyone. "And of course, the American people for producing so much trash, for never recycling properly, they have made it possible for all of us to be here tonight."

"Mom," Lila hisses. "This is not about you."

"I know that, Lila," Patricia says. "Nothing is about me. I'm aware!"

Gary's mother is still standing, confused, so Gary gets up to join her.

"Let's all hold hands," Gary says, and Lila rolls her eyes. But they all hold hands and say grace one last time.

"Now we're going to be late to the fireworks," Lila announces after.

"Can we really *miss* the fireworks?" Jim asks. "We can see the whole sky from up here."

"Yes, Jim, one can miss the fireworks," Lila says. "Because there is a setup down on the beach with a bonfire and blankets and a guy who is probably already making s'mores for everyone."

"Isn't the fun of s'mores that you make them yourself?" Marla asks.

Lila looks like she might explode, but instead she turns to Phoebe and Jim.

"Actually, I think we might have to cut your speeches," Lila says.

"Cut the speeches?" Gary asks.

"Jesus Christ, Lila," Jim says.

"What?" Lila asks.

"Jim worked hard on his speech," Gary says, visibly disappointed by Lila's decision.

Phoebe is disappointed, too. She didn't have a speech, but she was still looking forward to getting up there, speaking in front of the crowd, saying nice things about what Lila has meant to her this week, and really taking her place as Lila's friend. But maybe this is why Lila has no real friends, Phoebe thinks. She doesn't know how to keep them. She keeps trading them in for something else.

"Well, I'm sorry," Lila says. "We're paying a thousnd dollars a minute for those fireworks. And we're late already. You can email me the speech tomorrow if you like."

For a moment, Jim looks bereft, as if he might cry, as if this moment has become the moment he feared. He really will get cut out of the family's scheduled programming. But then he smiles to himself, as if he's just learned something vital. He folds his napkin, puts it on the table, and goes up to give his speech.

"Jim!" Lila hisses. But he doesn't stop. Doesn't pull out a piece of paper. He just begins talking.

"Well, Gary," Jim says, "we've been through a lot."

He begins by listing all the things they did together over the years, like riding horses in Wyoming and building a sandbox for Juice in the backyard.

"But the biggest thing we did together," he says, "was watch my sister"—and that's where Jim gets stuck.

He can't finish the sentence without crying. Lila holds her dessert fork tightly in her hand. Gary looks down at the table. Phoebe feels suddenly nervous for Jim, the way she felt when an unprepared student gave a presentation. Jim bites the side of his fist to keep from crying, and each time he seems ready to speak, he starts to cry again. Eventually, Gary's father stands up and starts clapping and says, "We're here for you, Jim." Then everybody starts clapping, everyone stands up, and this makes Jim cry and laugh at the same time. Finally, when Jim has composed himself, he finishes.

"I know I'm not supposed to stand up here and talk about my sister," he says. "But I don't know how else to talk about Gary. I've never known the kind of love that Gary has shown both me and my sister over the years. I never watched a man endure something so painful with so much grace. And on top of all that, he still has time to answer all your questions about whether the colors of your shits are normal—"

Everyone laughs. Lila blushes. Juice takes a sip of Jim's wine.

"I mean, the man even asks follow-up questions," Jim says. "'Would you say it's more of a mauve? Or a maroon?'"

The room laughs even harder.

"Gary is the best. We all love Gary. Everybody loves Gary. Gary is good. But the one thing he's not good at? Being a wingman," Jim says. He looks at the painting on display. "Because when we were at the gallery that day, I thought *I* was the one who was hitting on Lila."

The crowd laughs. They hear all of this as a joke—but Lila freezes. Lila seems to know it's not a joke.

"I thought, Who is this enchanting woman? Because that is one thing we know about Lila. She's enchanting. She has such a big personality. So many ideas. The most particular person I know, you know? Lila knows exactly what she wants. I mean, look at this place—look at these centerpieces, look at how amazing it all is."

The first firework of the evening goes off. It explodes behind Jim with a big red burst, but Lila does not see it. She's transfixed by Jim's words.

"Listen to that firework," Jim says, and the crowd laughs. "Who else would have had fireworks? Who else could have made this happen? Who else would have asked us to stay here for an entire week?"

"Six days, Jim," Lila corrects, and the crowd laughs again.

"Not including the travel days," Jim says.

They are good together. A comedy duo.

"See? Lila's bold—God, I really do love it. That's her great gift. That's what is going to make life with Lila so fun. So much bigger than the rest of us could dream for ourselves. And I'm so grateful to have been brought here, after a really dark time, to be given this chance to be included in that dream, to play my small part, to come together. It's what I've missed more than anything."

Another firework. Jim pauses, as if he's waiting for the lights to burn out of the sky. Then, he raises his glass. The whole room is moved, and Phoebe can feel it, too.

"A toast, to Lila and my brother Gary," Jim says.

Gary's eyes are bright red with tears. Everyone claps, and Gary stands to hug Jim. Juice takes another swig of Jim's wine just before he takes his place back next to Phoebe.

"You going to finish your fillet?" Jim asks.

"No," Phoebe says.

Lila just stares at Jim in silence as he finishes the fillet.

"That was so wonderful!" Suz and Nat say, and another firework goes off in the distance.

Phoebe looks at Lila. Points to her own teeth.

"Oh," Lila says. "Excuse me."

"Was Jim seriously just hitting on me during his best man speech?" Lila asks as soon as they are in the bathroom. "Why is he *like* that?"

"Because he loves you," Phoebe blurts out.

"He does not love me. He's had about fifteen girlfriends since I met him," Lila says. "He doesn't love anyone."

"That's not true, and you know it. Jim's actually a pretty good guy."

Lila turns to the mirror.

"God, why do I always get food stuck in this one little spot," Lila says. She blames this on her mother, too. Her teeth are too crowded in her mouth. Too big and white and shiny. She picks at her teeth, and the gesture is so familiar, it makes Phoebe feel like they are back having their first conversation in the Roaring Twenties.

"Well, you just don't say things like that in a best man speech," Lila says. "He never knows what's appropriate. He's like, feral or something."

"But isn't that what you like about him?" Phoebe asks.

"What do you mean?"

"That he just says things. That he calls you on your shit."

"My shit? What shit?"

"I mean, he tells you the truth. Makes a stupid joke about your mom's painting and makes you laugh."

Lila turns to Phoebe. "If he loves me, then why is he hitting on you, too?"

"Because you're getting married tomorrow!" Phoebe says. "I'm his backup plan. His consolation fuck."

"Wait, are you going to fuck Jim?"

"There's a decent chance I might, yes."

"So something really *is* happening between you two? I kept telling Gary that I couldn't picture it."

"Why not?" Phoebe asks.

"You're like, so not his type."

"What does that mean?"

"You're just very brainy. In a really lovable kind of way. But you're not a cheerleader type, you know? You're a little . . . well, suicidal."

Phoebe is shocked by how casually she says it. As if it's no big deal to be suicidal. To have shown up here wanting to die. As if this is just another one of Phoebe's lovable quirks.

"Yeah. And did you ever wonder why I was suicidal?" Phoebe asks. "Did you ever once ask me, Hey, what's wrong?"

"Well, I didn't want to pry."

"No," Phoebe says. "You just wanted to talk at me. You don't care what I have to say."

"That's not true," Lila says. "I literally asked you to stand up and give a speech at my wedding."

"Yeah, and then you cut it."

"I really don't have time for a fight," Lila says. "This is my rehearsal dinner."

So perhaps they aren't going to be friends. Perhaps they are back where they started, Lila obsessed with making sure that nothing ruins her perfect wedding, and Phoebe, always just about to ruin it. Perhaps there really is no such thing as friendship, just as Phoebe thought on the darkest nights back at home.

But Phoebe can't let herself fully believe this. It seems truer to say that friendship is just hard. It requires radical honesty. A kind of openness that Phoebe felt for the first time in her life that night she arrived at the hotel, so free and unburdened by anything. So ready to leave this world. But now she is no longer free—she is a person at this wedding, and the responsibilities of being a good friend have already started to change her. She can feel herself wanting to hide things from Lila. Nurture secret feelings in the dark of her mind, because total honesty is terrifying. It feels like it can ruin everything. And maybe this is what Patricia meant about saving yourself. What the Sex Woman meant when she said that Phoebe, for the rest of her life, would have to keep "checking in." Look in the mirror and repeatedly ask herself, Am I being honest right now?

"Can I be honest with you about something?" Phoebe asks.

Phoebe doesn't want to be like Mia. She doesn't want to pretend that her feelings for Gary aren't a real thing growing between them. But she doesn't know what being honest in this moment means. Is telling the bride about her feelings for the groom the most selfish act or the noblest act? She doesn't know. The only thing she can think to do is let the bride decide.

"I mean, when do you ever hold back?" Lila asks. "Isn't that kind of your thing?"

"Is it?"

"The first time I met you, you told me you wanted to kill yourself."

Phoebe nods. It seems unbelievable to her that she would have told a total stranger that, but now Phoebe can see it clearly as an act of desperation.

"I'm sorry I did that to you," Phoebe says.

"It's all good," Lila says. "But I seriously can't handle any more honesty right now after Jim's speech. I really just need the night to go smoothly. And some floss."

"But I thought you wanted to stop pretending."

"And I thought you were my maid of honor."

"I am," Phoebe says.

"So help me."

Phoebe opens her bag. "Here," she says. "Use this."

"Your table card?" Lila asks, but takes it. Starts using the sharp corner of the card to poke between her teeth. She gets it out. Victory. She reapplies her lipstick. Smacks her lips. Looks at Phoebe like she couldn't be more grateful.

"When we get back there, I want you to give your speech," Lila says. "I'm sorry I cut it. I really want to hear it. I just get so worked up sometimes, you know?"

"I know," Phoebe says.

BUT WHEN THEY return to the patio, they find it nearly empty.

"I told everybody to head down to the fireworks," Gary says. "We'll meet them there."

"But Phoebe hasn't given her speech!" Lila cries. "And we didn't even eat any of the palette cleansers, did we?"

"You don't eat palette cleansers, you *have* palette cleansers," Marla corrects.

"Jesus Christ, Marla, who cares?" Lila says. "We didn't eat or have any of them, am I right?"

"I do not recall a palette cleanser, no," Gary says.

"For the best," Jim says. "I'm stuffed."

He rubs his belly like it got bigger during dinner, which it didn't.

"But we paid for them," Lila says.

Lila signals for help, but it's not the waiter who comes over. It's Pauline.

"Yes, I'm so sorry," Pauline says. "The waiter came to me with your concerns, and we made the decision to omit the palette cleansers so we could get you all to the fireworks in time."

"You *omitted* the palette cleansers?" Lila asks.

"I am afraid we did omit them, yes," she says. "The meal was taking a little longer than planned, and we made an executive decision."

"Oh! As long as it was an *executive* decision," Lila says.

"Lila," Gary says. "It's okay."

"No, it's not okay! This is unacceptable. We ordered one hundred and sixty palette cleansers!"

"I hope you're donating them," Marla says.

"Do people donate palette cleansers?" Phoebe asks. "That just seems . . . cruel."

"Oh my God, can someone just tell me what a palette cleanser is?" Juice asks.

"Like a lemon thing on a spoon," Jim says.

"A lemon thing on a spoon?"

"I don't know. Ask the professor," Jim says.

"It's just what they always are," Phoebe clarifies.

"Pauline, thank you," Gary says. "We'll take it from here."

Pauline nods, leaves, and in her absence there is a lot of discussion about whether the hotel had the right to do that—to omit the palette cleanser, to make an executive decision without consulting the bride and groom.

Gary seems to think it is his responsibility as a kind person to forgive the waiter for whatever choices he made, because he was just a man with no good options, and Lila seems to think it is her responsibility as the bride to not have her dead father's money wasted on food they were denied.

"We paid a lot of money for this meal," Lila says.

"Okay," Jim says. "Here we go again."

"What do you mean, Here we go?" Lila asks.

"I mean, we know how this is going to play out, because this is how it always plays out, so why don't we just skip over it all and head down to the fireworks to enjoy our night?"

"How does this always play out?" Lila asks.

"You really want to know?"

"I don't think we want to know," Gary says. "Jim, I think you need—"

"No, I really want to know," Lila interrupts.

So does everyone else watching.

"You get upset about something very small and minor," Jim says. "And Gary takes deep breaths and says, Okay, okay, we'll fix this, and then he is going to fix it, and then you'll feel better, until tomorrow when you find something else pointless to melt down about."

"It's not pointless," Lila says.

"It's a lemon thing! On a spoon!" Jim says. "Who cares?"

"I care!" Lila screams. "I care! What is so wrong about caring? What is so wrong about wanting things to be done right? That's how you make big dreams happen, Jim. That's how you actually build a seaplane. You have to order all the parts and then make sure you get all the right parts, because if you are missing even just one, the seaplane doesn't work!"

"What does any of this have to do with my seaplane?" Jim asks.

"You don't even have a seaplane!" Lila says. "For two years, you've been talking about it like you have this seaplane, but you don't! You haven't even ordered the frame! Because you don't take anything seriously, not even your own dreams. You just sit around and talk about all the shit you're never going to do and all the people who aren't here, and I'm sorry your sister is dead, but you seriously have to move on and start building your seaplane! All of you do."

The family looks at Lila, a little stunned.

"This is tiresome," Jim says. "I'm tired of this."

"Tired of what exactly?"

"I'm tired of you overreacting like this," Jim says. "Yelling at everyone. And Gary just standing there. Look at him. He's just standing there."

They all look at Gary, and Gary clears his throat. But he doesn't speak. He just continues standing there.

"You're both better than this," Jim says.

Another firework goes off in the distance. "Good night," Jim says, and then leaves like this was the real speech he had been writing inside his head all week. All year.

Phoebe half expects Lila to yell for Jim as he walks away, but she says nothing, as if she's already trying to be her better self.

"Did you know that shrimp eat themselves from the inside?" Juice asks, holding a glass of wine in her hand.

"Are you *drinking*?" Gary asks.

Marla puts up her hand. "I'll handle it," she says.

"Juice," Gary says. "Why are you drinking?"

"I'll *handle* it," Marla says. "Go down to the Cliff Walk and enjoy the fireworks with your fiancée. That's an order."

Lila and Gary look at each other, a kind of helpless look, as if they have no idea how to enjoy the fireworks now. But they leave, and Oliver looks distressed, like he just realized that something is deeply wrong with the adults in his life. Phoebe remembers sensing the same thing as a child, seeing her father walk a woman to the door after dinner. Never inviting her to stay. Never allowing anyone into his life after her mother. He said goodbye to the woman, whoever she was, and Phoebe could feel him making a mistake, could feel that sometimes doing nothing was the biggest mistake of all.

But Oliver is just pointing at the nude painting of Lila's mother.

"Is that *you*?" he asks Patricia.

"That's me," Patricia says.

It's Juice who explodes, all over the table. Red vomit everywhere.

"Oh my God," Marla says, hand to forehead.

Marla looks at Phoebe.

"I'm sorry, I just can't," Marla says, and takes her husband's hand for the first time since he arrived. "Vomit makes me vomit."

JUICE WALKS SILENTLY under the wing of Phoebe's arm, all the way into the elevator.

"I'm so sorry," Juice says.

"I know," Phoebe says.

"I mean, I'm so sad."

"I know."

"I miss my mom."

"I know."

"I wish she could be here."

"I know."

Phoebe feels powerless to help. She imagines this is what mothers often feel. Powerlessness is part of the package. So she does what she can: She brings her to the room Juice shares with Gary. But at the door, Juice just cries.

"I don't *want* to be in my dad's room," Juice says, and it sounds like she is about to hyperventilate. Like she almost did that day at the wharf. "I just want my mom."

Phoebe feels Juice's cry deep in her heart—she feels it as her own.

"Let's go to my room," Phoebe suggests.

Inside, Phoebe gets her a glass of water. She takes off Juice's gold shoes. She puts a blanket over her. She sits at the edge of the bed and thinks, I would have been a good fucking mother, and then strokes Juice's hair.

"I'm sorry your mom isn't here anymore," Phoebe says. "But that doesn't mean you're alone."

Juice cries, curls herself into a ball, pulling the blanket up to her chin. Phoebe hopes Lila will grow into the role of mother. She hopes Lila will at least be stepsisterly. That the two of them will bond while watching shitty movies and eating cookies late at night.

"You'll be okay," Phoebe says. "I know you don't believe that now. But you will."

"How do you know, though?"

"Because I didn't have a mother, either," she says. "And I'm okay."

"You're okay?"

"I am okay," Phoebe says, and it feels true. I am okay. I am alive. I am here.

When Juice falls asleep, Phoebe looks at her phone. Three missed phone calls from her husband. He has lost control, she thinks. She starts to listen to the first message but is interrupted by a knock on the door.

"I couldn't just sit there watching the fireworks," Gary says. "Is Juice okay?"

"She's okay now," Phoebe assures him.

"I mean, clearly, she's not okay," Gary says.

"This is hard for her."

He sits down on the love seat. "I kept thinking that at some point it would be easier for her. Maybe as the engagement went on, this would all feel right. I thought my getting married again would be good for us."

The fireworks are loud outside, but Juice doesn't budge.

"She must be really drunk," Gary says.

They watch the green and red and blue explosions in the sky.

"Jim was right," Phoebe says. "There's no missing the fireworks."

"Jim is often right." He sighs. "Life is never what you think it's going to be, is it?"

"No," she says. "It's been a very surprising week."

He looks at her. "I certainly didn't expect you."

"I didn't expect any of you. Any of this."

"Phoebe," Gary says, like he is about to start up their conversation from earlier. "I think I'm making a terrible mistake."

But then there's another knock on the door. She can hear her husband's voice asking very loudly, "Phoebe, are you in there?"

"Matt," Phoebe says when she opens the door.

"Phoebe," Matt says.

Her husband is here. Because if she's being totally honest with herself, he is still her husband. When she sees him she thinks, Oh, my husband is here. He looks as he always did. He stands in the hallway like he has stood in every hallway she's ever seen him in.

"Hi," Gary says. "I'm Gary."

Matt must be so confused to see her here with this stranger behind her, this girl in her bed.

"I'm Phoebe's husband," Matt says.

She waits for Matt to correct himself, but he doesn't. She can't tell if Matt is the one who seems weird next to Gary or if Gary seems weird next to Matt.

"Nice to meet you," Gary says. He looks at Phoebe, as though trying to send a message with his eyes, but Phoebe can't pick up on it. Her husband's presence has short-circuited something. "Well, I should bring my daughter to her room."

They watch silently as Gary picks up Juice from the bed and carries her out the door.

When they are alone, Matt says, "Who were those people?"

But Phoebe doesn't answer. She refuses to explain the wedding people to him. They are hers, not his.

"You're my *husband*?" she asks.

"Sometimes it still feels that way to me."

Matt sits on the bed.

"Stop," Phoebe says. "Don't sit on the bed."

"I'm sorry," he says.

Phoebe feels very protective of her space. She doesn't like seeing him under the canopy. This is her room. Her hotel.

"What are you doing here?" she asks.

"I called you a million times, Phoebe," he says. He stands in front of the balcony door and answers into his hands. "I'm sorry to show up like this, I really am. I know it must seem crazy. But you have to understand that for a few days, I really was going crazy. I thought you might be dead."

"I'm not dead," Phoebe says.

"I can see that."

He comes up to her, like he wants to put his arms around her, but he is scared.

"You just disappeared, Phoebe," he says. "On the first day of the semester. You would never do that."

"You don't know what I would or wouldn't do anymore," Phoebe says.

"I know you wouldn't just take off without it being an emergency. We were all worried sick about you. We thought something terrible happened to you. Like Larry."

Larry was a professor who stopped showing up to classes without emailing. When they found him, he had been vomiting for days.

"You thought I had a stroke?" she says.

"I could only think the worst."

She was not in the house when he went to check, and there was nothing missing, no signs of any real departure.

"And then I couldn't find Harry," he says. "And you don't know what that felt like, finding him down there in the basement. Digging his little grave."

The thought of Harry snaps her back into her old self.

"Thank you for doing that," she says.

Matt starts to cry just thinking about Harry. "Why didn't you tell me?"

"Why would I tell you? You left."

"I loved Harry," he says. "You know that."

"You loved Harry?"

"I loved you, too. I still do. I always will. I know that now."

He takes her hands.

"When I saw you on Monday, I was so stunned. I wanted to talk to you, but I didn't know how. And then I thought you were dead, and I just . . . couldn't handle it. Why did you just leave like that?"

She doesn't answer. She doesn't have to say anything. He is technically not her husband anymore. She doesn't owe him the deep truth about her life.

"How did you find me?" she asks.

He says it was easy. Too easy. "You never took me off our bank account."

He saw the charge for the airplane and the Newport hotel, and he remembered the name, the Cornwall. He couldn't remember why it sounded so familiar to him, maybe they went there once, maybe they were supposed to go there.

"But why? Why leave like that, so cryptically, to come to . . . a wedding? And whose wedding is this?"

"Lila's," Phoebe says. "And Gary's."

"Gary? The man who was just here?"

"Yes."

"Oh," he says. "But it seemed like . . . I thought . . . never mind."

"And so you just fly here? After two years of living fifteen minutes away from you, never visiting me once, you fly all the way here to find me?"

"I missed you. More than you know. I've thought about you every day since we got divorced. I wanted to call or text. I wanted to say something, but I couldn't. I didn't know what to say. I was so awful to you. And then you were just gone. You weren't answering my texts or calls. And Bob said your email was really cryptic. I'm sorry, I just had to come. I had to make sure you were okay."

"I wasn't okay," she says. "I was . . . very upset. I've been upset since you left."

"I know. I'm so sorry I did that to you."

But now it annoys her that he thinks this was all about him. And while he was certainly a large part of it, he was not all of it. This was bigger than him. She knows this now.

"It's not just about you leaving," she says. "It's everything. It's about the way I've been my entire life. I've been so . . . contained."

"What do you mean, contained?"

"I mean, I just lived my life in such a small way," she says. "It was too small. I was so convinced there was only one way to live my life."

"I liked our life," he says.

"Apparently not."

"I was going through something, Phoebe. But I know that's no excuse. I know I could have handled it differently."

"Ha!" she says. "That's one way to put it. You were awful."

"I know."

"You abandoned me. Christ, you don't have to be with a person forever. But you don't have to abandon them. You were such a coward. I'm so glad I can see that now."

"I was a coward," he says. "I can see that now, too."

"I hated you," she says. "I still sometimes hate you."

Yet she feels glad that he tracked her down. Glad that he worried about her, glad to find out that his love did not disappear. And then she feels shame that she feels glad that a man has stalked her. Then she remembers she is not supposed to be feel shame, according to her therapist and Thyme. She is supposed to be kinder to herself, because this habit of tearing herself down every three seconds in her mind makes her feel ashamed. But at least she notices it. At least she is becoming aware of these things now.

"It would kill me if you hated me," he says.

"I don't actually hate you," she says. "Not anymore. I'm feeling better now. I really am."

"Because of that guy?"

"Don't even begin to get jealous."

He knows. He is ashamed about that, too. He is sorry he is jealous, sorry that he left. Sorry that he cheated on her. It was absolutely the wrong thing to do. But he felt like he was drowning and it's no excuse, yet he didn't know what else to do.

"Be honest?"

"I couldn't," he says. "After Mia and I slept together, I couldn't believe it. I couldn't believe I had done it. I couldn't imagine a more horrible thing to have done after I did it."

He had been so mad at Phoebe for being depressed and so mad at himself for being mad that his wife was depressed and also not to mention, a little depressed himself, and working so hard not to slip into that deep, dark hole with her, that by the time he found himself alone in a room with Mia, it felt like an opportunity.

"An opportunity?" she screams.

"To be a father," he says. "To be a good partner again. I felt like I was vanishing."

"So did I!" she yells. "Are you fucking kidding me?"

She yells it so loudly, she imagines someone might call, maybe Pauline, and maybe her father, to say, Calm down, this is too much, you are being too much. She expects her husband to walk out. But he doesn't. When she's done yelling, she feels calm. She feels sorry, too. She knows what it feels like to be vanishing. She can understand now what he means by opportunity. She feels it every time she looks at Gary.

"I'm so sorry," Matt says. "I'm so, so sorry."

"I know," Phoebe says. "I know."

"She made me feel alive. I just wanted to feel alive again and I didn't know how else to do it. It's a—"

"Terrible cliché."

She hates to hear herself say it. She doesn't want this thing with Gary to be a terrible cliché. She wants it to be more because it feels like it's more. But how does she know? Her husband thought he knew. Her husband was so certain when he left her.

But now he's here. Now he's sorry. Why would this thing with Gary be any different?

"I understand," she says. "I get it now."

He comes closer to her.

"You look beautiful," he says. "You really do."

His compliments make her feel smaller than she felt all week. She suddenly feels like an entirely different person than the one who just put Juice to bed. In her husband's presence, she feels like his wife again. He comes closer and touches her shoulder. She backs away.

"No," she says. "I understand, but I don't want that. I'm not the same person anymore."

She looks out over the balcony to see if she can find Gary in the darkness, but she can't.

"Neither am I," he says. "Most days, I wake up in Mia's house and I think, Where the fuck am I? I am here, with someone else's child, making pancakes on someone else's stove. A fucking electric stove that basically takes an hour to heat up. Mia and I, it's not right. I don't know what I was thinking. I wasn't thinking. I was being selfish, and I made a mistake, and our marriage has been the only meaningful thing of my life, if I'm really being honest about it."

"Then why didn't you call or text or write during that whole time?" she asks.

"I felt like I couldn't," he says. "The break between us was so hard. So official. God, that day on Zoom. Phoebe, that was awful. I cried for hours after. But I couldn't call you. I didn't want to mess with your head. I didn't even know what to say. I wanted to be sure about it when I finally spoke to you. And I'm sure."

"Sure what?"

"That I want to try again."

"Try again?" She laughs. "Are you kidding me?"

"I love you. I always will, Phoebe. What we had. It was the best part of my life."

"But that's over now."

"Don't say that."

"You said that!"

"We were *married*," he says. "I honestly don't think I realized what it meant to be married until I left. How do you know, until you can look back at what it was? After I left, I could see it so clearly. I saw this beautiful thing that I had destroyed."

He clears his throat. He sits down on the bed.

"But during it, I somehow stopped seeing the big picture. I was thinking so narrowly. I kept thinking everything had to happen a precise way. Like there would be something awful about adopting. Of course we can adopt. Of course we can do surrogates. We can do whatever. If we want a family, we can make it work. We can have a family, Phoebe."

She feels herself softening at the word *family*. The whole gang shows up in her head again—their little family. Their little noses. Their little laughs. Their little fingers, picking strawberries. Always their fingers, always their noses, never their whole faces. When she tries to imagine their faces, all she can see is Juice, throwing up at the table. The bright red chunks of it all.

"How about a drink?" Matt says.

"No," Phoebe says. "I need to go."

"Go where?"

"I don't know," she says. She wants to call Gary. She wants to finish their conversation. But when she looks up, Matt has already poured something amber in the little glasses.

"I should warn you that's like a million dollars," she says.

"Good," he says.

Maybe he is different now, too. She watches him take a sip. They sit on the love seat. Every time he leans forward to get a sip of his drink, their knees touch. She wonders if he is making this happen, if he keeps putting the glass farther and farther away from him on the table so he can touch her. It's like Matt to appear so casual, so effortless, but as his wife, she is the only one who knows how much time and effort he puts into appearing relaxed and easygoing. He does breathing exercises in the morning so he can face the day. He does eighteen drafts of his lecture so it can sound off the cuff. He looks in the mirror and says, Okay, here we go.

"Bob is utterly dumbfounded that you took off," he says. "The whole department is truly worried about you."

"They should be."

"They are."

"Good," she says. "They didn't worry about me enough."

"I know."

The more her husband speaks about their life, the more it reminds her he was her husband. He is Matt, who got her a beer on the first date. Matt who wrote her letters from Edgar Allan Poe's desk that month he was in Baltimore. Matt, whose brother used to bury him in the sand and put breadcrumbs around his head for the seagulls. She puts down her drink, reclines, and knows it's him, and yet she stares at her husband like he's someone she's looking at from very far away. He has gained a little weight, now puffier in the cheeks. But it's not just that. He is someone who has fucked Mia now. He parts his hair on the other side. He wears a shirt he must have bought after the divorce. And this all weirdly makes her want to touch him. Like this is really her fantasy now—her husband is a total stranger.

"Remember the eclipse, when I proposed?" he asks.

She nods. They were staring at the sky then, too. She listens to the fireworks in the distance. She feels that same feeling she had when they watched the eclipse, that same intense desire to make it meaningful, turn it into a metaphor. But she can't quite make it work: The fireworks are the opposite of an eclipse, man-made light bursting open into a dark sky. She doesn't know what it means.

He kisses her, and it makes her cry.

"I love you, Phoebe," he says. "I've loved you since the first second we spoke."

She hears the wedding people outside. She hears the fireworks in the distance. She feels the wedding going on without her. She knows that life, real life, is waiting for her on the beach. Yet in here, it is warm. Here is her husband.

He has learned a new way to kiss with Mia. He uses too much tongue. But when she turns away, he rubs his finger down her back. She can feel how he is ready to worship her in this moment if she lets him. She can see the whole thing, how he will spread her legs, how he will enter her, how good it will feel to touch this total stranger, even before it happens. It makes her feel excited and sick all at once. It feels like the worst part of her that wants him. But it has been so long.

SUNDAY

❧

The Wedding

In the morning, Phoebe wakes to see her husband in bed. There he is again, the man who gets exactly eight hours each night. The man who wakes up without an alarm. The man who puts on clothes right after sex and maybe that is why he looks so strange to Phoebe—so naked—like some caveman unearthed and transplanted to the Cornwall.

She looks at her phone. No messages.

Should she text Gary? Should she call him? Should she say anything at all?

She looks outside the balcony for evidence of something, and she sees Aunt Gina and Uncle Gerald in their wedding attire, drinking coffee. So the wedding is on. Life is as it should be. And yet something feels very, very wrong. She has made a mistake. She has lost her opportunity. Not to mention, she has betrayed Gary, abandoned him for her husband, but that makes no sense. Today is Gary's wedding day. And her husband is not her husband.

"Hey," he says, reaching for her.

She slinks out of bed.

"I need to go to the bridal suite to get ready," she says.

WHEN PHOEBE WALKS into the bridal suite, Suz and Nat are already on their way out with updos.

"We'll see you at the Breakers," Nat says.

They air-kiss Phoebe goodbye.

"Lila, the next time we see you, you'll be getting married!" Suz shouts, but Lila doesn't turn around.

Lila is unknowable, in a floral silk robe facing the big bay window overlooking the sea, which makes her look more like a widow waiting for something. She keeps her back to the room as the stylist curls the bottom parts of her hair.

"Your turn," another stylist says to Phoebe.

Phoebe stares at the woman with her tools belted to her waist. Eyeliners and brushes and lipsticks and curling irons. She pulls out a comb with the disposition of a surgeon. She is dressed much cooler than Phoebe remembers ever dressing in her twenties. High-waisted black jeans and a crop top and eyelashes as thick as quarters. Phoebe supposes it's part of her job to look cool in the way it was part of Phoebe's job never to look cool. To wear tweed. To push up her reading glasses and say, "I should really double-check my sources."

"I'm Tiff," the stylist says. "What would you like?"

"Dealer's choice," Phoebe says.

Phoebe wishes she had access to Lila's face. She wants to say something, but she feels the weight of the whole thing.

"You sure?"

"Yes," Phoebe says.

But Juice is much more particular. Juice has been studying Instagram photos all morning. She holds up a picture on her phone. Juice has no trace of a hangover or the shame that comes with one. This morning, she is just a kid again.

"I want this *exactly*," Juice says to her stylist.

Tiff makes general observations as she works on Phoebe's hair, like, "Your hair starts really far up on your head," and Phoebe says, "Is that bad?" and Tiff says, "Absolutely not," and then, "But do you ever notice how large your forehead is? Or how you're always putting your hair behind your ears?"

"Isn't that what people with hair do?"

"No," Tiff says, horrified. "You do that because you don't have a side bang."

"Do I need a side bang?"

"In my professional opinion, yes."

"Then give me a side bang," Phoebe says.

Maybe this is all she needed the whole time. Maybe this is the finishing touch of the grand makeover. Why didn't she think of it earlier? A side bang!

"You're so open! I love it." Tiff pulls out the scissors. "It'll keep the hair from falling in front of your face. Trust me."

She takes out a pair of red scissors and scoops the front of her hair into her hand. "This is fun. No one ever lets me cut their hair on the morning of a wedding."

Phoebe likes the warmth of Tiff's fingers and thinks how lucky her future daughter will be. To have a mother like Tiff who will give her every haircut. Who will know exactly what she needs with just one glance. Phoebe wants to turn around and hug her, but that's too weird.

"See?" Tiff asks.

Phoebe does see. Because the makeover scene always works. It takes one slight change. A side bang. And *bam*—a whole new face. A whole new feeling. She forgot how good she felt after a haircut. Like when she and Matt got new curtains for the house—the windows no longer depressing and barren, but cozy.

Someone knocks on the door, and this time it is Jim. He stands there with a tray of what looks like a hundred spoons.

"Jim, why have you brought us spoons?" Marla asks.

"One hundred and sixty palette cleansers," Jim says. "Or well, one hundred and fifty-nine to be exact. I had one in the elevator."

They all wait for Lila to react, but she doesn't turn around or say a word. She is steady as the stylist pins hair all around her head.

"I found them in the fridge this morning," Jim says. "And you were right, Lila. They were going to waste! They were just sitting there in the fridge, and the chef wouldn't even let me take them."

"So how did you get them?" Marla asks.

"I took them," he says.

"You stole them?"

"I salvaged them."

They wait again for Lila to say something, but she says nothing.

"Anyway, I just wanted to say I'm sorry for being out of line last night. I'm sorry for a lot of things. Hopefully you'll accept my apology in the form of . . . one hundred and fifty-nine spoons. They're actually pretty tasty. Very . . . cleansing."

After Jim leaves, Juice eats twelve in a row.

"How many palette cleansers do you have to eat until you're fully cleansed?" Juice asks.

"Sounds like a question for your other grandma," Patricia says.

Patricia is already fully poofed, starts to offer everyone champagne, and everyone accepts but Lila.

"I'd like to be sober for my wedding," Lila says, and Patricia looks confused.

"I can't see why anyone would choose that," Patricia says and pours her daughter some champagne that Lila does not drink.

Phoebe waits for Lila to lash out at her mother, but there is something serene and stoic about Lila this morning. Maybe this is Lila's better self. Or maybe something is wrong?

Phoebe wishes the others would go away. She wishes she could know what happened last night with Gary after he left. What did Gary do when he went back down to the fireworks? Did they sit under the exploding sky and hold hands and say very honest things and reaffirm their love for each other on the blanket? Did Lila confess to having a crush on Jim and did Gary confess to having a crush on Phoebe and did their confessions somehow make them stronger, the way that confessions usually do? Or did they say nothing at all? Did they just hold hands and smile at each other and proceed forward like normal? Is that why Lila is still here, in her bridal robe, the pastel flowers dotting her hair?

Phoebe doesn't know. She can't know. She must sit there, must tolerate Tiff's hot breath on her face and answer each one of her questions.

"A professor," Phoebe says. "St. Louis."

It's a relief when all the hair is up and off her neck. The other women are done, too, and headed out the door—Marla has ironed herself flat like usual in front of a tiny mirror. Juice has a series of braids woven into her hair. The three stylists pack up their things and say goodbye to the bride.

When they are entirely alone, Lila finally turns around. Phoebe stands there, waits for Lila to accuse her of something.

"How does it look from the back?" Lila asks.

Phoebe often thinks brides look cartoonish, and Lila is no exception on this morning. There is too much makeup, because it's not done for the people in the room. It's done for the photos.

"I went classic," Lila says.

"It's beautiful," Phoebe says.

"And the front?"

"Even more beautiful."

It's true. Phoebe walks over to the bride, helps her put on her dress. "It's Victorian," Lila says.

But not truly Victorian, Phoebe thinks. Lila wouldn't want that. Lila wants to be a Victorian bride, but without all the ruffles. Vintage, but hot. And this dress is hot. It has an entirely open back with delicate jeweled lace across the chest.

"Don't mess up the hair, please," Lila says, when Phoebe puts on the veil.

"I won't mess up anything," Phoebe says, and she means it.

Lila looks back out the bay window. "It's not even going to rain. It's a perfect day. I can't believe it."

"It really is."

"Nothing is going to ruin my wedding."

"No."

"Not even you."

"Not even me," Phoebe says.

"I was so certain something was going to ruin it," Lila says. "For two years, something kept ruining it. At a certain point, I was convinced it was never going to really happen. And when I saw you in the elevator that first day, I thought, Oh my God, this is it. This woman is going to turn my wedding into a crime scene."

"But I didn't," Phoebe says.

"Then I thought maybe Gary was going to call off the wedding. Because he gets like that, you know? He doesn't really get too invested in anything. Like if we're trying to make it to a concert on time, and we're running late, and then it rains, and everything gets too complicated, he gets overwhelmed and says, Okay fine, let's just not go? We're adults! We can decide to do things like that."

"But Gary would never call off a wedding," Phoebe says, and as she says it, she realizes it's true.

"You don't think so?"

"Of course not," Phoebe says.

"Why not?"

Because he doesn't break his promises. Gary has an insufferable sense of loyalty. Gary is a doctor who doesn't really like being a doctor and yet he continues being a doctor. He is a man who lost a wife and continues raising his child through the biting depression and dissociation and then goes out to shovel the driveway. Takes a drive just to try to admire a painting on his dead wife's wedding anniversary.

"Because he loves you," Phoebe says.

It's what Phoebe is supposed to say as maid of honor. She is ready to tell any lie. So the transformation is complete: Phoebe is one of the wedding people now.

"Do you really think so?" Lila asks.

But Phoebe can't bring herself to say it a second time. "It doesn't matter what I think. It matters what you think."

"I hate when people say that."

Pauline pops her head in. She announces details they already know: The new car will be downstairs in fifteen minutes. The champagne will be stocked.

"Thank you," Lila says. She stands up. "It really is such a beautiful day."

"It really is."

The wedding is happening. And what did Phoebe expect? Gary is not the type to call off a wedding, and neither is Lila. Lila has spent a million dollars on this. The champagne flutes were shipped here from France six months ago. Brides who plan weddings this expensive actually go through with them. People do what's expected. People get in their grooves and never crawl their way out. They make their decisions about plate patterns, then eat off them for the rest of their lives. She can't think of one real person she knows who ever called off their wedding the day of. And so that is it: Lila will marry Gary.

Yet Phoebe is in disbelief as they head for the door. She feels she is headed toward the wrong event, the wrong world.

"You look different," Lila says.

"Side bang," Phoebe says.

"No. It's something else."

Phoebe doesn't know what to say. Doesn't know how to explain the small and large ways this week has changed her.

"It's the side bang, I'm telling you," Phoebe says.

Lila stops just before the door. Looks at the one hundred and fifty-nine spoons. She picks one up. She eats it. She nods, like she's had an experience.

"Anything in my teeth?" she asks, smiling at Phoebe.

"No," Phoebe says. "Perfect."

BACK IN HER room, Phoebe looks at her green dress. Six days ago, she was ready to die in it. In some versions of this story, she would already be buried in it. But in this version, Lila had it laundered by the hotel staff. It shimmers on its hanger. It's green—just like the bridesmaids dresses. And it is remarkable to put it on for a different reason. Remarkable to have a beautiful side bang. Remarkable to see her husband here. There he is, in the shower. He is showering so they can go to a wedding together. It is all so familiar, the sounds of him humming "Yellow Submarine" without realizing it. His legs, which are still strong and muscular. She imagines they'll be the last thing to go on her husband; when he's older and losing parts of himself, his legs will be like the marble columns of Greece. So thick and strong, they'll last centuries.

But will she be there to see it? She doesn't know. Will she be there to hold his hand as he dies? They always imagined him dying first, something to do with him being a man, but also both his grandparents dying of lung cancer. They always imagined themselves as people who would never retire but would spend long summers on decadent cruises, going down the Nile while writing their books. Their children would be happy at college. And they have thought about this so many times, it's like it has already happened. She can see them, reading in the mornings, taking walks at four in the afternoon just before the sun sets in winter. Asking each other periodically, Do you think the kids are happy?

But she doesn't really want this now, after everything that's happened between them. She has spent too much time killing him off in her head. Killing herself off in her head. And now they are back, but they are different, because nobody comes back from the dead the same. You emerge always with a little bit of the underworld on you, the lesion, the scar, having seen unspeakable things.

"It occurs to me that I don't have anything nice enough to wear to a wedding," Matt says. "Should I stop to buy something?"

"I don't think there's time for that," she says. She wants to suggest he not come. But that seems cruel. He has come all this way. "Just sit in the back."

"These towels are amazing," he says, and rubs his face down.

She looks at herself in the mirror one last time, and it makes her want to cry. She feels such a relief—like when she returned home after a brutal day at work and turned on the lights—to be home again, to see the place she knows light up.

Her husband comes to put his hands around her. He kisses the back of her neck.

"You look beautiful," he says.

He seems to mean it. He has been trying to express himself more. He has started going to therapy. He has learned he was never really good at saying what he thought. He is learning now how to do this more. Learning how to actually talk. She turns around and looks at his belt. There it is, halfway through its life, smooth in parts, wrinkled in others. She feels the leather, expecting it to feel different, but it doesn't.

"Let's go," Phoebe says.

Downstairs in the lobby, Matt kisses her goodbye and takes the shuttle with the other people to the Breakers like he's been part of the wedding this whole time.

PHOEBE WAITS WITH the bride in the lobby for the new vintage car.

"The car is ready," a man in burgundy says.

As Lila walks out, Phoebe holds her train, all the way out the entryway, past the giant candles. But when they see the new car, Lila stops.

"I'm sorry, what is that?" Lila asks.

"Your car," the man says.

"I'm not getting in that car," Lila says.

The new car is an ordinary black town car. Like the kind Phoebe took from the airport.

"What's wrong with it?" Phoebe asks.

"It's like an Uber Black," Lila says. "Did Gary not ask for a vintage car?"

And suddenly it feels like they will never get to this wedding, like they're trying to get to Bowen's Wharf in traffic all over again.

"I asked for it," Phoebe says.

"Is there a problem?" Pauline asks, coming out the door.

"This is an Uber Black."

"I assure you this is not an Uber Black," Pauline says. "It's a 2022 brand-new Mercedes with a state-of-the-art sound system."

"But it's not vintage."

"I'm so sorry," Pauline says. "We had no more vintage cars available with such late notice."

They wait to see how Lila will react. For a second, she doesn't. But then without a word, Lila turns around. Walks back up the stairs, while Phoebe and Pauline follow, trying to protect the train.

"Lila," Phoebe says. "What are you doing?"

"I knew it," Lila says. She stops on the top of the stoop. She starts to rub her temples. "I knew something was going to ruin the wedding."

"I hardly think this will ruin your wedding," Phoebe says.

"Nobody can make me get in that car."

"Technically, that's correct."

"We need a new car."

"Absolutely," Pauline says without hesitating.

"No," Phoebe says.

"*No*?" Lila says.

"You don't need a third car," Phoebe says. "What you need is to be on time to your wedding. We're already late."

"So what? They can't start without me," Lila says. "I'm the bride."

"Exactly. You're the bride. It doesn't matter what car you drive to your wedding. It really doesn't. No one gives a shit. Everyone is already inside. They won't even see it."

"It matters to me."

"But why?"

"It just does!"

"God, you're being so ridiculous," Phoebe says.

"Don't call me ridiculous! I'm so tired of people calling me ridiculous!"

"Well, stop being ridiculous!" Phoebe says. "It's just a stupid fucking car! It's just a hunk of metal! It doesn't matter what it looks like!"

"Then you get in it!"

"Fine! I will," Phoebe says. She walks back down the stairs and sits in the car. It is, Phoebe thinks, a perfectly fine car. "Hey look, real leather interior. Smells like being inside a leather bag."

"That actually does not sound very appealing to me," Lila says.

"The Veuve Clicquot is in the copper ice bucket," Pauline interjects.

But Lila looks so confused in her dress. Lila looks at Phoebe the way she did when Phoebe first told her she had food in her teeth, sinking under the weight of the wedding's imperfections. Lila doesn't move in either direction. Phoebe holds up the champagne.

"Well, are you coming?"

Lila doesn't move.

"The car is just so . . . ordinary," Lila says. "It's just wrong."

She sits down on the stoop in the fluff of her own dress. Phoebe waits for Lila to get up again, but when she doesn't, Phoebe puts down the champagne, gets out of the car, and walks up the stairs to sit next to the bride.

"What's wrong?" Phoebe asks.

"You lied," Lila says.

"I swear I asked for a vintage car. I think."

"I mean, you lied about Gary," Lila says. "He doesn't love me. Not the way I want to be loved."

Phoebe doesn't open her mouth, doesn't risk lying again.

"And I don't love him," Lila says. "Not the way I want to love someone."

Lila says she's been thinking this for some time. Ever since her father died, she wondered if they were making a mistake. But she wasn't sure. The pandemic—life without her father—it was all very confusing.

"And I thought that maybe if the wedding was perfect, it could feel right again," she says. "Like it did those first few months. But it doesn't. And I'm glad something ruined it."

She puts her face into her hands like she did the night of her bachelorette party. But now it's different. She can't just turn over and go to sleep and hope it will all feel fine in the morning.

"What am I going to do?" Lila asks.

Phoebe feels the adrenaline of really being called into action.

"You're going to go upstairs and take a very long bath," Phoebe says.

"I can have Carlson start running it for you," Pauline says.

Lila nods. "But how am I going to get this dress off?"

"Pauline will help you," Phoebe says, and Pauline nods.

"That's not Pauline's job, though," Lila says.

"It can be," Pauline says. "Just for today."

"And then what?" Lila asks.

"Then you're free," Phoebe says.

"Then I'm *alone*."

"Then you can go wherever you want," Phoebe says. "Where is that?"

"Somewhere I've never been," Lila says.

But this is tricky for the bride, who has been almost everywhere.

"Except for like, Canada," Lila says. "And Russia."

"So you'll go to Canada," Phoebe says.

"I can use your credit card to book you a flight and into one of our Canadian hotels right now," Pauline says. "We have one in Montreal. It's basically a stone castle."

The bride nods. Takes off her veil. She holds it in her hands.

"What a waste," Lila says.

It is. A waste. A huge waste of money, which is exactly what Phoebe wrote in her maid of honor speech, which Phoebe realizes is probably what Lila needs to hear right now.

"Every wedding, even a successful wedding, is a waste," Phoebe says. "Every wedding is an egregious amount of money that could have, yes, been spent on much more practical things, like say, a house, a down payment, a school in a small, dying mill town. A wedding is always a fleeting spectacle that is one hundred percent going to become packed down into a teeny tiny garbage square that'll wind up in your father's landfill someday."

"None of this is very comforting so far," Lila says.

So Phoebe jumps to the final line.

"But it's also true that this wedding will never be a waste," Phoebe says. "Because I came here to die. And now look at me."

This is when they both start to cry.

No, Phoebe will never be a mother. Phoebe will never know what it's like to create life inside of her. But there are other ways to create. Other ways to love. Other reasons to live.

"Lila, every day this week, you gave me a reason to get up in the morning, to put on a beautiful dress and be part of something, and for that I will always be grateful."

Phoebe takes the Mercedes alone to the Breakers. The ride is so beautiful, and stocked with so much champagne, that even without the bride, it still feels like an event. Phoebe studies the mansions along the way and wonders how many of the people living in them are happy. She wonders what they wish for when they wish for different lives. She wonders if this is why she has always been interested in nineteenth-century novels about rich people—it's a giant human experiment. It asks the question: What does a person still need once a person has everything? What does a bride still desperately lack as she stands in the lobby just before her big, beautiful wedding?

It's Phoebe who walks down the aisle to tell Gary. Phoebe makes sure to look at him the entire time. It's tempting to look at the ocean behind him, but she doesn't want to be a coward. She doesn't want to hide from his eyes or leave him alone in this moment. He searches her face for some kind of information, even though he must already know. Why else would Phoebe be the one walking down the aisle?

"Lila is not coming," she whispers when she is at his side.

And of course, of course. He nods his head with the stoicism of a soldier who has just been shot. It seems the man will go down without a single expression. He nods, looks at his shoes, nods again and again, like now he's just watching the blood drip to the floor.

Phoebe turns around. Surely the wedding people know now, too. But someone has to say it aloud and make it official.

"Lila and Gary will not be getting married today," Phoebe says. It is good practice, speaking with finality. Being direct. Saying the hard truths in front of the wedding people. Phoebe wants to get better at that. Phoebe will get better at that. Phoebe knows this is the only way she wants to live. She must say the terrible thing, even when it's hard. She must think the terrible thing, even when it's scary. "She thanks you all for your support and love, the time and money it took for you to get here."

The crowd murmurs. Phoebe wonders how much they all spent. She wonders how many times Uncle Jim and Aunt Gina will say, "Five grand! Five grand just to watch someone not get married!" all the way to the airport.

"Jesus Christ," Patricia says. "What a production. Where is she?"

"At the hotel," Phoebe says. She imagines Lila in the bridal suite, slowly undressing until she is no longer a bride. "But then she's going to Canada."

"Canada?" Suz asks.

"What's in Canada?" Nat asks.

By the time Phoebe answers all the wedding people's questions, the same questions they would have had about Phoebe if she killed herself (But did she say why? Did she leave a note? What was she *thinking*?), Gary is gone. Gary has left the Breakers. He must have slipped out the other door. He must be feeling something terrible, but what? Phoebe wants to follow him through the door, comfort him, be with him forever, but it doesn't feel like her place to chase after him. It's too soon.

And there is Matt, standing in the aisle waiting for her. They wait until all the wedding people file out of the Great Hall, just as they waited on their own wedding day. Then Matt and Phoebe get into the ordinary car like husband and wife.

"So, what happened to the bride?" Matt asks in the Mercedes.

"I'm not going back with you," Phoebe says.

She has to say it right away or she'll never say it.

"To the hotel?"

"To St. Louis," she says. "I'm not returning. I'm just not."

It is her fantasy, finally playing itself out. She is leaving him. But it doesn't feel like her fantasy because he has already left her. And when she says it, he doesn't shout "No!" and she is glad for it. She doesn't want him to be upset by this. She doesn't want this to feel like an Ibsen play. She wants him to just say, Okay. I understand. For the first time since he left her, she wants him to actually be okay. And this feeling of goodwill—it's a promising sign.

"I was worried you would say that," Matt says. He asks her a series of reasonable questions like, Are you ever coming back? What are you going to do?

"I'm going to go on medical leave," Phoebe says, "assuming adjuncts can do that."

It's an old joke, an old feeling, this making fun of their university.

"Oh, I'm sure they can't, now that I think about it," Matt says, and they even laugh a little.

"I'm sure Bob will be like, Well, turns out, adjuncts aren't allowed to receive medical treatment," Phoebe says.

"Turns out, adjuncts have to pay the administration a small fee every time they get sick." He reaches out for her hand. "I love you."

"I love you, too," she says. "But you need to go home."

He looks out the window while she tells him what she wants—to sell the house, to live in the nineteenth-century mansion and write.

"Write what?" he asks. "Your book?"

"Anything," she says.

"Maybe it's for the best," he says. "I do have a lot of grading to do tomorrow."

It's a joke, his attempt to lighten the mood, but he bites his finger to keep himself from crying. He looks like a little kid. Like Jim standing up giving his speech. A little boy in pain. A little boy who wasn't expecting life to be this confusing. She squeezes his hand, which makes him cry harder, as if the idea of joking with her, of laughing together after all these years of not laughing, makes him sob again.

"Shit, I need to get myself under control."

"Why?" Phoebe says. "I don't care if you cry."

"I care," he says. "You know I look like shit when I cry."

"I'm not sure I ever really saw you cry."

"That can't be true."

"It is."

"I cried when the Phillies lost the World Series."

"My point exactly."

The analysis of his own tears has calmed him. Brought him out of his emotions and into his brain. That's where her husband likes to be.

That's where he's comfortable. But Phoebe can't live there anymore. Phoebe wants to be in her body. She wants to enjoy this beautiful dress. And her side bang. She almost forgot. She is embarrassed by how much of a difference it makes. But it's the small things. She leans over and grabs the champagne. Pops the bottle open. Why not? Nobody is going to drink it now, except them.

"What are we toasting to?" Matt asks.

"Your first adult cry unrelated to sports?"

"I'll toast to that."

They clink glasses.

"This is good champagne," he says.

She tastes it. "It actually is."

She wonders how much Lila spent on it. She takes another sip. She is happy that she has lived long enough to learn the difference between decent champagne and really good champagne, which she now knows doesn't just taste good on the first sip, but the entire way home.

The whole mood of the Cornwall is different without the bride and groom. It's too quiet, and it feels rude to still be enjoying the spa water now that the wedding has been called off. Even Pauline seems subdued, fielding questions with a solemn voice.

"Yes, the pool is now open again," she says, and, "No, I'm so sorry, but we cannot give you a refund for tonight," and, "Had I known your husband was allergic to oranges, we would have left them out of the spa water."

Phoebe gets in line behind Nat and Suz, who are already back in their high bun and neck pillow, making declarations about the wedding in low whispers.

"I truly can't believe it," Suz says. "And yet, I'm not surprised at all."

"I knew Lila wasn't in love with him," Nat says. "I just knew it."

"I didn't know that," Suz says. "But I knew something wasn't right when we were with the Sex Woman."

"Do you think Pauline will give us our money back for tonight if we really beg?" Nat asks.

"No," Suz says. "But at least we got our flights changed."

"You're leaving tonight?" Phoebe asks.

Nat misses Laurel. Suz misses the Little Worm. Then they both go on a long tangent about their own wedding days, how fun they were, how in love they were. But Phoebe is not ready to leave. Phoebe wants to stay at this hotel forever.

"Checking out?" Pauline asks Phoebe as she approaches.

"I'd actually like to stay tomorrow night if there is room," Phoebe says.

"I'm so sorry, but there are no more rooms available," Pauline says. "There's another wedding starting tomorrow. We're all booked."

"Oh," Phoebe says.

Phoebe feels stunned by the way Pauline said "We're all booked" with such a decisive tone, it left no room for debate. Pauline, too, has transformed this week—she wears a loose gauzy dress, with wavy beach hair cascading over her shoulders. And Phoebe feels proud, but also flustered; she is not ready to leave. Phoebe gives Pauline one more moment to make a miracle happen, to look at the computer and say, Actually, I made a mistake! But Pauline just blinks, her thick lashes like gargoyle wings. It makes Phoebe feel dizzy.

"I'll be staying just tonight then," Phoebe says.

"Checkout is at eleven," Pauline says.

UPSTAIRS, PHOEBE SITS on the balcony. She wonders where Gary is. She considers knocking on his door, considers texting him, but then considers that he probably wants to be alone right now, the way she wanted to crawl into the hole of her bed after Matt left.

But then she considers that this might be a very different situation. Maybe the last thing he wants to be is alone. Maybe he's just fine. Maybe he's scuba diving in St. Thomas right now. Maybe she doesn't really know him, and again, this is the problem: She worries she doesn't.

Phoebe watches Carlson fold up the tiny circular tables that he put out for the hotel after-after-after-party. He stacks them into one long ladder so tall it looks dangerous. He puts the ladder of chairs on his back and walks out of sight. In his wake, Ryun stabs the white and lilac balloons. He uses an obscenely large kitchen knife. Each pop makes Phoebe startle.

But then they are gone, and it's just the sound of the ocean and a white ribbon flying off the cliff into the darkness. A waste. The idea is always lurking behind every object, every moment. She imagines the ribbon sinking, and for a moment, she feels herself go with it to the murky bottom.

But then she gets up, walks to Gary's door. She knocks. When nobody answers, she turns around to see Marla.

"Where's Gary?" Marla asks.

"I don't know," Phoebe says. "Did he check out of the hotel?"

"I don't know," Marla says. "He just texted and asked me to watch Juice until he gets back. But he didn't say when that will be."

Oliver is by Marla's side.

"So why don't you teach Percy Jackson?" Oliver asks. "Do you not like Greek myth?"

The randomness of the question makes Phoebe and Marla laugh.

"Been a little busy," Phoebe says. "But you know what? I'll read one of his books soon and let you know what I think."

BACK IN HER room, Phoebe dawdles, drinks some Everybody Water, eats a complimentary macaron. In a strange way, she feels as she did that first night—unsure of what to do with herself. She will actually have to leave tomorrow, figure out somewhere else to go. Buy a suitcase.

The thought of leaving makes her feel nostalgia for the room. No, she feels love for it. She loves this room, the high ceilings, the marble bathroom, the old wood floors. She wishes she could take it with her, capture the feeling of being inside here forever, bring it everywhere she goes.

And maybe there is some way she can. She opens her notebook.

She rereads her wedding speech. As a speech, it's terrible. But as literary analysis of the curious absence of weddings in Victorian marriage plots, it's not bad. She likes the part about Jane Eyre getting married in under a sentence. And the paragraph about Jane's failed wedding being the only wedding that Brontë describes in actual detail. And why would Brontë do that? Why spend more time writing the failed wedding than the successful one?

Her phone dings.

Geoffrey is interested in offering her the job. And yes, she can have a small dog, as long as it's a breed common to the nineteenth century.

Reading the email gives Phoebe the same feeling she got when her father said she could go to summer camp one year. She wants to tell Gary. She writes out then deletes a series of possible texts.

~~Hey I got the job!~~

~~Hey there.~~

~~You okay?~~

~~Do you think I'd make a good winter keeper?~~

Instead, she downloads *Jane Eyre* on her phone. She rereads the scenes leading up to Jane's failed wedding. On the hotel pad, she jots down any line that seems to foreshadow the wedding's ruin. She tries to pinpoint the exact moment when the engagement became a trap; was it on the way to town after he proposed? Or did it start much earlier than that, long before Rochester proposed? Eventually she calls down for another pad. She writes all night. She does not smoke. She does not drink. She is energized by the thought of not knowing what she is even writing, of getting to decide it with every sentence.

MONDAY

❦

The Wedding Brunch

In the morning, Marla is in the conservatory. She says she is not leaving until she sees Gary. In the meantime, yes, she is absolutely going to eat the wedding brunch.

"Carlson is the one who put it out," Marla says.

"I didn't say anything," Phoebe says.

"Is there some rule about only getting to eat the brunch if the wedding takes place?"

"It just feels a little wrong, no?"

"What feels wrong is watching avocado brown right in front of your face."

"It feels like someone died," Juice whispers.

"Nobody died," Marla says. "This is just food. And somebody needs to eat it."

"Did it have anything to do with us?" Juice asks.

"We could have been nicer," Marla says.

"But that's not why she left," Phoebe assures them.

Soon, others join. The mother, the father. Marla's husband. Jim, too. But no groom. They eat cantaloupe and tell stories about Gary in his absence, stories that have nothing to do with Lila. Stories of Gary's past. That time he hid the statue of David when he threw a party in high school. When he was a small boy sneaking something off the counter. And Phoebe gets the feeling they are telling the stories for her.

"He was seriously in love with doughnuts," Marla says to Phoebe. "I mean, it was a problem. Our mother used to keep them up on the highest shelf above the stove, and he was trying to climb up to get them and somehow accidentally turned the burner on. He didn't realize it, though, went upstairs, and by the time he had finished the whole box of doughnuts, the house was on fire."

"Ever since that fire, Gary's tried to be Mr. Perfect," Gary's mother tells Phoebe.

Each time someone new walks in to join, Phoebe hopes it is Gary. But it never is. It's Uncle Jim. It's Roy.

"It's the whole goddamned family!" Jim shouts into the phone. "Get your ass down here, Gary."

"Is he okay?" Gary's mother asks Jim.

"Oh, leave the man alone!" Gary's father says. "He was just dumped."

But Phoebe pulls out her phone. She doesn't want to leave him alone. The man was just dumped. Right now, he should not be alone if he doesn't want to be. He should at least have the option.

You should know that the family is telling stories about you right now, she texts Gary.

Her phone dings right away. But it's just her ex-husband, texting to say he has made it back to St. Louis alive. She wonders when he will stop texting her proof of life. Perhaps that will be the true end of the marriage, when they no longer need to know: Are you still alive?

IN THE LOBBY, new wedding people are arriving with their titanium-strength suitcases, looking for places to store them while their rooms are cleaned, and it reminds Phoebe that she needs luggage.

"Custom Canvas is on Thames," Pauline suggests.

"Is there like, a Marshalls or something?" Phoebe asks, and Pauline writes down an address. Then Pauline goes to put up a new sign in the lobby: WELCOME TO THE WEDDING OF SOPHIA AND STEPHEN.

She is glad that Lila is not here to see it. Awful for the bride to watch another bride take her place—even if she is not really the bride anymore. She is just a woman who is eating poutine in Canada with her mother.

My mother keeps hitting on our waiter solely because he is getting a master's in pre-Raphaelite art, Lila texts.

The early birds mill around, some already holding little white welcome bags. Half the room is saying hello, half is saying goodbye. They are exchanging numbers, saying, Stay in touch, let's get together in a year, and she wonders if they will. She hopes they will but suspects they won't. Perhaps this week is just a special moment in time. All of them together here, in this lobby, never to be so again.

"So how long is too long to wait before we call them?" Jim asks.

Phoebe smiles. "I'm sure Lila will explain that to you in detail when you call."

"Well, Phoebe, I do hope we're not done with each other just yet," Jim says.

Phoebe hopes for that, too. So she does what feels like the most ridiculous thing to her: She gives him her number, hugs him, and says, "Let's be friends."

It makes her feel five years old in the best way.

"As long as you don't use me for my weed hookup," he says. "I'm never getting high with you again."

"Two weeds, please," she says.

Jim laughs. Phoebe watches him get in his Uber. He steps into the dark hole, just a person in jeans and a T-shirt. No longer the best man. An engineer on his way to Pawtucket, where there are apparently no more socks.

She wonders if this transformation has already happened to Gary. She wonders where and when he shed his tuxedo. She wonders if he is somewhere still wearing it.

IN MARSHALLS, SHE stands in a long line of other people buying things when she gets his text.

Is it the story about hiding the statue of David when I threw a party in high school? Gary asks.

Yes. And also the one about you lighting the house on fire.

So predictable.

Why did you hide your mother's statue of David?

This was pre-Wendy. I couldn't see art yet, remember? All I saw was a naked man sitting on my mother's console.

You definitely didn't use the word console then.

No, I just found out about the word, actually. I can't stop using it. Hey, where are you?

In Marshalls trying to decide what suitcase to buy.

What are the options?

Is this something you really want to know right now?
Anything helps.
Either a hard-backed case that could survive space travel or a soft shell that can somehow charge my cell phone.
Guess it depends. Are you going to the moon?
St. Louis.

She doesn't realize it until she types it. But she needs to go back before she moves into the mansion. She needs to say goodbye to Harry. She needs to clean the crumbs off the counter. Turn off the water. Pack up her things. Get it ready to sell. Set herself up for the next part of her life. She feels strong enough now to face it.

Oh, Gary writes. *That moon.*
Not forever, she writes. *Where are you?*
In the hot tub.
Don't move.

SHE TAKES A cab back, but there is so much traffic, she decides near the end that it will be quicker to run. But running with a giant suitcase is difficult, and she is tired and sweating by the time she makes it back to the hotel.

In the lobby, everything is so still and serene, she slows down. This is one of those really great moments, she thinks. This is everything she loves about life. She wants to savor it. She leaves the suitcase with Pauline. She trails her fingers on the wall like she is already the winter keeper, checking for dirt. She admires the trim along the bookcase. Flips a book around, then nods at the new wedding people. Pours herself a glass of the spa water, which she knows is just regular water with cucumbers in it. It's not magic water. But everything feels like magic inside of her.

Outside, there is Marla, two legs in the tub. Juice, submerged up to her ears. The clouds, protecting them all from the vast, unknowable void. And there, underneath it, the groom.

· · ·

THE GROOM IS no longer a groom. Now he is just a man in a hot tub, wearing an orange bathing suit so bright Phoebe can see it glow through the water.

"Don't tell me you've been here this whole time?" Phoebe asks Gary.

"It's become medically unsafe," Gary says.

"Dad's having a spa day," Juice says.

They laugh.

"He deserves it," Marla says.

"It's no Bourbon Bubbler," Gary says. "But it'll do."

Juice stands up. Her face is flushed. "I need to get in the pool."

"You should get out, too, Gary," Marla orders.

"I will, when my back stops hurting."

"You need to see a doctor about that when you get home," Marla says.

"He *is* a doctor," Juice reminds them.

"But you can't be the doctor of your own back," Marla insists.

"That's certainly not how I'd go around phrasing it," Gary says.

They all laugh.

"Hi, I'm Gary. I'm a doctor of my own back," Juice practices.

"See?" Gary says. "Doesn't sound right."

Marla gets out. "Time to go."

"Time for the pool," Juice says, and does a cannonball before Marla can reach her.

Phoebe dangles her legs in the water. She feels nervous for a moment but then remembers: This is Gary. It's okay to say anything to Gary. Gary has watched a woman die. Gary has been left at the altar. Gary is just a regular man in a hot tub.

"So," Phoebe says.

"So," Gary says.

They both laugh again.

"How are you doing?" Phoebe asks. "You know, besides your back."

"Oh," he says. "I'm feeling very weird right now."

"Weird how?"

"I have been having some very weird thoughts."

"Go on."

"Well, a butterfly landed on my forearm a bit ago, and I thought, Oh, how sweet. How nice. But then I thought, What if it's not nice?"

"What do you mean?"

"I mean, do we actually know why butterflies land on us?"

"I'd like to believe science has progressed beyond that point."

"Well, I've never heard any theories on it."

"Should we be suspicious about that, though?"

"Yes! We don't think it's sweet when flies land on our food. Because flies vomit every time they land on food. Did you know that?"

"That's not a myth?"

"No. They need to do it, to digest the food," he says. "So what if butterflies are like that, too? What if they, like, orgasm every time they sit on your forearm?"

"You think that's why they do it?"

"The horny bastards."

"And we think it's so sweet."

"And they're like, Uh huh."

"So I see things are going really well for you here, Doctor."

He laughs. "Now it's your turn."

"For what?"

"I said a weird thing so now you need to say a weird thing. Balance me out."

"Fair enough. Okay. Well. I don't wash my back unless I'm married to someone."

"That's not weird. Who washes their back?"

"Obviously not you."

"That's the worst you got? That's your secret? That your back is filthy?"

"Yep."

"I, for one, am scandalized."

A squirrel hops along the ridge of the hot tub.

"So where did you go yesterday?" she asks.

"The cemetery," he says.

He spent the night driving around, unsure of where to go. He just had to get out and away from all the people. He couldn't face them.

"I wanted to talk to you," he says. "But it would have been too confusing."

So he drove to the cemetery and sat by his wife's grave until he fell asleep.

"Jim was right," he says. "I was a totally different man with Wendy. A better person. Because I was *in* it. But with Lila, I really was just standing there. I let her run the whole relationship. Like she was my camp counselor or something. And I did love her for it. How could you not? I felt such . . . gratitude, if that makes any sense. Such appreciation. She made things happen. She performs life very well. If it's her birthday, she throws a party. If there's a week off, she'll book a grand tour of Europe. If she's getting married, she'll throw the goddamned most elaborate wedding possible. That kind of thing made me feel . . . part of the world again. Part of something bigger than myself, you know?"

"I know."

"But then all the people would go home or we'd be on the airplane, and there'd be nothing to say. Or I felt like everything I said annoyed or bored her. And I guess I kept trying because it felt like my fault. Maybe I was annoying? Or really boring? And here was this wonderful woman who was offering me a second chance at a normal life, a wonderful woman who just booked us a trip for two to Paris, and Germany, and all the places I dreamed of going, so don't screw it up. Don't sit on the plane and cry about your dead wife. Instead, I'd sit on the plane trying to come up with things to talk about at dinner. Would literally plan out topics of conversation. Like I was practicing being a person. And she was right to run away from all that. Lila was brave. I told her that back at the hotel. I told her she was very brave."

It occurs to Phoebe that maybe, in some way, they were all brave. Even her husband—not for lying, not for cheating, that was not brave. But for going after what he wanted. For being the one who could admit when something was wrong. For packing a suitcase and leaving the house because the house was sick.

"And Lila told me everything," he says. "How she had actually been interested in Jim, and Jim had been interested in her, and how much she hates art. Honestly, that was the part that confused me the most. She kept going on about how she didn't want to be in a marriage where she was expected to sit around and talk about the Cubists every day. Which was very confusing, since I don't think I've ever said one thing about the Cubists in my life."

"Now you have."

"And she wanted to go to Canada? Said something about learning how to ski."

"She doesn't know how to ski already?"

"I know, I was surprised," Gary says. "I was like, Wait, this whole time you didn't know how to ski! Had I known, I would have called the wedding off months ago."

"Obviously."

"It spooks me," he says, "that I didn't call off the wedding. After the rehearsal dinner, when I came to you, I knew something was wrong."

"So what happened?"

"I didn't trust myself. I didn't trust what I was feeling."

"Funny how you can live long enough, go through enough, and learn how to stop trusting yourself."

"And by funny, I assume you mean terrifying," Gary says. "Because I mean, I wasn't happy, but I didn't think that was a problem, because I was convinced happiness wasn't real. Until I met you. But I didn't trust that feeling, either. I just met you. It was my wedding week. And then your husband showed up, and so after I left you in your room, I waited for hours to see if you would text me. Like that would decide it. Like it was some kind of test of the universe. If she texts me, this is real. If she texts me, I'll call it off. I'll take the plunge."

"But I didn't."

"I should have done it anyway."

It is not an easy thing to do, walk away from what you've built and save yourself. Destroying Phoebe's marriage felt like destroying herself. Walking out of the classroom felt like killing the twenty-two-year-old who tried to save her own life by applying to graduate school. It is so much easier to sit in things and wait for something to save us. For the past two years, Phoebe sat in the bad things the way she used to sit in the snow as a child. An hour would go by and it would be very hard for her to get back up. Eventually she looked down at her toes and became confused: Why are they frozen? It was her father who picked her up, said, It's time to come inside. But now she has to learn when it's time to come inside. She has to learn to check in with her toes when nobody else is looking. To care for them when no one else will.

The new bride walks out onto the pool deck.

"The rain is going to be a problem," the bride says. "But the tent will be set up here for tonight?"

"Yes," Pauline says, taking notes.

The bride gives the two of them in the tub a look, like she is suspicious of them—they are strangers in a tub who do not give a shit about her wedding. They have the power to make the bride's wedding totally ridiculous with one glance, make the fuss of it all seem so unnecessary. Turn her into a queen or a fool, just like that.

But Phoebe smiles, and the bride smiles back. It's too easy to turn the bride into everything we want to be or everything we once were and can never be again. Too easy to forget that she is brave, too, her heels clicking as she circles the pool, dreaming up a whole life.

"I feel like we're supposed to get out or something," Gary says.

"We still have twenty minutes until checkout," Phoebe says.

"Good."

Gary leans his head back against the edge of the tub to look up at the sky, while Phoebe looks around at all that is before her. She feels the wind against her cheek and the warmth of her toes. She feels excited about the rain that is going to come soon. She listens to the birds in the trees and the sounds of other people's children swimming in the pool. Juice, who will one day grow up and forget what she ever loved so much about hotel pools. She will stay at beautiful hotels around the world and never once use the pool. She will look in the mirror and think, Who the fuck am I? Why did I ever want to be called Juice? My name is *Melanie*. She will have to practice saying her full name—all of them will. Because Gary is not wrong—becoming who you want to be is just like anything else. It takes practice. It requires belief that one day, you'll wake up and be a natural at it.

"I'm going to become a winter keeper," Phoebe says.

"Congratulations," Gary says. "Though I knew Geoffrey was going to give you that job."

"Because it's classic Geoffrey?"

"It's classic you," he says, and it feels exhilarating to hear him say that. To talk about her like he knows her. "Who else would be better at living in a mansion with terrifyingly large gargoyles on the roof?"

"In theory, the gargoyles will be there to protect me," she says.

"Is that in their contract?"

"Since the thirteenth century."

"I like that you know when gargoyles were invented," he says.

Phoebe laughs. "I like that you just used the word *invented*."

"Well, that's how it happened," Gary says. "Some little boy in the thirteenth century had a dream that one day he'd grow up and invent gargoyles and he did. Don't ruin this for me, Phoebe."

"They were basically just the plumbing at first," Phoebe says. "Just harmless, medieval gutters."

"Medieval gutters that happen to be shaped like monsters," Gary says. "How does that not scare you?"

"I don't know—it might," Phoebe says.

When they get out of the hot tub, Gary looks at her and she looks back at him. "You know I meant it about you calling me if you see a ghost."

"What if I don't see a ghost? Some in the scientific community might argue that there is no proof of their existence."

"Call me anyway," Gary says.

UPSTAIRS, SHE PACKS her suitcase. She likes her new luggage, how sturdy it is. When she leaves, she rolls it with ease down the hallway, past the copper sconce. By the time she's in the elevator, she is convinced it will do everything the label promises it will do.

In the lobby, she stops in front of the bookcase. She puts *Mrs.*

Dalloway back on the shelf, spine facing out. She is so good at predicting what will happen in books, so bad at predicting what will happen in life. That is why she has always preferred books—because to be alive is much harder. To be alive, she must leave this hotel, despite the uncertainty of everything. Walk down the long hallway of that mansion come winter, not knowing what will become of her, which is a thing that does scare her. But she also feels a thrill imagining the candles she'll light at night. Frank, the nineteenth-century yellow dog, who will sleep on her bed as she writes. The snow dusting the ocean.

She walks through the marble lobby, and it feels like something huge is ending, but she knows it's not. She knows this is a story that she will tell again and again for the rest of her life, and that one of these days, she'll tell it as a beginning. Some of the details will be long forgotten by then, but some will live on each time she and Gary bicker over the most unimportant parts, like what exactly is coastal business casual and why were all the books turned backward and are coconut pillows really better than regular pillows?

"Thank you, Pauline," Phoebe says, stopping just before the front doors to say goodbye. But Pauline is focused on the new wedding people, looking one of them so deeply in the eye, she doesn't see Phoebe wave and walk out through the heavy velvet drapes and into the bright light.

"Your car," the doorman says, and takes her luggage.

Phoebe pauses on the stoop for just a moment, tempted to see everything as she did when she first arrived, as if the people and the brick walkway and the trees are props in a play. But then she tips the man in burgundy and steps forward into the world.

ACKNOWLEDGMENTS

This book would not exist without my agents, Molly Friedrich and Lucy Carson, who were guiding lights at every stage of its development, especially when it was a mere proposal. Thank you to everyone else who works at (or alongside) the Friedrich Agency—Dana Spector at CAA, who literally makes dreams happen; Marin Takikawa, whose sharp editorial eye saved me at the eleventh hour; Hannah Brattesani, who helped make this book exist in other countries and languages; and Heather Carr, who patiently answers all my questions.

Thank you to Caroline Zancan for being a phenomenal editor and friend throughout the making of this book. Your brilliance, warmth, and humor are unparalleled; you make books better and you make writers better. Not to mention, it's just plain fun working with you. I'm equally grateful for the rest of the Henry Holt team: Amy Einhorn, thank you for believing in the manuscript. Caitlin Mulrooney-Lyski, you have made such a difference in my career. Lori Kusatzky and Leela Gebo, I'm endlessly in awe of how smoothly you make everything run. Hannah Campbell and the rest of the editorial team: I'm so grateful for your thoughtful attention to detail. Nicolette Seeback Ruggiero, I'm the biggest fan of your jacket design. Clarissa Long, thank you for the work you put in to get the book noticed out in the world. And to the design, sales, publicity, and marketing teams: thank you for the time and creativity you dedicate to getting people reading—not just this book, but all books.

Thank you to everyone who read some version of this novel and offered crucial feedback: Diana Spechler, for your superpower of knowing when someone "does that thing"; Shelly Oria, for your pitch-perfect sense of how people talk and think; Cristina Rodriguez, for all the conversations we've had over the years that gave me the courage to write a book like this (not to mention your editorial insight); Emily Pittinos, for being the poet in my life; Mark Polanzak, for talking with me on those Adirondack chairs about Lila; Stephanie Boeninger, for your scholarly expertise (and, of course, getting me to take surfing lessons with you); Keegan Drenosky and Elizabeth Bridghman, for offering your professional and scholarly expertise when I had questions; Teddy Wayne, for your support and last-minute edit; and Michael Andreasen, Sarah Lazer-Gomez, and Kerri Joller—your friendship and enthusiasm for this novel meant a great deal at a very crucial time. I am fortunate to have friends that I can share my work with—it makes writing so much less solitary to know that one day you'll all read it. But mostly, thank you all for being smart, funny, and loving people who talk and laugh about the weirdness of life with me. I always thought I'd get increasingly afraid as I grew older, but I'm not, and that's because I'm too excited by everything we have yet to talk about.

I owe so much to Virginia Woolf, Charlotte Brontë, and all the writers who have and continue to, as Woolf wrote, "cut" the literary road for women and work to keep "the path smooth." Thank you to the readers who give this book a chance and help my writing have a life out in the world—I love hearing from you. I am equally grateful for the booksellers out there who write early reviews and blurbs when they could be doing many other things.

Thank you to Alexis Gargagliano—it was special to come full circle and work with you again. Thank you to Providence College for the CAFR grant that supported this novel. To the Tiny Pool people—you are new bright lights in my life that inspire me to keep writing. And to my cat, who I realize will never read or understand this, but who quite literally sits by my side and keeps one supportive paw on my forearm while I write, an act that finally deserves a little public recognition.

To my parents, my brother Gregg, Andrea, my aunts and uncles— thank you for your unabashed enthusiasm anytime something happens with my writing. I tell everyone (and maybe don't tell you all enough) how lucky I am to have a family that reads my novels and then talks to me about them. It feels like a rare gift to bridge the gap between my writing life and my family life—something I'm only able to do because you're astonishingly open, curious, and loving about it.

Finally, to the strangers I've met over the years—the people who bought me nachos and made me laugh while stranded at an airport, the ones in coffee shops who asked me what I was working on, the ones on trains and planes who exchanged life stories with me when they could have just pretended that I didn't exist. You all helped me feel like a person during moments when I least felt like a person. You told me stories that reminded me about the many ways a person can live a good life, about how to start over, about how to make it through that impossible thing. I've never known how to express my gratitude to people I'll never see again, except maybe in this way. Consider this book a very long thank-you letter for saying hello.

ABOUT THE AUTHOR

Alison Espach is the author of the novels *The Adults*, a *New York Times* Editors' Choice and a Barnes & Noble Discover pick, and *Notes on Your Sudden Disappearance*, which was named a best book of 2022 by the *Chicago Tribune* and NPR. She has written for *Vogue, Outside, McSweeney's, Joyland*, and many other publications. She is currently a professor of creative writing at Providence College in Rhode Island.